THE KNIGHT OF THE CART

THE KNIGHT OF THE CART

A MERLIN MYSTERY

JAY RUUD

Encircle Publications, LLC
Farmington, Maine U.S.A.

Paperback ISBN 13: 978-1-948338-89-9
E-book ISBN 13: 978-1-948338-90-5
Kindle ISBN 13: 978-1-948338-91-2

Editors: Cynthia Brackett-Vincent
Book design: Eddie Vincent
Cover design: Deirdre Wait, High Pines Creative
Cover image © Getty Images

Published by: Encircle Publications, LLC
PO Box 187
Farmington, ME 04938

Visit: http://encirclepub.com

Printed in U.S.A.

DEDICATION

For Jenny and Christian, Gerry and Anne

ACKNOWLEDGEMENTS

The story of the Knight of the Cart appears first in a late twelfth-century romance by the major French poet Chrétien de Troyes called, as you might expect, *Lancelot*, or *Le Chevalier de la Charrette* ("The Knight of the Cart"). The poem is notable for marking the first appearance of Sir Lancelot in world literature. Lancelot went on to become the great hero of a lengthy cycle of French prose romances in the early thirteenth century, romances that in turn became the chief sources for Thomas Malory's fifteenth-century *Morte Darthure*, wherein Lancelot is the premiere hero of King Arthur's court. Malory retells the story of the kidnaping of Guinevere, and I have sometimes used his version of the story and sometimes Chrétien's in my reworking of the tale. The trap door by which Lancelot is captured may seem to some readers to be a kind of modern plot twist that stretches the limits of credulity, but I assure you it comes directly from Malory's version, though in Malory's, it is Meliagaunt who pulls the trick on the Great Knight.

The pathetic story of Elaine, the Fair Maid of Astolat, also comes directly from Malory, though he took it from the aforementioned French Lancelot cycle. As for the healing of Sir Urry, that is one of the few chapters in Malory for which he seems to have had no known source—and therefore he seems to have invented the story. So far as I know, I am the first (at least since Malory) to connect those three strands into a single intertwined story, and to turn it into a mystery to be solved.

Students of Malory will also certainly recognize that in my description of Lancelot in chapter five, which reads "He was motivated by love all his life, and therefore, though some high Church prelates or small-minded self-congratulatory moral arbiters might grudge it, I say without blushing that he had a good end," is lifted directly from Malory's description of Guinevere in his section on the "merry month of May," and this is of course a deliberate allusion—as, for that matter, is the last sentence in the section on Sir Urry.

The city of Caerleon has traditionally been the capital of King Arthur's kingdom since Geoffrey of Monmouth made it so in the early twelfth-century *Historia Regum Britanniae* ("History of the Kings of Britain"), and I have made it so in all of my Merlin books. But Geoffrey's Caerleon is in Wales. Because the requirements of this particular story made it necessary that Camelot be closer to Winchester (as it is in Malory), I've placed it twenty-five miles away, about the distance to Salisbury and Stonehenge, two other sites often associated with Arthur. My apologies to the actual Caerleon on the River Usk, whose ancient Roman origins made it a likely place for Geoffrey to place Arthur's court.

There was indeed, as described here, a thriving Jewish community in Winchester in the twelfth century, dating from at least 1160. From what the records reveal, the citizens of Winchester had a more tolerant attitude toward Jews than those of many other English cities, perhaps because the Jews of Winchester were more involved in the commercial life of the city. In 1271, however, when all Jews were ordered to leave England, the Winchester Jewish community ceased to be. "Jewry Street," however, remains to this day.

Gildas is the name of a sixth-century monk who wrote a book called *De Excidio et Conquestu Britanniae* ("On the Ruin and Conquest of Britain"), which gives us the first descriptions of Arthurian-era battles in written European history. Gildas's fellow monk at my (fictional) Saint Dunstan's Abbey, Nennius, was historically a Welsh monk whose *Historia Brittonum* is the first text to refer to Arthur by name as the British leader in their battles against the Saxons. I should note, however, that the historical Nennius lived in the ninth century and was not a contemporary of the sixth-century historical Gildas.

As usual, I need to say a few things about canonical hours, by which time is referred to in the novel. Before the development of accurate clocks, medieval people often thought of the day as broken up into the established times for divine office as set by monastic communities. There were eight of these hours or offices, and the bells of churches, monasteries, and convents rang out to call their members to sing the holy offices at those times. Assuming a day in spring or fall, with approximately equal twelve-hour periods of day and night, the office of prime would occur around sunrise, about six A.M. according to modern notions of time. The next office, terce, would be sung around nine A.M., sext would be around noon, none at about three P.M., vespers at six P.M., compline about nine P.M., matins at midnight and lauds around three A.M. These are the approximate times for events in the novel.

I want to reiterate my caveat that the novels in this series are not intended to be "historical" in the sense of presenting an accurate picture of the "real" King Arthur (whatever that may mean) in the sixth century, as so many modern writers do. Instead, they are intended to conjure the imagined world of the early Arthurian romances—a somewhat glamorized twelfth to thirteenth century— and to further make connections with contemporary lives, with the implication that these are people not unlike ourselves. So expect the occasional anachronism.

The chess match depicted here in chapter eight is, as in previous books, drawn from the website "Best Chess Games of All Time." This happens to be based on the E. Hurt vs. D. Baca match of 1987, and can be found at http://www.chessgames.com/perl/ chessgame?gid=107798.

CHAPTER ONE

THE FAIR MAID OF ASTOLAT

The great sword hung poised above my head for one brief alarming moment, and then began its terrifying descent as King Arthur's heavily muscled arms brought Excalibur sweeping down straight toward me. I bowed my head and flinched, but only slightly, as the flat of the blade struck home on my right shoulder, and Arthur pronounced those words I'd been waiting four years to hear: "I name thee knight of the Table Round. Rise, Sir Gildas of Cornwall!"

No I wasn't dreaming, though your faces tell me you think that must be the case. I was nineteen, it was Pentecost, and I was one of the new Round Table inductees. My road to knighthood had been shortened because King Arthur was replacing the knights lost during the quest of the Grail with the largest class of inductees since the Round Table was conceived.

I had been kneeling here with the other inductees since matins, so the hammer of the sword on my shoulder was nothing compared to the pain in my knees and neck from keeping my head bowed and pretending to pray for twelve straight hours. My master Sir Gareth stood behind me, where he had been since the beginning of the ceremony. He had already planted on my cheek the kiss of welcome into the order of knighthood (a point at which we very nearly broke out laughing as we stared at one another at that close range and tried not to blink). He had also fastened golden spurs to the armored heels of my boots.

Now as I stood, Sir Gareth picked up the sword he had so

generously given me—a fine tapering steel arming sword with a one-handed cross-shaped pommel and a 30-inch polished blade. As the son of a Cornish armor-maker, I was fascinated with, and highly appreciative of, a well-made sword, and Gareth's gift was a fine blade manufactured by one of the armorers of the Rhine, heirs to old Wieland the Smith. In fact, I had already given her a name: Almace, the name of the sword belonging to Turpin, Archbishop of Reims, in the legends of Roland. The Archbishop would only use his sword in defense of the right, of God's will, and I intended that such would be the case for my own Almace as well.

Sir Gareth girded on my sword from behind, just as, to my right, my old friend Thomas—or, I should say, *Sir* Thomas—was having his own new sword girded on by his sponsor, Sir Ywain, the Knight of the Lion, whose squire Thomas had been until, well, today, when he became a knight in his own right; and, to my left, Hectimere, Sir Gaheris's former squire, was having his own sword girded on by his own sponsor. Farther down the long line at the altar, Baldwin of Orkney, Sir Agravain's surly squire, was finally being bumped up into the Order as well, as Arthur was just now striking his right shoulder with the *colée*, and pronouncing the admonition "Let this blow remind you that knighthood shall bring you pain as well as honor." And the fifth of the Orkney clan squires, Sir Gawain's own son Lovell, was being inducted as well, so that Gawain and his brothers were changing significantly the balance of power in Arthur's Table.

Not that Lancelot's faction was faring badly in this ceremony. There was Meliot de Logres, a cousin of Merlin's beloved Nimue, the Damsel of the Lake; Lancelot had helped save Meliot's life after he had been wounded by the recreant knight Gilbert the Bastard, so he could be expected to be sympathetic to Lancelot. There were also Sir Tirre and Sir Lavayne, sons of Sir Bernard of Astolat, lord of Guildford, whom Lancelot had befriended before the last great tournament at Winchester. Lavayne had even fought by the Great Knight's side in that tournament, which Lancelot had attended in disguise to ensure that knights would spar with him, since no knight wanted to take on the world's greatest killing machine if he actually knew what he was getting into.

The ninth and final new member of King Arthur's valiant Order of the Round Table was a veteran knight named Geraint of Dumnonia. He was a young knight, but a petty king of that region of Logres called Dumnonia, and demonstrated his fealty to Arthur by joining the Order of Arthur's knights. And thus there were nine new inductees to the Table, nine worthies to replace those souls wasted so needlessly in that futile quest of the Grail.

Well, not so pointless, I supposed, for Perceval, who had in fact achieved the Grail and chose not to return to Camelot, losing his life in some other exalted cause there in the Holy Land. But certainly meaningless for my best friend Sir Colgrevaunce, dead trying to save Sir Bors from the violent madness of his brother Lionel. And pointless, too, for Lionel, whose own life was forfeit after those mad crimes of his. And Sir Safer, my friend Palomides' brother, slaughtered unarmed? For what? Sir Uwain, Sir Grummer, Sir Gliglois, even the vile Sir Ironside, all brought low. And most pointless of all, the witty and cynical Sir Dinadan, who only joined the quest to observe the folly of it, found that joining had been his own folly when he too perished. Of course, I do not number among the lost Sir Galahad, who was born, it seemed, only for the Grail, and whose seat at the Table, the Siege Perilous, had always been an addendum after all, bringing the total of knights to one hundred fifty-one only when he was present. The nine new inductees brought the total knights of the Round Table back to the customary hundred and fifty. And brought all back to normal. Or at least it was nice to think so.

But I had daydreamed long enough. The ceremony was finishing, as Arthur stepped back from giving the *colée* to Sir Geraint, and moved away to conclude the knighting ceremony by formally accepting all of us into his renowned Order: "As King of Logres," he intoned, "the Emperor of Ireland, Normandy, Brittany, and Gaul, as sovereign authority of the order of chivalry called the Round Table, I now admit you into that sacred Order. Draw your swords now, and salute your sovereign, as Knights of the Round Table!"

The huge crowd assembled in the great Cathedral of Caerleon— called Saint David's after the Welsh saint who had presided over a church council here some time back—all cheered as we drew our newly girded swords and held them high to our new liege lord. And now William of Glastonbury, the Archbishop of Caerleon, dressed for the occasion in his full ecclesiastical regalia—his cope and chasuble, his mitre and crozier—proclaimed to the congregation:

"On the first Pentecost, the Holy Ghost inspired the Apostles with the fire of faith, and they went forth and established the Church of our Lord. Now on today's Pentecost, let the modern heirs of the Apostles—you who do God's own work here in His fallen world—be inspired once more by His Holy Spirit, as you renew your vows with me, repeating the oath that you all took when you became knights, and that these nine new knights of the Table join us in repeating now…"

I already knew the oath by heart, having heard it at every Whitsunday ceremony every year I had been at Camelot. Now for the first time I said it in unison with all the hundred and fifty knights now present, each of them holding out his sword and saluting the king along with the ideals expressed in the oath:

"We swear always to follow the commands of our king: never to do outrage or murder; always to fly treason; never to be cruel, but in all circumstances to grant mercy to any who plead for mercy, or forfeit our own worship and the lordship of our lord King Arthur for evermore; and we swear always to give succor to ladies, damsels, and gentlewomen, on pain of death. And we further swear never to go to battle in a wrong cause no matter what law may try to force us to do so, and no matter what the worldly reward. All of this we swear, both old and young, the Knights of the Table Round."

And just like that it was over. The dignitaries began assembling in the apse of the cathedral, under the brilliant glow of dozens of candelabra alight for the occasion, and began to file out in a colorful procession to the delight of the spectators in the congregation, to exit the building and then to make their way out of the city and toward the castle of Camelot itself, where awaited the great Pentecost feast, the most sumptuous of the entire social calendar, as it always marked the anniversary and renewal of the Table. Archbishop William led the procession down the great nave, side by side with the king himself, who wore his most magnificent royal robes of state, purple edged with ermine, and his heavy imperial crown as well, so that from my vantage point as he passed I could see the sweat on his brow and the straining of his neck muscles as he worked to hold the royal head erect until the procession concluded. King and Archbishop were followed by the sponsors of the inductees, Sir Gawain and Sir Gareth leading the way, and all the Orkney brothers in cloaks of red and green Orkney plaid, fastened at the shoulder. Sir Lancelot, who had sponsored both Sir Lavayne and Sir Tirre, followed in his blue tunic and ermine-fringed cloak, walking with Sir Ywain, in his tawny tunic and cloak fringed with fox fur around the collar, making the Knight of the Lion look positively, and appropriately, leonine. Sir Bors and Sir Kay, sponsors, respectively, of Meliot and Geraint, came next, and the sponsors were then followed by the nine inductees themselves. I was in the first pair, walking next to my old companion Thomas, whose sandy hair glistened with sweat and who breathed a sigh of relief.

"Thank God that's over," he whispered to me. "I swear, when the king smacked me with that sword, I thought he'd broken my shoulder. Seriously."

"Bear up, boy, everybody's watching," I warned him, giving him a half grin. "The ladies-in-waiting like strong shoulders, you know."

And the ladies-in-waiting were indeed seated with the queen in the front row to our right as we began the long trek down the aisle. Guinevere gave me a subtle half smile and even—was I imagining it?—winked at me as I passed. But my eyes were drawn chiefly to the lady seated at the queen's right hand. Her eyes sparkled brighter than the stars on a soft, clear summer night; her long brown hair, kept in place by a net linen wimple, I imagined cascading like a mountain stream down her slim shoulders, shoulders that were protected from the chill of the cavernous nave by a light blue samite cloak edged with vair. Lady Rosemounde averted her eyes as I walked by, looking down but, I noticed, stifling a smile as she pretended to ignore me.

It was a bittersweet moment. I had begun the trek that brought me to this moment four years ago, and knighthood had not been an end in itself but only a means to an end: there was only one way a nobody like Gildas of Cornwall, son of a Cornish armor maker, could hope to wed Lady Rosemounde, sole legitimate child of Duke Hoel of Brittany, and that was by becoming a knight of the Table Round. But my social rise had come too late: that wimple hiding the glory of her hair was the public symbol of her wifely obedience—or, as I liked to think of it, her imprisonment, a daily reminder to me of her marriage to that boil on the backside of chivalry, Sir Mordred.

But I wasn't about to let thoughts of my lord Gareth's sorry excuse for a half-brother spoil my joy in the day. I took a deep breath and held up my head, taking in the beauty of the cathedral's sunlit interior: the new Gothic style allowed for narrow stained glass windows that rose some thirty feet in the air all along the left and right walls of the nave, washing the whole interior of the building with splashes of color. On my right hand the windows pictured scenes from the Old Testament— Adam and Eve in the Garden, Noah's Flood, Abraham sacrificing Isaac, Abraham with the three heavenly visitors, the infant Moses in the bulrushes. These were balanced on the left side by parallel New Testament scenes: Christ as gardener with Mary Magdalene, Christ's baptism across from Noah's Flood, Christ as the Lamb of God directly across from and paralleling Abraham and Isaac, the holy Eucharist across from the angels with Abraham, Herod's slaughter of the innocents from Moses found in a basket among the bulrushes. Above them all, in the apse itself, directly behind me as I made my way down the aisle, was the great fresco of Christ Pantocrator, emperor of all the earth—as Arthur was, under God, ruler of all he surveyed. I could almost feel the eyes of Christ boring into my back as I moved toward the exit, reminding me that knighthood was a holy calling, bulwark of the Christian commonwealth, where there were those who fought, those who prayed, and those who worked. My job, as knight, was to fight—to protect God's people. To uphold the great oath I had just taken. Not to seek to cuckold another knight, even if that other knight was Sir Mordred, who didn't care one jot for his duties to God—or to the king either, for that matter. But I wasn't going to think about him today. Really.

By now the procession had reached the western door of the cathedral, and as I was about to pass through with Thomas I noticed on my right, standing unobtrusively in the shadows, a tall elderly man dressed in brown worsted threadbare robes. He had long, unkempt hair and beard, with eyebrows that sprouted from his face like a tangled briar patch. He leaned on a long staff and watched me with eyes that seemed to be glowing in his wizened head. I blinked several times, thinking after the long watch and fast that had led up to this morning's ceremony I must be seeing things. He hadn't willingly left his cave without a direct summons in years, to my knowledge, preferring to curl up in a melancholy ball, shut away from the world that had deprived him of his beloved Nimue, the Damsel of the Lake.

"Merlin?" I cried in disbelief, as I realized it was indeed the old necromancer and not a figment of my imagination shuffling toward me with what almost looked like a smile on his rugged, wrinkled visage. "It is you! I thought my eyes were playing tricks. What on earth brings you here? What could have roused you from your cave?"

"God's belly, boy, can't I move around the king's demesne on my own, without your leave? Anyway, I've heard the Pentecost feast is going to be particularly fine this year, and I have a standing invitation from the king himself."

Feeling a bit abashed at having apparently overstepped my bounds, I began to stammer out a response, "Oh, well…yes…um, Sir Kay is rumored to have outdone himself with the preparations. Roast swan, I've heard, and…um…"

The old man cuffed me gently on the ear and interrupted, "You Cornish dunce, don't you know when you're being mocked? I'm here to see *you*, of course. You didn't think I would let my old partner in crime—or the investigation thereof, at least—be raised up to noble knighthood, the thing he's wanted since I first knew him, without coming out to witness such a vile blot on the fabric of chivalry?"

"Well, I'm pretty sure I'm being mocked right now, old man. How dare you call my knighting a 'blot on the fabric of chivalry.' Look at this sword! With such a sword even a knight of, shall we say, questionable skills, which I by no means admit describes myself, could hold off a whole bevy of infidels, or whomever we may be fighting in the near future." And with that I drew the blade carefully from its scabbard and displayed it for him to see, bending my arm to lay it across my elbow to give him a closer look.

The mage gave an appreciative whistle and focused his full attention on the sword. "Beautifully polished, well forged, and," with this he touched the edge of the blade gingerly, "carefully honed. With a sword like this you could cut through a reinforced shield... or decapitate a man before he knows he's been cut. A gift from Beaumains?"

Merlin always called Sir Gareth by the original ironic title Sir Kay had foisted on him when he appeared at Camelot in disguise and was given employment in the kitchen. "Of course," I answered him. "I can't afford such a weapon on my own."

"Norman?" he asked, his ponderous right eyebrow going up quizzically.

"German," I answered.

"Ah, fine smiths there on the Rhine. Well, I hope you live to wield it with honor and courage. I really do, young Gildas," and with that the old man placed his hand on my shoulder in a gesture of camaraderie I had never seen from him before.

"I call her Almace," I ventured, trying out the name aloud to see how it played. Merlin nodded sagely. Which was pretty much the only way he knew how to nod.

"After the famous sword of Bishop Turpin, eh?" He observed. Then his brows came down, in imitation of a looming storm. "That doesn't mean you're still thinking about entering holy orders soon, does it?"

I shrugged. "I had considered it for a while, it's true. But now I know I shall never do so as long as the lady Rosemounde draws breath."

Merlin's eyes rolled a bit and he began to walk with me out of the cathedral and off toward the castle, where the rest of the crowd was moving in the expectation of the promised sumptuous feast. "Lady Rosemounde of Orkney? Wife of the king's own nephew Sir Mordred of Orkney? That Lady Rosemounde? Don't you think you ought to be setting your sights on someone a little less lofty? And a little less married?"

"But she..." I broke off, biting my tongue. I had forgotten momentarily that Merlin knew nothing about my tryst with

Rosemounde, and only a very little of her showing me the marks of her vile husband's beatings—her pleading with me to learn well the craft of knighthood so that I might avenge her wrongs on that brute—who, at present, was still more skilled in arms than I was. Or at least more experienced. But Rosemounde had also cautioned me to do nothing at present, since as long as she stayed in Camelot and her time was spent in the queen's entourage, she was safe. But Merlin was only vaguely aware of this and, kicking a stone from my path, I continued our casual stroll toward Camelot, and steered the subject elsewhere. "Nephew? You say that with a straight face?"

The old mage shrugged. "He is King Arthur's nephew according to royal proclamation. Whatever you and I—or anyone else—might think otherwise, there has never been any official acknowledgement of any other relationship, and therefore he remains Arthur's nephew in all polite conversation. Certainly as son of the king's half-sister Margause, he must be Arthur's nephew. Paternity is much harder to prove."

"Oh yes, I daresay," I replied, quickening my pace just a bit. "Let's get moving! My stomach is growling. I'm famished! I've been fasting for days."

Merlin looked a bit quizzical. "Isn't it really just a day and a half? Thirty-six hours?"

"Don't burn me with the facts, old man!" I threw him one of his own favorite expressions. "I will get to sit at the Round Table itself for the first time today—instead of serving Sir Gareth at the feast. I intend to make a big dent in that roast swan. But will you be up in the Great Hall for your meal?"

The old necromancer sniffed, as if offended. "My dear young Cornish imbecile," he said in mock haughtiness. "When I said I had a standing invitation to the Pentecost feast at Camelot, I did not mean an invitation to eat among the rabble. As Arthur's oldest and—need it be said?—his wisest adviser, I am invited to partake of the feast at the Round Table itself, along with the hundred and fifty knights in the presence of the king. *Himself.*"

"So there will be an extra seat at the Table?" I wondered.

"Not at all," Merlin laughed at my incredulity. "I'll be sitting in the

Siege Perilous. It ought to be good for something, now that Galahad has left us for more heavenly environs."

"Well then, we'll have a great banquet together! And look, Merlin, if you intend to stay around the castle for a time after the feast..."

"I may," the old man glanced at me out of the corner of his eye, "if there's something worth waiting around for."

"There is!" I gushed. "You have to see Sir Gareth's *other* gift to me."

That piqued the mage's curiosity all right. The sword had been a typical gift, one that might have been expected from a chivalrous knight to his faithful and well-loved squire at the latter's elevation to knighthood. Something more must needs be something altogether extraordinary. "His other gift?" Merlin asked, almost warily. "And what might that be?"

I put my lips together in a close-mouthed smile and walked on at a brisk pace. "Move your feet old man, I'm hungry!" I remarked nonchalantly, ignoring his frustrated muttering.

"God's eyeteeth, Gildas!" Merlin finally exclaimed.

"All right!" I said finally, turning toward him and beaming. "It's Achilles!"

Merlin's jaw dropped and for nearly half a moment (unlikely as it may seem) he was speechless. Achilles was one of Sir Gareth's great destriers, the foal of Gareth's own powerful war horse Ajax. Gareth had actually bought both sire and foal in Spain, and Achilles was a powerful dark brown horse who stood some eighteen hands tall. I had ridden the great beast on several occasions when accompanying Sir Gareth on military business or, this past year, on his ill-fated quest of the Grail. But the gift was unparalleled, at least in the Camelot I knew. I would have had to save for years to amass the sum I would need to purchase even a mediocre war horse, let alone one of Achilles' quality. A good destrier could cost as much as a third of a knight's annual income, even a knight as wealthy as one of Arthur's nephews of the Orkney clan.

"Beaumains is a generous knight," Merlin pronounced. "Perhaps the most generous in Camelot, as this gift demonstrates. And since generosity is the chief characteristic of courtesy, it follows he is also one of the most courteous knights of the Table. And therefore a good role model for all new knights."

"My master has been my role model all along," I conceded. "Though I cannot say I've always followed him. But we'll go to the stable and I'll have Taber bring out Achilles to show you after the banquet."

"I'll look forward to it, Gildas my boy." Now Merlin looked ahead, squinting. We were drawing close to the castle now and could see the figure of Arthur waiting outside the drawbridge, nodding to the knights and clergy and townsmen who were entering the castle for his annual feast marking the renewal of the Round Table. Merlin sighed. "I see that the king has still not given up that old custom of his boyhood."

"No," I said grinning. "He still takes an oath every year that he will not sit down to a meal until he sees, or at least hears about, some great marvel."

But as we came closer and closer to the fortress we began to hear murmurs coming from below the castle moat, and when Arthur noticed something was happening at the river that flowed below the gate on the north side of Camelot, he himself began to jog boyishly down the slope to see what was happening.

A crowd had begun to form there by the time Merlin and I reached the riverbank, and we tried to make our way toward the shore through the gathering throng. By the time the king reached the bank, the queen and Sir Lancelot had joined him, followed closely by Sir Gawain, and the crowd parted to let them through. What they saw—what we all saw—as we stared out into the river was a small barge, covered at all points with black samite, which had been moving with the current, steered by a single boatman who peered mutely at the shore as he angled the barge toward the bank.

It wasn't merely the presence of the solitary craft that drew everyone's interest. It was the woman lying in the boat, her arms folded across her breast, her eyes closed as if in sleep. But she was not asleep. She lay upon the barge in a fair bed of soft down and fur coverlets, and she herself was richly garbed in a green samite gown with gold filigree, her long blonde tresses held in place by a gold circlet and light gold mesh crespine. She could not have been older than seventeen, and my heart sank when I saw her. What malicious star had shined on her infancy to bring her to this sorry place?

I had a nagging sense of déjà vu. Wasn't this an ominous echo of what happened a year ago, at the last Pentecost, when sir Galahad had arrived at Camelot and pulled the sword from the stone that floated on the river at this very spot? And hadn't Lancelot come down the river to Corbenic on board a boat in which floated the body of Perceval's sister? What did they mean, these repeated motifs? I couldn't help voicing my confusion to Merlin. "This has happened before. Is it a sign from God? Is He trying to send us through the same test as last year? Will He give us these strange quests until we get it right?"

Merlin lowered his brows and glared at me as if I had grown a second head. "Cornish dimwit, what have I told you? Random events occur constantly in our world. Occasionally two random events seem to happen in conjunction with one another, and we call these coincidences signs or omens. This is merely another random occurrence."

"Dead women lying in boats on Pentecost really doesn't seem all that random to me, old man," I responded.

"Quiet, boy, they've found something."

And peering over the shoulders of those in front of me pressing forward, I saw he was right. The boatman refused to speak, but only stood impassive, waiting for the members of the court to do what they would with the corpse. Lancelot's face had gone pale, and Sir Gawain noticed that a piece of parchment was grasped in the lady's right hand, placed there, I assumed, prior to the lady's death, so that her hand would stiffen around it as her body cooled. Gawain climbed aboard the barge and tenderly and carefully removed the message from the young woman's death grip, and the king called to him to read the letter aloud.

But before he could begin there was a great cry of alarm from farther back in the crowd. I turned to see a figure dressed, as I was, in armor lately hung with a new sword, pushing his way toward the barge in great distress. He was followed by a second figure, grim but less beside himself with grief. The first figure cried out, pushing his way onto the barge. "Elaine! Oh my dearest sister! What has happened to you?" He took the body of the lady, still beautiful in her finery, into his arms and let his tears fall freely onto that green samite gown. "You were alive and healthy when I left Guildford! What's happened? How could you...how could this..." but Sir Lavayne was unable to complete the thought in any coherent manner. His brother Sir Tirre followed him onto the barge, head bent in sorrow but more contained in his passion.

"Whatever has happened here, we will get to the bottom of it, brother. Rest assured. Our sister will not have died in vain, however it was that she died. The letter...let us hear what is written there. It is in my father's hand, I recognize it."

"If that is so, my lord, then it was dictated to him by this young maiden herself. By your leave, I will read her words now, shall I?"

"Please," Sir Tirre answered. Sir Lavayne only sobbed.

"Then hear all of you," Gawain began. He held the letter before him and struck an authoritative pose, his red hair uncovered and blowing in the May breeze, his green eyes flashing with concern over this unforeseen and unwanted interruption in the Pentecost celebration, concerning as it did two of the newest inductees in his uncle's storied order of chivalry. He flung back his Orkney plaid cloak so that his arms were free, and proceeded to read:

"Most noble knight Sir Lancelot," he began, and the assembled crowd all looked in the Great Knight's direction. Lancelot looked down, with more than a little suspicion, I was sure, of what was to follow. The letter continued: "Now death has parted us because of my great love for you." At that there was an audible gasp throughout the assembled crowd, and Sir Lavayne and Sir Tirre glared at Lancelot's bowed figure with dark faces. I could not see the queen's. "I was your lover," Sir Gawain read on, "called by many the 'Fair Maid of Astolat.' I call on all women to pity me, and I call on you, Sir Lancelot, to pray for me and to see that I am given a proper burial. This is my last request. I take God as my witness that I died a pure maiden. Sir Lancelot, you are without peer among all the knights of the world, so I ask you again to pray for my soul."

Now Gawain looked up. "That is the extent of the letter, my lord."

The murmuring of the crowd grew to raucous proportions as people glared at Lancelot, some pointing to him while speaking to others in the crowd. King Arthur squeezed his lips together and his brows lowered in concern. Still, I could not see the queen. Sir Lancelot, however, his trimmed brown hair ruffling in the breeze, his blue eyes (which matched so well the blue cape embroidered with fleur-de-lis that draped his broad shoulders) glancing downward in humble deference, raised his voice to a level that quieted the onlookers.

"My liege!" He called, addressing the king. "My Lord Gawain, my Lady Queen Guinevere, I am as shocked and saddened by this damsel's death as anyone here. Yet still, I protest that I never harmed this maiden. But there was nothing I could do: she loved me with a kind of madness, out of all measure. But you heard from her own letter that she was a pure maiden yet. Nor did I ever treat her with anything but the deepest respect, as I would the highest-born noble woman in the land. I call her own brothers to witness the truth of that statement." At that he raised his eyes to the two mourning figures on the barge and made a half-hearted gesture toward them with his left arm.

At that, Sir Lavayne, who seemed by his unrestrained passion to be the most moved by his sister's death, looked up. His tears were running uncontrollably down into his thin beard, his long, thin brown hair trailing onto his shoulders, his dark eyes looking almost crossed in the midst of his narrow face, looking down at Lancelot from either side of his long nose. But he nodded assent to Lancelot's words. In a voice choked with sobs he agreed: "It is true, my lords. Never did I witness any discourteous word toward my sister from Sir Lancelot."

As for Sir Tirre, he was far harder to read. His own dark eyes were hidden somewhat by his scowl, and his mouth turned down into his own brown beard. His close-cropped dark hair was too short to be affected by the breeze, as perhaps his own heart was too hard to be affected by Lancelot's excuses. He said nothing, but gave one small nod, which most of the crowd read as a kind of assent to his brother's words.

But Lancelot was hardly exonerated. For now I saw a figure stand forth from the surrounding crowd, stepping toward the Great Knight with an accusatory finger pointed into his face. It was the queen.

"Now comes Lancelot's real trial," the voice of Merlin whispered into my left ear.

"God protect him from her tongue," I muttered, sympathetically.

"You make your excuses, Sir Lancelot, and claim to have followed the letter of the law of courtesy in all things. But haven't we all heard, 'The letter kills, but the spirit gives life'? You might have shown her some bounty and gentleness that might have preserved her life!"

"Madame," Lancelot answered her, his temper broiling beneath the surface of his courtesy. "She insisted on being either my wife or my lover, and I was not willing to grant her either of those things. I did everything I could otherwise…why, I even offered her a thousand pounds a year as a dowry to have her choose another worthy knight to love!" At that the murmurs increased again—and if some around me were exclaiming at the great generosity of Sir Lancelot for a gesture that would have made this damsel one of the richest women in Logres, the others I heard were faulting the Great Knight for putting a monetary value on the spiritual quality of love.

But Lancelot continued: "For Madame, you will understand this if nothing else I have said: I refuse to be in any way constrained by love. Love cannot be forced, but can come only from the heart."

Now the king himself felt compelled to step between his queen and his greatest baron. "Of course, of course what Lancelot says is true. Where love is forced, it ceases to be love. But my lord Lancelot, I am certain you will accept the damsel's request at any rate. It will reflect worthily upon your own integrity to see that she is interred with all appropriate honors."

But the queen was not appeased. She muttered something *sotto voce* that few around her could make out, but that I, having been her page for years and knowing her as well as I did, was able to read on her lips. "Yes, you two men can congratulate each other while the woman suffers." But she said aloud, for all to hear, "Be that as it may, Sir Lancelot, I charge you to recall what you and the king and all the knights here present swear in your Pentecostal oath every year: 'to give succor to ladies, damsels, and gentlewomen, on pain of death.' Is that what you did in this case? If you hold woman's love in such low regard, I command you to void my sight. Come not near me again, unless you dare incur my wrath." And with that she turned heel and began making her way up the hill to the castle, her ladies-in-waiting, among them my own beauteous Rosemounde, picked up their skirts and bustled after her.

The king looked at Lancelot, raised his eyebrows and shrugged. Lancelot, striving with all his might to appear unmoved, rose to his full height and commanded, "Some of you men lift her from the barge and carry her into the chapel in the castle. I will work with Bishop William to see that she is given an honorable burial."

Now the large crowd began to disperse and move away following the queen toward the castle. Sir Gawain and the silent boatman lifted the Maid of Astolat, and Lancelot cautioned "Gently! Gently!" as Sir Lavayne followed, continuing to sob. Sir Tirre remained unmoving and unmoved on the deck of the barge, watching his sister make her final journey up Camelot Hill, his eyes piercing holes in Lancelot's back.

CHAPTER TWO

AT THE SIGN OF THE RED FOX

"Well, we won't be seeing Sir Lancelot again, at least not this side of October," Sir Gareth opined, sipping on his third pint of ale and waxing chattier as the evening wore on. "After that kind of rebuke from the queen? He'll be off tomorrow looking for some adventure where he doesn't have to answer to her sharp tongue."

It had been an unprecedentedly depressing Pentecost. The appearance of the body of the Maid of Astolat had dampened spirits at the feast both in the great royal banquet hall and at the Round Table itself. And while there had initially been a plan for all the new inductees to meet and celebrate our ordination here at the sign of the Red Fox—the most popular public house in Caerleon—what with Sir Tirre and Sir Lavayne hurled suddenly into a state of mourning, no one else was in much of a mood to celebrate either. Gareth and Merlin were not about to let my induction as Knight of the Round Table pass without some kind of libation to mark the occasion, though, so the three of us were sitting around the table at William Bailey's inn, and Gareth was just warming up. The story of Elaine of Astolat was on everybody's lips, but few had any of the real details. Sir Gareth was one of those few, having had the story directly from his brother Gawain, who had been there himself to witness the maiden's naïve obsession with Lancelot.

"So you remember the tournament at Winchester that King Arthur called this past Assumption Day?" He began. "Where he and the King of Scots issued a challenge to joust against all comers?"

Merlin scoffed. "Remember it? How could I forget a challenge that foolhardy? Kings risking life and limb on some silly whim?"

"Chivalry, old man, chivalry!" I goaded him. "It's all about the impression you make, right? How you fashion yourself, present yourself."

"Poppycock, you Cornish blockhead. Chivalry is about manly virtue in the service of righteousness. That's all it is. Not this phony play-acting."

"Do you want to hear this or not?" Sir Gareth, slightly annoyed, broke in. I turned polite eyes on him, and Merlin crossed his arms and snorted through his nose, which was his way of saying, "Go on."

"So again, you might remember that Lancelot stayed behind instead of going with the king to the tournament. Well, turns out he really just wanted to come in disguise. You know, being Lancelot is not an easy thing. You go to a tournament and what happens? Nobody wants to fight with you because no one has ever beaten you and odds are you're never going to *get* beaten. So everybody at the tournament avoids fighting you and you end up riding around the field by yourself. But how does a knight earn a reputation for chivalry?"

"By doing deeds of valor in defense of justice," Merlin said matter-of-factly, glancing in my direction.

"By creating a perception of exaggerated gentility," I countered.

"Will you stop with this?" Gareth burst out, frustrated. "You get a reputation by doing deeds of worship on the jousting field." Merlin snorted again. I shrugged. Gareth continued.

"So Lancelot follows after the king a day late, and he's planning to fight in the melee in disguise against the side of King Arthur."

"Against the king? But why?" I asked.

"The greatest knights in the world are the knights of the Round Table. You don't build up your worship by beating up on knights obviously weaker than you. Anyway, Lancelot has to stay in the town of Astolat on the way to the Winchester jousting fields, and he is able to get lodging in the palace of Lord Bernard, the baron of that town. The old guy is courteous and welcoming, but he's never been close to the court here and he doesn't recognize Lancelot on sight, or by the coat of arms on his shield, the three golden *fleur-de-lys* on a field azure—the best-known shield in Christendom. But he offers Sir Lancelot a good meal and a bed for the night, which the Great Knight is glad to get. But he asks Bernard for one more favor: his shield, he says, is easily recognizable and he really wants to attend the great tournament anonymously. Might the old baron have some unknown or unmarked shield lying about that Lancelot might just borrow for the tournament? He promises to bring it back afterwards and will leave his own with Sir Bernard while he's gone. And guess what?"

Merlin's eyes rolled. "I'm guessing he gave him a shield."

"Right!" Gareth cried boisterously as he took another big gulp of ale. Gareth didn't feel the need to speak quietly or inconspicuously at the moment, and fortunately there were only a few others in the inn that night, to the disappointment of William Bailey, who had counted on a big crowd from the Pentecost celebration.

"Sir Bernard tells Lancelot that he's got these two grown sons, see, who have just recently been knighted, and so their shields are simply a blank, pure white. And it so happens that Sir Tirre is injured and couldn't ride to the tournament even if he wanted to, so Bernard says Lancelot can use Tirre's shield and no one will be the wiser. But Bernard wants a favor in return: 'My younger son,' he says, 'Sir Lavayne really would love to prove himself on the jousting field. He has the makings of a noble knight,' and that he would love to have his son ride along with Lancelot to the tournament and learn something from the veteran jouster."

"So that's how Lavayne became so close to Lancelot so quickly," I mused, nodding.

"That's how," Gareth agreed. "Now Lancelot, of course, he agrees to all this because it's exactly what he's looking for. Not only would he be unrecognizable with the blank shield, but if he appeared at the tournament with Sir Lavayne, then everybody'd think the two were brothers, and that would make it even harder for people to recognize him. Especially if Lancelot left his own horse there and borrowed one of the Lord Bernard's, his own tall black horse Minuit being perhaps too well known to the other knights of the Table. And so Lancelot, pretty pleased with himself at how all this is turning out, sits down to a fine dinner with his host and his two sons, and seated right across from their lovely young sister, Elaine le Blank."

Merlin looked over at me with eyes narrowed. "That's 'Elaine the White' for those of you who don't speak French."

Now it was my turn to roll my eyes at him. "I'm working on it, old man. Let me get comfortable with Latin first."

The Mage shrugged at that, conceding, "Yes, well that's more important, truly. That's where all the learning is. About all you can read in French is exaggerated romances of love at first sight and such drivel."

"Precisely Elaine le Blank's problem," Gareth added, moving us back to his story. "At least according to Gawain. Her mind was so swayed by romances of knights doing great deeds in the service of ladies, and ladies besotted with handsome, bold, and chivalrous knights…"

"Chivalrous in what sense?" Merlin raised his eyebrows at Gareth.

"She immediately saw Lancelot as the one she was destined to love and be loved by," Gareth went on, ignoring the old man's jibe. "And so she spends the whole meal batting her eyes at him and mooning like a sick calf. Well even Lancelot, dense as he is about such things, notices this, as do the two brothers, who are embarrassed for their sister, especially as it seems that Lancelot only wants to be left alone, and politely but noticeably ignores the maid's inviting eyes. Still, she is the lady of the house, it seems, the baron's wife having died some time ago, and it is a tenet of chivalry—by *any* definition of the term," Gareth glared as both Merlin and I had prepared to renew our debate at that point, "to honor ladies and to be courteous in serving them. And so, of course, Lancelot made the usual polite and complimentary observations about the lady's dress and her conversation and her skillful management of the feast. It was just polite small talk, but Elaine le Blank had never been treated so courteously before, and misinterpreted Lancelot's courtesy for love-talk, and her head was turned."

"Sad," Merlin shook his head, "how easily we are fooled in matters of love by what we wish to see." I looked over at him, wondering if he was thinking about his own obsession with the nymph Nimue, or if he even recognized the blatant irony of his comment.

"Well, Lancelot spent the night on a pallet in the room with the damsel's brothers, and in the morning, he and Sir Lavayne made their preparations to leave for the short trip to Winchester, grabbing a bit of bread and cheese and small ale to tide them over until they reached the lists. And as Lancelot picked up the unmarked shield, the fair maid came down, dressed in her finest gown of green samite, the sleeves hanging down to her knees. She was desperate to have some sign from the Great Knight that he reciprocated her feelings at least to some extent. And again, he was just as polite and attentive as courtesy demanded. Then he saw his shield where he had set it in the dining room, and, having no idea how she would interpret the request, asked the maid Elaine if she would keep it for him until he returned."

"Now that was careless," I muttered. "I mean, if he could see how she was acting the night before, how could he not think she would take such a commission as a lover's request? Why didn't he ask the baron to hold it for him?"

"Well, he didn't," Gareth said flatly. "Who knows why? I suppose there's something soothing to the ego of a knight approaching middle age to entertain the idea that a fresh young seventeen-year-old virgin idolizes you—and for Lancelot even more flattering since the girl didn't even know who he was, so he could be certain she was not simply enamored of his great name. And I suppose he thought he was just giving her a little something, throwing her a bone, you might say, by giving her charge of his shield. But what happened afterwards was much worse."

"So it must have been," Merlin agreed, "if it drove her to her death."

"And so it was," Gareth continued. "She produced a red sleeve, embroidered with pearls, and held it out to him. She had obviously been planning this all night, and his request that she keep his shield emboldened her to make her own request of him. She would keep his shield, she told him, on the condition that he do her a favor as well, and promise to wear her sleeve on his helmet in the tournament."

I was taken aback by this. "But Lancelot never…" I began.

"No, and that's the point!" Gareth cried with increasing emphasis. "He has never worn a woman's token, and that's exactly what he told the girl. 'I have never done so much for any woman,' he says to her. And then she entreats him again and even goes down on her knees to plead with him. And all this time he's thinking, well, *everybody* knows that I have never worn a woman's token in any tournament or joust in all my days as a knight, and so if I truly want no one to recognize me, or even to guess that I may be in disguise, if I wear the token, no one will even entertain the idea that I am Lancelot du Lac himself. And so he finally gives in, and tells Elaine yes, he'll wear her sleeve, and worse than that, he even thoughtlessly says to her, 'Now you can say that I have done for you what I have never done before for any woman.'"

Merlin slammed his hand down on the table in vexation. At that, William Bailey rushed over, thinking we wanted to order more ale. That hadn't been the point, but Merlin, abashed at having given the frustrated innkeeper the wrong impression, said "Three more pints, my good man, if you please!" And William called to his new barmaid, Lucy, to bring over three pints and be quick about it, then went off smiling. But as soon as he'd gone, Merlin's great brows lowered and he growled, "Sheer idiocy. God's cheekbones, what on earth did he imagine she was going to think of that?"

"Well, to be fair," I reasoned, "many knights wear ladies' tokens just out of respect or friendship. Several knights, for instance, have worn the queen's token, usually at her request, to show their loyalty or their support or their love for her as queen. The king has never looked upon these requests as anything but courtesy—and neither, of course, has she."

"But this maid was not a queen!" Merlin chided me. "Nor was she in any way familiar with the manners of court. For her, with her head filled with romances and her heart with infatuation, his wearing her token could symbolize nothing but his mutual love for her. She believed Lancelot was declaring his love for her right then."

Gareth nodded. "Without question, that is what she believed, as

Lancelot and Lavayne rode off that morning to Winchester, and she retired to her private rooms to dream of her golden knight's return.

"Well, I don't suppose I need to go into much detail about the tournament itself. Gildas was there. Merlin, you must have heard about it somewhere."

The old man shrugged. "I picked up bits and pieces here and there. I gather that the two kings' jousts went off without any difficulties…"

"Yes, the first day of the tournament was dedicated to the kings who had promised to joust against all comers. But you know, if Lancelot suspected no one would want to joust with him because of his reputation, you can guess how it must have been for the kings. Nobody wants to show up his king, and so none of the greater knights would dare to pick up a lance to use on his own sovereign. Only a handful of the younger knights, expecting to lose but wanting to make a name for themselves as those who actually challenged the king, went to the lists, and of course they were all roundly defeated. Lancelot had kept Lavayne out of the fray, cautioning him that it would be much better to do well in the melee that would follow the next day than to challenge the reigning monarch. And so the first day passed without incident."

"It was the second day, as I remember, that things began to unravel for Lancelot," I continued. "What I remember best—what led me to suspect that something very strange was going on—was that King Arthur started the day by forbidding Sir Gawain to take part in the tournament. Why on earth would he do that, I wondered."

"Exactly," Gareth added. "Arthur had glimpsed Lancelot himself the night before when he walked by one of the pavilions outside of Winchester where the knights were quartered during the tournament. Lancelot and his young companion were just moving their things into an obscure pavilion on the edge of the encampment, and the king had chanced to recognize him, and also recognized that the livery one of the servants wore who was helping them get settled there was the livery of his old vassal, Sir Bernard, lord of Guildford. The king deduced immediately what was afoot. He knew, of course, that Gawain would see the prowess of this disguised knight and want to test his mettle himself, and he worried for Gawain's safety if he seriously challenged Lancelot."

The barmaid Lucy came to the table carrying our three fresh pints on a tray, and placed them unceremoniously before us, bending down to give us all a glimpse of her ample cleavage. Then she tucked the tray under her arm and, giving me a surreptitious wink, bustled off to see if Master Bailey wanted her in the kitchen.

"And actually, the king was very concerned about all of his knights," Gareth continued, and I forced my attention back on him. "Especially in the wake of that Grail quest that decimated his vassals. So he was careful to lay down explicit rules for the tournament. Knights were limited to four lances: if they broke all four, they could not joust with a fifth. Other weapons—axes, flails, and maces of all kinds, and all thrusting weapons like short swords or dirks or long daggers—were forbidden. Aside from his lance, a knight could carry only his one-handed arming sword, to be used for battering, never for thrusting. The king's motive in all this was to eliminate accidental deaths or serious injuries in the melee. Any knight that was unhorsed must retire from the field, unless his opponent was also unhorsed and he was the first to clamber back into the saddle—into any saddle. By such means did the king ensure that the tournament was for sport, not for simulating true warfare. You remember, Gildas, you were there."

"That I was, and I thought the rules were sensible even if I didn't expect them to prevent serious injuries. You have hundreds of armed and mounted warriors charging each other with lances and whacking away at each other with swords. It's a pretty good bet that somebody's going to get hurt. And so somebody was. It's just lucky nobody was killed."

"Well you remember that Arthur, the Scottish king, and King Anguisshe of Ireland put their knights up against the vassals of the King of North Wales, the King of Northumberland, the King with the Hundred Knights, and Sir Galahalt the Haut Prince, and when the heralds blew 'Unto the Field,' ah, what a sight it was to have all those well-armed knights—three hundred on a side—lined up on their destriers to charge one another." Gareth's eyes took on a far-away look, and I had to agree that seldom had I seen the like of that great mass of chivalry gathered together in one glorious place.

Merlin cleared his throat. "They were playing a game. God's bodykins, there was nothing glorious about it. It was a playing field. They were exercising. It meant nothing. True chivalry *means* something."

"Well, in this case it meant charging knights and clashing arms," Gareth continued, unfazed by the dim view Merlin was taking. "The trumpets blew again, and at that signal, three hundred knights on one side charged in a mass formation toward three hundred knights on the other side. When they came together, good Lord, what a sight! At least fifty knights down on each side, and that meant dozens out of the fray after the first charge. Most of the knights who remained on horseback had splintered their lances, and rode in haste to the sidelines to their squires to take up another and to attack or defend against one another in smaller groups, or on a more individual basis."

"I recall you came to where I was keeping your lances and grabbed one, and then joined with your brothers, Gaheris and Agravaine, and galloped off to take on a small contingent of knights from the King of North Wales' company."

"Your memory is better than mine, Gildas. I was so fired by the whole experience that I don't even recall needing a second lance. But now that you mention it, I do remember wondering where Gawain was—at the time I didn't realize that King Arthur had commanded Gawain not to take part in the melee, and that he was sitting with the king in the royal scaffolding overlooking the field. And what they saw of me and my two brothers was our demolishing of seven of those knights from North Wales, and three of those I had dispatched myself. I began to think that I might be in good position to take the prize at that tournament, what with Lancelot out of the picture, and Gawain apparently not on the field either.

"But at the same time I saw that my old friend Sir Kay, along with Sir Bedivere, Sir Griflet, Sir Lucan the butler, and about eight or ten other knights, including my other brother, your much-loved Sir Mordred," at that I coughed and nearly lost my latest swallow of ale, "were riding into the great mass of the King of Northumberland's knights and hurling down anyone that came into their path. It was beginning to look like a rout, for the knights of the Round Table simply were in a completely different category from those on the other side."

"And that was the moment that I noticed the knight with the red sleeve," I took over the story. "He and his companion had been holding back through the initial assault. They had, in fact, been hiding in a small patch of trees outside the lists. Now suddenly they came in and surprised everyone on both sides, but they made a direct line for Kay and his large knot of knights, and with a single spear the knight with the red sleeve smote down Kay, Griflet, Lucan, and that sorry excuse for a human being, your half-brother."

Gareth nodded. "That he did. And from my spot on the field I could see him turn and bear down three more knights of that group, seven knights and all of the Round Table. I had seen the like before only three times: Sir Lamorak, Sir Tristram, and Sir Lancelot were the only knights I had ever heard of who were capable of such a feat. Now it seemed we must add a fourth to their number, this anonymous knight, who bore no device on his shield but was recognizable only by the red sleeve."

"I know I was pretty astonished myself, watching from the sidelines," I added. "His companion was doing well himself—he had unhorsed a couple of Round Table knights of his own, including Sir Bedivere, who's been in more tournaments than anybody else in Camelot, if I'm not mistaken."

"Yes. Sir Lavayne, as it turned out. He made an impressive debut. But the knight with the sleeve, now he was a wonder. It could not be that he was a new knight like Lavayne. He was the most skilled knight on the field. Gawain told me later that, up in the stands with Arthur, he had told the king with much excitement that this knight was one of the greatest he had seen, and since Lamorak and Tristram are both dead, he would swear it was Lancelot himself if it weren't for the red sleeve: Lancelot, he knew, had never worn a lady's token, and for reasons suspected if not commonly known, was never like to."

Merlin cleared his throat in a cautionary way, as if alluding to Lancelot's relationship with the queen, even here where there were few ears and no one seeming to care much about what we were saying, was not advisable, and that Gareth had better tone it down.

Gareth went on as if nothing had happened, but left any conjecture as to Lancelot's motives in wearing, or in *not* wearing, ladies' tokens hanging in the air. "This knight with the red sleeve was having his way with anyone who stood against him, up and down the field, until no individual knight would even approach him anymore. That was the point where Bors de Ganis decided he had had enough."

"Yes, Sir Bors does take offense if he thinks the honor of the Round Table is at stake," I remarked.

"And he is also jealous of his cousin's reputation, and when it seemed as if this upstart 'Knight of the Red Sleeve' was beginning to reach the point where he might be calling into question Lancelot's preeminence, Bors was going to shut this down. Always kind of a killjoy, that Bors, but a pretty doughty knight for all that. He joined together with Lancelot's own brother Ector, and other kinsmen, Sir Bleoberis and Sir Blamor de Ganys, and five others, so that nine knights of his own country now rode at Lancelot, with no idea who he was except that he was knocking every Round Table knight in the melee onto his well-armored arse."

"But what a sight it was when Bors, at the head of his company, hurled himself headlong at the knight with the sleeve," I continued. "The shock stunned that borrowed destrier the Red Sleeve Knight was riding and it stumbled, and in that second, Bors' lance drove into that knight's side, breaking the lance there and even leaving the head in his flesh."

"And by the rules of the tournament, the Knight with the Red Sleeve would have been out of it had not Sir Lavayne, at the same instant, knocked Sir Bleoberis off his own horse and quickly brought his red-sleeved counterpart the new horse to mount again. And he was on it, wound and all, before anyone could count him out of the tournament. He was able to grab himself what was his last lance, and ride back at Sir Bors with such fury that he knocked him off his horse, and in a kind of frenzy, turned, leaned down and yanked the helmet off of Bors' head, drawing his sword to have a swing at Bors' unprotected pate. But he returned to his senses quickly enough, and let Bors go. Seeing who it was that wounded him no doubt cooled his rage, though at the time I just thought he was being chivalrous."

Merlin snorted. "He rode away from the encounter and, though few marked it, rode off the field itself and back through the trees from which he had entered, followed by Sir Lavayne."

"And this you call high chivalry," Merlin scoffed. "Arthur's greatest knight plays a silly game, pretending to be somebody else, so that he can knock some of his friends off their horses in a larger game. In the process gets himself severely wounded and then almost kills his own kinsman in a rage over the squabble, the point of which is what? To brag about who won the game? How precisely does this conform to *anything* in the great Pentecost oath? What does it have to do with defending the right against forces of evil? With giving succor to ladies? With advancing the king's law? What good does it do to *anybody*?"

Gareth shrugged. "Maybe none at all, in itself. But you know, skills in battle against those same forces of evil don't come from nowhere. God doesn't just make a great knight. Lancelot doesn't just turn into a great warrior through some magic spell of yours, Old Necromancer. It takes training. Hours and hours of training. Gildas can tell you that. And part of that training is meeting other knights one-on-one in mock battle. It's the only way. And yes, sometimes knights are hurt or wounded. But there's no other way to hone our skills."

Merlin raised one side of his mouth along with his substantial hedge of eyebrows. "I grant you that there is merit in practicing martial arts. And though it seems silly to glorify the practice, I won't dispute the necessity to make the knights take the practice seriously. But how serious can it be when Lancelot plays these kinds of games? And how is being nearly killed by his cousin's spear point going to make Lancelot a better warrior? These things have nothing to do with what you call chivalry!"

"Look, do you want to hear the rest of this story or not?" Gareth huffed. "So the tournament comes to a close, and all the kings call it a draw. And they also unanimously vote to give the tournament's big prize to the Knight with the Red Sleeve. But of course by then he had gone and no one knew where. We had a great feast anyway, and everybody drank to the noble Red Sleeve Knight. Everyone was curious about where he could have gone or why he didn't stay around for his prize, though Sir Bors knew he had wounded him, maybe gravely."

"So where was he, then? Gone somewhere to be healed, I daresay," Merlin asked.

"There's an old knight of the Table, Sir Baldwin of Brittany, who became a hermit and has a cell near Winchester. He's a learned man in the healing arts, and Lancelot knew it, so he compelled Sir Lavayne to take him there with all due speed. Now recall, I had all this much later from Sir Gawain, who had learned all after the fact. The hermit Baldwin took one look at Lancelot's face and, in addition to recognizing him as the Great Knight, could also see that unless he got that truncheon out of his side, the king was going to have one dead champion on his hands.

"When he pulled it out, Lancelot fainted from the pain, and maybe that was best. Baldwin used all his healing arts, searched his wound and put together some kind of poultice that he thought would give Lancelot a chance to live, and bandaged the wound to staunch the blood. And Sir Lavayne sat outside the hermit's cell biting his fingernails.

"Meanwhile back in Winchester at the great feast, the kings and great barons were speculating as to who their champion knight could have been, and why he didn't stay for his award. Gawain and I were with them, so I can tell you this for certain. At the time, Arthur just assumed that Lancelot had slipped away in order to preserve the secret of who he was, although that didn't make any sense to me: I mean, if you're going to go to all that trouble to disguise yourself in order to gain the honors you would have missed otherwise when nobody would fight with you, what possible reason could you have to keep the secret afterwards, when it was time for you to claim those honors? Anyway, it was Galahalt the Haut Prince who told Arthur that none of the leaders on his side had any idea who the Knight with the Red Sleeve was either, but that he was pretty sure he'd seen him sorely wounded by a lance, and that he had looked like he had one foot in the grave when he'd ridden out of the melee with his companion. At that, Arthur blanched, and it was too much for Gawain. Gawain was so impressed by the knight's chivalry"—at the word he glanced over at Merlin, who merely, once again, rolled his eyes a bit—"and so distraught over his severe wounding, that he vowed then and there to take off and find that knight, to make sure he was alive as well as to find out just who he was.

"Well you know how impetuous Gawain is. He had jumped up and was ready to go after the Knight of the Red Sleeve right then, but the king got up and laid a hand on his shoulder before he climbed down from that scaffold. 'I have reason to suspect that he lodged last night at Astolat, with Sir Bernard. Ride to his lodgings first, and see what you can find out there. I would not for half my kingdom have anything happen to this knight.'"

"You overheard this?" I asked at that point.

"I did," Gareth responded, grinning. "It was clear from that point that the king certainly knew who this champion was, and I had no little suspicion it was Lancelot. I mean, who else?"

"So what happened when Gawain got to Sir Bernard's house?" I followed up.

"Well, about what you'd expect. Gawain asks about the two knights with the blank shields, and Sir Baldwin tells him it was his son Lavayne and another knight, who wouldn't tell anyone his name. And Elaine, the fair maid, is there, and clamors to know the outcome of the tournament, and how the Knight with the Red Sleeve comported himself, and Gawain—who never met a woman he didn't want to flirt with—is more than willing to tell her what she wants to hear, and informs her that the Knight with the Red Sleeve was the clear champion of the tournament, and she says well, she knew it, and then tells my brother that the red sleeve was her own token, that she had given it to the knight, who, she now claimed, she loves more than life itself."

"But what about the shield?" I wanted to know. "She had Lancelot's shield in keeping, right? Didn't Gawain see that?"

Gareth had paused to down what was left in his cup, and signaled to the innkeeper for another round. Which signaled to me that his story had a few more episodes left before he'd be done. "Just getting to that, Gildas my lad. Elaine told him about the switching of the shields and the knight's desire to enter the tournament as an unknown. Of course, when Gawain got a look at the shield the knight had left he knew it was Lancelot's right away and he started to laugh. Well Elaine didn't know how to take that, but Gawain apologized and told her it was a laugh of joy, not derision. The paragon of courtesy that is my brother Gawain apparently bowed to her and praised her for her good judgment: 'You've given your love to the man of most worship in the whole world,' he told her. 'This is the shield of the one true bulwark of the Round Table: the incomparable Sir Lancelot.'

"Well I guess that really got her going, crying things like 'I knew it! I knew he was worthy of my love!' And old Sir Bernard was pretty impressed as well. Because you know, they say that nobility alone makes one worthy of love, and that only the truly noble can truly love. It follows that the nobler your lover, the nobler you are, since you are naturally drawn to that nobility. Ergo, Elaine of Astolat had demonstrated her own noble nature in recognizing the nobility in Lancelot without even hearing his name. And that just made her love him all the more."

"Sheer poppycock," Merlin muttered. "Sentimental clap-trap. Or worse: fairy stories that aristocrats tell each other to convince themselves they deserve their exalted station in life."

By rights, I should have probably been on Merlin's side on this question, since I was myself just the son of a Cornish armor-maker, lucky enough to be appointed a page at court. But being in love, as I was and always would be with the beautiful Lady Rosemounde, heiress of the powerful Duke Hoel of Brittany, I took comfort in the belief that such a love ennobled me, too, and made me the worthy equal of any knight in Camelot, even my lord Gareth, nephew to the king.

Gareth shrugged. "That's one point of view. But Elaine of Astolat is a pretty low-ranking aristocrat. Her love of Lancelot is to her credit. But Gawain did make one thoughtless comment: he mentioned that he didn't recognize Lancelot on the field because of the sleeve. 'Lancelot had never worn any woman's token in any tournament before,' he said, and all that did was make Elaine think Lancelot must be in love with her as well."

"So it got her hopes up," I murmured.

"Did it ever. But still, nobody knows where Lancelot is except Sir Lavayne, and he hasn't been home yet either. Gawain leaves the girl and heads back to Camelot. He figures once he spreads the word it was Lancelot who was so sorely wounded at the tournament that some of his kinsmen might know where he could have gone. So when he gets to Camelot, he talks to me and some of Lancelot's other friends, and then goes to Sir Bors and Sir Ector.

"When Bors hears that the Red Sleeve Knight that he ran his lance into was his own cousin and lord, he becomes really distraught. Gawain says he's never seen Bors so emotional. Which isn't saying much—Bors could have frowned and you could say you've never seen him so emotional. But Bors says right away he knows where Lancelot must have gone: he knows the old hermit just as well as Lancelot does. And so he's on his horse and heading off toward Winchester before Gawain has even had a chance to have a drink after his own long ride."

"Well, I remember Gawain coming back," I added. "I remember, too, how angry the queen was when she heard that Lancelot had worn another woman's sleeve. She was out of sorts for days. Even made comments to the effect that if Lancelot died of his wounds, it was no great loss, that obviously Bors was the better knight or he wouldn't have been able to wound Lancelot so gravely."

"She was indeed," Gareth agreed. "I scrupulously avoided her for a few days there—my friendship with Lancelot was not going to do me any favors in the queen's sight at that point."

"Smoke with no fire," I told him. "I know the queen better than anyone. Well, except perhaps for Lancelot and a couple of her ladies-in-waiting." (I had Rosemounde in mind chiefly). "I knew she was only frustrated and a bit jealous, but she knew why he had done it, so the sleeve didn't bother her that much. And she didn't want to let her concern for him give away the secret they've kept hidden for so many years. She was petrified, mad with concern for his life. But Master, tell me about the girl. Isn't that the point of this whole long discourse? What was Elaine of Astolat doing all this time?"

"Well, Bors, as I said, was the only one in Camelot with a clue as to where Lancelot might be, but remember the only knight who actually *knew* where he was was Sir Lavayne, and once Lancelot seemed out of immediate danger, Lavayne left him in the hands of the hermit and rode home to Astolat, vowing to return after he had brought news of the tournament and Lancelot's fate to his father and siblings. So, by the time Bors arrived at the hermit's cell, the maid was already there, nursing Lancelot with an eagerness that made Bors blush. The way Bors tells it, she never left her patient's side except to go get him some broth to keep up his strength, or to get new bandages or salve from the hermit to work on his wound, which was beginning to heal properly.

"So of course, Bors gets down on his knees and he says something like, 'Oh, my lord, I'm overcome with shame that my hand could lift a lance against you, let alone wound you so sorely with it. I deserve to have my fingers cut off at the elbows for lifting a weapon against you,' or some such thing, and Lancelot, of course, is all forgiving and tells him, 'No, no, Cousin, it was all my fault, my pride led me to take part against King Arthur's knights and you were only defending the honor of our liege lord. You didn't know who I was,' and so on and so on, and Bors says, 'That's right, I didn't, and don't you think maybe you should have told me at least?' And Lancelot says 'Oh, don't worry, I will next time.' And Bors says '*Next* time? You mean you're going to do this again? Didn't you learn anything from *this* little adventure? I nearly killed you!' and Lancelot says 'This? Just a scratch, just a scratch, don't let it bother you,' and Bors finally says 'Oh yeah? I'll give you a scratch…'" Merlin's eyes rolled back in his head. "You're making all this up, aren't you?" he sighed.

"Well, mostly, yes, but I'm just giving you the gist of what transpired. Anyway, Bors stayed there with Lancelot, sleeping in the hermit's cell for weeks, until Lancelot was almost ready to mount a horse again. And through it all, Elaine stayed as well, attending to him so that the hermit, old Sir Baldwin, told Bors that Lancelot might not have recovered so well or so quickly if it weren't for the girl's nursing. And Bors, getting ready to return to Camelot and expecting Lancelot to follow him within days, gave Lancelot a stern warning before he left. 'This girl,' he said, 'is going to expect something from you that you will not be willing to give.'

"Lancelot was skeptical, but soon discovered how true Bors' words were. When Sir Lancelot was finally able to mount his horse, he courteously escorted Elaine back to her father's house, thinking to simply bid her goodbye there and return to Camelot, which he had sorely missed in the six weeks or so he had spent recovering in Baldwin's cell. They were welcomed, of course, by Lord Bernard and Sir Tirre, and Lancelot was made much of, now that they knew who he was. He banqueted well and stayed the night, and in the morning made ready to go, collecting his shield and arms and getting Minuit saddled.

"Now I had the rest of this direct from Sir Tirre, who was there for most of it, and I apologize if it's not as detailed as Gawain's and Bors' stories, but Tirre just gave me the essentials."

At that I yawned and drained the last leavings of my cup. "Well, you've gone on forever as it is, so a quick end might be a good idea— we've got to get back to the castle and to bed." Merlin, who'd been pretty quiet for awhile, gave a nearly inaudible grunt.

"But this is the most important part," Sir Gareth warned. "Elaine, seeing her knight getting ready to leave, and apparently without speaking to her alone as she had imagined, took matters into her own hands and cornered him while he was tending to his horse. There in the stable she propositioned him as bluntly as a woman ever did a man: 'Marry me,' she says to him. 'You know that I love you, I have never left your side these six weeks. And I know you must feel something special for me as well, since as you told me, you never in all your career wore a woman's token in a tournament.' At that you can be sure the Great Knight turned red and flinched. But she went on, 'I am not from one of the great families of Logres, and can bring you nothing but my love and my maiden body. Please speak with my father before you leave…'

"So how was he going to answer that? Well, you know Lancelot, he stammered a bit but he did come out with the truth unvarnished: she had his eternal gratitude, he says, for seeing him through his recovery, and he would always bless her name. He loves her, he says, like a sister…"

"He did *not* say that! Not *that*!" I shook my head in disbelief. How could somebody that naïve and clueless about women have ever won the heart of the most prominent woman in the kingdom—the queen herself? But he had, that was the known quantity in this equation. "Did he just leave it at that?" I prompted.

"No, he goes on to say that his heart belongs to another, and can never be his to give again, or some such rubbish. But apparently even that didn't daunt her. She goes down on her knees—her *knees* I tell you—and begs Lancelot to take her as his lover, then, because at least she'll have something from him. And that's when things turned tricky."

"*That's* when they turned tricky?" I raised my eyebrows.

"Lancelot left the stable and came out to the middle of the courtyard of Lord Bernard's house, and he called the lord and Sir Tirre there to speak with him. First, he assured them that he had never touched the maid Elaine in any improper manner, or encouraged her to any lewdness, but had only the deepest respect for her. But he said he could not marry her—the heart cannot be coerced, he asserted, and he simply could not be made to love her, nor would he marry her. That's when he made the generous financial offer that you heard him declare at the river when the body turned up this morning. Sir Tirre thought it was rather insulting, as if his sister could be bought off. But in any case, Lancelot made the offer and bade them farewell, and returned to Camelot. And she, as we know from this morning, managed to die of a broken heart, and in that boat to bring it all back home to Lancelot's door."

I looked down at the table and weighed the whole story. "Merlin would say," I ventured, glancing over at the mage, who was not stirring, "that no one has ever died of a broken heart. People grieve to the point of destroying themselves through neglect or deliberate action, but it isn't the grief itself that kills them. Isn't that true, old man?" I kicked at Merlin's chair to awaken him if he had fallen asleep, but got only a low groan.

Merlin's face had turned an ashen gray, and his eyes were skewed, so that one squinted while the other seemed to bulge unnaturally from its socket. He put his head into his hands and swayed from side to side. I could interpret these signs. It was one of Merlin's spells. They came upon him periodically, when the pain in his head became too much for him and he collapsed in exhaustion. There was nothing to be done but to let him sleep until the pain passed, which might be overnight or it might be three days later. I called to the innkeeper, "Mister Bailey, my companion is taken ill! Do you have a room where he can spend the night?"

William Bailey came over and fussed sympathetically. "Oh, my lord Merlin! Of course, of course…"

Sir Gareth had leapt up and was at Merlin's side, helping him to his feet. As he supported the mage's right side, I held up his left, and together we moved the unresisting—and nearly unresponsive—Merlin toward a room in the back where William Bailey was leading us. We got a few curious looks from the smattering of customers still sitting in muted conversation around the tables of the inn, but they soon looked away, assuming it was just another old man who had drunk too much of Master Bailey's ale and was going in the back room to sleep it off.

But just as we came to the threshold, Merlin's head jerked up. "Listen!" He said in a slurred voice. "The boot that tramples the white lily impedes the laurel!"

Gareth looked at me in surprised bewilderment, perhaps believing the old man had finally lost his wits altogether, but I just shrugged and gave him a half-smile. "Just one of Merlin's prophetic moments, I'm afraid. I have no idea what it means either."

CHAPTER THREE

THE LUSTY MONTH OF MAY

I wasn't just being flippant with Gareth. I really didn't know what Merlin meant. Those spells of his were always accompanied by some kind of gibberish that never seemed to make any sense until much later. This is how Merlin had gained his reputation as a seer or prophet. He'd mumble something about a great whale swimming in a tub of wine and three weeks later, if an obese abbot or bishop became tipsy while banqueting with the king, someone would remember and say, "Aha! Merlin predicted this would happen! The abbot is fat as a whale, and he drank a tub of wine!" And so it went.

The fact was, though, that occasionally Merlin's "prophesies" had helped us out in our investigations, like the time he had muttered in his trance that "the green limb is black," and after some time we realized that Sir Florent's shield with the black tree could have been mistaken in the dark for Sir Tristram's with the green tree—and saved Florent from hanging. Or the time he prophesied "the dog turns on his master," which pointed to who was really responsible for the death of La Belle Isolde. What his ramblings were about this time I had no idea, but since we were not on a case, I ignored them and so did Gareth, and Merlin was fully recovered by the next day.

Things in Camelot got really interesting for me in those few weeks after my knighting ceremony. Yes, Lancelot had taken off—Gareth was absolutely right about that—and no one, not even Sir Bors, seemed to know where he had gone. "Seeking adventure" was the official word. "Sulking" was probably more like it. But the queen was not having it: she was not going to show a face to the world that was not self-sufficient, serene, and royal. She was also dead set on doing something special for her favorite former page to welcome me into the ranks of the aristocracy upon my elevation to knighthood, and what she came up with was this:

A proclamation was presented to the knights at Camelot that the queen wished to create a new sub-order of knights from the Round Table, an elite core of eight valiant knights who would vow to be of particular service to the queen and her household, and to be on call when she wished to employ them on her business. I assumed she had set the number at eight because she had at the moment eight ladies-in-waiting, and wanted an equal number of knights so that on state occasions there would be a balanced number around her on the dais. The proclamation stated that knights who wished to be considered for such a role should apply directly to the queen. But the fact is, she already had certain knights in mind for this honor, and I was one of them.

Sir Palomides, the Moorish knight, was among them as well, and I suspected the queen had him in mind all along, if for nothing else than for his talent for composing songs of love with which he might entertain us. Sir Agravain, Gareth's older brother—who resembled his brother Gawain in his red hair and green eyes, but his brother Mordred in temperament—was chosen, I'm certain, to please the Orkney clan and their powerful faction in the court. Sir Brandiles, a longtime close friend and ally of Lancelot, was another choice, clearly intended to gratify the Lancelot-Bors bloc in Camelot. Another choice, and one that surprised me, was Sir Kay, Arthur's seneschal, one of the earliest of all the knights to ally himself with the king, and one who had been, in fact, the king's foster-brother in their youth. Most people thought him something of a boor, and I was no exception. But politically, it was a brilliant appointment on the queen's part, since with it, she pleased the most important member of the court—the king himself.

The other three Queen's Knights were, like me, relatively new to the Table. This, I assumed, was to allay any suspicion that the whole thing was simply a way for Guinevere to clothe me, her favorite former page, in underserved honors. She also elevated my good friend Thomas, former squire to Sir Ywain, and Sir Tirre, brother of the ill-fated Fair Maid of Astolat—both of whom, you'll recall, had just been knighted with me. To round out that total of eight honored knights, the queen chose another relative newcomer to Camelot, the knight named Sir Pelleas, who was known, for reasons that probably don't need explaining, as "the Lover."

May had come to Camelot, and with it, the primal desire to be off in the countryside enjoying the soft breezes, the newly green fields, and the sweet perfumes of the wild flowers that grew in the woods north of the castle. And so, the queen declared that our first official duty as members of the honorable order of the Queen's Knights was to assemble on a Friday morning late in May in a clearing in the woods that was familiar to all, a clearing that surrounded one of the oldest trees in the forest—a large beech tree that everyone called the "Fairy Tree"—in order to welcome the summer with dances on the green and the crowning of a May Queen from among her retinue.

We were warned to meet in the middle bailey at prime, and to come dressed in green and prepared to celebrate the new life of spring with all due merriment. Like the other knights, I wore brown hose and a dark green tunic without a hood, so that the mild western breeze tousled my long, brown locks—oh yes, I was somewhat vain about my hair in those days. The queen had provided each knight with a gentle palfrey, and each knight rode into the wood holding one of the ladies-in-waiting before him in the saddle. The queen rode her own horse, and next to her, Sir Kay rode with my lady Rosemounde before him. This, of course, caused me no end of envy, but I realized that Guinevere was protecting me from any suspicion by letting the king's own seneschal escort her primary lady, the wife of Sir Mordred, the king's own nephew. I and Thomas, bringing up the rear of the procession that left the castle for the woods, were escorting a pair of sisters newly come into the queen's household, the nieces of King Arthur's senior knight, the good Sir Bedivere, whose father was a minor lord in Winchester. Lady Mary, my own charge, was a sprightly, thin blonde with flashing blue eyes and an animated demeanor that made her head jerk about whenever she saw anything that to her seemed new and exciting—and to her fifteen-year-old eyes everything looked new and exciting. Her sister, Lady Elizabeth, was all of thirteen, and was a darker, plumper version of her sister physically, but her opposite temperamentally, as she rode most of the way with her head down, too shy or too insecure to say much in that very noble, and significantly older, company.

"I'm going to weave myself a garland of flowers for my hair so fine it will look like a royal crown. Oh, who do you think will be the Queen of the May? Truly Bessie, do you think it might be me? Wouldn't Father be ever so proud if I could write home and tell him that's happened? But he'll be tickled in any case when we tell him all about this picnic, don't you think? Who'd have thought we'd be celebrating the May first here at court the way we did back home? But escorted by such handsome knights as well, how could it be more romantic?" Lady Mary chattered like a magpie as we ambled out of the castle gate, under the barbican, from which I thought I heard Roger Kempe, captain of the king's guard, call a sympathetic "have fun, boys," as we passed under the guardhouse.

I admit I reddened visibly when Lady Mary talked about romantic, handsome knights, and when she rolled her eyes back toward me, I glanced over at Thomas, who rolled his own skyward. The lady Elizabeth just pursed her lips and murmured, "If you say so, Mare-sy."

And so we passed the half hour it took our small party to amble its way the mile and a half through the new blooming birches and oaks that lined our path through those woods, Lady Mary babbling away in expostulations I had long since stopped listening to, Lady Elizabeth adding an occasional morose response, and Thomas and I communicating our mutual long-suffering reactions through squinting eyes and writhing lips.

The fresh sunshine glistened off the dew as we arrived at the clearing around the old beech. Ducking my own head to evade the flailing pate of the boisterous Lady Mary, I laughed and dismounted, reaching up to help the lady down from her perch in the saddle while her mouth rattled on. "Oh look at that old tree! It must be hundreds of years old. Do you think it's really the home of fairies? It's even bigger than the one back home, isn't it Bessie? Oh I do hope we'll have music and dancing, don't you? I just adore dancing around the Maypole. Bessie does, too, don't you Bessie?"

Bessie, or the lady Elizabeth I should say, was preempted in her response by the queen herself, who was now dismounted and in the middle of the clearing, commanding the scene. Sir Kay, who seemed to have been in on the planning for the occasion, was distributing to each participant long ribbons, pink for the ladies and green for the gentlemen, and the queen was making her wishes known. "We'll welcome the May first with the traditional dance! Take your ribbons, tie them to the branches of the old Fairy Tree, and dance about it! Sir Palomides, you will please accompany us!"

It was then that I noticed Sir Palomides had donned a green mask, covered with woodland leaves but provided with eyeholes to enable him to see his instrument, and, sitting cross-legged beneath the great tree, began to play a lively tune on his gittern. The rest of us, strange as it seemed to be frolicking on command, did as the queen bade. I tied my ribbon to one of the tree's low branches and began, with the other knights, to dance to Sir Palomides' sprightly tune, gamboling around the tree in one direction, while the ladies all cavorted going the other direction. Each time I passed Lady Rosemounde, she flashed me her familiar smirk and made me sigh. And each time I passed Lady Mary, she batted her long eyelashes in my direction, which made me sigh in a different way.

Well before terce, we had exhausted the energy of the morning, and all lay flushed and spent, supine in the grass under the great beech tree. I reclined near Sir Palomides, who had removed his "Green Man" mask and was huffing and puffing, having tired himself with his musical exertions and, perspiring from the hot mask, was wiping his green sleeve across his dark Moorish forehead. "Ah, spring!" he exulted, looking over at me and laughing at my weary countenance. "The mating season! When a young man's fancy turns to thoughts of his beloved, does it not, my young friend? Before this afternoon is over, I'll sing you one of my new compositions on just that very subject!" He laughed again, and he was not the only one caught up in the rites of spring. I noticed some serious flirtations developing among some of my companions. The lady Mary, it seemed, had despaired of getting me to notice her, and had moved on to Thomas, who somewhat abashedly was responding with some interest to her garrulous advances.

But we had come now to the central part of the outing. Queen Guinevere stood again in the midst of the clearing, and instructed us to go into the woods and do homage to May: "Ladies," she exclaimed, "be off! You must find yourself your own perch among the trees, there to await the coming of whichever knight happens upon you!" With a rush of skirts and a chorus of youthful giggles, the eight ladies all sped off in different directions. It seemed clear they were ready for this game, and I supposed the queen had discussed it with them before they had ever left her chambers. There was certainly no reluctance on the ladies' parts, and as they ran off, I noted the direction taken by the lady Rosemounde, as I had no doubt she expected me to do.

Now the queen prepared to give us knights our own instructions, and Sir Kay once again had visited his horse's burden, this time coming out with eight small baskets made of rushes. "These are the rules, by my royal decree!" Queen Guinevere called when each of us had basket-in-hand. "I am charging you all to do homage to May by picking a basketful of the most colorful flowers you can find in the woods! Your task is to gather these flowers and to find one of my ladies in the woods, and she is to weave your flowers into a garland for her hair! But you must all return here before sext, for I have a delicious picnic banquet being loaded in a wagon as we speak, and being brought here by my kitchen staff even now. The lady with the most beautiful of garlands will be chosen Queen of the May! Now go, seek your flowers and your ladies, but even if you fail to find a lady, return before sext—that is the overriding rule!"

With less giggling and a lot more murmuring, the eight of us started off to follow the queen's instructions. I knew which way I was heading: the same direction that Rosemounde had taken, off to my left, which was south and toward the running brook I knew snaked through the woods toward Merlin's cave and Lady Lake. Thomas, I noted, took off in the opposite direction, the way the chattering Lady Mary had scampered. I reasoned she would not be hard to find, since her sister went in the same direction, and the lady Mary was sure to be nattering all the while. Sir Palomides, whose own love for La Belle Isolde had been well-known, had foresworn any flirtations since that lady's untimely death, but still trudged gamely among the trees, aware that in court, one must play whatever game is afoot.

Leaving the clearing behind, I caught sight of a number of daisies near the base of a birch tree, and I quickly grabbed them for my basket. And the farther I walked, the more flowers I found. It was curious: I had scarcely paid attention to these glories of the woods before, but now, forced at the queen's whim to gather flowers, I became aware of the great variety and beauty of those wild denizens of the forests of Logres. A few early spring flowers—delicate pink primroses and bouncing yellow daffodils—could still be found in some places, and I added several of these to my basket. Tall clusters of bright yellow cowslips had sprung up in some of the boggier areas of the woods, and I gathered a bouquet of these on my walk. Small white bunches of cow parsley were growing in the less shady borders of the wood, and I snatched up some of these, and in the shadier and drier places, I was glad to find sprouts of bright purple columbine. In one of the most ancient tracks of wood, I found a virtual carpet of deep blue or violet bluebells. To these I added some of the creamy white flowers of the native woodbine or honeysuckle, and my basket was nearly full by the time I reached the brook, where I stopped and, taken aback by what I saw, nearly dropped the basket unto the forest floor. For there, reclining on a large flattened rock at the edge of the stream, her bare feet dangling in the water as she gazed in my direction, was my lady Rosemounde. I—and my basket—quickly and wordlessly joined her.

Her deep brown eyes looked up at me with a piercing darkness, the corners crinkling in amusement as her mouth formed her signature smirk. The light garland that already encircled her long, loose hair gave off a faint perfume that merged with her breath, which smelled of apples as I leaned toward her. That breath grew heavier as she closed, then opened her eyes, and looked again into mine, and I was aware without touching it of the softness of her pale skin and the roundness of her breasts under the laces of her loose smock. The pile of fresh flowers in my lap camouflaged my rising ardor and, unable to restrain it, I put forward my trembling hand to caress her alabaster cheek as it tilted toward me until, without thought or premeditation, I drew her toward me and met her lips with mine, pressing against them so hungrily that I could feel her teeth pushing against mine before they parted, yielding to the onslaught of my tongue. My left hand moved onto her right leg and slid furtively up her thigh, till with a start I realized she was wearing nothing under her smock. I drew my face back and scrutinized her. "You planned this?" I asked.

She flushed and looked down, though her smirk remained. "No, no!" she replied. "But I did…anticipate?"

And so, though I hesitate to confess this here, that was the point at which I committed the sin of adultery with the lady Rosemounde for a second time. God knows I have confessed this before and done penance, but I must admit once more that I have never truly repented that sin. I tell you sincerely that I have prayed devoutly to feel true contrition. But God does not always answer our prayers in the ways we expect.

***

"You already have your garland, I see," I murmured in her ear as we lay languorously at the edge of the brook, each with a hand dangling playfully in the cool rushing water.

"Yes," she breathed. "I didn't want to waste time weaving it later. How much time have we got before sext? Maybe I can weave a few of those bluebells in—I didn't have any of those when I made this."

I looked up at the sun and scowled. "Time went a little faster than I anticipated, I'm afraid," I answered her. "I think it's time we found our way back to the queen's picnic."

"Oh, well. I suppose I'll have to give up any hope I had of being Queen of the May."

"For me, you're the queen of every month," I told her. "Anyway, why not let the young Lady Mary have it? It seems to mean a whole lot to her."

"Yes, poor thing," Rosemounde said. "She has so little, anyway.

Let's give her that at least."

I looked up at her as I gathered up my remaining flowers and bound them into a nosegay to hand to Rosemounde. "What do you mean, she has so little?"

"Well," Rosemounde shrugged and looked slightly abashed as she accepted the bouquet I handed her. "It's not widely known, and you must promise never to let on that you know, but the queen has really taken on the lady Mary and her sister as a kind of charity case, and out of respect for Sir Bedivere and Sir Lucan."

"A charity case?" I echoed.

"Yes," she continued slowly as we began the walk back to the clearing around the great beech tree. "Her father, you see, was shamed irredeemably by…by another knight to whom he owed a great sum of money that he could not pay. My…this other knight had Mary's father—who goes by the name Lowell of Winchester— paraded through the streets in a cart like a common criminal to the center of the city and had him flogged, which the law allowed. There is no way to recover from such a humiliation, and the citizens lost all respect for Lowell. He sits in his house alone, without servants or money, letting what is left of his manor fall to ruin around him. Needless to say, the girls had no prospects for marriage. What man of honor would ally himself with such a house? It is probably a blessing that their mother, Lucan and Bedivere's sister, died more than a year ago, and did not have to witness the fall of her family."

"So the queen has taken the girls on out of the goodness of her heart, eh?" I pondered this, turning over in my mind what Rosemounde had said. Taking a clue from her, I said, "This other knight you mention, it was certainly a churlish act on his part to shame Sir Lowell in that way. What kind of low boor would do such a thing? Not a member of the Round Table, I would hope?"

Rosemounde seemed flustered, avoiding my eyes and hanging her head, regretting now that she had ever brought this up. "It…yes, I'm sorry to say…"

"Not a member of the king's own family, is it?"

At that she looked up at me and knew I had guessed the worst of it. "Yes," she said bluntly. "I don't need to confirm it. It was my husband."

There's nothing that takes the blush off the rose when you've been gleefully performing the rites of spring like coming face to face with the reality of the lady's husband. I'd been blissfully unconscious of the existence of the vile Sir Mordred from the moment I had glimpsed Rosemounde at the brook, but now her revelation about Sir Lowell had brought that dark stain on Arthur's Table back into the forefront of my mind.

"He has always been partial to flogging, as I recall," I observed drily, uncertain of what else to say. "Your back, I notice, has healed quite nicely." My brain had gone straight from mention of Mordred and flogging to the memory of Rosemounde's back after that swine of a husband had beaten her in their home in Orkney. "Nor did I see any fresh bruises on the rest of your body." Indeed, her soft flesh had appeared flawless in the gentle May sun that had lighted our precious dalliance just now. I had not, until this moment, realized the significance of that.

"No," Rosemounde whispered. "As I've said before, as long as we stay in Camelot and I am a part of the queen's train, I'm safe. Now faces blank, my lad, we're entering the clearing!"

Most of the other knights and damsels had returned to the clearing by the time we arrived. Thomas was there with the lady Mary, her garland beautifully woven. Sir Tirre had managed to come across Lady Elizabeth, though she didn't look particularly excited to be seated beside him in the grass. Not that she was likely to have looked very excited in any case. Sir Agravaine sat with one of the other newer ladies-in-waiting, Lady Alison, a diminutive dark-haired beauty from Bath, whose father was an alderman of that town. Agravain looked at me sharply, his green eyes boring a hole in my face, and I knew that it would not be prudent for me to be seen acting too friendly with his brother's wife. Of all the Orkney clan, Agravain was closest to Sir Mordred. I often felt it was by default, since Gawain and Gareth were so close, and Gaheris—well, he had his own dark side, but he always gravitated toward Gareth, whom he saw as the image of his better self. But Agravain, devoted as he might be to the queen as a member of her select band of knights, valued nothing more highly than blood, and so, was fiercely loyal to his uncle the king, and to his closest brother, Mordred.

This much we knew, and without needing to consult, we split up on entering the clearing, Rosemounde to go seat herself in her usual place at the queen's right hand, and I to sit next to Sir Palomides, now seated in the grass under the great beech tree where he had sat before. He was now in the process of tuning his larger instrument, his lute, in preparation for another performance, I assumed. He had apparently not returned with any of the ladies-in-waiting, not that I would have expected him to be particularly flirtatious with any of them, not after the loss of Isolde.

Sir Pelleas had returned with not one, but two damsels, escorting one on each arm: the lovely young Lady Barbara, a teenager nearly as young as Elizabeth, and the formidable Lady Anne, Queen Guinevere's longest-serving Maid of Honor, who was a good ten years older than the gallant Sir Pelleas. But he seemed in his element, and was equally courteous to both ladies. Within minutes of his return, he began entertaining them and the rest of the group by doing a Morris Dance in honor of the May.

As Sir Palomides began accompanying him on his lute, Sir Pelleas demonstrated a sword dance of the sort practiced in his own home town of Glasgow, far to the north. I glanced at Sir Agravain, knowing that the Orkney clan were familiar with this sort of entertainment, known in the north as the *Gillie Callum.* Agravain's eyes were bright with anticipation as Sir Pelleas placed two broadswords crossways on the ground, forming them into an "X" shape. He proceeded to dance around the swords, arms raised above his head and legs kicking about him in all directions. Sir Palomides quickened the tempo of his music, and the pace of Sir Pelleas's dancing picked up accordingly. Now on his toes, Pelleas began to dance within the quarters of the X created by the swords. When he had dazzled everyone with his footwork, Pelleas, still moving with the rhythm of Palomides' quickening strum, bent over and skillfully picked up a sword in each hand, ending his dance by swinging one sword over his head with his left hand, narrowly missing his own skull, then swinging the other under his feet with his right, leaping over the sword and landing with a flourish on two nimble, rhythmic feet.

The whole company laughed and applauded Pelleas's performance, and he bowed to our acclaim like a prancing juggler, a few beads of sweat dripping from his chin as he grinned and winked at his two ladies, Anne nodding back to him graciously and Lady Barbara squealing with delight at his flirting, though I noticed at the same time Sir Agravain stifling a yawn. But now, as Pelleas sat himself near Sir Kay, close by the queen's place, I saw that Sir Palomides was retuning his instrument, preparing to regale us with one of his own compositions in the style of the troubadours. When the whole circle was silent, he struck his lute, lifted his eyes and his voice to the heavens, and began this tribute to Love and to the month of May:

> *The flowers of May*
> *Their colors gay*
> *Burst forth with life anew*
> *Just as my love*
> *In this sweet grove*
> *Bursts from my breast so true.*
> *I cannot calm the urgings of the spring,*
> *Which give me joy that only love can bring.*
>
> *The birds of spring*
> *Rise up and sing*
> *A song that warms my soul*
> *And so my heart*
> *Sings its own part,*
> *Part of the loving whole.*
> *For precious jewel, I give you all of me.*
> *Do what you will, your slave I vow to be.*
>
> *The sweet breeze from the west*
> *Inspires me in the quest*
> *To seek my lady here or anywhere.*
> *Wherever she may go*
> *I lay my pride full low*

Beneath her feet, her dainty feet so fair.
I cannot hope without humility to win
Her passion and her life, her love that moves within.

A hushed silence descended on our circle then, broken only by a few sighs issuing from some of the courtly ladies there, when suddenly I was startled into alertness by the whinny of a horse coming from the trees behind me. And then I was aware that there were horses coming slowly upon us from every direction in that forest—we had been so enthralled by Palomides' performance that we had not noticed a score of fully armed and mounted knights who had crept up on us through the forest and now had us surrounded.

They sat on horseback with visored helmets closed, an eerie, silent force, and at a signal from the one that had emerged directly behind the queen and who seemed to be their leader, the knights drew their swords and held them out in a threatening manner.

The leader spoke out from behind his helmet's visor, a rich low voice that seemed somehow familiar to me. He spoke directly to the queen. "You must yield to me, your majesty. You see we are well armed and your knights have no weapons. Yield now and there need be no bloodshed. But I will have you as my own, whether you resist or not. Your knights can remain safe with all their limbs intact, or they can be slaughtered or maimed by our arms. The choice is yours."

We were all taken aback, and the queen herself was momentarily too shocked to speak, but what happened next happened so fast that we had little time to react. Sir Kay, moving with the instinct of decades of knightly training, leaped from the queen's side and snatched one of the swords Pelleas had been using for his dance, and stepping between Guinevere and the leader of that mounted threat, spat the armed knight's words back in his visored face. "Yield to you, you prancing poltroon? Not today. Come, boy, come—see what you can do against a true knight of the Round Table instead of hiding like a coward behind your armor and shield. Can't face a man, eh? Craven and traitor, recreant knight who makes war upon defenseless women, even your queen? Get down from there and come get the beating you deserve!" Kay's greasy hair flew back in clumps from his head as he shook it, curling his fleshy lips over his yellow teeth in a sneer of defiance.

Now I had known Kay for years and knew him to be a blowhard, a self-involved social climber with a vastly inflated opinion of his own knightly value. But that day he won my grudging admiration and respect for what Sir Gareth would have certainly called his chivalry. And his gallant stand against deadly odds brought the rest of us to life as well. Sir Pelleas grabbed his other sword and moved to stand beside Kay. I had no weapon—I was kicking myself for not having the foresight to bring my exquisite new sword Almace along on this picnic, and for one brief moment thought what a shame it would be if I perished here, never having had a chance to use it. But I shook off that thought and found a branch on the ground that might serve as a club, and I moved to stand in front of the lady Rosemounde. The other ladies-in-waiting now all huddled together near the queen, and the eight Queen's Knights formed a circle around them, some holding knives, some sticks or large stones, Sir Palomides holding up his lute as if it were an axe to bring down on any attackers' heads that came in range. We all knew it was, at best, a symbolic defense, since we could not hope to defend our queen from armed and mounted knights with sticks and stones. And the leader of those brigands was not about to take up Kay's offer and meet him in a fair fight.

Instead of giving Kay an answer, he spurred his horse forward, knocking Kay down and slashing him with his sword. At the same time, the other armed knights moved forward to mow down the rest of us, but before that happened Guinevere finally found her voice.

"Stop this madness at once. I command it!" she shouted over the din. She was standing now, her eyes flashing and her hair flying in the breeze so that she looked like a goddess of the winds with an aspect that demanded to be obeyed. "Queen's Knights, stand down! Let there be no more useless bloodshed. And you *sir,*" she spat the last word as if it were an insult, looking up at the visored face of the knight who commanded this band of renegades. "Though you have treacherously ensnared me and my loyal knights, you win nothing thereby but shame and dishonor. Yes, you shame all knighthood, yourself, and me as well by this unprovoked assault. You have wounded Sir Kay grievously, and I warn you, if he should die, you incur the unending wrath of King Arthur himself, who is his foster brother." Indeed, Sir Kay lay in obvious pain, his head propped against the Faerie Tree while Lady Anne, who had rushed to help him when he fell, was tearing off strips of her shift to serve as bandages to staunch the bleeding. I could see a long gash that that started at his shoulder and sliced across his chest. It did not look deep but it spewed blood like a fountain, and Lady Vivien had now come to help Lady Anne, staunching the blood with a handful of moss as Anne tried to wrap Kay's chest in cloth. Kay's eyes were closed in the grey pallor of his face, and I could see that he was barely conscious.

The unnamed knight gave a grim laugh. "So it's Kay the king will resent, do you think? It won't be the fact that I will have his queen for my own?"

With that the queen paled, and looked for a moment as if she would falter. At her right hand, Sir Agravain colored nearly as red as Kay's blood, and I saw his jaw set in hate and anger as he glared at the mounted knight who threatened his uncle's, and hence his family's, honor.

Recovered from her momentary alarm, Queen Guinevere stood again to her full height and with an icy calm taunted her captor. "You wouldn't dare to touch one hair on this head, villain. And be assured that I will never suffer you to shame me. I would sooner cut my own throat than be dishonored by the likes of you."

Again the grim laugh, which sounded like a heavy boot grinding on gravel. "Your resistance will merely make the ravishing all the sweeter when I have had you." He paused a moment, his visored face moving from side to side as if he were glancing around, measuring his surroundings. "Perhaps I will have my men guard our sorry defenders and drag you off farther into the woods. You can spew forth all the disdain your haughtiness can think of once we're alone, but I'm willing to bet it's not for one moment going to stop me from getting those royal skirts up over your waist. What do you think, boys?" There were a few scattered guffaws at that, but I had the feeling that even his own men were uncomfortable with this kind of abuse of so exalted a figure as Queen Guinevere of Logres.

By then, I had had enough. Unarmed and vulnerable as I was, I was still the queen's knight and owed her allegiance. As her former page, I also owed her my faith and loyalty. Besides which, I loved her. And nagging at the pit of my stomach was the feeling that, if that bastard could treat the queen herself so, what might happen to her ladies-in-waiting with so many other armed knights around? I couldn't hold it in any longer.

"You motherless swine!" I railed in impotent exasperation. "Cowardly capon! Make a move to touch her and we'll have you down off that horse and throw you in the river, armor and all!"

The knight's head started back for a moment, then came that gravelly laugh again. "Why, Gildas of Cornwall, I thought you had known better than to meddle in matters that are beyond your rank. Or is it *Sir* Gildas now? It is, isn't it? You're one of the new crop of Round Table Knights just sprung up after the quest, is that it?"

Now everyone's ears had pricked up. This was no strange knight. It was someone familiar with Camelot, someone who recognized the lowly new-made knight Sir Gildas of Cornwall from earlier times. Someone whose voice had finally clicked into place in my memory.

"And you, Meliagaunt! I thought you had washed your hands of the Round Table and all its affairs when you and King Bagdemagus begged off from the Grail quest. What are you doing now? You, whose own sister was Her Majesty's lady-in-waiting and married Sir Degore? You think this would make your father proud? One of Arthur's earliest and longest faithful allies, to have his own son shame him in this manner, and insult his liege lord?"

Meliagaunt, unmasked, put up his visor, since it was pointless to wear it any longer, and his face was red underneath—perhaps from shame at being called out, perhaps merely from the heat under the helmet in the warm May weather. His identity revealed, he became laconic. "It's *Sir* Meliagaunt now," he declared. "My own father has knighted me." He sat awkwardly and looked around, as if, now that he was known, he could no longer go through with his original plan. But he set his jaw determinedly, and snapped out an order: "All of you mount your palfreys. You are my prisoners now. We are riding to my father's lands, the kingdom of Gorre."

With that he turned his horse, but the queen called to him, somewhat more courteously now that he had backed off his original threat. "Sir Kay is grievously wounded. He will not be able to ride. And we cannot simply leave him in the midst of the woods, even this close to Camelot. It is at least a two-days' ride to Gorre, and he may not live. For your courtesy's sake, let him be brought back to the castle with my ladies-in-waiting."

Meliagaunt turned back toward her. "My courtesy's sake?" He scoffed. "Don't try to flatter me, you silly woman. Make a litter to haul him in if you must, but nobody is going back to that castle. And mind that you keep up, or we'll cut him loose on the way." With that he spun off. The queen began to weep, comforted by Lady Anne and Lady Rosemounde, while Palomides, Agravain and I quickly put together a litter of branches and tied it behind Palomides' horse, as the twenty armed knights goaded us to hurry with drawn swords. We lifted Sir Kay unto the litter and his fat lips peeled back from his protruding yellow teeth as he sighed with pain. "We'll get you there, old sot," Palomides whispered to him as we laid him gently down. "The king will have something to say before this whole thing is done."

I mounted my own palfrey, placing the trembling young Lady Bessie in front of me in the saddle while just behind, Thomas was holding the still-chattering Lady Mary, whose comments were now little more than a whisper. "Why did they have to come when they did? Now I'll never know if I was to be crowned Queen of the May or not."

As we left the clearing behind and rode off deliberately away from Camelot, I saw in the distance the wagon from the castle's kitchens, coming to bring us our promised picnic banquet. I supposed we wouldn't be getting a square meal any time soon and grieved for that, but I was certain later on that it was the driver of that wagon that must have carried the news of Guinevere's abduction back to the palace, and so brought about all that was to come.

CHAPTER FOUR

THE WATER BRIDGE

I didn't know till much later what happened at Camelot after Roger, the castle's head cook, burst into the king's chamber demanding to see King Arthur with news of the queen's abduction. That was, of course, because I was being dragged off to King Bagdamagus's Kingdom of Gorre at the time, but I think it's important to understand the reaction at court when this news broke, so here's what I was told much later by my friend and old master Sir Gareth, who was in on it all from the beginning.

The king was in his private chamber, holding council with some of his closest advisors at the time, including Gareth and Gawain, as well as Sir Bors and Sir Bedivere. Gawain's new squire, Peter, who until recently had been the queen's page, was in attendance as well to wait on his new master. They had just reached a crucial question about whether it was a good idea to exempt the clergy from a newly imposed tax on windows (at least that was what Gareth *thought* they were discussing. "I had just dozed off, to tell you the truth," he told me later) when Sir Ywain—who was serving, as he often did, as Arthur's chamber guard—moved into the room and stood next to the door at attention, waiting for the king to address him. King Arthur, a bit annoyed at the interruption, looked up and demanded testily, "Sir Ywain, you have something to report?"

"My lord," said Ywain. "Roger the cook begs immediate audience with you."

It was so unprecedented an announcement that Arthur merely

stared at Ywain for a moment open-mouthed, until Ywain, who had of course screened the request before bringing it to the king, added, "He has news of great—and immediate—import, Your Highness."

After another beat, the still-skeptical king looked around the room with a bemused expression and asked Ywain to show Roger in. "Let us hear what culinary emergency has arisen in Camelot," he quipped. For him, that was a quip.

Sir Ywain stepped out and immediately followed Roger into the room. The cook was obviously abashed, never having set foot in this unfamiliar private territory of the king before, and refused to raise his eyes—Gareth remarked that it was affecting to see Roger, so clearly the master of his own domain in the kitchen, made abject by this change of venue. Having worked in the kitchens himself incognito when he had arrived at court years ago, Gareth was the one person in the room Roger must feel somewhat comfortable with, and accordingly, my old master tried to set him at ease. "Speak up, Roger old boy," Gareth said. "Something important has brought you here. What is it, man?"

"M'lords," Roger began quietly. "It concerns 'er majesty, the queen, it does."

"The queen!" Now Arthur was quite serious again. "She went a-Maying this morning, didn't she?" He looked around the room for affirmation, and everyone nodded.

"With her new 'Queens' Knights,' including Gildas and Palomides," Gareth had said.

"And her ladies-in-waiting—my nieces were to go with her…" Sir Bedivere added.

"And Sir Kay," Arthur stated with finality, and he glared at Roger, waiting for the cook to continue.

"That's it, yer 'ighness," the cook went on. "I was to bring 'em all a fine banquet for their picnic lunch, as per the queen's express command, sir, do y'see? And that's why I was on the road to that 'ere clearin' in the woods north of the castle, if yer know where that be." He looked questioningly around the room.

"Yes, yes," Sir Gareth hurried him along. "We all know where it is…"

"Around the old Faerie Tree it is, sir, you know…"

"Yes!" Gawain had cried as the king closed his eyes, trying to remain patient. "Get on with it! What did you see there?"

"Well, I was still a furlong shy of the place, yer Grace, when I saw all the fine ladies and courtiers, all in their picnic garb, a'ridin' off to the north, surrounded by a whole company o' mounted and armed knights, like they was herding 'em, you might say."

"Armed knights!" Sir Bors exclaimed. His face paled, and Gareth guessed he must be calculating now how quickly he might get word to Lancelot whose whereabouts were still a mystery.

"Right, sir. Must 'a been a score of 'em, I should say. Didn't look like the queen was any too happy to be goin' with 'em either, and one of 'er group, it looked to me like Sir Kay, was being 'auled along in a litter, looked like, like 'e was sick or maybe wounded, your 'ighness. Well I knew that looked bad, so I figgered I'd better come straight 'ere, though a' course it wouldn't generally be my place…"

The king could no longer contain himself. "Abduct my queen!" He roared. "From under our very noses? The unmitigated gall of those villains. Who were they, Roger? Did they bear any banner? Any coat of arms?"

Flinching at the heat of the king's wrath, Roger held up his hands, whether in a gesture of calm or a shrug of ignorance, Gareth could not say. But Roger managed to blurt out, "They bore no devices on their shields, yer Grace, nor any banner nor colors that I could see. Their armor looked like British work, as far as I know. Nothin' foreign nor outlandish about it."

"So, we don't know who these men were or where they are taking the queen," Gawain said. "There isn't a moment to lose—somebody's got to go after them and see where they are heading and how the queen might be rescued…"

"And report back here while I assemble the knights," the king added. "We don't need an army to fight twenty brigands, so it shouldn't take long to assemble the knights of the Table now in residence and march off after them. But Gawain is right, someone must go immediately to track them…"

"I'm on my way now," Sir Gawain said as he pulled on his cloak and stood. "Which direction did they go in?"

"North, sir," Roger said. "Due north!"

"I'm with you, brother," Gareth had added, and Sir Bedivere rose, his teeth clenched.

"Count me in as well," the old knight fumed. "Those are my nieces the bastards have taken with the queen. I must help them."

"Stay," Arthur told his old friend, placing a hand on his arm. "You'll be needed here, to help me get the knights assembled and mounted. We'll go after them together, but Gawain and Gareth can move much faster alone, and what's needed in that pursuit is speed."

Sir Bedivere, aware that he was being told in the gentlest of terms that he was too old to be running after bandits in the woods and must leave such japes to the younger folk, nodded with some chagrin, while Gareth and Gawain, with the squire Peter, were already out the door and moving toward the stables. Gawain shouted to Peter to run and fetch his sword and shield, and Gareth's as well, while the brothers saddled the horses.

In not much more time than it takes to tell about it, the Orkney brothers and their young squire were out the gate, over the drawbridge and off into the woods north of the castle. When they got to the Faerie Tree clearing, it was not difficult for them to see the trail left by the thirty horses that had left that space less than an hour before, and they reckoned that without pushing their horses too far, they could catch up to the kidnappers in half a day, assuming they did not lose the trail among the trees and the sometimes rocky paths of that forest.

But it was slow going as it turned out, and there were places where the path between the trees was narrow, forcing them to slow down. After a few hours they were finding it more difficult to recognize the kidnappers' trail because of other traffic through that area, and they were beginning to despair of catching them in time to see where they were taking the queen. That was when they saw, perhaps two furlongs up ahead, bouncing along the uneven forest trail, an old horse-drawn cart, driven by a little man with a long white beard, his head covered with a blue hood. The cart was a wooden box perhaps eight feet long and five feet wide, with sides made up of wooden rails four feet high and spaced eight or nine inches apart. It rode on two large wheels with twelve spokes apiece, at least half as wide as the length of the cart's bed. The dwarf held a lash with which he encouraged the single horse—a tired looking old chestnut nag—to keep moving at a pace not a great deal faster than walking.

"G'wan there, Daisy," the dwarf called.

"You there! Dwarf!" Gawain cried. "Hold up! We need to speak with you!"

"Name's Thorvald," the little man responded, neither slowing down nor turning to face his pursuers.

"Well, Thorvald, then," Gawain said. "Hold for us, will you?"

"You're on horses. I think you can probably catch up."

Flustered, Gawain and Gareth spurred their mounts on until they were riding on either side of the slow-moving cart, with Peter trotting along behind.

"Why does it have to be 'Hey you! Dwarf!' You can't say 'You, Driver!' or "Carter!' or even 'Old Man!' I *do* have a white beard, after all. Why does everyone have to say, "Hey Dwarf!' I mean, look, what if I just looked at you and said 'Hey Carrot-top! Go shake your ears!' What would you think of that?"

Gawain didn't know quite how to respond to this tongue-lashing from a common carter—and a dwarf at that—but Gareth stepped in with a bit more charm and wit. "Well, Thorvald then," he sidestepped the issue. "I take it you've been on this road for awhile."

"Can't hide anything from the likes of you, can I, Tow-head? Sharp as a tack, you are."

Gareth laughed as if the dwarf had said something appropriate, and said, "We just want to know whether you've seen a large group of horsemen pass this way not long ago—about twenty armed knights, who may have been guarding seventeen unarmed captives? They would have been hard to miss, if they came this way."

"Oh really?" Thorvald answered. "As if maybe I dozed off and might have slept through forty horses passing me on this dirt road? Of course I seen 'em, numbskull. Recognized 'em, too—that was

Meliagaunt, son of the King of Gorre, riding up front. Told me to get out of the way if I didn't want to lose my cart. Always a kind word for everybody, has good old Meliagaunt."

"Meliagaunt—King Bagdemagus's squire?" Sir Gareth cried.

"His son," Gawain corrected. "But why on earth would Meliagaunt want to kidnap the queen?"

"The queen?" Thorvald exclaimed in his turn. "Is that who that great imperious lady was? Guinevere herself, big as life? She sat that horse like her arse was too precious for saddle leather, a-looking down her nose at ol' Meliagant all the while. Ha! Wouldn't I like to be a flea on that horse's ear right now, to hear what kind of a conversation is going on there! Kidnapped her, you say? Didn't think Meliagaunt had that kind of backbone. Taking her to Gorre, I suppose. That'll be a sight, the king trying to get into that place."

"What do you mean?" Gawain asked. "I've never been to Gorre…"

"Few have," the carter replied. "Me, I've been there a few times professionally, and I know a thing or two about it."

"Professionally?" Gareth mused, looking into the bed of the cart, which was nearly empty but for a small sack, presumably holding the dwarf's personal effects, and a length of rope. "What are you, some kind of itinerant merchant? You don't seem to have any goods to sell."

Thorvald snorted. "A peddler? Me? Don't you know what kind of a cart this is?" He waved his arm as if displaying the nonexistent wares in his empty vehicle.

Gareth and Gawain both shrugged, but Peter, following the gist of the conversation from the rear, called out, "It's a prisoners' cart. The kind you drive felons around a town in to humiliate 'em before flogging 'em tied to the back of the cart. Or before hanging 'em if that's the sentence. Everybody knows that."

"That's what you do?" Gareth asked, eyeing the length of rope once again. "So you actually do the whipping and the…the hanging, too?"

Thorvald shrugged. "Somebody has to do it, and it's kinder to the condemned if its somebody who knows what they're doing, 'stead of some amateur who makes a hash of it and prolongs the victim's suffering, am I right?"

Gareth wasn't completely convinced, though Gawain gave a grudging nod of his head. "So you've been to Gorre in your role as, uh, executioner. But you say it will be a problem for King Arthur to get the queen out of that place? What do you mean?"

"I *mean*," Thorvald stretched that last word out as if he was talking to the village idiot, "that the land of Gorre is an island, and that Meliagaunt is going to take himself and his prisoners, and all his armed men, onto the island on a raft they keep on the shore. But when they want to make sure nobody can get onto the island, they keep the raft on the Gorre side. The only way to get to the island then is by one of two bridges—the Water Bridge and the Sword Bridge—and only a single person can cross either bridge at one time."

"These bridges are difficult to cross then?" Gawain asked.

Thorvald let out a heavy sigh. "Difficult? You hain't ever seen the like. The current is so strong there no man has ever swum it, and the Water Bridge is a crossing that takes you through an underwater tunnel narrow enough for a man to get stuck in, then spits you out the other side still far enough from shore that you still might get carried off if you're not a strong swimmer. Of course, you'll only make it that far if you can hold your breath longer than anybody I've ever seen."

"Sounds like the Water Bridge is right out," Gareth suggested. "How about this Sword Bridge?"

"Well, that one is pure suicide," Thorvald told him. "A sharp steel blade suspended two hundred feet above a craggy gorge and a river with a raging current. It's some thirty yards across and you've got to balance on the blade itself, keen as a razor. Nobody has ever crossed that bridge—you either cut off your hands, or fall onto the rocks to be crushed, or into the river to be drowned."

"Right, then, the Water Bridge it is!" Gawain decided.

"Thorvald, be a good chap and tell us how to get there, will you?" Gareth asked. "We need to get there in time to head them off if we can."

"Going to have a whack at that bridge are you? That'll be a sight. Don't like going to Gorre myself. They don't seem to like me. Matter of fact, most places don't seem to like me. Bigotry toward dwarfs, I calls it."

"So you think people don't like you because you're a dwarf?" Gareth answered. "You don't think that, oh, I don't know, your profession might put some people off? Or maybe your personality?"

"My personality?" the dwarf seemed genuinely confused. "'ow could that…"

"No matter, no matter," Gawain interrupted. He was beginning to show some of his characteristic impatience. "Tell me how to get to this Water Bridge. There's really no time to lose."

"Well here," the dwarf said, a touch of irony in his voice. "I'm heading in that direction. Why don't you tie your horses to the cart and hop in the back, and I'll give you a ride there, quick as you like."

Gawain looked stumped. He hadn't expected that. "Well, er…" he stammered. "Look, it's a kind offer, I'm sure, but to tell you the truth, I know I can get there faster on my horse, and speed is of the essence here."

"Don't want to be seen riding in a cart, is that it?" The dwarf goaded him.

"Well, now that you bring it up, how would that look? A knight of the Round Table, riding in a cart meant to carry miscreants, thieves and murderers? I'd never live it down. My reputation would be as the knight who rode in the cart of shame. No thank you, I wouldn't put my honor at stake for such a thing. No, no, just tell me, for your courtesy, where I can find this Water Bridge?"

"Well, it's easy enough" Thorvald answered, stroking his chin. "Keep on this path you've been following. It's going to take another day and a half of riding, most like, but it's not hard to follow—this road comes to only a couple of crossroads before you get to the river. When you get there, turn to the left and follow the river for another two furlongs. There you'll find a clear path that follows down into the water. You really can't miss it."

"Then I'm off. Peter, with me. And brother," Gawain told Gareth, looking at him intensely. "Only one man can cross this bridge at any time, so you must allow me to do it. Your company can do me no good now. But we know who has taken the queen and where the villain is taking her, and the king must be informed of that. You must ride back as quickly as you can and help Arthur get the Round Table assembled to come after. I'll get across this Water Bridge if it can be crossed, and challenge this Meliagaunt where he lives."

Gareth protested, of course, arguing that Gawain's loss would be a blow from which the king's court could not recover, but once Gawain got something into his head it was pretty hard to argue him out of it, and besides, they were in a race to beat Meliagaunt to the river and it would have been foolish to stand there arguing for long, so Gareth of course, gave in.

"I'll send Peter back to let you know if I've caught up with Meliagaunt, or how I've got on with the bridge if I haven't. Get to Arthur as soon as you can. Come on, Peter." And with that Gawain was off toward the river, Peter trailing after him like a puppy. Gareth, turning around to head back to Camelot as soon as he could, heard Thorvald grumbling to himself as he lashed his horse one more time. "Coupla rude gents there, Daisy. Not even a civil 'farewell' for the likes of me. Ah, it's tough being a dwarf."

***

The great oak and beech trees we rode through towered above us, their great branches stretching skyward over our heads like the great Gothic arches of Saint David's cathedral in Caerleon. The dead leaves of a hundred autumns past lay scattered and moldering between the hard timber trunks, and a thick carpet of green moss lay under the leaves, in many places covering the path we followed northward through that old forest. The moss made me smile. Once the queen's absence was noted and searchers from the castle came to find her, tracking the movements of a company this large should be easy for a pursuing group of knights.

Meantime, I wanted to assess the situation we were in right now.

"Your Highness, I'm well acquainted with this Meliagaunt from before, from the days of the Grail quest. This behavior is, well, it's not anything I would have expected of the fellow I knew then."

"Well, Gildas, I wonder why that doesn't make me feel any better?"

The queen responded testily. Not that she didn't have every right to be testy, kidnapped as she was out of the blue by someone who might have been thought to be close to the court. I had sidled up to her left on my palfrey, carrying the dreary Lady Elizabeth before me in the saddle, to try to see what might be done to bring a little comfort to her in this trying situation. What I was more interested in was comforting my lady Rosemounde, riding on the queen's right side, though of course, I didn't feel completely free to do this because we were right under the eye of Sir Agravain, who rode directly behind Rosemounde, so I focused my attentions on Her Majesty.

"With your permission, your Highness," I continued, ignoring her last remark, "I'd like to address him in private, kind of, you know, feel him out, see if I can gather what exactly he has in mind with this madness. It would help if we could understand what his motives are."

"Motives?" the queen raised an eyebrow in my direction. "All of your sleuthing with that old necromancer Merlin has seeped down into your vocabulary, it seems. Well, go on," she waved her hands vaguely in the direction of Sir Meliagaunt at the head of our procession. "Talk to him if you think it will do us any good."

"Thank you, Your Grace," I nodded. "At least we may be less in the dark afterwards." And I was about to spur my horse ahead to catch up with Meliagaunt when I noticed the lady Elizabeth's large eyes staring back at me, a quizzical expression on her face. "Oh!" I started. I couldn't exactly talk to Meliagaunt privately with Elizabeth in between us. That was when Rosemounde spoke up.

"The lady Bessie can share my horse," she offered, for she was riding alone, her escort Sir Kay being carried behind on his litter. "That is, if you think your conversation with Sir Meliagaunt would be better conducted in absolute privacy."

"Why, yes," I agreed, more than happy to be rid of the encumbrance of Lady Elizabeth, not only because it freed me to be completely open with Meliagaunt and, I hoped, he with me, but also because, frankly, she was not exactly pleasant company, being given to tears and whining and the occasional "Oh, what's to become of me?" lament at the least opportunity.

Having divested myself of that tearful adolescent, I trotted forward, passing a few horsemen on the way who murmured and drew their swords, though I raised a hand to assure them I had no intention of trying to escape or of harming their leader. That didn't really quiet them, but when, hearing the hubbub behind him, Meliagaunt glanced around and saw it was me approaching, he waved them off, so the guards sheathed their swords and continued their silent ride.

"So, Gildas," he growled at me, sounding only slightly annoyed, and not particularly surprised to see me. "They've chosen you as a spokesman, have they?"

"Well, uh, not exactly," I answered, aware that I was treading on some fairly fragile eggshells. "I took it upon myself, you might say, to put forward a few questions to you…"

"Probably want to know where I'm taking you, I suppose, is that it?"

"Well, you did say the Land of Gorre…"

"Right. Ever been to Gorre?"

"No," I answered, trying my best to remember whether anybody had ever even told me where King Bagdemagus's land actually was. "Is it far?"

"Two days' ride," Meliagaunt told me. "And you haven't missed much. There's not much there. But it's a well-fortified island, and it's almost impossible to get to the island from the other side of the river if you don't already live there and know the secrets."

"Not exactly welcoming to visitors, then, I take it?"

Meliagaunt gave a grimace of a smile in spite of himself. "No. And when Arthur brings his men to besiege us, it won't be very welcoming for him either, I'm afraid."

"I'm sure," I said, clueless as to how else I might answer. "Assuming he ever actually learns where the queen is. But for now, I think we have more immediate concerns. Like how are we going to make this two days' journey? Is there food? Shelter for the night?"

"We have some rations. Didn't expect to be bringing back a whole army. Everybody is going to have to be on half rations. As for shelter—well, we're going to have to sleep out under the stars, I'm afraid. Can't take a chance on stopping at some inn or convent."

"Because…?" I encouraged him.

"Well," he burst out, irritated with me, or perhaps with himself, "as you might appreciate, I'm not keen on anybody knowing about this if we can help it. At least not until we're safe in Gorre."

I seized on that moment of candor to goad him about his actions. "Well, of course," I said. "Doesn't that give you a clue that what you're doing is reprehensible? I mean, what's it about? Why would you put your reputation as a knight at risk in this manner? This doesn't seem to be action worthy of the squire to King Bagdemagus—a knight of the Round Table for God's sake!"

"Round Table! Right. You've hit it right there!" Meliagaunt burst out with surprising hostility. "My father was one of Arthur's first allies, and then one of his first knights of the Table bringing an entire petty kingdom under his sway. And what did he get for it??"

I was at a loss. "Arthur's undying gratitude and friendship?" I ventured.

Meliagaunt scoffed. "Try paying your retainers on Arthur's friendship. Hard to eat gratitude, I'll tell you that. But my father isn't going to complain, is he? But what about me? Answer me that. I was my father's squire for years. Years! Then King Bagdemagus retires from his seat at the Table. Not only that, but what, eight more knights die on that fruitless quest of the Grail? They have to have a mass induction, that includes, among other worthies, Sir Gildas of Cornwall, squire to the king's nephew for what, *two* years?"

"Three," I corrected him. But I was beginning to see his point.

"And Gawain's son, what, a *year's* service? I have served longer and have better knightly skills than any squire that was raised to knight at Pentecost. And my father's long service to Arthur should have guaranteed me a seat at that table as his replacement even if the other weren't true. So, where was my invitation to knighthood from the king? A bit late in arriving, wouldn't you say?"

"Well, I can understand your disappointment, your resentment even, sure," I told him. And I did. "But what gave you the idea that kidnapping the queen would win Arthur over to your side?"

With that, Meliagaunt began waving his arms about wildly, now reaching a point of near hysteria, it seemed to me. I glanced around to see whether his knights were paying any heed to this, but they seemed oblivious. Maybe they were used to it. "You think I planned this?" Meliagaunt said at last. "This was the last thing I wanted! I was forced into it when you recognized me. I just wanted to get the queen alone…"

"Well, apparently to rape her, from what you said, which, I hate to mention it, is not really a direction I'd go in if I wanted to get Arthur to consider me for knighthood."

Meliagaunt winced at that as if I'd stabbed him in the ribs. "That's not what I intended," he rasped through clenched teeth. "I was going to get her alone, show her that even though I had her completely at my mercy, I would never do her harm, and beg her to plead my case with His Majesty."

"Well, why do it that way? Why not just get down on your knees and beg it of her as a favor?"

He bristled at that. "I'm the son of a king! I do not kneel like a peasant for favors. Besides, I thought the drama of it all would impress her."

"*Impress* her? You thought threatening to ravish her and then not doing it would make her think well of you?"

"*Well*," he grimaced again, "maybe I didn't think it through all the way. It doesn't sound so smart when you say it like that. But I was pretty riled up. I wasn't thinking clearly. That's why my father knighted me himself—thought it would take the edge off. It didn't."

"Well, look," I said, "you can still get out of this without destroying yourself or your father's kingdom. Let us all go now, say it was all a kind of May-time prank gone awry, no harm done. Maybe people will think you're a little unstable, what? But not a recreant knight devoid of courtesy, which, let's face it, is what people are going to think right now."

Meliagaunt's face grew stony at this and he stared ahead with a grim determination in his eyes. "Too late for that," he said. "When I struck down Sir Kay, I cut the cord of mercy from Arthur's hands. He could never just let me go now, queen or no queen, prisoners or no prisoners."

"But look, Kay is wounded sorely. If he dies, you can have nothing from the king but his enmity. Let us go now, and we may find a holy convent in these woods with a good infirmarian who may be able to search his wounds and heal him. Drag him all the way to Gorre and he may not live through the journey."

He shook his head. "His wounds are not so grievous that he will die that quickly. We have a physician at my father's castle who can heal him if anyone in Logres can. But from me, Arthur will want only vengeance, whatever my course now. If I have the queen and all of you in Gorre, and the king only able to sit across the river and seethe in his own ire, there is only one course available: he will have to send a warrior to fight me in single combat for the queen. That is what I will demand of him. And it will have to be Sir Gawain or Sir Ywain or even Sir Lancelot himself. If I can defeat one of them—and then restore the queen to him unharmed after all—he will have no choice but to recognize me as a doughty knight worthy of a seat at his Table."

My eyes nearly rolled out of my head at the absurdity—and the absence of self-knowledge—apparent in his plan. "Are you insane? Maybe, sure, you can get a lucky blow in against Gawain or Ywain or even my old master Sir Gareth, but the odds of your beating them are pretty slim. And if it's Lancelot who comes against you—and believe me, that is a strong possibility in this case—you're up against a killing machine against whom there is no defense. You're going to die if you persist in this, Meliagaunt."

The poor fool shrugged in a kind of hopeless stupor. "I wanted to die of shame when I wasn't recognized for the Table," he replied. "And I'm as good as dead now because of my own recklessness. Either Arthur will kill me or I'll live the rest of my life in shame and dishonor. I have a chance to get back some portion of my honor this way, so that's the course I've set. There is no turning back for me."

I could see there was no reasoning with him. His mind was set, what little of it there was, and the rest of us were just pawns in the mad game he was trying to play. "This cannot turn out well," I murmured to him as I slowed my horse and let him ride ahead, dropping back to move in beside Guinevere again. I sighed as she and Rosemounde both looked at me quizzically.

"Hold on to your wimples, my ladies," I told them. "This is going to be a bumpy ride."

What I didn't mark at the time was that, as I was doing that, Meliagaunt had turned and whispered something to one of his followers, and that five knights then dropped back to the rear of the company and had stopped there, bringing out crossbows that had been hanging from their saddles.

***

I didn't know it at the time, of course, but about that same hour Gawain and Gareth had encountered the dwarf in the cart, and as I told you before, Gawain sent Gareth back to Camelot to let Arthur know where the queen was being taken. Meanwhile, Gawain rode off with his squire to attempt the dangerous Water Bridge. He and Peter told Sir Gareth all about it, and Gareth told it to me later, so I'm sure every word of this is true.

"When Gawain left me, he rode till darkness had fallen and his exhausted horse could gallop no further," Gareth told me weeks after these events were over, when we were back in Camelot having a mild repast before having a go at the quintain in the jousting practice fields outside the castle's bailey. "He was forced to stop then, and I know that Peter cautioned him that if he rode his horse to death, he'd have a much slower go of it. But Gawain was restless, anxious about the wellbeing of the queen, and eager to get to Gorre in time to shield her from harm, if possible. But it was a two-day ride, Peter reasoned with him, and they had to rest. Or if they didn't, at least their poor horses did."

"So they did actually get some rest then?" I asked. "We were forced to lie on the ground in the woods overnight. Meliagaunt wouldn't have it any other way, and I can tell you, I dozed off and on for maybe five minutes at a time. The queen and her ladies were so angry in the morning at having to go on looking disheveled that they wouldn't ride with us at all—they all shared horses and we knights did as well. Rosemounde said they would not allow themselves to be seen close up by any knight looking the way they did."

"Well, Gawain slept for maybe two hours, and then Peter says he was up pacing around the campsite hours before dawn. Finally Peter got up, too, since he couldn't sleep with Gawain clomping around the way he was. And so Gawain told him they might as well leave, but said he'd walk for a few hours and give his horse a break from riding him too hard."

"Obviously, he never found us. And if he was riding that hard, and riding for much of the night, I can't see how he could have failed to catch up. But turns out it's a good thing he did fail. Those five archers that Meliagaunt had left behind I'm sure were meant to stop anybody following us. Gawain may not have gotten off with his life."

Gareth shook his head. "If Meliagaunt wanted to get back in Arthur's graces, ambushing his nephew and heir-apparent would have been a pretty bad idea. I suspect they were intended to slow him down. But traveling in the dark must have thrown him and Peter off the main road, and so they failed to pick up your trail after they'd stopped. And I understand they kept veering to the left, or so they told me, and I suppose the main road you were on was veering to the right. Anyway they couldn't have gone too far off course, because they did get to the river by after tierce the next day, and followed it to the left, as the dwarf told us to go, and by a little before compline had arrived at the Water Bridge.

"That was a fearsome sight, as Gawain told it. A set of man-made steps of stone descended from the forest down the embankment and continued into the river itself. But that was white water roaring through a deep rift a quarter mile wide and twice as deep as Gawain is tall. There was a beauty to it, too, Gawain says. The sunlight flickering on the crest of each ripple of that rushing water was like stars glittering on a moving background of sky. He and Peter made their way down to the bank, tethering their horses to a tree above the embankment.

"So Gawain is standing there staring at those steps disappearing under the river and he's wondering how he's going to cross this stretch of water, 'bridge' or no. And Peter is saying, 'Don't do it Master! There's no way a man can cross that! Even if there's an underground tunnel like the dwarf said, what happens when you get out the other side? It doesn't look like you could climb out over there.' And Peter was right as he pointed to the opposite bank, which proved to be only a rock face at this point in the river, rather than the smooth embankment they had just come down.

"'And leave the queen to whatever fate awaits her? I would be shamed, and justly, too,' Gawain told him. 'Help me grab this great branch here. I want to throw it into the water to see just how the current treats it.'

"So they took this old oak branch they'd found, as tall as Gawain and three or four inches thick, and heaved it into the river. The current took it like it was a little twig, rushed it along and ricocheted it against several boulders until finally pinning it against the rocky face of the opposite bank. 'Ouch,' Peter says sympathetically. 'Yes,' Gawain mused, 'but it tends to push toward the other side. Not sure why. Maybe it's deeper over there, or the river curves up ahead.'

"So Gawain starts to take off the chainmail he's been wearing. 'Can't have this weighing me down in the water,' he tells Peter as he hands it to him. 'But I'll keep my sword at least. Pretty sure I'm going to need that when I get to the other side.'"

"'But Master,' Peter says, as Gawain piles his armor into his squire's arms. 'Are you a strong enough swimmer to survive that current?'

"Gawain just shrugs. 'The kingdom of Orkney is made up of twenty islands,' he says. 'My brothers and I used to swim in the sea, sometimes, in the Bay of Skaill off the main island when we were kids.' He shivered at the thought of it. 'It was awfully cold water, even in the summer, so we didn't do it often. But I think I should be able to stay afloat. Watch me closely, though.' He looked his squire deep in the eyes. 'You may need to tell people what's happened to me.'"

"And did you? Swim, I mean?" I asked Gareth as we watched Peter himself mount a horse and pick up a tilting lance to take aim at the quintain.

"Aim for the center and give it a good wallop!" Gareth called out, encouraging his brother's squire. "Sure we swam," he returned to my question. "Maybe once a year. On a dare, to see if we could stay in that icy water for more than a few minutes. But the sea's waves came into that bay pretty strongly. Gawain? If he ever stayed afloat in the water more than five minutes, it was before I was born. He had no business tackling that river. But then, there was no one else, and there was no other way. Or so we thought. It was the queen, after all."

"Oh, bad luck, that," I winced as Peter, striking the quintain, failed to ride through fast enough and was clobbered from behind as the sandbag balancing the wooden figure swung around and caught him before his horse galloped out of the path. Peter held on, barely staying in the saddle but managing to right himself after all.

"Good!" Gareth called to him as he trotted on with a chagrinned look on his face. "You kept your seat, boy, and that's what'll keep you alive in a battle! Now give it another try, and gallop through faster this time! So…where was I?" Gareth returned to his theme. "Yes. Gawain, holding up his sword, stepped into the water and started inching his way down those steps, careful to keep his feet against that onrushing current. The water was cold, but not nearly as cold as the sea off Orkney, so he quickly got used to that. But as he stepped lower and lower into the river, he could sense no trace of that underwater tunnel the dwarf had described. He was out thirty or forty feet and the water was up to his neck, and the current washing around him and like to knock him off his feet, so finally he could see nothing for it but to plunge under the surface and see if he could find it. And so he did."

"Just like that?"

"Well, he figured to take a look under the water to see if he could espy that tunnel, and then pop his head back up for an extra breath when he had seen exactly where he needed to go. But the current was tumbling him about so that he couldn't stand again. And he had seen a dark opening as soon as he stuck his head under. So he says he kicked to the bottom and kind of groped his way along there to the tunnel. What he didn't know, of course, was how long he'd have to be underwater in that tunnel since he couldn't see where it came out, and he didn't know how long he could hold his breath. But he couldn't fight that current for long, so he decided to try poking into the tunnel, figuring he could come out and try to get to the surface if it was no go. But when he ventured into the tunnel, he realized that the water there was perfectly calm and he didn't have to fight against the torrent outside the tunnel, so he decided his best chance was to use the tunnel and try to get to the other side before his lungs burst."

"Well, my lord, I can hold my breath for maybe two minutes—I suppose two and a half if my life depended on it. How long was Gawain going to take to get through that tunnel? You said the river was, what? A quarter mile across?"

Gareth shrugged. "I'm just going by what Gawain told me. Peter confirms the story. Don't you Peter?" He called out to his brother's squire, who was just readying to have another go at the quintain, but Peter jerked his head back at us when he heard his name, causing the visor of his helmet to clang shut, blinding him for a moment and making him careen awkwardly about, trying to regain his balance and get back control of his horse.

"Never mind," Gareth called back to him. "Anyway," he resumed his tale, "Gawain may not have been the strongest swimmer, as I said, but as far as his breathing goes, he had trained himself pretty well, swimming in that Bay of Skaill back home in Orkney, and could hold his breath for a good four minutes if pushed."

"Hmm," I answered, without conviction.

"Peter was pretty concerned, though, after three minutes or so had passed and he could see no motion under the water to suggest there was a swimmer under there. He was just trying to decide what he should do if Gawain failed to come out of this—run back to find the king's army, or try to take the tunnel himself and see if he could save his master—when Gawain himself finally poked his head out of the water on the far side of the stream."

I knew, of course, having been there myself, that Gawain had not rescued the queen, but I didn't know exactly what had stopped him. "So Gawain actually did pass the Water Bridge! Then what prevented him from getting into the kingdom of Gorre and challenging Meliagaunt?"

Gareth chuckled. He could laugh now, since Gawain was alive and well, though I imagine at the time he'd have been as frantic as Peter apparently was. "Peter says Gawain came up gasping and choking, coughing up water, and so wasn't in sufficient control of himself to fight the current, which took him and flung him downstream before he could try to scale that sheer rock on the other side. By now, of course, he'd lost his sword. What saved him, apparently, was that branch they had thrown into the water earlier. By then it had snagged itself on a protruding rock downstream and a good fifty feet from the other bank, and Gawain was able to grab onto it before being swept away completely to who knows what end further downstream. He hung there, grasping the branch for dear life, bobbing up and down in the water, helpless against the current. There was nothing that Peter could do."

"Except go for help?"

"Which he did, leaving Gawain to hang there in the water, suspended between life and death."

And that's where he left him.

CHAPTER FIVE

THE SWORD BRIDGE

S ir Gareth had trotted halfway back to Camelot when, coming
through the forest the other way, he met a grim-faced and
determined Lancelot du Lac, galloping so recklessly that he nearly
ran down Gareth before he saw him. Stopping so suddenly that his
horse reared up, Lancelot demanded with an uncharacteristic lack of
ceremony, "Where have they taken her? Tell me quickly, I haven't a
moment to lose!"

"My lord," Gareth more courteously replied. "Her Majesty
the queen has been abducted by Sir Meliagaunt, the son of King
Bagdemagus of Gorre. It is to that kingdom he is even now bearing
her and her companions away."

The Great Knight paused long enough to ponder that. "Gorre?
Never been there. It's up this path you've come down?"

"Yes. Sir Gawain is on his way there now. From what we are told,
we understand there are only two ways into the kingdom, both very
treacherous: the Water Bridge and the Sword Bridge. Gawain has
gone toward the Water Bridge, deeming it the more quickly passed
of the two."

"Me for the Sword Bridge, then," Lancelot announced with quick
decisiveness.

"That bridge lies over a chasm…"

"No time for long explanations. If I move quickly enough, I can
overtake them before they reach that stronghold. Get the news to the
king!" And without another word, Lancelot spurred his destrier past

74

Gareth along the path from which he had just emerged. Gareth learned, after reaching the court, that Sir Bors had sent an immediate message to Lancelot in care of the Lady of the Lake, at whose palace he had been raised, and where he sometimes stayed if he wanted to avoid the court. It was Bors'—and the queen's—good fortune that such was the case in this instance, and that the Lady's palace bordered on these woods just as Camelot did. Gareth's spirits rose considerably, for while Sir Gawain was a noble and formidable knight, he was not Lancelot. Nobody was. And with Lancelot chasing after the queen, Gareth knew the king would breathe a lot easier over the next few days. And Gareth knew better than most that Lancelot held the queen dearer than his own life.

But of course, Gareth had no idea what happened to Lancelot after he disappeared into the woods. That much, you'll understand, I had to put together later from Lancelot's own laconic recollections, and from the dwarf Thorvald—yes, I met the carter, too, later on.

But before Lancelot met Thorvald, he came in range of those five archers that Meliagaunt had left behind, concealed among the trees. Their orders were to slow down any pursuit, but not to assassinate the knights who came after them, for Meliagaunt, you recall, wanted the opportunity to fight one of the great knights—Gawain or Lancelot or anyone else—who came in pursuit, but did not want anyone tracking him down before he was safe in his father's kingdom, for he felt he might have an advantage in single combat in his home castle. And so without warning, the charging Lancelot heard the sudden whistle and thud of a crossbow dart, whizzing out of the trees and into the flank of his great warhorse. The horse reared again and flung his head from side to side, when another dart and then another buried itself in his smooth brown haunches, and he fell, throwing his noble rider.

Lancelot cried out in inarticulate rage, sputtering until he could form words. "Cowards! Recreant knaves!" He screamed into the silent forest, drawing his sword and holding up his shield. "Come and fight me like men, you white-livered bastards!" But his answer was only several more whizzing darts—all of them into the shoulders and neck of his fallen steed, whose eyes rolled about in terror before they lost their light at last.

The steed was not Lancelot's own great war horse, but one he had borrowed from the Lady of the Lake as the one closest and already harnessed when the urgent message had come from Bors that the queen had been surprised and ravished away from her woodland idyll. But the horse had sprung to the task and had given his all to help his new master in his quest, and Lancelot was always one to appreciate the noble efforts of any living thing, to see God's spark in every creature. There was that goodness in him that sought always to ease suffering, whether of man or beast, to aid the fallen or the dispossessed, to right wrongs. Lancelot du Lac was the pure essence of chivalry, whether you defined it as Sir Gareth did, or as Merlin did. Even when he was exposed as the Great Adulterer, his sympathy never waned for the suffering of others. He was motivated by love all his life, and therefore, though some high Church prelates or small-minded self-congratulatory moral arbiters might grudge it, I say without blushing that he had a good end.

But I'm getting way ahead of myself. Lancelot, I say, was shocked at the cruelty done to his horse, and mourned the poor beast as if it had been his own brother, and he bellowed in inarticulate rage at the silent trees, for those soulless bowmen of Meliagaunt's had fled as soon as they'd stopped the Great Knight's pursuit. They rode quickly to catch us, and overtook us when we had stopped for the night en route to Gorre.

And so, his tears rolling down his cheeks, Lancelot sheathed his weapon, squared his jaw, took a deep breath, and did what he had to do: he set off at a brisk walk, determined to find whatever conveyance he could, but committed, if need be, to walk all the way to Gorre.

***

Just as he had pushed his poor horse nearly to the breaking point with galloping along the path, so Lancelot seemed bent on wearing himself out, running for as long as he was able, then walking briskly until he was able to breathe evenly again, which was the cue for him to resume his run. Carrying his sword and wearing his chain mail hauberk made such a regimen quite grueling, but he did not know whether the hidden archers were waiting for him somewhere further along the path, and reasoned he would need his armor to block their darts. Still he forced himself ahead, for nothing could deter Lancelot from pursuing the rescue of his Guinevere. Then, after two hours of this punishment, when it seemed that he must rest or faint, he saw ahead on the path a wooden cart of the sort used to convey prisoners to their execution, or to castigation by flogging.

Lancelot rubbed his eyes, bent over panting, then raised his right arm and shouted out, exclaiming between pants: "You there! Driver! Stop!"

The driver heard the cry, and at first thought he might have heard it wrong. He stopped the cart and looked back over his shoulder, watching the knight stumble toward him. "Eh?" he said as the knight drew closer. "What'd you call me?"

Lancelot scowled in irritation. "Uh…driver? Carter, if you prefer? Sorry, I don't know your name, but I'm in a great hurry. I'm trying to catch up to a group of riders…"

"A-carryin' away the queen. Yes, I know. On your way to Gorre then, are ya?"

"Right," Lancelot replied. "Obviously you've seen them. How long ago was it?"

"Oh, got to be several hours by now. You're never goin' to catch them on foot, ya silly muckwit."

"I'm aware," the knight replied, leaning on the back of the cart and breathing deeply. "Listen, what would you think of selling me your horse? I don't have a great deal of gold with me now, but truly, I will give you almost anything for that horse. Look, I have a small castle near the Dover coast, called Joyous Gard. The deed of the castle is yours if you but let me have that horse of yours. He looks young and strong…"

"Sure, 'e's a pip. But I ask ya, what good's a castle gonna do me if I die out 'ere by myself tryin' to pull this cart by 'and? Answer me that!"

Of course, another knight would have pulled his sword, told the dwarf he'd cut him into pieces if he interfered, and taken the horse. But in those days of the Round Table, Arthur's knights were bound by the Pentecost oath, and such a thought would not have occurred to them. Well, at least it wouldn't have occurred to Lancelot. But seeing the knight's chagrin at his refusal, Thorvald gave Lancelot a counter-offer.

"I'll tell you what," he proposed. "I'm 'eadin' in that direction anyway. Hop in the cart and I'll give you a ride all the way to Gorre. No charge, it'll be my treat. I'd like to see old Meliagaunt get 'is comeuppance, and it'd probably be a good thing to rescue the queen, after all, even the snooty haristocrat that she is."

The dwarf gave his horse a cluck and the cart slowly lurched forward while Lancelot—well aware that the reputation of anyone riding in such a cart of shame was forfeit and that he might nevermore be honored among knights as he had been once word of this disgraceful ride had spread—hesitated for half a step, then hopped up into the bed of the cart. Reputation or no reputation, he must get to the queen.

As Lancelot settled into the bed of the cart, he stripped off his chain mail and relaxed, his shoulders against the wooden poles that formed the bars of the cart's cage. Exhaling a great sigh of relaxation, content that he was heading relentlessly now in the right direction, Lancelot turned to his driver. "All right, Coachman, tell me what you know of this Sword Bridge."

***

Some hours later, with twilight coming on, Thorvald turned the cart down a path he knew that branched off the main road. "It's gettin' on dark," he told the knight. "The 'orse needs rest and 'is supper, and so do we. We'll get to Gorre sometime around none tomorrow, but two miles down this branch is a small village with an inn I've stayed in before. We'll 'ead there for now."

Lancelot bit his lips in silent frustration. "Maybe I should take leave of you here. If I keep going on foot, and if they stop for the night, it may be that I can catch up with them when they don't expect it, and snatch the queen before they have a chance to react…"

The dwarf was shaking his head as he replied, "You don't know where you're goin' and you'll probably lose your way in the dark. And even if you don't, they'll 'ave guards with crossbows around their camp just waitin' for you. And if they don't cut you down when you approach their camp, you'll 'ave to fight all twenty of 'em when you get there, and perhaps the queen's knights'll want to rise up to 'elp you even though they're unarmed. It'll be a bloodbath 'owever it turns out. No, no, much better if you cross that Sword Bridge into Gorre and challenge Meliagaunt to single combat for the release of the queen and 'er people. 'E'll never be able to stand against you."

The Great Knight weighed what the dwarf said, but remained unconvinced. "But you told me no one had ever succeeded in crossing the Sword Bridge."

Thorvald shrugged. "Yeah, I said that, sure," he said. "But mostly I was tryin' to scare ya. When you come down to it, nobody's ever crossed the Sword Bridge mainly because nobody's ever tried."

"What?"

"Sure. I mean, really, 'oo'd be crazy enough to grab onto a razor sharp blade an' scoot along thirty yards of it while 'angin' two 'undred feet over a gorge? You'd be the first one loony enough to try it, an' I figure you may just be loony enough to make it. See, I know from what you've told me that you don't care a rat's arse for your own life. The queen's all you care about. And that's gonna get you across."

Lancelot was perturbed and feeling pent up and ineffectual, wasting time in this cart, but he could see the wisdom in Thorvald's words, and leaned back against the side of the cart with an exasperated sigh. "I suppose you're right," he told the dwarf. "But I want to be back on the road before daybreak, and I'll walk alone if you are not willing to rise that early."

"Never mind," Thorvald said. "I'll wager I'm up and ready before you are!"

When they pulled up to the doors of the inn, the sign of the Fox and Hens, two serving men came to pull the cart into the barn and tend to the horse, while Thorvald stepped down and walked in the door, followed by Lancelot. But when they stepped across the threshold they were met by hard, unwelcoming eyes from the landlord and from three travelers dining near the fire in the candlelit interior.

Thorvald raised his chin quizzically. "Is there something amiss, Master Porter?" He addressed the innkeeper.

"You're welcome as usual, Master Thorvald," the landlord told him. "But we want nothing to do with a man who's ridden in a penal cart. My other guests won't have it—they refuse to be in the same room with the likes of him."

Now it was Thorvald himself who told me this story, and he was honest in telling me that he wasn't too surprised by this reaction— he'd seen it before. The onus of riding in one of those carts was usually enough to ruin a man's reputation for the rest of his life, so great was the shame of it. Furthermore, Thorvald insists that he had never demanded Lancelot's name, that not being the polite way for a host to treat a guest, even if it was only the guest riding in your cart. So he was pretty sure that his protests would be in vain, but he protested anyway.

"Ah, come on now, Jack, this is a noble knight I've got 'ere, not some common criminal. Somebody I picked up in the forest, 'oo's 'orse was shot out from under 'im! Give 'im a room and a meal, now, can't ya?"

"Well, he can't be such a noble knight if he cares so little for his own worship as to jump in that cart of yours without a thought for the shame of it!" Master Porter boomed out from his barrel chest. Then, in a much lower voice, he leaned down toward the dwarf, saying, "Look, Thorvald, I'll send him a plate for his dinner, but he's got to sleep in the barn. For your sake I might give him a room, but these guests won't stay here—they feel it'd be a shame to them to be under the same roof with him."

Now of course, Lancelot could have put a stop to all of this, merely by stepping forward and declaring himself, saying that he was Lancelot du Lac, greatest knight of King Arthur's Round Table, and implying that if he thought it worth his while, he could carve every man in that place into mincemeat. But he just stood in silence, an ironic smile on his face, contemplating what an insubstantial thing reputation was, to hold such inordinate sway in human affairs. Chivalry, he thought, had some influence on reputation, but was itself an independent and more tangible quality. It existed in itself, apart from reputation or any other product of broad rumor, an ideal in the mind of God to which Lancelot subscribed. He nodded his head and went off to sleep in the barn.

They'd given him a plate of hard brown bread, a piece of cheese, and a thin slice of cold mutton with some small beer in a wooden cup, all of which he devoured in minutes, sitting on a pile of hay on the floor of the barn next to Thorvald's horse, who was munching on his own fodder in silent companionship. With the edge off his hunger, Lancelot turned his attention to the horse. "Well, fellow," he cooed to the solid beast, stroking his long grey nose. "I didn't catch your name, but then I never told you my own either, so I suppose we'll leave it at that. I'll just call you 'horse,' and you can address me, should the need arise, as 'knight of the cart.' Though I'm pretty sure that phrase won't hold for you the same implications it does for some of our two-legged brothers."

The horse snorted, and Lancelot gave him one more tender stroke along his masticating jaw while the horse nuzzled him gently under his arm. With a light laugh, Lancelot lay down on the bed of straw he'd gathered for himself and, finally realizing how tired he was after his long day's quest, closed his eyes against a last worried thought of the queen. The horse closed his eyes as well.

***

I was sitting with Sir Agravain and Sir Tirre that same afternoon, just a few hours after we'd arrived in Gorre. Meliagaunt, feeling charitable, had allowed us to walk freely about the castle grounds under the watchful eyes of his armed guards while he took his prize catch, the queen herself, to his father's presence chamber. Meanwhile, as good as his word, he had sent the faint and failing Sir Kay to be searched by his own surgeons. Sir Pelleas, who'd been wounded slightly in the brawl in the forest, had gone with him. The ladies-in-waiting had all gathered in the castle's lesser hall, where King Bagdemagus's seneschal had arranged for some cooling drinks to be brought to them while they rested from the journey, and the rest of us were instructed to amuse ourselves in the bailey if we liked. Meliagaunt had little to fear, since we could all see that the only way off the island was the raft on which we'd come, and that raft was outside the castle walls and under heavy guard.

While I certainly would have preferred the company of Thomas or of my old friend Sir Palomides, I took this opportunity to bond with Gareth's brother, in whom I was at pains to allay any suspicions he might have had about me and my lady Rosemounde. At the same time, I was keen to get to know that newcomer to Camelot whose late sister had been the focus of so much excitement and controversy at the Pentecost ceremony. Not that either of these things was an easy task: two more reticent and laconic knights I had never found at Camelot. Before or since. That's why it was so ironic that Agravain ultimately got the reputation of being "Agravain the Open-mouthed," as Gawain dubbed him. But that was because…well, never mind. I'm getting way ahead of myself.

Strolling about the green middle bailey, the castle's great hall with its dark stone turrets on our left, and the round tower of the tall, imposing keep on our right, Sir Agravain spoke his heart aloud, as if we were in the middle of a conversation.

"He'd better not lay a hand on her, that's all."

By this I assumed he was referring to Meliagaunt and the queen. Seeking to reassure him, I said, "No. This is his father's castle, and King Bagdemagus would never sanction such a thing. Besides which, King Arthur will surely learn of this. I wouldn't be surprised if he were already on his way here with an army. Meliagaunt will wither like a plucked rose when he sees the king camped across the river."

"Or," Sir Tirre proposed, "Meliagaunt may figure that the king will draw and quarter him no matter what happens from now on, so he's got no reason to leave Guinevere alone…"

I scowled at Tirre, but Agravain sniffed and put his nose in the air, his face beginning to approach the color of his fiery hair. "If he tries it, I'll find a way to slit his throat myself," he said. "The royal blood must be kept pure!"

It struck me as an odd position for Agravain to hold. Sure, he was the king's nephew and for that reason had some stake in the clarity of the line of succession, but after a quarter of a century of marriage it seemed highly unlikely at this point that there would ever be any direct heir out of Her Majesty's womb. And nothing could mar the fact that his own brother Gawain, as Arthur's eldest nephew, was heir apparent to the throne of Logres. If he was thinking of his own blood relatives, Guinevere's purity or lack thereof could have no effect, since she was kin to him only by marriage. His own mother, Margause, it must be said, didn't care a fig for "purity," whatever that meant, for she had notoriously been caught by Agravain's elder brother Gaheris in an adulterous bed with the Welsh knight Sir Lamorak and lost her head to Gaheris's sword stroke—a fact that Agravain himself was well aware of, having taken part with Gawain, Mordred and Gaheris in Lamorak's subsequent ambush and murder. That crime was the worst-kept secret in Camelot. The best-kept secret also involved Agravain's mother: prior to his marriage to Guinevere, Margause had seduced her unwitting young half-brother Arthur into another adulterous liaison, the product of which, as Sir Gareth had revealed to me, was Agravain's younger "brother" Mordred. Whether Agravain was privy to that information I did not know, but given his mother's adventures it seemed ironic to me that Agravain had such an attitude toward the queen. Or maybe it wasn't such a strange thing after all: if Margause herself had failed to live up to Agravain's image of the Virgin Mother, perhaps he had replaced her in that ideal category with his aunt by marriage, the incomparable Guinevere.

"Yes," I said cautiously. "It's important to protect the queen."

"She is like an alabaster statue of the Blessed Virgin. Inviolable."

"Yes," I repeated in a neutral tone, while Sir Tirre gave an audible snort—whether of derision or of grudging agreement, I could not tell.

Just then, we were interrupted by a cry from one of the castle's guards from a battlement atop the outer wall of the castle facing the rushing river. "A knight has arrived at the Sword Bridge," the guard called. "And listen to this: he's come riding in a cart!"

There was a great deal of laughter and agitation in the bailey, and a few pages ran in to the building to inform the king and Meliagaunt. Tirre, Agravain and I made for the stone steps rising inside the wall to watch from the battlements, where Palomides, Thomas, and a couple of the queen's ladies were already standing. As we reached the platform, Lady Anne was saying, "This has turned into an inane comedy. Is it the dwarf or the disgraced felon who plans to assail the bridge? Are we supposed to believe that a knight without honor will have heart enough to cross that bridge with nothing to save him when he falls?"

"I think we need to prepare ourselves for a pretty gruesome death on those rocks," Sir Brandiles said, coming up behind us. "Nothing but dishonor and failure can be expected from a knight who's been forced to ride in a felon's cart." And then he caught his breath. Brandiles squinted and then held his right hand over his brow, straining his eyes to see exactly who was stepping down from the cart and, stripping himself of gloves, shoes, and armor, was preparing to have a go at the razor-sharp blade that spanned the rocky gorge. Then Brandiles gasped again. "That knight! Unless my eyes are failing me in this light, I believe it is my lord Lancelot himself!"

It was way too far for anyone to recognize the face of the knight of the cart, but Sir Brandiles had been a close ally of Lancelot's since shortly after the Great Knight's first appearance at Camelot and was, in fact, one of the knights Lancelot rescued from the renegade knight Sir Turquin. Brandiles had been devoted to Lancelot since that day, and could recognize him by his movements alone. I watched the knight in the cart closely, unsure whether to believe Brandiles or not. I had to admit there was nothing in the way he took off his armored boots and his metal gauntlets to leave his feet and hands bare—the better to grasp that sharp sword edge on which he must cross—nothing in his manner as he removed his mail shirt to give him less weight to carry across that narrow gorge, nothing in the way he wrapped the shreds of his surcoat around his knees—on which I perceived he planned to balance himself on that precarious span—that could have made me recognize Lancelot du Lac. And of course, without his surcoat or a shield bearing his coat of arms, there was no way that any of us could have been certain that this knight of the cart was in fact the Great Knight himself. But Sir Brandiles had spoken true.

All of us on the wall were silent as we watched the knight carefully, but without hesitation, kneel onto the Sword Bridge, resting his weight on his bandaged knees and gripping the sides of the blade with his hands and his feet. He quavered for an instant until he caught his balance, and then began the slow and excruciating crawl along that blade suspended high over the dangerous chasm. Inch by inch the Great Knight crawled, shredding his hands and feet, I had no doubt, and probably cutting away what protection he had managed to wrap around his knees, but still holding on for dear life, since a plunge to the rocks below would most certainly be fatal. Foot by foot, yard by yard, on came the knight, swaying occasionally with the breeze, but never to the point of losing his balance. Not a knight or lady of Arthur's court standing there on that wall even dared to take a breath as he neared our side of the gorge, and when after what seemed eons, he made a final lunge, grabbing on to the small platform at which the bridge ended, the battlements erupted into a loud cheer.

It was at that point that I glanced back to the opposite bank, and noticed that a young man had come riding up to the dwarf on the other side of the river. I was curious because he seemed to come rushing along the bank from well upstream, and he was apparently quite agitated about something. The dwarf appeared to give him a positive response of some sort, then began following the lad as he urged his horse back along the bank in the direction from which the boy had come. I couldn't be sure, but to me the young fellow looked something like Gawain's squire Peter, but as I say, it was too far away to be certain of anything.

And I suppose it was because I was distracted by that side action that I didn't notice that Lancelot had been met, once he stepped off the bridge onto the land of Gorre, by a group of twenty or more squires and pages, as well as King Bagdemagus's own physician, and had been carried, bleeding from his hands and feet, into a small closet in the castle to have his wounds tended to. Bagdemagus himself was standing close by us prisoners on this same battlement, along with Sir Meliagaunt who, I now realized, had not seen the face of the man who had crossed the bridge—if he had, he wouldn't have been so insanely confident in his response to his father, who had apparently just declared that Meliagaunt was to leave this knight alone until the knight was recovered from the gashes on his hands and feet.

"I will not!" Meliagaunt was shouting. "He has come to challenge me for the queen? Let him do so then, immediately! I will not be put off by some unknown knight riding in a cart. He's clearly a recreant felon of some kind, with no honor to his name! No one rides in a cart like that for no reason. A knight in a cart has no worship and deserves no courtesy. He is outside the laws of chivalry, and I'll dispatch him quickly. Let the news get back to Arthur that he must send true knights to fight me, not villains on carts."

"Whomever this particular knight of the cart is," Bagdemagus argued, "you've seen what he just did, eh? With your own eyes? Bloody hell, that was a feat if I've ever seen one! And believe me, I've seen one or two. Some feat, I tell you. And nobody is going to bother that lad until he's ready himself. So cool off your zeal, son, you gain no honor yourself from fighting a wounded man."

"I get no honor for fighting this man in any case. Nobody can gain honor by defeating a knight who has no honor himself. All I want to do is to send this one packing and force Arthur to send a real champion against me."

"I tell you no one but a true champion could have crossed that bridge!"

"A trick!" Meliagaunt answered his father. "This knight of the cart is some wandering acrobat, a juggler. Put a sword in his hand and you'll see his real worth."

"Not until he is ready," King Bagdemagus said. "That is final."

***

He was ready.

One brief hour had passed since the Knight of the Cart was carried into the castle. Word was that he requested to have his hands and feet bandaged and to be given a sword and shield, helmet and a mail coat, insisting that he was fit to do battle and challenging the queen's abductor to single combat. No one in that room had ever seen Lancelot du Lac, and neither Bagdemagus nor Meliagaunt, who *did* know the Great Knight on sight from their time in Camelot, had seen the Knight of the Cart except from a distance or, when he emerged from the physician's quarters, helmeted. So Meliagaunt could hardly be blamed for not recognizing him.

But you certainly *could* blame him for his reckless overconfidence. For him—and to be honest, for pretty much all of his vassals who had helped him in his kidnapping of the queen and the rest of us—this was just a knight who had ridden in a cart, and so was a negligible person to be swept aside as soon as possible.

King Bagdemagus, yielding to the importuning of his impetuous son and of the Knight of the Cart as well, granted an immediate trial by combat to take place on the middle bailey, the broad lawn between the keep and the barbican that stood guard over the front portal of the castle. Every resident of the fortress had drawn around to witness the battle, the prisoners from Camelot huddling for the most part on the east side of the lawn, the barbican on their right and the keep on their left—all but the wounded Sir Kay, who watched from a window in the great hall. Servants and tradesmen lined the other side of the bailey, with Meliagaunt's knights watching the dispute from above. Bagdemagus himself sat on a modest throne on a raised dais directly before the keep, with Queen Guinevere, an honored prisoner to be treated with great courtesy, seated in state at his right, with the lady Anne at her right shoulder and my lady Rosemounde bent over her left, whispering in her ear.

It was clear that Meliagaunt was confident, strutting around the lawn and cutting an impressive figure in his close-meshed hauberk, his pointed nasal helmet, and his Reuleaux triangle-style shield bearing his family's coat of arms: a chimera rampant, black on a field of red, or *gules* as we would say in heraldry. For him, this duel was a warm-up, he thought, to a more significant combat later on, when Arthur would send a true champion for him to deal with, not this meddlesome Knight of the Cart. His followers on the wall cheered him on, mocking Lancelot with a derisive chant that somebody up there thought exceedingly clever, and riotously funny:

Knight of the Cart!

Ain't worth a fart!

It was not by any definition of the word chivalrous, but then it was assumed that a knight forfeited any expectation of courtesy when he had suffered the ignominy of a cart. Meanwhile, the Queen's Knights and her ladies from Camelot, convinced by Sir Brandiles' comments, stood in joyful expectation of Lancelot's inevitable victory. But we all kept silent, unwilling by any slip to give away the identity of this challenger. For I recalled Gareth's words about Lancelot's difficulties in tournaments: his inability to get any other knights to challenge him, thus the necessity for him to enter tournaments in disguise to achieve any honor at all. In a way his mistaken, or at least misinterpreted, identification as the Knight of the Cart worked to his advantage here in Gorre, and none of us wanted to see the Great Knight lose that element of surprise.

Lancelot, in borrowed chain mail and a battered bucket-shaped enclosed helmet, gripped a rounded triangle shield made of wood covered with leather and painted white without any device, like the shield of a squire or a novice, untested knight. The bandages could be seen on his hands, and he slumped, leaning on his sword and obviously spent after the ordeal of the Sword Bridge. Looking at him, Meliagaunt grinned in anticipation of a quick victory and a vanity-stroking burst of adoration from his vassals, his father, and the local folk, plus at least an acknowledgement of his worth by the stony-faced queen.

Normally one would have waited for the lord of the manor to call for the combat to begin after going through the formal step of asking whether the two parties might be reconciled peacefully, but the Knight of the Cart, impatient to begin his rescue, the sooner to have the queen out of danger, leaped over that formality and issued an abrupt challenge:

"Sir Meliagaunt of Gorre," he began. "I say you are a vile and recreant knight, a blight upon the rose of chivalry, having duplicitously and villainously abducted Queen Guinevere and members of her household, and I demand that you yield her and all her fellow prisoners into my protection immediately, or be chastened by the edge of my sword."

"And I say you lie in your teeth, you lickspittle little whelp of a cart-riding cur. Enough of this pretense of chivalry. Kneel down and ask my mercy and I promise I won't kill you. I'll just cut off your ears as a sign to other upstart little villains not to get above themselves, and send you back to the king with a message to send me a real challenge next time." And while Meliagaunt preened like the cock of the walk, his supporters increased their jeering taunts.

But no one had noticed the queen. At the sound of the Great Knight's voice she had frozen with immediate recognition, and as Meliagaunt crowed she rose very slowly from her seat until, reaching her full height by the end of Meliagaunt's rant, she cried out in a clear, strong voice, "Lancelot du Lac! Humble this ass's pride and set my people free!"

The cat being out of the bag, so to speak, the queen's household cheered as one with all the nervous energy that had been building up inside us since the moment of our capture days before.

At the sound of that name, though, all taunting ceased, and Meliagaunt's supporters stood mute as stone. Meliagaunt himself froze, and though I could not see his eyes, obscured by his helmet, I was sure that the lower half of his face had turned a sickly shade of green. That's not to say that Meliagaunt was a coward: he was beyond question egotistical and could be something of a bully when the odds were on his side, but he had been wanting precisely this kind of showdown since the moment it entered his head to snatch the queen, so he could not shy from it now. It had simply come upon him unawares, and he wasn't quite ready for it.

Lancelot wasted no time, but brought his shield before him with his left arm and, raising his cruciform-shaped arming sword high over his head, marched steadily toward his motionless foe. Stirred to action by the threat of Lancelot's onslaught, Meliagaunt crouched down in a fighting stance, bringing his own Damascus steel knightly sword around in a sweeping arch, trying to surprise the attacking knight with a swipe at his midsection. The Great Knight parried that sweep, allowing the sword to glance harmlessly off his shield, then brought his own sword down with enormous strength, enough to split Meliagaunt's helmet asunder if it had landed. But Melieagaunt was nimble and sidestepped the blow, though the sword did glance off his shoulder, sending bits of metal chainmail flying and drawing blood. "A scratch, a scratch," Meliagaunt called out with a nervous laugh, provoking a few scattered cheers from his supporters on the wall. But

Lancelot pressed toward him further, coming on like an inexorable force, his sword drawn back again for another blow at Meliagaunt's head, landing it square on the rivets of Meliagaunt's shield as the younger knight swung his crimson-painted defense round to block that hammerblow again. Lancelot had driven his opponent close to the edge of the field where we were standing, and I could see after that blow a small hairline crack begin edging down the center of Meliagaunt's shield.

Now both combatants swung swords at once, clanging them against one another like the clash of two charging bulls. But they were close enough that I could see blood oozing from the bandage around Lancelot's right hand, and it seemed to me that his blows lacked the power they had shown when the Great Knight first assaulted his rival. Meliagaunt, too, seemed to notice this and to take new courage, pressing his attack with blow on repeated blow against Lancelot's proffered shield.

To see the Great Knight put on the defensive like this was more than the queen could bear, and I could see the anguish in her face as she called out, "You must end this, Lancelot! Finish him!"

And Lancelot, stung by the queen's words as by a whiplash, jerked his head back at the sound, actually turning his eyes to see the queen's face while his hands, machine like, continued to ward off Meliagaunt's blows with his shield, or parry them with his sword hand.

Lancelot's face was completely encased in his helmet, but I had seen his look of grim determination so often in the lists at Camelot that I fancied I could see it here, through the rounded steel that covered his head. With renewed vigor he redoubled his efforts, pushing forward against his foe, shoving aside Meliagaunt's sword blows with his borrowed shield like so many cobwebs, and hammering away at Meliagaunt's own shield with blow after blow like a barrage of Jove's thunderbolts. After a dozen or so of those sledgehammer blows, the crack I had noticed forming in Meliagaunt's shield gave way, and the reinforced oaken board splintered into a hundred shards, sending Meliagunt to his knees.

At that point I glanced over at the dais in time to see King

Bagdemagus go down on his own knees, turning to Queen Guinevere, and though at that distance I could hear nothing, it did not take an Aristotle to deduce that the king was pleading for his son's life with the only person present who might be able to stop the killing machine that was Lancelot du Lac. The queen, recognizing that she was captive no longer and that power had now shifted to her, could be generous in victory: I saw her nod to the king and turn toward the battle, where Lancelot had now battered Meliagaunt's sword from his failing hand and was about to swing at his helmet as Meliagaunt flinched and held up his mailed arms to further protect his head.

"Lancelot!" She called out. "You have prevailed! Spare his life now."

And just like that the Great Knight ceased his onslaught. In mildest courtesy he gave his head a slight bow toward the dais and stepped back, his sword placed point-down before him. His battle was over.

But without warning, Sir Meliagaunt snatched up his fallen sword, leapt to his feet, and hurled himself full force on the startled Lancelot. The Great Knight lifted his shield to ward off Meliagaunt's treacherous attack, then continued to fend off blow after blow as the weaker knight battered the white shield with unrestrained fury. Lancelot neither retreated nor advanced, but stood his ground, defending himself only with his shield, his sword remaining point-down before him, held in place by his bloody bandaged right hand.

The prisoners from Camelot cried out in sympathetic rage at this base betrayal, while Meliagaunt's own supporters gasped in a kind of embarrassed chagrin. Now King Bagdemagus, shaking with frustration and anger, charged down from the dais and moved as quickly as his advanced age would let him to stand between Sir Lancelot and his son. Meliagaunt, quivering with ire at being prevented, shrieked at his father. "Get out of the way, old fool! You'd stop me when I'm on the verge of beating him? You always stand in my way!"

"Beating him? You're striking a man who will not defend himself, who had already plainly beaten you. In what fantasy world were you winning this fight? Find another person here who thinks you were beating him and I'll send you both to the Bedlam madhouse you must have escaped from. Put your sword down before you lose all honor. These prisoners," the king now called out to all present, "are hereby freed, by my command!"

Cowed and denied, Meliagaunt let fall his sword arm. But his teeth were still clenched as he muttered, "I will leave the field in deference to you who are my lord and sire. But know this…" he blinked and then, as his father had done before him, raised his voice to a bellow as he turned around, addressing everyone present at those lists. "Know this: I did not yield to this Lancelot, nor will I acknowledge him the victor. For me, this battle is not over."

And with that Meliagaunt stalked off. We all looked at one another with sweet relief. We were free. The queen was rescued. Lancelot had won the day. Despite anything Meliagaunt might say, the battle was over.

CHAPTER SIX

ADVENTURES IN EQUIVOCATION

Sir Gawain arrived the next morning. So did Arthur and his knights. They camped on the other side of the gorge, a bit upstream from the other end of the Sword Bridge, and sent Gawain across the river on the barge with Thorvald and his cart, who tagged along to see whether there might be any business for him in Gorre.

I mentioned, didn't I, that amidst the excitement over Lancelot's crossing of the Sword Bridge I had seen someone across the river approaching the dwarf from upstream? Well that was Peter, it turns out, Gawain's squire. He found Thorvald and asked him to come help rescue the king's nephew. I'm not sure how it was done—I wasn't there—but Thorvald did have that big length of rope in his cart, and I think they tied it to a large branch they let float out into the middle of the stream, and Gawain was able to make his way to the branch and grab it. Then Thorvald and Peter tied the rope's other end to the cart and what with the horse pulling and Peter and Thorvald helping, they were able to drag poor Gawain out of that deathtrap.

They built a fire on the riverbank and dried Gawain out, and meantime Peter was actually able to catch a good-sized perch for Thorvald to fry up in a pan over the fire for their dinner. It was enough to refresh Gawain, though by then it was sundown and they decided to sleep out in the open again for the night. Thorvald slept in his cart, as he did fairly often when there was no inn that he knew nearby, but he couldn't interest Gawain or Peter in getting into the cart themselves.

They were up before prime the next morning and Gawain was eager to get started. He knew that by now Gareth must have encountered the king and his household and led them back through the forest in the direction of Gorre, and in fact they must be nearly here by now, since they could not be more than a day behind his own pace. The dwarf had, of course, filled him in on Lancelot's miraculous conquest of the Sword Bridge, but Gawain couldn't have known what success the Great Knight, weakened and bloodied, could have had in the interim, or what kind of welcome he might receive when he reached Gorre. Find the king, besiege the castle, and get in there to see where things stood—that was Gawain's checklist at the moment.

They had traveled less than an hour back along the path Gawain and Peter had come by when they heard coming toward them a good number of horses and riders, many with arms they could hear clanging as they rode. As you can imagine, there was a joyous reunion when Gareth found Gawain alive and well, and joy when Gawain saw the king with a score of his knights—Bors and Hector, Bedivere and Geraint, and some dozen or so others who happened to be in the castle at the moment Arthur determined to pursue the queen. They had come with tents and supplies, whatever they might need for a short siege, including workmen who could design and build siege engines. Gawain doubted the value of such engines considering the stream that barred any direct route to the castle, but considered that such builders might be set to work constructing sturdy rafts, depending on what might have been happening behind those walls since the arrival of Lancelot.

And so by midday the king and his entourage had pitched pavilions on the bank of the river, a bit downstream from the Water Bridge but perhaps a furlong upstream from the Sword Bridge, in easy view of the castle's barbican and almost directly across from the main gate and from the pier at which the castle's own great raft was tethered. It was Thorvald who had led them to this spot, knowing from his own experience that it was the point from which the castle's guard could most easily fetch them with their raft, if they had a mind to. And, as it turned out, they did.

King Bagdemagus was not about to offend Arthur any more than had already been done, and when he saw the king's banner with its three rampant gold dragons on a field of scarlet, he very quickly dispatched a messenger to his guards to send the raft across the river and bring back the king, or his representative, to parley. The king sent Gawain, and Gawain came attended by Peter, and by Thorvald with his cart, who somehow prevailed on Gawain—"I did save your life, after all"—to let him come across, cart and all, on that raft.

Meanwhile, Bagdemagus had prevailed on the queen to meet with him and Arthur's lieutenant, hoping that she would help smooth things over for him. With that goal in mind, he expressly forbade Meliagaunt from attending the meeting, and though he would have liked Sir Lancelot to have been there as well, the Great Knight had been so exhausted after his ordeal and had lost so much of his own blood that he had had time after the duel only to kneel briefly before the queen and pledge her his eternal loyalty, which she had very formally acknowledged and given him her blessing (neither, obviously, could demonstrate their true feelings in that formal, public display). Then he had been given a bed in a small private solar above the Great Hall and passed out. And so the queen, feeling the need to have a knightly supporter of her own at this conclave, if only for moral support, tapped her favorite former page for the honor. I was most happy to oblige.

We sat in a small room adjacent to the castle's throne room, around a board that had just been brought in to make a table, with King Bagdemagus at its head, Guinevere and me on one side, and a place for Sir Gawain on the other. Peter stood behind his master like a good squire, and Bagdemagus had a squire of his own standing over his shoulder. Gawain had been delighted to see the queen, kneeling to her in respect and murmuring, "My lady! Your safety and welfare have been the concern of all of Camelot these past days. I rejoice to see you well and without distress."

"You may rest assured, my treatment has been most courteous here in Gorre, under the eye of my lord King Bagdemagus," Guinevere confirmed, as Gawain rose and took his seat opposite her at the table. "I cannot say the same for my earlier treatment at the hands of his ungentlemanly son, Sir Meliagaunt." Bagdemagus made some gurgling sounds, a few grunts, and a few actually audible "my lords."

"Indeed," the queen continued, "one would think, after taking your own daughter Lady Constance as my lady-in-waiting, and seeing her well married to a knight of the Round Table, I could expect more courteous treatment at the hands of your family." Bagdemagus only hung his head.

Gawain went on, addressing King Bagdemagus. "And Sir Lancelot? I understand he made his way across your cruel Sword Bridge yesterday. Has his treatment here been equally courteous?"

Bagdemagus sputtered, "Well, you see, Sir Lance…that is, he, uh, arrived…I mean to say, when he came to the Sword Bridge he was, well, riding in a cart, don't you know? I mean, the idea! What were we to make of it, sir? Hmm? A knight without honor. Even when he crossed the bridge, well, Meliagaunt, impetuous boy, that's all he is…well, he still thought the Knight of the Cart was of no consequence…"

"So what happened to him?" Gawain asked, an edge of impatience creeping into his voice.

"Lancelot still challenged him, I mean Meliagaunt, even though he was bleeding from wounds to his hands and feet…I mean Lancelot's. And they fought for the queen's freedom, as it were."

Sir Gawain, in his role of royal negotiator, tried very hard to keep a stony, serious expression, but I certainly noted an insistent smirk straining to come to the surface of his face. He knew better than most just what the Great Knight was capable of, particularly when the queen was involved. "And what," he asked, "was the result of that contest, my lord?"

While Bagdemagus hung his head, searching for the right way to say it, I couldn't help blurting out, "Lancelot thrashed him like a schoolboy up and down the lists!" And when the queen raised her left eyebrow at me, I grinned at her and added, "Would have killed Meliagaunt, too, if the queen hadn't stepped in and stopped the fight." I knew that my contribution was not expected or required or, for that matter, even desired in so august a company as sat around that table, and Guinevere's scowl told me so in no uncertain terms, but sometimes you just have to describe things just the way they are, and Lancelot's victory over Meliagaunt had been a sweet, sweet revenge for how he'd treated the queen, me, Sir Kay, my lady Rosemounde, and everybody else, and sometimes you just need to gloat. At least you do when you're nineteen, which is what I was at the time.

King Bagdemagus didn't appear to be angry. In fact, he seemed relieved not to have to describe the battle. He rushed ahead, pleading his case: "And thus Sir Lancelot du Lac is resting now from his travails, which is why he is not here with us right now. So you see, my lord Gawain, the queen is quite free to go. Along with young Gildas here, and all the other knights and ladies taken captive with her, and, well, Sir Lancelot himself, of course. Free to go. Definitely not prisoners here now. Guests! Honored guests, eh, what? So, the king has no call to find fault here, we can send him the queen back on the same raft that brought you here!"

"With all due respect, King Bagdemagus," Gawain answered. "Your son laid violent hands upon his sovereign queen. He dragged her and her retainers for two days through the forest, with little food or water, and imprisoned them here on this island with little hope of rescue or succor. And what about Lancelot? I heard all about it from that dwarf, that Thorvald. Your son's archers were so unchivalrous as to kill his horse in the woods and leave him without any means of transportation. That's why he got into that cart when Thorvald offered it to him—it had nothing to do with any spot on his honor, he just needed a way to pursue the queen, and he only hesitated for a step or two before getting into that cart! Can't say I'd have done the same." At these words I saw the queen turn almost instantly crimson, though with great effort she kept her own countenance free from any change in expression. Gawain continued, "The king is in a great fury over all of this. He will certainly not let Meliagaunt off lightly!"

And that was when the dam burst. Clearly this was Bagdemagus's motive in having Guinevere present at this meeting. "My boy," he sobbed, tears welling up in his ancient eyes. "He is my only son. He is all I have left—his mother, you know, died years ago. Take him from me and I have nothing any more. Not even my heart." He broke down completely, his head in his hands on the board. The queen reached over and touched the old man's shoulder, not with as much tenderness as one might have wished—she had, after all, just been kidnapped—but with formal, and royal, protection.

"Be comforted, my Lord Bagdemagus," she told him. "Too much blood has been spilled, but no lives have been lost in this foolhardy enterprise. I will speak for you, and for your wayward son, with the king. No doubt I can prevail upon him to be merciful, and I would not have it said that any man of noble blood—even a jackanapes like your son—was killed for my sake."

Bagdemagus breathed an audible sigh of relief, and Gawain sat back with some satisfaction of having successfully negotiated an end to this touchy affair. "Then, Your Majesty, are you ready today to return with me across the river to Arthur's encampment? We can send the raft back to begin bringing your ladies and knights when we have you safely back in the king's pavilion."

"Yes!" King Bagdemagus exclaimed. "The sooner the better!" Out of sight, out of mind, I could see, was his attitude. Sweep it all under the rug.

But the queen was shaking her head.

"It may not be," she asserted. "You forget, King Bagdemagus that your son, in his *abduction* of me," Bagdemagus winced at the word, "wounded two of my knights—Sir Pelleas and Sir Kay. Pelleas' wound is slight, and will most certainly mend. But Kay, the king's own foster brother, suffers from a much more serious wound, a sword cut across his chest. Before we leave this castle, I must be assured that Kay is healthy enough to travel. Until Kay leaves this place, I shall not be going anywhere." And with that she glanced over to me and gave me an almost imperceptible wink. It was her way of getting a dig in to Bagdemagus. Even though as queen she must be the embodiment of mercy in the realm, she was not about to let anyone forget that this seizure of her knights was a violent outrage.

With that, Sir Gawain rose from his seat, saying, "I understand, as well, that Sir Lancelot has sustained wounds in crossing the Sword Bridge, and we should learn whether he is fit to travel as well. Let's go, then: it seems we must pay a visit to the queen's entourage, to see what damage has been done among her knights and ladies. We cannot bring them back to Camelot if they need to recover from their harms. King Arthur will be particularly interested in the welfare of his foster brother. If Kay is seriously wounded, even the queen may be unable to hold back Arthur's wrath. Gildas, will you be my guide and bring me to visit your fellows?"

"Gildas will certainly come," Guinevere answered for me. "But I will lead you. I want to see Sir Kay's condition for myself to see whether he can be safely moved. Come! Follow me!" And so we all tramped out behind the queen, with King Bagdemagus bringing up the rear, wiping the sweat from his brow with his ermine sleeve.

***

A visit to Sir Kay was the first order of business. In a large room on the castle's ground floor, the queen had been housed upon her arrival in Gorre, and in this room a luxurious curtained bed had been set up to accommodate Her Majesty last night, after Lancelot had ensured her freedom. There were iron bars in the window of this room, not to keep her in, but to protect her from anyone who might seek to do her harm during the night. King Bagdemagus had insisted on this, no doubt with some justified suspicion of Meliagaunt or, more likely, some of the thugs he employed. Across the width of this room the queen had caused a large, heavy curtain to be hung, effectively dividing the room into two living quarters. On the other side of the curtain from the queen's bed, Guinevere had demanded Sir Kay be laid on a comfortable pallet of his own, so that she would know immediately if he suffered any setback or needed the attention of a leech. King Bagdemagus employed a monk from the nearby Benedictine Abbey of Saint Frideswide as physician and surgeon for his folk, and this Brother Clement had been tending Sir Kay's wounds since yesterday, so that he was at Kay's side when we arrived. The king's seneschal lay as if asleep.

"Well, Brother Clement, how is the patient today, eh?" Bagdemagus began as we stepped into the dimly lit room. There was no window in Kay's half of the room, and what light there was came from a pair of candelabra near Kay's bed and from the six inches of space above the curtain through which a bit of light from the queen's barred window was seeping. "This is Sir Gawain of Orkney, Brother, King Arthur's own nephew. Wants to how our Sir Kay fares. Ready to put on his armor and ride at the king's side back to Camelot is he?"

There was a hopeful tone in Bagdemagus's clowning manner. Brother Clement, it appeared, was not inclined to be amused. Or else he was a man inclined only to the literal. "Goodness no, my lord! He must rest! He's in pain and he's also weak from loss of blood. I've cleaned his wound and changed his bandages. I've given him a dressing of honey to try to ensure that the wound does not fester and putrify. But I cannot be responsible for his bouncing along on a horse. Surely that would reopen the wound!"

Kay himself opened his heavy-lidded eyes and licked his thick lips, revealing those yellow teeth that seemed too large for his mouth. "Quiet, little man," he croaked out. "What are you but a monk? Can't you see this is Gawain himself, and Guinevere, Queen of Logres? If the king needs me, I shall ride, even into the flames of hell itself. Tell him I said so, will you Gawain?" And with that Kay closed his eyes.

Brother Clement clicked his tongue and looked at Gawain. "He is in pain, I think. And he is weak with loss of blood. He cannot ride."

"The queen must leave with her retinue as soon as possible," Gawain argued. "She was brought here against her will and so naturally would like to leave without any difficulty. And the king is anxious to have her back. Kay must come with her."

"He was brought here on a litter," I interjected. "Could he not leave in the same way?"

The monk frowned. "It is not advisable to move him at all. Still, a litter would certainly be better than riding a horse. But only if you take him directly to the king's camp across the river, there to let him rest further. And only if he stays here for one more night, to allow his wound to knit a little more before trying to move him anywhere."

"Then that is what we shall do," Guinevere decided for us all. "Now come, Sir Gawain, you will want to meet with the rest of my household and with Lancelot to make sure there are no obstacles to their leaving this place tomorrow morning if Kay can be moved. Come on, then!"

Gawain nodded, the shadow of a smile on his face, amused at himself, I supposed, for having thought for a moment that he was in charge of this situation.

***

In two adjacent barrel-vaulted lesser halls on the castle's second level, separated by an archway framing a tapestry depicting the classical story of the rape of the Sabine women, the ladies and knights of Guinevere's personal household were being housed. I had slept here last night with the rest of the queen's knights, while in the room beyond the tapestry lay my lady Rosemounde and the rest of the ladies-in-waiting—tantalizingly close but alas, without any opportunity for privacy. Besides, any notions that may have flitted briefly through my ardent mind were squelched by the even closer proximity of Sir Agravain, who, unwitting as it may have been, was as good a chaperone as Argus with his hundred eyes. In another small, private chamber adjacent to this one, Sir Lancelot was housed, and Gawain, of course, planned to visit the Great Knight as well, to judge for himself Lancelot's health and fitness for travel.

The remains of a light midday meal were scattered about the room when we arrived: Bagdemagus wanted to keep Guinevere's knights away from his own to reduce the chance for frictions to develop, but of course he wanted to ensure that the knights and ladies did not complain of their treatment here, and so had sent a few meats along with some bread and cheese and flagons of ale, hoping to be able to send his "guests" packing soon after. But it seemed that was not to be.

Everyone sprang up when they saw Sir Gawain, almost as if Arthur himself had walked into the small hall. But Gawain walked immediately over to Sir Agravain and gave his brother a relieved embrace. When Guinevere followed him in, they all bowed formally out of respect and duty. When I entered, they ignored me, which was pretty much how they treated the rest of the party, including Bagdemagus. In the other room, there was an excited stirring, and all eight of the queen's ladies came through the tapestry, having dressed as best they could under these circumstances, and considering they had not had a change of clothing in three days. Lady Anne led the ladies in, followed closely by Lady Rosemounde, who flashed a covert look at me from under lowered eyelids and remained standing well away, with Anne and Lady Vivien along the wall to my right. Lady Mary, I noticed, came directly over to stand beside Thomas, who leered at me as he looked in my direction from the corner of his eye. Lady Elizabeth trailed after, looking bored, and I could hear Lady Mary's chatter rise above the general hubbub in the room: "If Sir Gawain's here maybe we're about to leave then? I'm certainly ready to, I can tell you that. What kind of host gives his guests bread and cheese *en masse* in a back room? And when will they let us bathe, for heaven's sake?"

"Sh…," Thomas inserted, anticipating some kind of speech from Sir Gawain.

"My friends," Sir Gawain began in a voice that overpowered whatever murmurs were still ongoing. "King Arthur has brought a small party of knights and has set up his pavilions on the opposite bank of the river. Your host, King Bagdemagus, is eager to return you all to your sovereign lord, who is, after all, his own liege lord as well. If all goes well, if Sir Kay is hale enough to be moved, we can arrange to have you all leave Gorre tomorrow and join the king's party, to make our way back to Camelot in comfort and at leisure."

Several folk cheered for Gawain in gratitude, but the king's nephew, never comfortable dressing himself in borrowed robes, held up his hands to deflect any thanks. "I would love to have been responsible for your deliverance," he told the room. "But I failed in my efforts to cross the Water Bridge and come to the queen's rescue. No, you all must realize that your freedom is owed solely to the heroic efforts of Sir Lancelot du Lac."

From somewhere in the midst of the crowded room, I heard a snort, and a mocking voice said quietly, "the Knight of the Cart." The room fell silent, though there was a low ripple of laughter, some of it coming, I noticed, from Agravain's vicinity, and looking past Gawain's brother I realized the remark had come from the new knight Sir Tirre. Looking around, I saw the queen's eyes glaring and her jaw clenched, and noticed Sir Gawain beginning to bluster, not knowing what to say. I also saw Lady Mary grasp Thomas's arm and bite her lip, tears welling in her eyes, and I remembered what she had said about her own father's mortification. But to the surprise of everyone in the room, it was the lady Elizabeth who stepped forward to address Sir Tirre in no uncertain terms.

"That's not funny, sir. My father was forced to ride in a cart and to be flogged and humiliated. And he was a noble man and did not deserve such treatment. He was shunned by everyone afterwards, even his oldest friends would not talk to him. To be seen with him was an embarrassment to them. And what was his crime? He owed a powerful knight money and was not able to repay him. The money was to buy himself a noble destrier and armor so that he might ride well-equipped in his lord's wars. But after Arthur's last war with the Emperor Lucius, my father's lands were wiped out by disease and he had no harvest. The cruel knight demanded payment, and when my father could not pay he was humiliated and brought to public shame. He does nothing now but sit alone in what is left of his castle. And all because of this cart thing? A man's worth should be based on what he has inside, not on what he rides outside. How shallow are you people? Is this your idea of chivalry? Don't you know that chivalry involves loving your fellow man and not just his reputation?"

By then her anger had run its course, and she stood panting, as if she'd just raced a furlong or two. The room was hushed momentarily, as surprised at her outburst as they had been by Sir Tirre's ill-timed comment, and Elizabeth's sister had moved to her and taken her in her arms, cooing softly, "That's all right, Bessie. You gave them all a schooling, didn't you?"

Sir Tirre, now somewhat abashed, reddened and stammered out, "Rest assured, you have my apologies, my lady, it was discourteous of me..." and the hub-bub in the room increased again, as we all returned to our previous conversations and others vied for Sir Gawain's attention with various questions. Sir Tirre, however, continued to grouse to Sir Agravain, in whom he seemed to think he had found a sympathetic ear. "So no one can say a word about the Great Knight, can they? It's Lancelot of the Lake, the fair-haired boy all the time. Always must be the center of attention." Agravain said nothing, but I began to wonder why Tirre should have taken so hostile an attitude toward Sir Lancelot, who after all had sponsored him and his brother for knighthood. I imagined it as pure jealousy: only the greatest knights could keep from envying Lancelot at least a little. Sir Gawain was never jealous. Mordred always was.

But my wondering hadn't progressed far when suddenly Lancelot himself appeared in the doorway.

His blue eyes were dulled and the lids drooped as if he had only just risen from his well-earned rest, but his square jaw was clenched and his face bore a frown that would have worried anyone unfortunate enough to be in the lists with him at the time. His hands were both heavily bandaged but he had them curled into fists as he stepped into the room. I was fairly certain he had heard something of the chatter that had been taking place in this room in the past five minutes. Yet he spoke courteously.

"My lord Gawain," he began. "I rejoice to see you unharmed. I was worried when I heard that you had gone off to assail the Water Bridge. I commend your great courage."

With unfeigned humility Sir Gawain bowed his head, saying, "My lord Lancelot, my own failure is offset by your great courage and prowess in conquering the Sword Bridge. No other knight could have been capable…"

Lancelot shrugged and brushed off the compliment. "I'm not here for praise," he said, looking past Gawain toward Queen Guinevere. "And I apologize for interrupting this august company, but it has recently occurred to me that my choice of transportation for my journey to this place may be misconstrued by some ill-informed folk. Your Royal Highness," and with this last word he went down on one knee before the queen. "I submit only to your own judgment. My horse had been ruthlessly killed by Meliagaunt's archers, and I must either pursue you and your abductors on foot, which would have delayed your rescue by days, the thought of which I could not abide; or I could ride in that cart, kindly offered me by the driver, Thorvald, and thereby reach you by the fastest means possible. I know that, no matter what anyone else says, you will understand where the dictates of courtesy had to lead me in that choice."

The queen looked at him, looked around at the rest of the room, and then, pulling herself up into her most imperious stance, her haughty nose almost vertical, she intoned through it, "If you truly loved me as you should, you should not have hesitated those two steps before entering the cart!" And on that word, she spun on her heel and stalked out of the room, followed closely, after a shocked pause, by Lady Anne, and then, with a quizzical and bemused look thrown at me, by my lady Rosemounde as well.

I rushed to Lancelot's side and put my hands on his shoulders to steady him, and saw his face frozen, mouth agape in stunned silence, before he sighed and in a quiet voice audible only to me, whispered, "My God! She's absolutely right."

***

Now I don't want any of you to get the wrong idea, and go misinterpreting just what it was the queen had done with that snub. At the time, pretty much everyone in that room—with the exception of me and Sir Lancelot himself—was thinking what an ungrateful bitch Guinevere was: after all, here Lancelot had just raced to her rescue, got a horse shot from under him, shredded his hands and feet crossing a razor-sharp bridge suspended over a deadly gorge, then fought for her in mortal battle to free her from her would-be ravisher, and she chides him over a two-step hesitation? But I knew what she knew— that the only way to stop people from fixating on the humiliating ride in the cart was to reject their frame, and to change it radically. What her rhetoric did in that instant was reinvent the cart, making it something admirable—the means by which Lancelot could rescue his queen—instead of something reprehensible.

And I also knew what nobody else in that room knew, that the queen was totally indifferent to whatever anyone present there thought of her. She was above it. She was unaffected by their adoration or their scorn. What she did care about was Lancelot, and what the rest of the world thought of *him*. It was important to Lancelot that the world see him as the Great Knight, and for him she was prepared to do anything to ensure that this state of affairs continued.

But even more than the queen, I also knew what Lancelot knew, and better than anyone, I knew how he felt. He loved the queen truly, wholly, completely, and when she told him that if he truly loved her as he should, he knew that she was talking about *that* kind of love, not the devotion of a loyal subject to his queen (which is how everyone else in that room understood her comments). And he knew that if indeed she was the love of his life, then any reluctance to enter the cart was selfishness, was concern for his own fleeting reputation and not for a love that was forever, and so *of course* he reacted when she chided him. Those two steps were worms in the heart of true love. True love must be absolute. *That* was courtesy. *That* was chivalry.

I knew that Guinevere intended to cow the rest of us by her comments. I wasn't sure whether she knew what effect her words would have on Lancelot. But as it turned out, that whole scene was just foreplay anyway.

***

Sleeping arrangements for one more night in Gorre had to be made that evening over a light supper that King Bagdemagus had arranged, trying to make up for his gaffe with the midday dinner. Bagdemagus had boards set up in the castle's great hall, and he himself sat at the head of the table at which he served roasted swine on trenchers with a thick gravy sauce in dipping bowls around the table, capped with a dessert of fresh seasonal fruits. Bagdemagus offered Sir Gawain his own private quarters close by Sir Lancelot's small solar. The queen's ladies would remain where they were, while the queen's knights for the most part would sleep where they had last night. But Guinevere wanted to further assure herself of her safety in what she still regarded as a hostile castle, and she also wanted to ensure the safety and health of Sir Kay, whom no one thought it advisable to move for the night. And so the queen requested that Sir Agravain and Sir Palomides be enlisted to stand guard before the door leading to her quarters. Those two knights readily agreed, but it was still not enough for the queen. She wanted someone she trusted completely to be in her quarters on the other side of that privacy curtain, both to watch the night with

Sir Kay in case he would take a turn for the worse, and to be at her beck and call should anything disturb her during the night. Since this confidante would need to sleep in the room with Sir Kay, it would not appear proper to have Lady Anne or Lady Rosemounde sleep there, but who could be more appropriate for this role than the queen's own faithful and trusted former page? And that's how I ended up in the queen's chamber that night.

So it was that shortly after compline, the hour of peace, I found myself stretching out on a pallet not far from Sir Kay's own, on which he rested somewhat fitfully. I could see he was uncomfortable, and though I knew him to be a pompous, vainglorious ass most of the time, and a bully when he was able to get away with it, I had seen that he was no coward, and that his loyalty to the king and to Guinevere was unparalleled. Here in the privacy and darkness of that small candlelit chamber, he was just an uncomfortable wounded comrade, and one who needed a drink.

I'd brought down a pitcher of wine from the dinner table and now poured it into a cup that I put to Kay's lips. He curled them up to reveal those prominent yellow teeth. "Thank you, Gildas my lad," he croaked. It was the first time he'd ever called me anything as pleasant as "my lad." I could see he was not himself.

He swallowed down the entire cup in just a few gulps, and with his nodding encouragement I poured him another. "Dulls the pain," he confided in me. "Hurts like the very devil. But I think it's mending. Doesn't smell like putrefaction, as far as I can tell. You?"

I wrinkled my nose at the thought, but told him honestly, "No. You're going to be all right. You know they want to move you out of here? To bring you across the river to Arthur's pavilions tomorrow?"

"Good," Kay said. "Don't want to die here." And to my great surprise the seneschal had tears in his eyes. "You know, Gildas, I just want to be worthy of him."

I wasn't ready for that, and I waited as he drained the cup once more. While I poured him his third cup, I prodded him a bit, assuming that's what he wanted. "Who?" I asked. "You mean the king?"

"Nobody knows better than I what a great stroke of undeserved luck I had being foster brother to the king. Who knew at the time?

He was just a bratty little foundling brother who unexpectedly pulls that sword out of the stone and suddenly he's king. And by virtue of our relationship, I become head of the royal household, Arthur's own seneschal."

"And you do it well," I told him sincerely. "Nobody could keep the grounds of Camelot as orderly as you do, or fill our larders more skillfully with supplies of all kinds."

The tears would not go away. "Is that all my legacy will be, though? I am not Lancelot. I am not Tristram. I am not Gawain, or even Gareth, the *Beaumains*. But I am no craven, and if death must come I want it to come on the battlefield, not in this backwater slum from some scratch like this." And he downed the rest of that cup.

"You're going to be all right," I reassured him again. "This wound is not your last. You're going to survive it, and I predict you'll live to fight and maybe die at Arthur's side in battle. If that's what you really want."

Kay gave a wan smile and then rolled on his side. "You're not a famous seer like your master Merlin," he told me. "But I choose to believe you anyway. Tired now. Don't wake me till morning." And within a few short minutes, Kay was snoring heavily. I lay down on my pallet and rolled toward the wall, thinking to join him in slumber as quickly as possible.

How long I had been asleep I don't know, but in the still of the night, with only Kay's snores for company, I heard the whisper of a sound on the other side of the curtain. It was a voice, I realized, at Queen Guinevere's window.

Immediately my senses were piqued. I crept to the curtain and put my right ear against it, straining my ears to hear what those voices were trying hard to ensure that no one outside that chamber heard. But I did. It was Lancelot.

"My lady," he murmured at the window. "Will you deign to speak with me, your devoted servant?" Oh boy, I thought. He's in that *fin amors* mode, is he?

"My love! Is it truly you?" the queen answered. I saw she had softened her tone somewhat since that afternoon.

"My lady, I have blasphemed against your love. As you pointed out this afternoon, my hesitation at the cart was an indefensible sin against love itself." Oh Lord, this making a religion out of your love for a woman was a game of sorts, I knew, but some people actually took it seriously, and Lancelot was one. I won't say I was another, but I understood the feeling. Rosemounde was for me more inspiring, more precious, than any cross or altar or reliquary.

"Dearest Lancelot," the queen purred quietly, "what I said was in jest, merely to throw those little gossips' minds off your humiliation." But I knew how he would feel about that: no act done for one's beloved is ever a humiliation.

"It was true none the less," Lancelot insisted, as I knew he would. "How can I expiate the sin? Give me some penance I may perform, some act to wipe away my falling short of your expectations." This seemed to be getting out of hand. What was wrong with Lancelot? Had the strain of the past few days driven him into some sort of fanaticism? I mean, he was talking like someone who'd lost touch with his reason.

But then, that was also an aspect of love sometimes, wasn't it? I should know.

"Then I command you..." the queen hesitated. I knew she was trying to figure out just how to handle this lunacy that had come upon the bulwark of the kingdom during this dark night of his soul. "I command you to come into this chamber with me. Find a way to do it that remains secret, but find a way. I command you to come to me." Not your best inspiration, my queen, I thought as she said it. I mean, I know she was making this up as she went along, and I know it made a lot of sense to get Lancelot safely inside where he was unlikely to harm himself or others, but this particular command—with her window fixed with iron bars and with two knights guarding the outer door through which he'd have to come, and then with Kay and me in this outer part of the chamber, it seemed frustratingly hopeless for anyone to get in to the queen.

Turns out I'd misjudged my man. But the queen hadn't. "Nothing can keep me from coming to you, my love, if you have commanded it," the Great Knight pronounced, and within seconds I heard an odd scraping of metal on stone, the grunting of Lancelot's straining efforts, more scraping, and a final deep groan, and I knew with certainty that Sir Lancelot du Lac, bloodied, bandaged hands and all, was using every ounce of his strength to pull those iron bars from that window, enabling him to crawl through that space and into the guarded chamber of his beloved.

What I heard after that was muted, and there were no more words. I sighed, shook my head, and returned to my own pallet. Sir Kay had never ceased his snoring. I hoped that Lancelot would be able to put those bars back before he left, and that he'd listen carefully for the morning song of the lark.

***

A commotion outside the door wakened me, and the dim light I could make out above the curtain informed me that it was past prime. Kay groaned on his litter and wondered aloud, "What the devil is that racket?"

"I'm about to find out," I answered, opening the door into the corridor, where Sir Palomides and Sir Agravain were restraining Meliagaunt from entering the room. Meliagaunt, dressed in a fine blue tunic covered by a gray woolen cloak lined with ermine, was glaring at them arrogantly and, as he was backed by three of his own stooges, it did not look like a situation that would end well.

When he saw me, Meliagaunt relaxed a bit. "Ah, Gildas," he said. "At last someone with some sense. I'm here to say farewell to the queen and to send her on her way. The sooner you are all out of Gorre, the better, that's how I feel. I'm here to speed you on your way, starting with Her Majesty."

I never knew how to take Sir Meliagaunt. It seemed that when he got something into his head, you couldn't reason him out of it. But then he'd change in an instant, latching onto some new obsession. He was mercurial, that's how I saw it. Now, having seen that his abduction of the queen had failed, he wanted anything that reminded him of that failure gone and gone immediately.

"Her Majesty is not yet arisen," I began, but then without warning Meliagaunt pushed past me and strode toward the curtain.

110

"Rise, Your Highness, rise and greet the day of your deliverance." He said this with a mocking tone in his voice, as if, after all, his little escapade had been nothing more than a prank that she—and by implication Lancelot and the rest of us—had been foolish to consider threatening in any way. "Come, I have the raft ready and waiting to take you and your ladies across the stream to my lord King Arthur, waiting on the other side. Then we'll bring it back to ferry the rest of your household across afterwards."

All the time he was speaking he was inserting himself further into the queen's chamber. But the queen, for modesty's sake if nothing else, made no answer, nor had she drawn aside the canopied hangings around her bed, but remained within those opaque bed curtains as if they were her fortress. With his accompanying soldiers, I followed Meliagaunt into the chamber, though my first thought was to glance at the window. I could see that the iron bars had been somewhat hastily and sloppily shoved back into place, though they didn't look as if they could withstand any force at all from the outside any more. I prayed neither Meliagaunt nor his minions bothered to take a good look at them.

Agravain and Palomides rushed into the queen's chamber after us, calling Meliagaunt to desist. "Cease this for shame, Sir Meliagaunt!" Palomides chided. "I ask you, is this courtesy? Is this chivalry? No, this is villainous, I tell you!" I realized then that neither Palomides nor Agravain had a weapon: the queen's knights were still not armed, though they had been set to guard her door that night. Meliagaunt and his three companions all carried swords. All Palomides had were words to stop Meliagaunt's insolence. And they weren't enough.

With his profane hand, Sir Meliagaunt actually reached out, took hold of the queen's bed curtains, and crying "Come, come, your grace, and greet the dawn," yanked them aside, to the collective gasp of everyone else in the room.

The queen sat bolt upright in her bed, her face a mask of pale, haughty rage. Her eyes glared at Meliaguant with cold hatred, piercing as if she meant to drill holes in him with her stare. The effrontery of the man was something she had never been exposed to in her life, and her lip actually curled in disgust at the sight of him. "You low-born villain," she said with quiet loathing. "Take your filthy hands away from my bedclothes."

Meliagaunt, however, was paying no attention to the queen or her words. His eyes were fixed upon the sheets that Guinevere was holding up before her like a shield. My eyes were drawn to where his were directed, and soon the gaze of all the men in the room had focused on those sheets, which were streaked with blood.

At that sight my own blood drained from my face and I nearly swooned. Glancing up at the queen I saw her look at me with a puzzled expression, her eyes questioning as I covertly moved my head slightly from side to side. But Meliagaunt, after a moment's shock, exploded.

"Aha!" He cried out in a high-pitched voice that smacked of a kind of madness. He reached out and snatched the sheet from the bed and out of the queen's trembling hands, and began to wave it about. "So this is our chaste consort of the great King Arthur, is it? Look at the blood on these sheets, all of you!" And he staggered to the opening in the curtain that led back to the sickroom behind the queen's. "It was you!" he pointed an accusing finger at the wounded Sir Kay, still lying on his cot with a clueless scowl upon his face.

"What in the name of sense are you jabbering on about, you demented cur?" Kay responded to the knight's bizarre outburst.

"You were in the queen's bed last night! You were rutting your liege lord's bitch and broke open your wounds in the heat of passion. Don't deny it—here's the proof!"

"You fool, I can't even get up out of this bed!" Kay responded. "Ask Gildas there, he was with me all night."

"How do we know you're not just feigning how weak you are? Yes, you would do that, wouldn't you, the more to make me seem the villain for wounding you. But young Gildas must have slept sometime during the night, didn't you Gildas? And you would have been oh so quiet, you and your randy queen, if you saw a chance to slake your traitorous lusts!"

I'd never seen Sir Palomides at a loss for words before, but the enormity of these accusations made on the flimsiest of evidence had him tongue-tied, and he merely gurgled in frustrated rage. Sir

Agravain had another response—the chagrinned look on his face led me to believe that he was beginning to doubt, after all, the purity of his uncle's mate, and therefore the honor of his bloodline. As for me, I know I could have handled things better, leapt to Sir Kay's defense more quickly, but the fact that I knew Sir Meliagaunt's charge to be true in its essence—the queen had, in fact, been with another man that night, Meliagaunt had simply accused the wrong man—made me slow in answering the charge. "N...no," I stammered. "I mean, of course I slept for a time. That is, I...uh... slept very lightly. I would have heard Sir Kay get up, certainly. He never did, I'm sure."

"Of course you'd say that!" Meliagaunt cried. "You'd say anything to protect your precious queen, wouldn't you? Well not this time!" And with that Meliagaunt took the stained sheet in his hands and, waving it behind him like some bloodied banner of war, rushed out of the chamber, heading for the middle bailey in the midst of the castle, and I followed quickly behind him in the vain hope of talking some sense into him, while he muttered, "If *my* name is going to be a hissing, by God, I'll make sure *hers* is as well!"

"Don't do this, Meliagaunt," I tried to reason with him. "Stop now before you get yourself into something you can't get out of. You will never get your name back after this!"

"I will if I muddy hers," he told me *sotto voce*. Then out into the bailey he lurched, waving the sheet about and screaming like a madman. "Come and see the proof! Your queen is a slut, a whore and a traitor! I've seen it with my own eyes! See for yourself!"

Most of the castle was just getting up to face the day, and of course, they were drawn to come out to the courtyard, or to look out through windows, to see what all the fuss was about. King Bagdemagus and two of his servants came out on a balcony with a quizzical look on his face. Across the courtyard, Sir Gawain had come out on his own balcony, looking at Meliagaunt with a thunderous brow after hearing something besmirching the queen's name. The queen's knights looked out their window from above the bailey, and several of the queen's ladies looked from another window, though I saw

Lady Mary, Lady Anne, and my own Rosemounde coming out the door to stand with offended disdain in the courtyard, offering a silent challenge to Meliagaunt's claims.

By now Meliagunt's three underlings had followed us outside, and Agravain and Palomides had, at Sir Kay's request, carried the wounded knight out into the courtyard, his arms draped about their strong shoulders as he sagged weakly and wheezed. The rest of the castle's occupants had emerged from within, surrounding the courtyard, and I even saw Thorvald the dwarf, peering tentatively out from one of the lower windows across the bailey. Finally, the queen herself, a royal blue samite cloak thrown hurriedly about her shoulders, stepped with undaunted bravado onto the open lawn.

Meliagaunt had what he wanted now, a large audience before whom he could act the part of a shocked loyal subject of the king, who at the same time was, perhaps, something like a wrongly rebuffed suitor. "This vixen is now revealed for what she truly is!" He proclaimed to anyone who would listen. "She, who acted the part of the pure, virtuous queen who must needs be saved from *my* evil intentions by her bully of a protector, the great Lancelot! She, who would have you think she was too precious to eat the same food, sleep in the same bed, even breathe the same air as the rest of us vile mortals! Well look at this bloody sheet, will you? Indisputable evidence that she spent the night rolling about in swinish lust with this wounded knight, Sir Kay, the king's own foster brother, who shared the same chamber with her!"

In the shocked silence that followed I saw a number of faces looking curiously at one another, their eyes puzzled as they weighed the possibility that Meliagaunt might be speaking the truth. After all, wasn't there proof positive on the queen's sheets? Only Rosemounde and Anne looked angry, their eyes challenging Meliagaunt to support his claims with something more than this tenuous "evidence."

Then I glanced at the queen, who had never looked fiercer. She stepped forward with no hesitation, with no fear or timidity or yielding in her voice. "By what principle of chivalry does a knight enter any lady's private chamber, let alone his queen's, and thrust himself among her bedclothes? Such a knight is not worthy of the name. And am I to defend myself against charges brought by such a one? It is beneath me even to answer. But I am sure that all reasonable persons know but have better manners than to discuss why a woman's sheets might be bloodied during certain phases of the moon. Let us call it, for delicacy's sake, a nosebleed."

At that all the men in the courtyard looked down abashed, while the queen's ladies, shocked at such boldness but convinced she had bested her challenger in one swoop, tittered self-consciously behind their hands or upraised nosegays. But Meliagaunt was not done.

"Nosebleed mine arse," he said with discourteous vehemence. "I invite anyone to look closely at this sheet and tell me these are not bloody handprints that I see here. I tell you they are the hands of a wounded knight!"

The queen seethed with anger, sparks flying from her eyes, when Meliagaunt was challenged from another direction.

"I cannot stand idly by and let this vile insult to the queen's honor, and my own, go unchallenged," Sir Kay rasped through his clenched, yellow teeth. "Give me a sword, someone, and I'll prove my lady's innocence and give this upstart crow the lie in his throat. We'll see if he can still rant so loudly with my steel in his belly."

Clearly Agravain and Palomides were astounded by Sir Kay's outburst. "My lord," Palomides cautioned him quietly, "you cannot do this! You are in no condition to even lift a sword, let alone fight… you must stand down."

But King Bagdemagus, smelling an opportunity for his son to get out of this mess with his name at least partly unsullied, was already grasping at that straw. "A trial by combat!" He proclaimed. "You have heard the formal challenge Sir Kay has made to Sir Meliagaunt. To determine the truth of these charges made against the queen and this knight, a trial by combat is proposed and I hereby accept it on behalf of my son and my house."

Amid the excited buzz that greeted Bagdemagus's assessment of the situation, I looked to the queen, and she looked back at me, all pride drained from her face. She realized the implications of this trial: if Kay were to lose the battle, then Meliagaunt's claims would be deemed accurate, for it was assumed that God would uphold the right in such a trial. Adultery by and with the queen was considered an act of treason, and punishable by death. This trial would put her life in the hands of Sir Kay. And he could not even stand up on his own.

A fact that was not lost on Sir Gawain. "Silence!" The king's nephew and representative commanded. The buzz stopped. "This man is in no condition to defend himself in the lists. His wound—a wound churlishly inflicted on him by the very man he has now challenged—precludes this being by any measure a fair fight."

"God will be in my sword arm, for I fight in a just cause!" Sir Kay wheezed up toward Gawain's balcony.

I could see in Gawain's face that he knew as well as I did that in trials like these, God could be counted on without fail to uphold the stronger knight with the more effective sword arm. And that was not going to be the sorely wounded Sir Kay. "You shall not tempt the Lord your God!" Gawain shouted back, surprising the breath out of me, for I had never known him to quote scripture—didn't know he knew any to quote! But this line sure came in handy. "In the name of King Arthur, I call a halt to these proceedings. He must approve any trial by combat that involves his honor and his queen in any case."

"He's across the river," Meliagaunt called up to Gawain. "We'll send a raft to him right now!"

"Sir Kay cannot do battle now, that much is clear," Sir Gawain insisted.

"No. But I can fight in Kay's place, as his champion," came a new voice from below. A knight in full armor and carrying a massive broadsword emerged from the door below the queen's knights' quarters. It was, of course, the voice of Lancelot. Now Guinevere's eyes lit up, and she rose to her full height once again. King Bagdemagus, however, was quite deflated. Having saved his son from slaughter at the hands of the Great Knight just the previous day, he did not relish exposing Meliagaunt again to the uncertain mercy of the queen's own champion.

"Sir Lancelot, then you are making a formal challenge?" Gawain prodded him. "What do you claim?"

"I say this," Lancelot replied steadily, "and swear it by all the saints: despite this perjurer's lies, Sir Kay is completely innocent of any liaison with the queen. And I further declare that the queen has never betrayed her lord the king with Sir Kay, and the blood on that sheet is not Kay's at all."

How careful Lancelot was in the wording of his oath. I looked across at the lady Rosemounde and saw her looking back at me with her signature smirk I had seen so rarely of late. I looked to the queen and saw her looking down, hiding her own expression of relief and of complicity in Sir Lancelot's precise and prudent summary of the situation. Maybe trial by combat always went to the stronger arm, but it couldn't hurt to be innocent as well. And Lancelot had so worded his defense that, yes, the queen was indeed technically innocent according to the letter of the law. Though she was guilty as sin according to its spirit. And at this my eyes flitted again toward Rosemounde, *As am I*, I thought.

"But Sir Lancelot's wounds are nearly as dire as Sir Kay's," King Bagdemagus now asserted. "He must be given time for his wounds to heal! Several weeks, at least!" I could see what Bagdemagus was doing. Put this trial off for some weeks and perhaps he could talk his son into backing off and taking back the accusation. Or maybe King Arthur would step in and forbid the trial by combat outright. Or perhaps Sir Kay's wounds would be so well healed by then that he would insist on fighting his own battle and take over from Sir Lancelot—and that, Bagdemagus was certain, would give his son a fighting chance. Something could be done to save his son. Given time, something could be done.

And Gawain concurred. He certainly did not want to see anyone killed this morning, just when he thought things had been settled peacefully. Nor did he want any kind of trial taking place without the blessing of King Arthur himself.

"This, then, is how it shall be," Sir Gawain proclaimed. "Today is what? The last day of May? The feast day of Saint Petronilla, is it not? Saint Peter's daughter? Then let us say in a month—make it the third day in July, the feast day of Saint Thomas the Apostle—when these two parties, Sir Lancelot and Sir Meliagaunt, will meet at the lists in Camelot before the king, who must needs give his blessing to this trial before it is legal. The battle will be to the utterance, the lives of the guilty or perjured being forfeit to the crown. If either party fails to appear in the lists when called upon on Saint Thomas's day, then he is to be deemed to have lost the trial, and his lands and life are forfeit—again, with the approval of the crown. Now let this assembly disperse, and let the queen and her household depart this castle, before more mischief is hatched!"

I breathed a sigh of relief. Sir Kay collapsed into his supporters' arms. Sir Lancelot bowed slightly to Sir Gawain to acknowledge the terms of battle. Bagdemagus had bought his son some time, but there was no question that in a month, a healthy Lancelot would be the killing machine of old. The queen was safe, or as safe as she could be for the moment. And we were all going back to Camelot to wait for the feast day of doubting Thomas, who insisted on seeing something with his own eyes before he would believe it.

CHAPTER SEVEN

CRISIS

"The object is to stay on the horse, featherwit!" Sir Gareth called his version of encouragement as Peter missed the quintain on his next pass and flipped backwards off his horse. Fortunately, his shoulders took most of the impact, and his helmet protected his head. Peter would be mighty sore tomorrow, but he wouldn't have any broken bones and would be quite capable of getting back into the saddle and having another go at that elusive quintain. This morning, Gareth had just been relating to me his version of how Gawain had dealt with the Water Bridge, a tale I hadn't heard before, though we'd been back in Camelot for some three weeks now.

As we helped the chagrinned squire get to his feet and hobble off, his arms over our shoulders, I told him quietly that I had had the same misfortune with the quintain as he, and that while bruising to the body as well as the ego, one could come back from it having learned a great deal about what *not* to do in a joust. "Look at me," I said. "Two years ago, no one—including my master here, Sir Gareth— would have predicted I'd ever become a knight of the Round Table. And look at me now!"

Peter, who by now had removed his helmet and was seated on a bench at the side of the tilting field, looked up at me from the corners of his eyes, his mouth in a kind of grimace, as if he was tempted to tell me what he *really* thought—that I had been lucky to be at the right place at a time when the Table was decimated by the Grail quest. And of course he'd have been right. But I felt determined to show off a little bit, for Peter as well as for Sir Gareth, and stepped back to my new destrier, the tall brown war horse Achilles.

Achilles and I were old friends, and now that he was mine I spent regular time with him in the stables, feeding him apples and stroking his nose on a daily basis, and taking him out for his exercise when I had the time to do so. And by now he'd learned to trust me and even respect me a little bit, though probably not nearly as much as I respected him.

I swung up into my jousting saddle—one with a raised cantle in back to guard against my being flipped over the rear as Peter had just been, and a high pommelto in front that protected against low lance thrusts when in actual combat. Jousting saddles were narrow and had particularly low-hung stirrups, to give riders more of a standing posture in the lists.

I fewtered my lance—holding it straight up as it rested in the leather support on the side of the saddle—and trotted Achilles out to about a hundred yards from the quintain. Achilles, knowing exactly what was expected of him, stamped his right foot with some impatience, something I'd seen his sire, Gareth's Ajax, do a hundred times. I lowered my helmet's visor, and couched my lance under my right arm, setting it at about a thirty-degree angle that was ideal for jousting. Then I gave Achilles his nudge with pressure from my thighs, and off he galloped, bearing down on the quintain with increasing speed and power. I pushed my feet down heavy into the stirrups, from which I should derive the power of my thrust. The quintain had a red bull's eye painted at its center, approximating the position of the four rivets a knight was likely to have in the center of his shield, and it was toward that red spot I aimed all the force of my lance's blow.

Achilles thundered into that quintain with all his speed and weight, and my lance struck it perfectly in the center so that it spun rapidly around like a windmill in a gale. I let Achilles ride well past it before bringing him to a stop with a touch of my rowel spurs, and then trotted back to where Gareth and Peter waited at the bench.

When I raised my visor to look at Peter, I raised my eyebrows as well, as if to say, "You see how it's done, boy?"

But all Peter did was shrug, hang his head, and mutter, "Looked to me like it was all Achilles' doing."

I threw down my lance in exasperation and had just started to roar, "Why you little…" when a sharp cry from behind startled me.

"Sir Gildas!" came a slow, high-pitched voice I'd heard before. "I've got an important message for you!"

I turned to see the young Lady Elizabeth standing expectantly behind me. She wore a simple green wool gown with white trim around the neck and without the stylish, wide hanging sleeves, clearly everyday attire for one of the queen's own ladies-in-waiting. She wore no cloak either, the late June weather being unusually warm today. In courtesy, I knew that I must dismount and do her deference, though I must say I found the girl somewhat annoying. Except for that time she schooled Sir Tirre about her father and the cart—that had showed some gumption. And then, as I swung my right leg up over my saddle and dismounted, I had a sudden disturbing thought: I had also found Lady Rosemounde annoying at first. And look how that had turned out.

"Lady Elizabeth," I said in my most courteous voice, removing my helmet and offering her a polite if mechanical bow. "What a delight it is to see you again. May I say that you are looking most lovely this morning."

The thirteen-year old girl was carrying a nosegay, and pushed her face into the flowers as she responded to my easy and frankly insincere compliment, as if my words had an unpleasant odor about them. "Well, I suppose I can't stop you from saying whatever you like," she responded. You see? Annoying. In a maddening kind of way. But, well, you know, with gumption.

"I'm to tell you that the queen demands your presence immediately," the girl continued. Then she turned and began to walk back to Guinevere's rooms without a glance back. I looked at Sir Gareth, who gave a sideways jerk of his head as if to say, "Get going," and Peter looked up at me and said, "I'll stable Achilles and make sure he gets taken care of." And so I figured I'd better scoot off in Lady Elizabeth's wake, still in my armor and carrying my helmet. When the queen said "immediately" she was not speaking figuratively.

Now there are some things that chivalry demands about which there is no wiggle room, and one of these was that one does not allow a lady to walk off by herself without an escort if one can possibly help it. I trotted to catch up with her as she briskly made her way across the middle bailey, and even called, "Lady Elizabeth! Please, allow me to escort you back to the queen's quarters!"

"Don't bother," she called back over her shoulder. But my legs were longer than hers, and within a few steps I had gained on her and took my place at her right side. She threw me an indifferent sidelong glance and then, eyes front again, pointed to the helmet I still carried and asked me, "What do you expect to do with that?"

I glanced dumbly down at the bulky thing myself, and realized I must look rather foolish carrying it around with me for no purpose, and I could feel my cheeks begin to burn. Rather than answer her (I figured the question was probably rhetorical anyway), I decided instead to change the subject and, perhaps, to put *her* on the defensive. "Lady Elizabeth, have I done something to offend you? If I have, I wish you would tell me what it is and allow me to make amends."

With that word she stopped abruptly in her tracks and turned to face me. By now we were approaching the courtyard of the lower bailey, and passing the kitchen and the great hall on our right. Smells of succulent roasting meat wafted toward us from the kitchen as the cooks prepared the mid-day meal. "I have no feelings toward you one way or another. To me you are just another knight. I do the queen's bidding and the queen has bidden me come and fetch you. I am not privy to why, but I gather some crisis has occurred and she has a notion you might be of some use. As for giving me offense, I know of no specific action of yours I can point to that has offended me. But as a knight, born into that privileged class of arrogant gossipmongers that has grieved me daily since I've come to this ungodly place, there are frankly ways in which your very existence offends me." And with that she sniffed and turned away.

Now my eyes were stinging. I wasn't sure whether it was smoke from the kitchen burning them, or tears of frustration fighting to escape. She thought I was a highborn noble? Well, I suppose being a Knight of the Table and hanging about with the Orkney clan could give someone that impression.

In retrospect, it was probably the smoke. But I decided to disabuse her of her mistaken notions about me. We resumed our walk, moving into the courtyard and starting up the stone steps leading to the queen's private chambers. "Lady Elizabeth, you mistake me," I told her. "My father is an armor maker in Cornwall. You yourself are far more noble than I, being niece to Sir Bedivere. I was born a commoner, but my father was well acquainted with several Cornish knights, and through them was able to procure a position for me as page in this court. I worked my way up from being Queen Guinevere's page to being Sir Gareth's squire and then," I paused, remembering Peter's humbling estimation of my promotion to the fellowship of the Table. "And then I became the luckiest armor-maker's son in Logres when so many knights were lost in the Grail quest that Arthur became desperate enough to bring the likes of me into the Round Table." Lady Elizabeth turned to me now at the foot of the steps, and looked at me curiously with her bright blue eyes. She pursed her lips and tilted her head so that her light brown hair hung down over her left shoulder. She seemed to be examining my face for clues to my low birth. I expected her to apologize. Or perhaps to laugh at my charming self-deprecation. But in fact all she did was give me a quiet, snorted "Hmmph," stick her face back in her nosegay, and climb the stone steps. I followed, abandoning any efforts at conversation, and entered the wide doors leading into the corridor, where I followed Lady Elizabeth to the entry into the queen's private rooms. I began to wonder just what it was that Guinevere found so urgent that she had to see me immediately. I was used to being at her beck and call for myriad minor concerns back when I had been her page, but these days she had other confidantes, most notably my dearest Rosemounde. Apparently she did not yet confide in Lady Elizabeth or, I supposed, her sister. And with that thought I made a conscious effort to put the lady Elizabeth out of my mind.

Master Holly, the queen's aged clerk who also served as her doorkeeper, sat hunched over his desk trying to make some kind of sense out of Guinevere's royal account books when we arrived in the outer chamber of the queen's quarters. He looked up but relaxed when he saw Lady Elizabeth and me arriving. "The queen…" I began, but Master Holly just waved me in through the curtains that separated the outer from the inner chamber, and went back to his books.

Lady Elizabeth led the way through the curtains, and when I entered the space usually occupied by all of the queen's ladies-in-waiting, I found only Guinevere herself, my Lady Rosemounde, and, to my great surprise, Sir Gawain, all seated as if in close private conference. Now my curiosity was really piqued.

"Here's the one you wanted," Elizabeth announced blandly. I noticed an almost imperceptible wince at the lack of courtesy in the girl's demeanor as the queen responded quite formally, "Thank you, Lady Elizabeth. You may go and join the other ladies. They've gone down for dinner." To Elizabeth's questioning look Guinevere responded, "We'll be down directly. This will not take long."

When the girl had left, Guinevere dropped her stiffness and revealed a more harried expression "Sit, Gildas, sit. Thank God you're here. We're not sure what we're going to do."

It was difficult to sit in any comfortable manner while wearing chain mail, but I managed to get myself propped on a wooden chair facing the other three and, not sure what to do with my bulky helmet, placed it in my lap. Lady Rosemounde's eyes sparkled as she smirked at me, and to tell you the truth, I'd have undergone any amount of awkwardness for just a few seconds of that pretty smirk. But I was not there to juggle helmets or to bask in smirks, and accordingly I looked to the queen and asked, "What is the crisis of which Lady Elizabeth spoke, your majesty?"

Seeing the queen's face, her red eyes and the deepened line of worry between her brows and along the frown of her face, I was very quickly taken up with the seriousness of the situation. Yet it was not Guinevere but Gawain who answered me.

"Lancelot has disappeared," he told me gravely. I looked at him blankly. I wasn't sure what he meant, or why it was of such concern.

"But…he often goes off on his own, looking for adventure or for something to interest him. He's restless when he hangs about the castle…"

"But he would have let the queen know if that's what he was doing," Rosemounde put in.

"Unless he had quarreled with her…" I started, then cut off, thinking there may be too much of a suggestion in that as to Lancelot's relationship with the queen, but Gawain did not take any note of it.

"There was no quarrel…" Guinevere blurted out, in what I now heard was a panicked voice.

"Besides, I've already talked to Taber in the stables, and he says Lancelot's horse, Minuit, hasn't left his stall in the last week, and surely Lancelot would have taken him if he was going off on some adventure. Lancelot said nothing to Sir Bors either," Gawain added, "and no matter what else was happening, he would have let Bors know his plans." And I knew that was true. Ever since the incident in the tournament when Bors had wounded Lancelot, the Great Knight was careful to let his closest kinsman know his designs. If Bors had not been informed, then Lancelot had not planned to leave the castle for any length of time.

"How long has he been gone?" I asked.

"No one has seen him for three days," Rosemounde answered.

"And in five more days it will be the Feast of Saint Thomas," I muttered, putting my finger on the main concern in the room.

"Exactly!" Sir Gawain cried. "This trial by combat over Meliagaunt's accusations against the queen and Sir Kay is due to take place in five days' time, counting today, and the knight pledged to defend the queen's interests is not here to answer the challenge! We run the risk of losing the case by default, which means…"

"Which means I am found guilty of adultery and treason. And sentenced to burn at the stake!" Guinevere sobbed.

"As, for that matter, is Sir Kay," Rosemounde added, somewhat anticlimactically.

"And Kay, who originally challenged Meliagaunt and could legally reclaim the right to fight him, is still not fully recovered from his wounds," Gawain said.

"Well, that can't be allowed to happen," I insisted. "Look, if Lancelot doesn't show up for the trial, I'll defend you myself, my queen. As would any one of your knights!"

"It's not that simple," Gawain stopped me. "In the first place, and I mean no offense when I say this, but Sir Meliagaunt is a doughty knight. Of course, he's a blowhard and something of a spoiled child about getting his own way, but make no mistake, he has been in some mortal battles before and it would be taking a great chance to have you face him—we might lose you along with Sir Kay and the queen."

"Even with God on my side?" I asked, mostly ironically. "The queen's innocence being certain, I should have nothing to fear. Maybe we can trust in that."

"I would rather trust in a good sword arm," Gawain replied calmly but firmly.

"Then Sir Palomides will defend her," I suggested. "Or you yourself, my lord Gawain, you were there at the time and heard the charge. Couldn't you step in and take up the challenge? Meliagaunt would have no chance against a knight of your prowess."

It wasn't idle flattery but Sir Gawain brushed it aside as if it were. "No, Gildas, as I started to say before, it's not that straightforward. The king *could* allow such a substitution, to be sure, but it would have to be agreed upon by all parties involved. Meliagaunt is likely to insist on the letter of the law, to insist that he fight Lancelot or Kay, or failing those options that the queen be found guilty. The king can refuse to issue a judgment, but Meliagaunt could complain that the king is unjust and twisting the law for personal reasons, and impugn his honor."

"Let him! It's better for Arthur than losing his queen!" I cried.

"Never," Guinevere whispered. "I will never allow the king's honor to be besmirched on my account."

I thought about this for a few moments. "Look, I think we're mistaking our man, here," I said at last. "Meliagaunt isn't in this because he wants the queen killed or shamed. What he wants is respect and recognition of his own knightly prowess. He wanted to win a great victory over one of Arthur's best knights. Even fighting him to a draw would be fine with him. If he could fight Sir Palomides or better yet, Sir Gawain, he would be perfectly happy with that."

Sir Gawain pressed his lips together in skepticism. "I don't know about that," he mused. "He's the one that set this whole process going, and to have the battle forfeited to him is still a victory as far as the law is concerned. If he has the advantage that way, why would he give it up?"

"We have to find another way," the queen sobbed.

"We have to find Sir Lancelot," Rosemounde added.

I thought for a moment and then stood up. "And that means I'll have to go find Merlin," I said, and with a bow each to Sir Gawain, Queen Guinevere and Lady Rosemounde, I took my leave.

***

Merlin's cave was located on the shores of the Lady Lake, through the woods north of Camelot. It was in a cliff honeycombed with caves, so that if you didn't know the right one to approach, you might look there for weeks without finding the old necromancer. I knew the right one. It was the fourth cave to the right of the one closest to the shore of the lake. To get there, I had to wade across a very cold stream that fed into the lake—that same stream that ran past the castle and had carried the body of the fair maid of Astolat weeks ago at Pentecost. Fortunately, I had taken the time to drop by my lodging in the castle and remove my armor, stripping down to a hooded brown tunic and hose, and, knowing this stream was going to be in my path, I had put on a pair of leather shoes with laces that I could easily remove. I removed them now and waded gingerly into the water, icy even in the warmth of this late June, cursing as I did to punctuate each step: "Why! Hell's! Name! So! Bloody! Cold!" Re-shoeing myself on the other bank, I grumbled as I climbed toward the old man's cave: "Can't live at the castle like a normal bloke, oh no, he's got to live in a bloody cave like a bloody wild man of the woods or some such foolishness...." But I quieted down as I got nearer the opening. Merlin was the wisest man in the kingdom, and he and I had been partners in solving all kinds of questions for the king and queen on various occasions, but I never knew what kind of welcome I'd meet when I got to his cave. He could be morose, moody, brooding one minute and jubilant, exuberant, even tempestuous the next. You never knew if you were going to get a pleasant welcome or a rude rebuff when you called. So, arriving at the cave mouth, I peeked gingerly around the corner into the cave and just as I did, was pleasantly aware of the scent of a tender venison stew coming from within.

"Well don't just stand there, boy! I've got dinner on, grab a bowl and sit!" Said the old man, bending over the fire and stirring a pot that was simmering over it. The fire glinted off his bright eyes, so that he appeared to be shooting red flames at me from under his considerable brows. "I see that your exalted status of knight hasn't prevented you visiting your poor old friend. Hasn't improved your stalking skills any, though. I could hear you coming a mile away—like a barbarian horde approaching down an echoing canyon, eh?"

"So you had time to put the pot on when you heard me coming?" I asked.

"God's eardrums, Gildas, I could hear you for miles. I had time to kill the deer, skin it and dress it, cut up the vegetables and simmer it into a stew by the time you got here!"

"Right," I said playing along. "And I suppose Nimue didn't send you this dish herself from the Lady of the Lake's household. You were out hunting yourself with your own crossbow and hounds?"

The old man shrugged. "She drops me a crumb now and then, I admit." I knew that much was true. Merlin's great love, the Lady of the Lake's nymph Nimue, for whom Merlin had nursed a deep but unrequited love for years, had stopped visiting him regularly when she had taken Gawain's son Sir Florent as her lover, but she did think enough of him to drop by, or send by messenger, some special treat occasionally. Otherwise Merlin was too eccentric to even think about eating until he suddenly felt hunger pangs, reminding him he hadn't eaten since breakfast the day before.

There was a small table in the cave, with two wooden chairs pulled up to it, and I took a bowl from Merlin and sat down in one of them, letting my eyes adjust to the scant light coming in from the cave entrance and the scanter light put off by the small fire. I liked to admire the tapestries with which Merlin had lined his rather cozy cave, which left barely an inch of the cave's rough wall exposed. What with the furnishings—Merlin's own pallet, a small bookcase containing several manuscripts he liked to peruse while falling off to sleep, his other small table on which sat his well-worn chessboard, and the fire that drafted through a hole in the stony ceiling, it was only that high dome of rock that gave this space away as a cave and not a room in a great stone castle.

I spooned some of the venison stew into my mouth rather greedily, my stomach just now remembering I had been sent off on this mission right at dinnertime. But as I chewed, I looked at the tapestry on Merlin's left wall on which was depicted King Pelinore, one of the first leading knights of Arthur's Table in the early days, subduing what I had always assumed was a mythical creature, the Questing Beast, a monster with a snake's neck and a leopard's body, a lion's haunches and a deer's legs. Pelinore was rearing his horse and driving his lance toward the beast's heart. I didn't know whether the subject was history or legend, but certainly the tapestry had been in Merlin's cave ever since I had been coming here. Yet, Pelinore himself was long gone, slain by Gawain and Gaheris after he killed their father, King Lot, in battle. Pelinore's son Lamorak, one of the three great knights of the Round Table, had died as well at the hands of Gawain and his brothers (except Gareth), and his younger son Perceval had died on the Grail quest.

And the Grail was the subject of the tapestry on Merlin's back wall: the golden cup was depicted there floating above the figure of Joseph of Arimathea, and in the background, an army of knights all armed in white, pursuing the cup. Though the tapestry predated the quest, it was a kind of presaging of that mad pursuit that ended in the deaths of so many knights along with Perceval and Galahad, the ideal knight.

On the right wall was Sir Tristram, second of the three great knights of Arthur's brotherhood, slaying a dragon in Ireland in his youth. It was said that he first met La Belle Isolde when she saved his life after he'd been poisoned by the dragon's venom in the wake of his famous battle. Now he, too, was gone, and Isolde with him. Merlin and I had seen the aftermath of that affair ourselves.

"So many gone," Merlin, seeing where my eyes were going and reading my expressions, spoke for the first time since sitting down to sup.

"There have been three great knights in the history of Arthur's Table," I mused aloud. "Three great knights, and Galahad, the purest and truest…"

"And least fit for this world," Merlin reminded me.

"But they are all gone now, save Lancelot," I said. "Are we reaching the end of chivalry? Are those Pentecostal vows soon to become meaningless and pass from the earth?"

"Who knows whether other great knights will appear?" Merlin argued. "Gawain is a great upholder of courtesy. Sir Gareth is as chivalrous as any. God's anklebones, boy, even you could develop into something given an infinite amount of time! But so long as Lancelot lives, and so long as he is willing and able to defend a noble cause, chivalry still lives. What has you in such a melancholy mood today?" And suddenly his great shaggy brows shot skyward and a look of sudden enlightenment crossed his face. "Oh that, of course, is why you're here. Something has happened and they've sent you to me to ferret out the facts again, is that it?"

"Well…" I began.

"King or queen this time?" the old man wanted to know.

"The queen again. Her life is in danger. Again. This trial by combat…"

Merlin had heard all about the impending trial, but like everyone else in Camelot, he saw it as no real danger to the queen. "But that's absurd, boy! Lancelot will make mincemeat of that blithering idiot Meliagaunt. Tell her to save her worrying for something truly upsetting, like that new Lady Mary's voice. Have you heard it? Like a squawling cat's, and I'm not exaggerating," and with that he gave a histrionic shiver of mock horror.

Things were too serious for me to humor Merlin's eccentricities, and I quickly brought the conversation back to the serious matter at hand. "Lancelot cannot be found," I blurted out. "Anywhere. No one has seen him for days. The queen and Sir Gawain suspect foul play."

"But surely Sir Bors…"

"Bors knows nothing," I told him. "And if Lancelot doesn't meet Meliagaunt to defend the queen's honor…"

"She'll be burnt. Or the king will be dishonored by protecting her."

"Which seems the better choice," I argued. "But it's a choice that does not have to be made if we can discover what has happened to Sir Lancelot."

Merlin gave a thoughtful sigh, and answered with unusual sincerity, "So it's as I said, then. For chivalry to survive, Lancelot must be willing and able to defend the queen in this honorable cause of hers." Raising just one of his considerable eyebrows, he threw me a sharp look, saying, "And it *is* an honorable cause, dear Gildas, is it not?"

I looked away from his eyes, down and toward the fire at my left. I took one last spoonful of stew and savored it for a moment or two before I answered. "Queen Guinevere is completely innocent of betraying the king with Sir Kay."

"Ah!" Merlin said, a cynically satisfied look crossing his face. "Congratulations, Gildas, since your promotion to knight, you've become as skilled an equivocator as any politician at court."

"But Merlin, listen, Meliagaunt can't…"

"Oh, I agree completely," Merlin said, holding his hands palms down to shut off my argument. "For the good of the kingdom and the future of the Round Table, Meliagaunt's accusations cannot stand. Lancelot must defeat him, and defeat him decisively. But you may remember what I told you a few weeks ago at the Red Fox Inn: I said there that chivalry was manly virtue in the service of righteousness. It has nothing to do with reputation. All of that 'honor' stuff is playacting. This trial by combat is just more playacting."

"But without it the Table will fall. And without the Table there will be no chivalry as you define it either."

"It may diminish," Merlin acknowledged. "But Camelot is not the only place that virtue can be enlisted in the cause of righteousness. It does thrive here, though," he sighed, "and so we will find Lancelot."

"Good!" I cried, rubbing my hands together in anticipation of the task. "Now I figure we talk to Bors first, to see…"

"White or black?" Merlin brought his chair over to the chessboard.

CHAPTER EIGHT

A GAME OF CHESS

Well, I knew one thing: we weren't going anywhere until I'd slaked Merlin's appetite for a good game of chess. Or at least as good as I could give him. Besides, I knew this was his way. He wasn't one to rush into anything without having thought it through carefully first, and if he was going to investigate the disappearance of Sir Lancelot, he was going to consider it from every angle he could think of first, and then decide on which steps to take. I had been through this before. So I sat down at that small table with the chessboard and, as Merlin pulled up his chair from dinner, told him, "White. Obviously. I need any advantage I can take."

"Of course you do. You'll always be a Cornish blockhead, and a dubbing from Excalibur isn't going to magically change that. Now make your first move while I see if I can get my brains lined up to think this Lancelot case through. As far as we know, he disappeared from the castle without informing anyone that he was going away, or whether he'd be back. Since we know he would not deliberately leave the queen in any danger from these serious charges brought against her, we must conclude one of two things: either he was taken against his will, or he was persuaded to go very suddenly and assumed that whatever he was summoned to do would be completed well before the queen's trial. If it is the first possibility, we must try to imagine who could possibly have overpowered Lancelot and taken him by force."

"That answer is easy enough," I told him. "No one. So that leaves the second possibility. And I'll start with king's pawn to king four."

"Oh, I'll follow suit. Pawn to king four as well. But what you say does not really follow. Just because no one could have overpowered Lancelot in a fair fight doesn't mean that someone, and again, it would have to have been someone he trusted, tricked him into letting his guard down, or into some kind of trap in which he was injured or imprisoned. The same is true of the second possibility—that he was lured somewhere away from Camelot and then trapped or set upon once he had left the castle. We know that he was not riding his war horse when he left. Did he have someone else's horse? Or was he being carried off?"

"Well if either of those things is the case, then what we have to worry about most is that he's been—or is now being—spirited away to some distant fortress from which even if we find him or he escapes, he'll never be able to get back here to Camelot in time for the trial by combat. And that dooms the queen, and Sir Kay. And, uh, king's bishop's pawn to king's bishop four."

"That's not at all what we have to worry about most, boy! What we have to fear the most is that they will kill Sir Lancelot. Or, even worse, that they already have."

An icy chill crept up my spine at that thought. "Good lord, Merlin, I don't know if I can bear to think of that! But you're right—if these people, whoever they may be, are planning to see the end of Guinevere and Kay, too, then why would they have any qualms about killing Lancelot?"

"Well, they wouldn't," the old mage replied. "If, in fact, that is their goal. We may have to hope that it's not. Pawn takes pawn. I'll take your gambit, young Gildas. Where'd you learn that little tempting move, boy?"

"Just something I've seen you do in the beginning of the game. So, we assume that Lancelot is alive, is that what you're saying?"

"Well, I think we have to act as if he's alive, as if we will find him. Otherwise we lose the urgency of the chase, and let up, perhaps, on the pursuit."

"There's still plenty of urgency if we want to save the queen," I countered.

"That's really less of an issue, I think," Merlin told me. "As I'm sure the king will not allow the possibility of the queen's burning."

"He did once before!" I exclaimed, recalling the case of the poisoned apple that had killed Sir Patrise at the queen's fatal feast a few years earlier.

But Merlin looked peeved. "It never got to the burning stage in that case," he said. "Lancelot got there in time, and besides, we proved her innocent."

"They were ready to light the fire!"

"Well, they didn't light it, did they? Anyway, that case had a dead body and a poisoned apple. A pretty clear cause and effect. The evidence is slimmer this time. We have to make a lot of inferences from blood on the sheet to get to adultery with Sir Kay. And make your move, will you?"

"All right, all right, uh…king's knight to king's bishop three," I said. "So what's the first step? Do we want to talk to Bors, or Sir Hector, Lancelot's brother? One of them might be the last to have seen him."

"Pawn to king's knight four," he countered. "Let's question them. But let's see if we can answer any questions by ourselves first. We don't know who did it, and we don't know how they did it, but let's see if we can guess *why* they did it."

"Well, that's easy. They did it to keep Lancelot from defending the queen against her accuser. Pawn to king's rook four."

"We assume that, but it could be coincidental timing, and so, it could be a plot to get at Lancelot that has nothing to do with the queen. Pawn to king's knight five." Merlin tapped his nose and lowered those cumbersome eyebrows as he thought. "But it's certainly most likely that it has to do with the queen's trial. If that's true, who is most likely to want Lancelot to miss that trial?"

"Again, it goes without saying. Meliagaunt, of course. Who else? His own life is in peril if he fights Lancelot. Still, as I've said before, Meliagaunt started this whole thing because he wanted to prove himself worthy, and he thought the best way to do that was to hold his own in combat with one of Arthur's greatest knights. Why should he then pull the rug out from under his own plan?"

Merlin stared at me a moment, then flicked his eyes downward toward the board.

"Oh, and knight to king five," I added.

"King's knight to king's bishop three," he countered, and then added, "I think we still need to keep Meliagaunt as a prime suspect. He stands to gain the most by winning his case. And whatever his original intentions, the prospect of meeting Sir Lancelot in the lists single-handed, especially having been bested by him once already, could easily erode the confidence of even the most self-deceived egoist—which is what this Meliagant seems to be. Even if he is unstable as a three-legged horse."

"Maybe," I acknowledged, unconvinced. Having been the only one to actually talk to Meliagaunt about his original plans, I couldn't see him being happy at the queen's demise, and said so. "I still can't see him wanting Guinevere punished. Or Kay for that matter. That wasn't his goal."

"But it would suit him to see the king dishonored, would it not? A kind of tit for tat after the king overlooked him and failed to give him the honor of a seat at the Table?"

Now *that* I had to concede. "Yes, that I can see," I said. "And pawn to queen four."

"So, who else had a motive to kidnap Lancelot? Queen's pawn to queen three, by the way. Threatening your knight."

I snorted at that. "Ha! My knight is quite threatened, if I can call Lancelot my knight. But who's the pawn that's threatening *him*?"

Merlin pursed his lips and suggested, "Maybe not a pawn at all, but a king? What about King Bagdemagus himself? What would you think of him being behind this scheme?"

I nodded in agreement. "Bagdemagus has the clearest motive here. He doesn't want to lose his son and he knows a healthy Lancelot will beat him in an instant in the lists. Bagdemagus would, I'm sure, do no harm to Lancelot himself, but if he could trap him somewhere and imprison him until the trial is over, he'd save his son. And for him, that's the most important thing in the world. Here, my knight is going to retreat to queen three."

"Then I'll take your pawn. Knight to king five and there he goes. Hmmph. We need to consider another possibility: that Lancelot is just a pawn in this, and that the real target is the queen. Or the king." Merlin drummed his fingers on the table for a moment, and then asked, "Who might have a vendetta against the queen herself? Who would stand to gain if the queen were dishonored and perhaps even put to death?"

"Well, you left your own pawn open then. Queen's bishop to king's bishop four, capturing your pawn. So there." I felt a little quiver of satisfaction at the idea of taking any piece at all from Merlin. But as I thought of Merlin's question the memory of Sir Agravain's face flashed into my head. "You know, old man," I said, thinking out loud. "The thought that the queen may in fact be guilty of infidelity to the king might truly be upsetting to any number of people."

"Not least the king," Merlin whispered.

That brought me up short. "Wait…you're not suggesting that King Arthur…"

Merlin shook his head decisively. "No, no, we're just brainstorming here. The king would never do anything to subvert justice, and it would be in his interests to have the queen proved innocent in a trial by combat. No matter what he thought the truth was."

My head was swimming with that one. But going back to my original thought, I mentioned, "Look, Sir Agravain was visibly shocked and distraught at the accusation that the queen was not completely pure."

"He has always had a kind of religious devotion to the queen. That's one reason she made him one of her knights. He would protect her from any harm."

"Unless he thought her purity was besmirched," I added. "So Lancelot must be removed and she must be punished if she's guilty."

"Queen to king two," Merlin said. "Threatening a discovered check. The knight protects the king."

"As Lancelot protects Arthur," I mused. "You mentioned that maybe somebody is actually trying to get at Arthur? Making him have to make the decision between the life of his queen or his own honor as king if he fails to execute the law?"

"And who stands to gain from the king's humiliation?"

"Mordred, of course," I answered without hesitation. "I can

certainly see him trying to use this whole Meliagaunt situation to his own advantage. Make a case that the king is unfit to rule if he won't burn his own queen at the stake, and try to assert his own claims to the throne? Who could put it past him? And, uh, queen to king two. Your queen's in grave danger!"

"She certainly is," Merlin said, "but so is yours. So here, let's do queen's knight to queen's bishop three. You know, there's even a possibility here that Sir Agravain and Sir Mordred could see an advantage in conspiring together in this sort of thing: capturing or kidnapping Lancelot ultimately damages both King Arthur *and* Queen Guinevere, so long as Lancelot is not able to fight in the lists for the queen."

"I hadn't thought of that either," I admitted.

"Of course you hadn't. Move," Merlin said. "And we still haven't exhausted the possibility that the target is really Lancelot after all, and the queen's case is merely coincidental?"

"Ah, pawn to queen's bishop three. Any knight as powerful and influential as Lancelot must have some enemies, I suppose. But there are a good number of knights of the Round Table who owe their lives to him, from when he got them out of one scrape or another. So while there may be plenty of knights jealous of him for his reputation and prowess, they aren't likely to plot against him because they really do recognize his goodness. I suppose some folks of the Orkney clan might resent his influence with the king, which they see as a kind of family right of their own, but Gawain is Lancelot's greatest admirer and champion. And Gareth nearly worships him—it was Lancelot, not Gawain, you remember, who Gareth wanted to knight him. Gaheris wouldn't do anything the other two would disapprove of..."

Merlin tilted his head. "Margause?"

I flushed for a moment, remembering how Gaheris had beheaded his own mother when Queen Margause was found in bed with the late Sir Lamorak. "That was a long time ago," I argued.

"Point taken," Merlin said. "Queen's bishop to king's bishop four. But that does bring us back to Agravain and Mordred, if we think that the Orkney clan has something to gain from imprisoning Lancelot."

"Well, I can't see it," I said. "Queen's knight to queen two. Mordred maybe. But I can't see Agravain acting against the others. Unless, of course, Mordred would egg him on."

"I am forced to agree with your reasoning, though it pains me to say it. I think I'll castle here."

"I think I'll do the same," I responded. "Look, what about this whole 'knight of the cart' thing? It seems to me that some of the knights, even some who were taken with me and held in Gorre, were less than disappointed at Lancelot taking a blow to his pride and his reputation by riding in the cart. It even seemed to be a point of celebration for some of them. Isn't it possible that one or more of those lesser knights, happy to see the paragon brought down even a little bit, contrived to shame him even more by making it impossible for him to fulfill his obligation to the queen?"

The old necromancer mused on that, finally just saying,"Rook to king one. Supporting my queen."

"She does need our support, for sure! Here, pawn to queen five. Your knight's under attack. Just like Sir Lance…"

"God's whiskers, boy, can we stop with all these allusions to Lancelot and Guinevere as if they're chess pieces? I *get* it already. It's becoming tedious!"

Slightly chastened, but feeling a little victorious that I was rattling him a bit and maybe throwing him off his game, I smiled slightly as I apologized. "Sorry old man. But what do you think of the 'jealous knight or knights' possibility?"

He shrugged. "Plausible, I suppose, but again, why would someone wanting to shame Lancelot put the queen at risk as well? It would need to be someone who had a grudge against both. But look, it could easily be someone we would never think of. I mean, think of Elaine of Corbinec and her father King Pelles. We had absolutely no suspicion of their hatred of Lancelot, yet they came close to undoing him as well as King Arthur during the Grail quest. Sometimes there are depths of resentment that may be beyond our detection. Knight to queen's bishop six."

I looked at the board and saw I was in trouble. "Either your queen or your rook is lost," he told me. As if I couldn't see that.

But something had just occurred to me that I wanted to ask Merlin about. That, and I had also seen a way out of this chess quandary.

"Listen," I said. "Do you know what I was just thinking?"

"The fact that you were thinking *at all* comes as quite a shock to me. I don't know whether I dare consider the actual *topic* of that thought."

"Well, first, I was thinking that I'm not just going to let you take my queen. If I'm going down I'm going to take you with me, so I'm taking your queen. And by the way, I can checkmate you in one move from here!"

Merlin's mouth twitched up a bit at the right edge, and I knew by that reaction that I'd done just what he had wanted me to do. Not that I had much choice.

"But the other thing I was thinking about was that night we were celebrating in William Bailey's inn after my induction."

"And why, pray tell, would that evening come into your little brain at this point?" Merlin asked. "Did I reveal some of my chess secrets in a fit of drunken frankness?"

"You had one of your spells," I reminded him. "And spewed one of your famous prophecies."

The old man snorted at that. "My 'famous prophecies,' as you call them, have never done me a bit of good. They tend to make sense only after the events they prognosticate come to pass. Which doesn't help anybody much while those events are unfolding."

"There've been clues there in the past," I reminded him. "And this time, what you said was 'The boot that tramples the white lily impedes the laurel!'"

"Ah!" Merlin exclaimed in feigned excitement. "That explains all! Clear as mud!"

"Well, I think we may get something out of it if we puzzle it out."

"Waste of time when we need to focus on finding Lancelot," Merlin said. "Just like your taking my queen. Here: knight takes queen's rook's pawn, with check to your king."

"Well," I said, moving my king to queen's knight one with chagrin, "I'm going to put it in the back of my mind to ponder anyway. I mean, the white lily might be identifiable if I set my mind to it."

"*Now* I'll take that queen," Merlin said, moving his knight to king two and pretty much sinking my big plans. "Do what you want with your mind, boy, but leave enough of it available to help me save our own queen. We can talk to any of the suspects we've named, but Meliagunt and Bagdemagus are two days' ride from here, and will most likely be on their way here even now, so we can't waste time trying to get to them and back before Lancelot is due at the lists. We'll have to see if anyone here can give us a clue."

I looked at the board and sighed. "King to queen's rook two, taking your knight," I said, thinking to fight to the bitter end. "I just can't see how Lancelot would have left the castle and disappeared without anyone seeing anything."

"Knight to queen four, taking pawn," Merlin said.

As I looked at my king's vulnerable position I rethought my "fight to the bitter end" attitude. "Well, look," I began, "I'm in no position to do anything here. I think I'm going to have to re…"

Before I finished that thought, the old Necromancer had leapt up with a sudden burst of unfeigned excitement, sending the chessboard and its pieces flying in every direction. "God's earlobes!" he cried. "Let's talk to Robin Kempe first! The guard in the barbican must have seen anybody who left through the gate. If anyone saw Lancelot leave, it was Robin or one of his guards."

"Unless he was disguised," I suggested. "We know he wasn't riding Minuit when he left."

"They would have made it their business to find out who was leaving the castle," Merlin said. "Anyway, we need to visit them first. Come on!"

I looked at the shambles of what had been our chess match. "What about your game?"

"We'll pick it up later, when we get back. You were about to resign anyway, weren't you?"

"Maybe…" I vacillated.

"You might as well," he shrugged. "You were lost. Let's get to the barbican, we're burning daylight and the queen doesn't have much of it left."

CHAPTER NINE
QUESTIONS WITHOUT ANSWERS

"Is that the famous Sir Gildas down there, as I live and breathe?" The voice of Robin Kempe, Captain of the King's Archers and head of the watch, came floating down to me as Merlin and I stepped over the drawbridge and passed under the barbican. "And I believe that 'Sir' is spelled *c-u-r*, is it not?"

"I see the king still hasn't found a real captain for his guard, since he still allows his court fool to man the barbican," I responded in kind to my nemesis. All in good fun. Or at least I always assumed so.

"And you've brought your superannuated nanny along, have you? Doesn't he ever get tired of dragging you around when he's trying to work his magic?"

"What I get tired of," the mage growled, "is meaningless drivel from your lips, Robin Kempe. We're here on the king's business, and foolish as it may seem, we want to talk to *you*. We'll come up there to the barbican—so tell your guards not to loose any arrows at us by mistake as we climb the steps. We're not assaulting your position."

Robin's tone became a shade more respectful as he called down, "Stay where you are, old man. I don't want your hoary heart giving out coming up that steep entryway. I'm coming down!" And with that we stepped over to the side of the castle's great heavy gate, and in a few moments Robin emerged from the small door at the bottom of the stone passage with the circular stairway leading to the guard tower above the portcullis.

Robin was dressed in the loose-fitting forest-green tunic that was the uniform of the king's archers, and his beak-like nose threw a shadow onto his long blond mustache and his strong, thrusting chin. His shaggy blond hair hung in unruly locks onto his shoulders and down his back, and his dark eyes looked at me with real concern from within their deep sockets.

"So what is this king's business you're about then, Lord Merlin?" Robin asked with surprising deference. "Though I suspect," he added glancing at me and raising his left eyebrow a bit, "that in fact it is the *queen's* business?"

"Indeed, it chiefly does involve the queen, and her upcoming trial," Merlin acknowledged.

"Tut, the outcome is a foregone conclusion," Robin scoffed. "The charge is obviously false. I mean, Kay of all people? I'd sooner believe that the queen slept with you, Gildas of bloody Cornwall. Besides, Lancelot could whip that little bugger with his right hand tied behind his back."

"That's precisely the problem," I said, and Merlin looked down at me with a scowl. I'd forgot myself: Merlin liked to handle all interviews himself. I was still just his assistant when it came to investigating mysteries. And always would be, knighting or no knighting, I could see that. So I bit my tongue and gave him free rein.

"What my young colleague means," Merlin continued, turning his gaze back on Robin, "is that Sir Lancelot has gone missing. He has not been seen in the castle for several days. Neither the queen nor Sir Bors is aware of any plan Lancelot may have had to leave, and with less than a week till the feast of Saint Thomas, there is grave concern in the queen's household."

Robin Kempe gave a low whistle. "And the king's as well, I'd guess. So, you want to know if I've seen Lancelot riding forth any time of late?"

"He would not have been riding, in all likelihood," Merlin said. "His destrier, Minuit, has not left the stables, according to Taber."

"So, he'd be what? Walking?" Robin raised his eyebrows. "Or carried out somehow against his will…" he gave voice to my own fears. "But look, obviously I haven't seen him, since I keep asking you all these questions. Haven't seen anything else that I can think of that would suggest his being carried out in a wagon or…"

"A cart?" I suggested, with a sudden inspiration.

"Cart? Why on earth would a knight of Lancelot's caliber risk his entire reputation by riding in a cart like a common criminal?"

"He'd already done it," I told Robin. "You didn't hear the story? That's how he got himself to Gorre to rescue the queen after Meliagaunt's stooges shot his horse from under him. If he was trying to sneak out of the castle for some reason, I don't see why he wouldn't have done it in a cart. In fact, he seemed to be very friendly with that dwarf, that Thorvald fellow, who drove him to Gorre in the cart. He could have left with Thorvald of his own free will…"

"Seems like a long shot to me," Robin said, his left eye squinting in disbelief. "Besides, I've seen a few wagons coming in and out with supplies for the kitchen in the past couple of days. I've seen hunting parties going out and coming in—Sir Gaheris and Sir Bleoberis are out on one right now with our huntsmen. But I don't recall seeing any cart moving in and out, at least not when I've been on duty, and that's pretty much all the daylight hours from prime to compline."

"And who, may we ask, has been on duty from compline to prime, then?" Merlin asked. "We'll want to talk to them. My young colleague may be on to something here, and we need to follow it up quickly. If we have to go chasing around the countryside looking for Lancelot, we don't have much time."

I had only an instant to register the fact that Merlin had actually called me "colleague" twice, when Robin answered, "All right, old codger, keep your leather *braies* hiked up, will you? Corporal Alan of Winchester would have been in charge of the barbican the past few nights, and he's asleep in the keep right now. I hate to wake him…"

"But you will because you don't want the queen to flay you alive and turn your tanned hide into a new pair of leather *braies* for her favorite old soothsayer?" I urged him in words he could understand.

"Well, if you put it that way, follow me, gentlemen. And don't step on the bodies of any guardsmen on the way upstairs."

The great stone keep was in the midst of the bailey, the very center of the castle. Conceived as the last, impenetrable refuge if the castle were ever captured by an enemy army, it was some ninety feet tall and fifty feet in diameter at its base, tapering to perhaps thirty-five at its crenelated top. The walls of the keep were three feet thick at its base, narrowing to eighteen inches at the top. There were no windows, but only cross-shaped slits through which defenders could launch arrows if under attack, and this meant that even in the brightest daylight, the keep was dark inside. Nor would there have been much to see if the lighting were brilliant. The spare, functional, military interior comprised bare stone walls, and a succession of stone staircases between levels. Robin entered the door at the base of the keep, nodding to the two guards who stood on either side of the heavy iron entryway, and grabbed a torch from the wall just inside, leading us up the stairs to the second level. Here, at least a dozen of the castle's garrison—the night guard—slept on pallets around the outer rim of the building. Robin went from sleeper to sleeper, holding the torch low enough to get a look at each man's features and receiving in return, grunts, moans, and a good number of heartfelt curses for the bloody idiot shining a fiery light in their faces when they were trying to sleep, damn it.

At length Robin found the man he was looking for. Alan of Winchester was a brown nut of a man with greasy black hair and a pinched, sour-looking face that looked no sweeter when Robin shook him awake and whispered to him to come outside and talk to these gentlemen there, so as not to wake the fellows sleeping around. "Do I have to?" Alan groaned in a whiny tone, at which Robin gave him a gentle kick in the ribs and said, "Come on, boy, sooner you answer their questions, sooner you can come back and finish that dream you were havin' about Lucy the barmaid at William Bailey's place."

Grumbling incoherently, Alan rose to his feet, hanging his head and shaking his hair like a dog coming in from the rain. Then, smoothing it back, he told Robin, "Wasn't dreaming about her at all," then added, "Was thinking about her, though!" And with that his face broke into a huge smile, and I could see that he still had a large number of his teeth, just not so many in the front.

Downstairs, back in the daylight outside the door to the keep, Robin shook Alan again to make sure he was all there. "Listen Alan, this is important. In the last—what? Three days?" He glanced at Merlin and received a nod in reply. "In the last three days, have you seen Sir Lancelot leave the castle at any time during your shift in the barbican?"

"Lancelot?" Alan twisted his face, which apparently meant he was thinking it over. "No sir. Lancelot hasn't ridden in *or* out of here, armed or unarmed, any time that I recall—no, not since he come back with the queen and all her household, along with old Gildas here." I didn't realize that members of the guard knew me by name, since I knew only a few of them, but I realized that it was their job to be able to identify friend or foe, particularly Arthur's own knights of the Table. Besides, Robin was forever engaging in his favorite pastime of Gildas-baiting, so they may well have all known me through that sport. But Alan wasn't really getting the point.

"We have some reason to believe that Lancelot may actually have been smuggled out of Camelot, or that he left in some kind of disguise," I told Alan.

"Yes," Merlin continued. "In fact, it is possible he may have left the castle riding in a cart, a cart driven by a dwarf. Think now, man, did you see anything like that recently?"

Alan stood with his head hanging down, unmoving. He stood that way for several seconds until I was convinced he had actually fallen asleep again on his feet, and my patience stretched thin as fine parchment. I was ready to shake him myself and tell him to focus when he finally lifted his head and answered, "Three nights ago."

Merlin's eyes were the size of cartwheels when he looked at me dumbfounded, shocked that my hunch had actually proven true and that it had been so easy to verify. I shook my head, in disbelief myself, as Alan continued.

"It was just at dusk, after I had come on duty at compline but well before matins. The portcullis had actually been lowered for the night when the cart appeared and the dwarf came to the gate demanding to be allowed to exit. I shouted down to him that it was highly irregular, but of course, I really didn't have any reason to force him to stay, since the castle wasn't on alert or anything, and it was a peaceful night."

"But think now," Merlin urged him. "Was the dwarf alone? It's very important."

Alan looked at the old necromancer like he'd lost his wits. "I didn't forget in the last two seconds that it was Lancelot ya were looking for! There was some hooded bloke in the back of the cart. He wasn't armed or anything, and the dwarf just said he had orders from the queen to take this bloke somewhere right away. I didn't really believe him, just thought he was trying to get me to open the gate, but I couldn't see that anything was fishy, so I had the boys crank up the portcullis and let them go."

"Did you see which…"

"North, Sir Gildas. The cart went north."

And that meant we were heading north. Though how it was going to be easier for us to track down one small cart than it would have been to find Lancelot alone I couldn't say. And before doing anything we needed another meeting with the queen. And quickly.

***

So it was that a second meeting of an expanded number of interested parties was hastily arranged in the queen's quarters a little later that afternoon. Next to Guinevere and Rosemounde we sat in a tense circle, with Sir Gawain, Sir Bors, and, lastly, Sir Kay, looking pale and thin but much improved since I'd seen him last. The lady Elizabeth stood languidly to the side, in morose attendance on her queen, should Her Majesty desire anything.

"My lady," Bors was saying. "I offered once before to serve as your champion when you were falsely accused, for my lord Lancelot's sake. Forgive me if I do not do so again, but this time you have other better knights willing to do so. My only concern right now is finding my cousin. The rest of you may do what you will, but I will ride to seek sir Lancelot immediately."

"And you'll be looking for a needle in a haystack," Gawain countered. "Do you have any notion where to look, or are you just

146

planning to stop at every house until you find a knight who doesn't happen to belong there?"

"My odds of finding him out there are a lot better than finding him while sitting here," Bors responded, ready to bolt at any moment. There was no particular love lost between Gawain and the brusque and stolid Bors. Bors thought Sir Gawain was too interested in the ladies, too concerned with *appearing* to be courteous, while at the same time dangerously vengeful, as demonstrated in his ambush of Sir Lamorak. Gawain thought Sir Bors was boorishly blunt and lacking in exuberance—in a word, dull. They were probably both right. But both at this moment wanted to find Sir Lancelot and save the queen, so they were forced to work together here.

"At the moment," Sir Kay interrupted, focusing on a different question, "the only knight Sir Meliegaunt is bound to accept as a substitute for Sir Lancelot in this trial by combat is myself. I was the one he originally challenged, I am the one that must meet him if Sir Lancelot fails to return."

"With all due respect," Sir Gawain answered. "I've no doubt that a normally healthy Sir Kay could deal with this upstart Meliagaunt in a fair fight. But my lord, you are visibly weaker, and not fully recovered from your wounds. Suppose your wounds open again during the combat? Where are we then?"

"I don't need my full strength to drown this puppy," Kay urged with false bravado. "Besides," he said his large lips protruding in a prodigious pout, and his bovine eyes focusing on the floor to our left, "God will protect the right, isn't that what we must believe?"

There was a silence broken by throat-clearing from a few sources before Merlin said, "God is far likelier to protect the right if Lancelot is the one defending it, I'm afraid. But Sir Kay is right about the king: his only choices if Lancelot fails to show up are to allow Sir Kay to defend his own honor and the queen's, or to refuse to allow the trial to take place, which puts him in the position of flaunting the laws of his own realm, and what will look to others like ignoring crimes that are inconvenient for him to acknowledge. And this is a king who every year demands the renewal of an oath whereby he pledges never to defend a wrong cause. Kings have been brought down by lesser things."

"What about the option of an open trial before the court?" Rosemounde suggested innocently. "Forget this barbaric custom of trial by combat, where the biggest, strongest knight is presumed to be right because he can beat up anybody who says he's not? Can't the king demand that this matter be decided with *evidence* after all? That, instead of fighting, we just look at the facts?"

What my lady Rosemounde said was, of course, eminently sensible, and seemed to be convincing to some around the room, as I noticed Bors, Kay and, momentarily, Gawain begin to nod their heads. But then Gawain stopped and squinted, and I knew he was remembering Meliagaunt's furious certainty, and the actual stains on the sheet that Meliagaunt had most surely kept. I felt a hot rush of blood to my cheeks as I glanced at the queen, whose blood had, conversely, drained completely from hers, but Merlin came to the rescue.

"The evidence of the sheet is, I'm afraid, far too prejudicial," he remarked.

No one understood what he meant, and Bors said, "Come again?"

"I mean that the sheet, as I understand it, actually contains bloody handprints. Such marks might be explained in any number of ways, but the one most likely to be assumed by the court or by any jury the king is liable to appoint is that they are from the wounded Kay's bloody hands. An open trial is too great a risk. There is a better chance of Kay's winning the combat."

And we all knew what chance there was of that.

"Lancelot must be found," Sir Bors insisted again. "Meliagaunt or his father is most likely behind this, and so this is what I propose: they are likely on their way here even now, since the combat is in four days. I will take the road to Gorre and waylay them until they admit to their crime and produce my kinsman. If Meliagaunt challenges me, I can say in all humility that the problem of this trial may be over before it begins."

"Provided you find them on the road, and provided they are coming directly here…" Gawain said.

"And provided they are the guilty ones," I added, far less certain than the others. "Why would Thorvald be helping them?"

"You saw yourself that he was well known in Gorre," Gawain argued.

"Winchester is in the direction of Gorre," Guinevere suggested. "And it's less than a day's ride. Meliagaunt's sister Constance has a manor outside that city with her husband, Sir Degore—not a castle but a smaller stone manor. Would not King Bagdemagus and his son be likely to rest there for a while on the way here, if they were taking their time?"

"And might not a manor in easy ride from Camelot be an ideal place to imprison a knight you wanted to keep locked up for a short time?" Bors asked, as animated as I'd ever seen him. "By God, that is my first stop!"

I was still troubled by the direction this was taking and I could see that Merlin was as well, but the old man was quicker than I was in responding. "Thorvald's cart!" he reminded us all. "That cart is the key here. What does the dwarf have to do with this, and where are we to find that cart?"

"Winchester." The answer came slowly and cautiously from an unexpected source. Lady Elizabeth, leaning impassively against the chamber wall, said it as if everyone but a complete fool knew the answer. When all eyes looked quizzically upon her, she shrugged and continued. "That's where he is headquartered. That's where they made my father ride in that awful cart of his. He goes to other towns when they want him for hangings and such things. But Winchester is where he spends his time when he isn't traveling around making other people miserable. Or dead."

"God's neck bones, then that's where we shall seek him!" Merlin said. "With your majesty's permission, Sir Gildas and I will be on the road by prime tomorrow. We'll find that dwarf and his cart or we'll turn Winchester upside down."

"You do what you want," Sir Bors said, standing up. "I'm leaving right now."

"But Sir Bors," the queen intervened. "Surely it would be better to wait until morning. You could not reach Winchester for many hours, and the city gates will be locked. You can bully your way past the guards, I suppose, but everyone in the city will be asleep. How can you find this dwarf in that situation?"

"Not Winchester, your Grace," Bors responded. "I'm not looking for the dwarf. I'm looking for Lancelot, and I say he's as likely to be at Degore's manor house as anywhere else. And if he's not, then that cur Meliagaunt will be, and I'll have the satisfaction of calling him a villain to his face. Majesty," he bowed slightly and stalked out.

There was a moment of silence before Sir Gawain remarked, "Bors has always known his own mind, and when he's made it up, it's like talking to a stone."

"Well I, for one, feel about as useless as a three-legged war horse sitting here," Sir Kay blurted out, his lips stretching over his protruding yellow teeth in a sincere grimace. "Maybe I should tag along with young Gildas and the mage tomorrow, see if I can be any help there…"

"No, no," Sir Gawain was quick to insist. "I mean to say, Sir Kay, that while your advice might be invaluable, you really must not leave Camelot at this time. You need to continue to heal the next few days, and you need to be sure to be on hand should you in the end be called upon to fight in this trial. If indeed it comes down to you as our last resort, we need you here and we need you whole."

Kay pursed those large lips and then nodded. He could see the sense in this. Then rising, he bade farewell to the queen, and wished Merlin and me luck in the morning before ambling off to his dinner. The queen, visibly shaken by the strain of these developments, bowed out herself and retired to her private closet. Sir Gawain, having risen when the queen departed, stepped to Merlin and me with a bowed head and said in a confident whisper, his eyes motioning toward the retreating figure of Sir Kay, "Saved you from an unwelcome millstone there, didn't I?" Then he added, "Gildas, the Orkney clan will be having a private supper in our rooms in a bit. Come join us, won't you? Gareth will be interested to hear what you've been up to."

I stole a glance at Merlin, and Gawain was quick to add, "Oh, the invitation extends to you too, old man, absolutely!"

Merlin snorted, replying, "I'm not going to carouse with you lot tonight. If we're leaving at the crack of dawn tomorrow, I need all the rest I can get. I'll be turning in early. But Gildas can do what he wants," and with that the old man made his way out the door, planning to sleep in the lesser hall where my own pallet was usually set up near the other minor knights.

But when Gawain looked back to me I still hung my head, not meeting his eyes, and at last he understood my reluctance. "Oh, and Sir Mordred will not be present, did I mention that?" he added. "Something about looking after some property interest of his, he had to travel out of the castle overnight. Said he'd be back tomorrow. In any case, it will just be Gaheris, Gareth, Agravain and me, with Lovell and Hectimere, if they are about. Gaheris had some luck hunting today, so we're looking at a venison feast and we'll need your help to eat it all!"

I looked up to see Rosemounde apparently waiting for me on one hand, and the lady Elizabeth, with a strangely pensive look on her face, on the other side. "All right," I consented, my chief objection erased with Mordred out of the way. "Your rooms, then?"

"At vespers," Gawain agreed, then followed Merlin out.

That left Rosemounde, who remarked casually, "I'll see you out, Sir Gildas," as she latched on to my right arm and guided me toward the curtains that separated these quarters from the queen's outer chamber.

Lady Elizabeth said nothing, but I nodded to her in friendly fashion as we passed and said, "Thank you for your contribution, Lady Elizabeth. Knowing that the dwarf's home base is Winchester was important for us all, and I appreciate your volunteering it!"

She pinched her face up and scowled at me. "Shocked that I might have a working brain, are you? Go on, I don't need your phony good will." And with that she stuck her nose in the air and turned her back, moving languidly to sit before the queen's private chamber door, where it was apparently her turn to sit attendance on Her Majesty, who had shut herself in and seemed to desire to be left alone.

I waited until we had passed out of the queen's rooms, then turned to Rosemounde in exasperation. "That girl!" I said trying to keep my voice down. "She never has a kind word for me! She seems to be challenging me every time she speaks to me! What is going on? What have I ever done to her to make her so…so…rude?"

The left corner of Rosemounde's mouth twisted upward along with its attendant eyebrow, and she giggled through her smirk as she whispered back, "You mean you really don't know? You haven't a clue what's been going on?"

I was truly lost, as Rosemounde could read quite clearly in my blank face, and, giggling a bit more, she grabbed my hand and walked me down the corridor until we were in a private corner well out of range of the queen's chamber, so that we could not possibly have been heard. Then Rosemounde, holding both my hands and looking conspiratorially into my curious eyes, asked me aloud, "You know that the queen has taken in Lady Elizabeth and her sister Lady Mary as a kind of charity for old Sir Bedivere…"

"Yes," I said, "all of Camelot knows that much. What of it?"

"Well, one of the things she has promised is that she will find appropriate husbands for both girls."

I shrugged. This was pretty common among these aristocratic families, and of course, I knew Guinevere had done so fairly recently in the case of Meliagaunt's sister, the lady Constance. "I suppose that's to be expected," I said. "But I still don't understand what that has to do with…"

"Well, who do you think the queen has in mind for our young Miss Elizabeth?"

I stared at her for a moment while her meaning sank in. "You can't mean…"

"Of course, silly!" Now Rosemounde's laughter was full throttle. "The handsome young brand-new knight of the Round Table, Sir Gildas of Cornwall! Eligible bachelor who won't object to a wife without great dowry because he comes from humble beginnings himself!"

Still my mouth hung open like a beached fish. "But it can't be. I mean, the queen knows that I love…"

"Who? The wife of King Arthur's…what? Shall we say 'close kinsman'? A situation that isn't about to change any time soon, barring murder or insurrection. Not exactly a match she's likely to openly endorse. She'll always strive to make the best of things as they are. Don't be so shocked, Gildas of Cornwall. In love or not, you are fair game until you are married, and matching allies together is a favorite pastime of queens and other nobles."

"But…"

"Oh for heaven's sake, where's your sense of humor?" She herself had stopped laughing completely by now, and looked more stern than happy. "At least your spouse isn't going to beat you bloody on a whim, or try to use you to spy on the court. This Lady Elizabeth is young and unassuming. I think she could be the perfect wife for you."

"You mean she won't get in our way?" I asked with just a hint of sarcasm. Rosemounde reddened, and I immediately regretted it, and quickly added, "But I still don't understand why she is so rude and unfriendly to me. She is angry that the queen is thinking of marrying her to me?"

Rosemounde heaved a sigh as if men were the densest creatures on God's earth, and told me, "No, silly. She doesn't want you to think she's easy, for one thing: she wants to be difficult to win, and so, valued the more. But she also feels inferior since her father's disgrace, and has it in the back of her head that any time you meet her you must be evaluating her, and so she resents any question you ask since she sees it as some sort of test. And besides all of *that*," Rosemounde was now coming to her chief point and pronounced it like a priest reaching the climax of a sermon, "she is really afraid you're going to reject her, and so is setting things up so that she can show anyone with an interest, herself included, that she has rejected you first. It's as simple as that."

I pursed my lips, shaking my head. "As simple as that, is it? Well, as soon as I'm able, I intend to have a talk with the queen about all of this, and ask her to give me just the slightest warning, if she could, about who she's planning to marry me off to, at least a bit before the actual wedding ceremony, thanks very much. Unfortunately, since Merlin and I are leaving in the morning, it will have to wait until I get back. And now I'm going off to sup with the Orkney clan, with venison fresh from the hunt, and not a single woman present. It will be so refreshing to be with men, who can be counted on to actually say what they mean. Good evening, my lady."

"Oh yes, I've never known a man to lie. Particularly one of the

Orkney clan…" said the wife of Sir Mordred of Orkney as she started heading back to the queen's chamber.

***

Dinner in Sir Gawain's rooms was a raucous affair, lubricated by a tun of wine he had tapped for the occasion. The rooms were quite sparse, with bare stone walls and only a few candelabra set around for lighting, but Gawain had set up boards heaped with meat and creamy side dishes. He'd also hired a wandering jongleur to entertain us as we stuffed ourselves with venison, blancmange and Bordeaux, and though the quality of the singing and playing was not stellar—I found myself longing for Sir Palomides' more refined performances—it passed the time and gave me space to consider what Merlin might wish me to make out of this opportunity.

For we had talked earlier about possible motives that Sir Mordred or even Sir Agravain might have for wanting the queen or Sir Lancelot shamed or eliminated, and I would have felt I'd let an opportunity slip away if I didn't try to gather anything I could about what those two brothers were up to. Since I spent the evening mainly in Gareth's company, I first broached the subject with him.

"So where's Mordred tonight? Gawain said something about some property interests? He was pretty vague anyway."

"Well, so was Mordred. I didn't pay much attention. But perhaps you'll run into him tomorrow in Winchester, and you can ask him yourself."

"Winchester?"

"Yes. That's where my charming little brother said he was going." That certainly piqued my interest. I suppose it could have been a simple coincidence, but it was surely a very curious one. If the dwarf and Mordred were in the same place, was there a connection between them? And thus with Lancelot's disappearance? But I didn't want to push it, even with Gareth, and so, kept that information in the back of my mind to inform Merlin of it tomorrow.

Gawain, always fond of apples, had provided a basket of them for dessert, and I grabbed one as the basket went by, biting into it and letting the tart juices cleanse my palate after a surfeit of the gamy taste of Gaheris's venison. We sat on stools around several small tables where our cups of wine rested, and Gaheris and Agravain were seated at a table next to ours. They were engrossed apparently by the jongleur's song about the intrepid Wade and his famous boat—a story so well-known I don't need to repeat it here. But I knew this was my last chance to feel Agravain out about his feelings for the queen, and see whether he seemed capable of a plot against Lancelot, so I endeavored to engage him in some small talk to start. Passing the basket of apples to their table, I specifically addressed Sir Agravain with the well-thought-out opening salvo, "Apple?"

"Thanks," Agravain said, snagging one and biting into it. He resumed his focus on the jongleur and I knew I needed to follow up with something non-committal that might encourage him to open up.

"So, are you recovered from our ordeal in Gorre? Feeling like things are back to normal around here, are you?"

Agravain looked at me with a blank stare, his mouth slightly open, and then, after a few moments, answered, "Sure." Then his attention returned to Wade and his boat.

"Of course," I went on, as if he had actually displayed a modicum of interest, "we still have the queen's trial to get through..."

And that, it turned out, was the one thing I could have said to get him going. "Trial? Pah!" Agravain spat. "How dare that villain Meliagaunt besmirch the queen's name! As if a paragon like herself would ever even consider letting a boor like Sir Kay touch her. It's preposterous! But it won't really be a trial, it'll be a slaughter. Lancelot will cut that Meliagaunt into a thousand pieces and serve him up for hash at the evening meal."

While I winced at the rather disgusting overtones of the metaphor, I felt some relief in seeing that Agravain, unless he was one of the world's great actors, did not even have a notion that Lancelot was missing, and so, seemed utterly without guilt in the matter of the Great Knight's abduction, if that's what it was. Well, scratch him off the suspect list. But Mordred still must remain there, particularly considering his suspicious trip to Winchester.

I did think it would be a kindness to let Agravain in on the problem of Lancelot's disappearance, since he was clearly uninformed. At that he showed some profound distress. "No! But Sir Kay can't be allowed to fight this battle on his own. He's unwell, and besides, he's clearly not capable of beating sir Meliagaunt. Lancelot must be found to fight for the queen. She *must* be saved!"

"I don't disagree," I said. "But unless you have some idea where he could be…"

"No," Agravain said. "I wish I did. I mean, I know people say that Lancelot is proud and overbearing, that he can do anything he wants because the king needs his sword arm, but it's certain that no one is better in a fight than…"

"Who says such things about Lancelot!" Gareth butted in, the wine perhaps making him belligerent. "If I ever heard anyone say such things about the man who knighted me, they'd have to face my sword before they opened their mouth again!"

Gaheris, on the other side, answered. "And that, brother, is probably why you haven't heard anything of the sort. I've certainly heard such things. And in our own circle—why the squire Peter has been known to make such remarks, attributing them to other, veteran knights like our brother Mordred."

Again that name. I scowled and looked down. "And where else have you heard these things, Sir Agravain?"

He shrugged. "Couple of the lads in Gorre with us—Sir Pelleas? Sir Tirre? Sir Thomas?"

"Thomas!" Now this seemed to be going too far.

"Well," Agravain backed off, "I can't say that for certain. But he was there, at any rate, when others were talking and didn't contradict them. But look, I'll say it again, Lancelot needs to be found and brought back here! The queen needs him! You say you and the old necromancer are going to search for him, are you? Anything I can do to help, just let me know! Truly." And with that he turned again toward Gaheris, and I, having come to the end of my usefulness as far as I could gauge it, and knowing the morning would come very quickly now that my head was so cloudy, rose to leave.

"Good evening, sirs," I addressed Gareth, Gaheris, and Agravain, and taking a final bite out of my apple, tossed it deftly into the fireplace. "And to you, Sir Gawain," I called across to the other side of the room. "I thank you for your kind hospitality," I continued, the jongleur having paused to down a draught of the Bordeaux. "I must be off, to rise at dawn. I wish you heavy slumbers," and with that I swayed out, the sound of good natured hoots behind me. I would have a ravaged head in the morning, but I'd have a few items of interest to run by Merlin. But first my bed was calling. Very, very loudly.

CHAPTER TEN

WINCHESTER

I lay on my pallet in the lesser hall next to a snoring Merlin when I heard the bells of the Convent of Saint Mary Magdalene tolling prime the next morning. *Oh, bother*, I thought. We'd hoped to be up and gone by this time, and instead the wine had gone to my head and I'd slept in. My only consolation was that the mage hadn't awoken yet either, and when I had dragged myself up I poked him in the ribs and whispered, "Let's go old man, it's time we were on the dwarf's scent!"

At the sound of my own voice I suddenly formed the mental picture of my devoted borzoi hound, Guinevere, whom I had not taken out hunting for at least a week, and who I knew would be up for the adventure of a trip to Winchester this morning. "And listen, Merlin, I'm going to bring Guinevere along. I…I mean, my dog, not the queen. She won't be any bother, and maybe she'll chase us down a rabbit for lunch."

"Well, I'm not chasing *her* if she runs off to tree a squirrel," Merlin vowed. "This is serious work we're about, and we can't have her getting in the way…"

"I suppose she was in the way when we captured Tristram's killer in Brittany?" I reminded him. "Or when she found Brother Nascien on the Grail quest?"

Merlin raised long-suffering eyes to the heavens, as if bewailing his fate in having been paired with me again for the duration of this investigation, but he kept silent as he noted a dark shape appearing in the doorway of the hall. That shadowy figure looked around him at the several sleeping knights scattered about on their cots, then saw me standing and came toward me. As he drew closer in the dim light, I recognized him as Alan of Winchester of the castle guard, and he was carrying a satchel over his shoulder.

"G'day to ya, Sir Gildas," Alan intoned in his whiny voice, pulling a greasy black forelock at me in deference. "Robin told me to bring this to ya before I came off duty and went to bed in the keep. Some bloke brought it in for you from Cornwall last night."

Puzzled, I reached for the satchel. "For me? Well, who on earth would be...." But then I felt the weight of the satchel, and heard the clanking of metal within, and as the blood drained from my face and settled like a great lump in my stomach, I knew. Slowly I set down the bag, and lifted from within a magnificent, flexible garment of steel mesh, fashioned with a coif of the same material and reaching down past my knees as I gently held it up to my torso.

It was a hauberk, finely made by a master craftsman, formed of more than a hundred thousand tiny interlocking rings, each of which connected to four other rings in amazing intricacy. The best armorers, those of Chartres with whom my father had trained, would spend months on such a mail coat.

For the gift was certainly from my father. He could neither read nor write, and so had sent me no note, but would have known that I must recognize it as his gift. A gift he must have spent time on daily, each evening after his regular paid work was through, because he wanted his son to have a hauberk as magnificent as any knight in Christendom. And he must have started work on it years before I was ever made knight, in hopeful anticipation.

Merlin watched me without a word, his eyes narrowed as he tried to read what was going on inside my head. But how could he? Waves of emotions washed over me as tears began to form in my eyes. I could see him, master armorer Myghal of Launceston, his burly arms, the sweat gleaming on his dark brow or running into his black beard as he worked over his charcoal forge, bending the fine iron wire into the ringlets that ultimately became an entire hauberk.

In my mind I was twelve years old again, watching him work at his forge with his journeyman David of Frampton while his two apprentices manned the shop. David had been a great coup for my father, since he had connections with the iron miners in south Gloucester, in the Forest of Dean, who shipped premade iron wire down the Severn to Boscastle near the old Ducal fortress of Tintagel. There, my father and David bought it up, brought it overland to Launceston, and turned it into the best-made mail armor in Cornwall. I was getting to the age where my father might have wanted to make me an apprentice in his shop and start me down the road to carrying on the family trade. But it turned out my father had other ideas.

Having observed for years the wealth and privilege of armed knights and their families, my father had vowed that his only son would not follow in his footsteps and learn the armorer's trade, but would find a way to break into that rarified class of movers and shakers to whom he was just another churl, despite his artisan rank and considerable income. And the first step in that direction, as he saw it, was giving me an aristocratic education in letters and such. So it was that he paid a local Augustinian canon, Father Cynfor, to tutor me every day at the new Launceston Priory, a branch of the great house at Bodmin. Cynfor gave me some rudimentary instruction in grammar, and I can remember him now, sitting at his desk with me on a stool before him holding a manuscript of Priscian's *Institutes* on my lap, wearing his black habit with his white-laced rochet, the linen over-tunic that was the sign of his order, like an apron reaching to his knees. Father Cynfor was impressed when he found me to be quick and clever, but the biggest boon of his tutelage turned out to be his connections at the court.

"Father" Cynfor, you see, used to be "Sir" Cynfor, a knight in the service of Leodegrance, lord of the petty kingdom of Cameliard in south Wales. Sir Cynfor, having seen many years in faithful service to Leodegrance, retired when the old king died and, like many another landless knight who'd never had time or income enough for a wife and family, he chose to devote himself to God's service. Like my father's premade wire, he came down the Severn, disembarked at Boscastle, and joined the Augustinian canons. He knew my father, who in the old days had made him his first mail armor, and he had one major connection in Arthur's court: Leodegrance's own daughter, who now happened to be Queen Guinevere of Logres. With my father's encouragement he wrote me an introduction to the queen, under the seal of Launceston Priory, and the next week my father sent me off at the age of thirteen, in a new suit of clothes and accompanied by a few priests of Cynfor's order traveling to Caerleon on business of their own. It was that letter of the old Sir Cynfor, which brought tears to the queen's eyes as she remembered him in his youth in her father's court, that brought me into the queen's household. And set me on the road that had brought me to this place.

Merlin was pointedly leaving me alone, moving Alan off to the side to ask him details about the geography of his native Winchester, where we were heading today, as my face, I imagine, registered each new emotion with undisguised rawness as they bubbled up from the depths where I had kept them buried for six years. That was how long it had been since I'd seen my father or my home. I had taken to my new home in the queen's household like a duck to water, as my father used to say. After all, I had lost my own mother at the age of five, when she had died giving birth to my little sister, who had outlived mother by just a single day. In the queen I had found a new mother, and in her household a flock of sisters that were a refreshing change from the all-male world of my father's shop with his journeymen and apprentices, and Father Cynfor's schoolroom. Life seemed a holiday, and in comparison my father's world a purgatory I was happy to escape from. I had dutifully written him a letter each yuletide season, even though I knew he couldn't read it. I assumed he would get some local priest, perhaps Father Cynfor himself, to read it to him. This Pentecost, however, I'd written him a special letter announcing my elevation to the exalted rank of Knight of the Round Table, knowing that this had been his dream for me from the very beginning. And now he had sent me this magnificent work of his own hands, this beautiful new hauberk, to mark the occasion. I made a silent vow to visit him when this business of Lancelot and the queen was over. And to wear my new hauberk when I did.

With solemn dignity I began to arm myself for what I now saw as my very first quest as a knight of Arthur's court, and one that had the potential of saving or dooming his queen, or his premier knight. I took up my habergeon, my padded under tunic, from where it lay on a shelf against the wall near my pallet, and donned it first. Then I pulled the new hauberk over my head and around me. It had slits up the side to make walking easier, but it weighed a good forty pounds and so would take some getting used to on the long ride to Winchester. Over the hauberk I slipped my white surplice. It had yet no blazon, since my house was not historically noble and had no traditional coat of arms. I must choose one for myself, of which the king might approve. But I felt I should first earn such a badge by actual knightly deeds. Of which as yet, I had none. And so my shield, too, was pure white and unadorned when I picked it up. But I set it aside for the moment, taking up my new sword—Sir Gareth's gift—in its scabbard, and fastened its belt around my waist: Almace, like the sword of the famed Bishop Turpin, to be unsheathed only in the cause of right.

"God's whiskers," Merlin exclaimed as I fastened my sword belt. "What a sight you are, you young Cornish brat. Now don't stand there admiring yourself, we should have been on the road half an hour ago. Let's not burn any more daylight!"

***

I sat astride the magnificent liver-chestnut war horse Achilles, Gareth's other generous gift, at an easy pace on the road to Winchester. His dark brown coat contrasted with the light gray palfrey we had borrowed for Merlin to ride, and I towered over the old man atop my great destrier, some eighteen hands high. We expected to cover the twenty-five miles in about five hours, plus a stop for a bit of lunch on the road. We'd brought some bread and cheese from the royal kitchens, but frankly, expected some bit of meat to be provided along the way by the hound Guinevere, who lived to chase down small game.

The dog had been ecstatic to see me that morning, and nuzzled Achilles as an old friend when we had picked him up from Taber in the stables. And now, on the forest road through the thick beeches and oaks, she gamboled about our horses' paths, making figure-eight

162

loops around us as we trotted along the muddy road. If our noise flushed out a nest of birds, she'd follow them and leap into the air as if she could catch them on the wing. And she could strike so quickly I would not have been surprised to see her snap up a starling or sparrow. But I'd rather see her bag a partridge or a grouse, something we could make a good feast of for lunch.

"So Merlin, my lord," I began after we had gone a few miles from Camelot and the sun had begun to rise toward terce. "Have you got an idea where we might start looking for this Thorvald once we get to Winchester?"

"In fact, I don't anticipate its being very difficult," the old necromancer replied. "I mean, think about it. How many dwarves driving felons' carts do you suppose inhabit a town the size of Winchester? He's not exactly going to blend in, is he?"

"I suppose you're right," I conceded.

"Of course I'm right, numbskull!" He shot back. "When I'm wrong, I'll let you know."

"Well, I mean to say, of course, Thorvald is not exactly going to have a low profile, is he? I mean, no pun intended, but Lady Elizabeth knew right where he was from when we mentioned him, didn't she?"

"Yes," Merlin said. "And I was talking with our friend Alan the guardsman while you were ogling your new toys, and he tells me that our most likely place to find him is a popular inn at the sign of the Red Ox. Alan says it's right on the edge of town on the main road from the west, and they've got good food and rooms to let at reasonable rates, so we can probably stop there overnight ourselves as well."

"And I suppose his own brother is the proprietor..." I mumbled cynically under my breath.

"Alan says that his cousin runs the place," the old man continued. I smiled discretely to myself. "It's on the High Street, he says, just inside the West Gate into the city. Should be easy to find."

"I've never been to Winchester," I told Merlin after a short space. "But I have heard that the cathedral there is an impressive structure. Puts the cathedral in Caerleon to shame, they say."

Merlin scoffed. "If size impresses you, I suppose, yes," he said. "The longest nave in all Christendom, they say. Still, I fear they were in too great a hurry to build it on the soggy ground near the old minster. The tower actually collapsed soon after they built it, and it has yet to be repaired. Still, people from the length and breadth of Logres visit the site to see the relics of Saint Swithin, bishop of the place in the old days."

"So I've heard. Do you suppose we'll run into a lot of pilgrims on the road as we get closer?"

"No doubt of it," Merlin said. "This time of year? And a sunny day at that? It will be a great excuse for plenty of them to polish off their piety and pop over to see the local saint. Seems to me that his feast day is coming up soon, too—the second day of July, if I remember right. And they even say this about Saint Swithin's day: Whatever the weather is on that day, it will last for forty days. But you don't hold with that rubbish, do you my boy?"

I shrugged my mailed shoulders and said, "Why not? I mean, the bit about the weather is just silly superstition, of course. But these saints are holy martyrs or miracle workers, and so they must have better access to God Himself than we poor mortals do, don't you think? It can't hurt to ask them for their intercession, can it? Stands to reason."

"Stands to idiocy, you Cornish knucklehead," he shot back. "Even granting you that there is such a thing as a saintly person recognized as such by God Himself—a premise I think is very much in question but which I'll pass over for now, since I can only handle one harebrained idea at a time—how can you imagine that some set of moldering bones is more sanctified than any other set of moldering bones, just because it's locked away in some church's reliquary? Whatever sanctity might have existed in the life that animated those bones is long since fled, to the bosom of Christ or wherever it is such sanctity finds a home. You want to pray to that sanctity, it'll hear you just as well in Camelot as it will in Winchester. Or Jerusalem. Or the waters of Babylon."

I shrugged again. "Being in the presence of the saint's remains concentrates the mind," I suggested. "It helps the penitent focus. It's not magic."

Merlin gawked at me as if I'd suddenly sprouted angels' wings and a halo of my own. "God's bloody wounds, Gildas, there are actually times I don't lament your feeble-mindedness." That, for Merlin, was high praise.

"Well, it sounds like you know something about this Saint Swithin, old man," I teased him. "What can you tell me about his life? How'd he become a saint?"

Merlin scoffed. "Twaddle and codswallop is all it is, my boy," he told me. "I mean, like all of 'em, he had a great reputation for living a charitable life. They say when he was bishop here he would throw great, luxurious banquets, but that he wouldn't invite the nobles or the rich merchants to his table, but only the poorest residents of the city."

"Well that's praiseworthy, isn't it?" I suggested.

"It might be. If we could believe it. But in the same breath they will tell you that he repaired churches and public works and paid for them out of his own pocket."

I mused again, and said, "Also pretty saint-like, wouldn't you say?"

"Charitable, at any rate," Merlin said. "What gets him appointed saint, though, is miracles. And here's Swithin's: they say that one day, as he was walking over a stone bridge that he had built and paid for himself, leading across the ditch before the west gate of the city, he saw an old woman who was crossing the bridge jostled and manhandled by a couple of rowdy young pranksters who caused her to drop and break a basketful of eggs she was bringing to town to sell for her daily pittance. So what does our good Bishop Swithin do? He doesn't do anything about the ruffians who caused the ruckus in the first place. Instead, he takes the woman's basket, places all the pieces and detritus of the dozen broken eggs in it, waves his hand over the basket and boom! Just like that, the eggs are whole again. It's a miracle."

I pulled a face at Merlin and couldn't resist teasing him. "And you mean to tell me you don't believe the story about the eggs?"

The mage shook his head in bewilderment. "Whether I do or don't isn't the issue," he said. "The issue is that none of Swithin's generous works, which seem to have been myriad, gained him the Church's recognition. But pull a magic trick with some eggs in a basket, and presto, you've got yourself a bona fide saint. No, Gildas," he shook his head again. "I don't think I'll be paying his shrine a visit while we're in town."

"But we will be able to cross that stone bridge when we get there, won't we? Coming from this direction, it's probably the west gate we'll enter by, right? Anyway that's where this Red Ox Inn is. Maybe I'll keep my eyes peeled in case I can see a few egg shells left on the bridge...." As I needled Merlin to the best of my ability, I noticed Guinevere's ears shoot straight up, and her head rise erect as she bored a hole into the woods with her stare, then without a pause she zipped like a crossbow bolt into the trees. "Well," I said. "Looks like we're about to get lunch."

When Guinevere emerged from the trees a quarter hour later, it was a furlong or so ahead of us, and it was with the body of a good-sized rabbit dangling from her jaws. She pranced along in front of the horses for a bit, showing off, and then, deciding that wasn't enough, ran circles around them for several minutes, still holding the rabbit but with her mouth stretched out in what was unmistakably a self-congratulatory grin. Finally, having decided it was as good a time for lunch as any, I held up Achilles and got down from the saddle, picking up a few dry branches to build a bit of a campfire alongside the road. Merlin got down as well, telling me, "Give me those sticks, boy. I'm not skinning that thing. I'll start the fire." And so the three of us had a jolly picnic, figuring to get to Winchester by dinnertime.

***

It was, in fact, a little before vespers when our mounts ambled across the bridge heading for the west gate of the city of Winchester. Even Guinevere was tired by then, and the spring in her step was little more than an imperceptible bob as we approached the gate. Our own shadows were growing long, and preceded us over the bridge, where I really did glance around a bit, looking for leftover eggshells. We passed through the gate without a challenge, along with several other pilgrims coming to the city in advance of Saint Swithin's day, and were immediately looking down the length of the High Street. On our right, close by, was the great fortification of Winchester Castle. Perhaps five or six furlongs farther up on the right I could see another structure with tall stone walls, which I'm sure must have been the great cathedral, though since the tower had fallen, it was not so easily recognizable from this distance. What was quite recognizable over on the left side of the High Street was an inn with the sign of a red ox hanging outside. Alan had not been exaggerating—his cousin's inn was very easy to find.

Merlin and I dismounted and guided our tired horses to the inn's wide new stables, where we told the livery man that we intended to stay the night in the Red Ox, and asked that our mounts be groomed and fed and watered, and kept comfortable for the night. I further asked that Guinevere be allowed to stay in Achilles' stall with him, the horse and hound having formed a fairly close bond in the times they had spent together.

As Merlin and I were about to exit the stables, I happened to glance to my left and noticed, stomping his foot as if impatiently waiting for his evening helping of oats, a great, brown, powerfully muscled Tuscan destrier standing some fifteen hands high and weighing a good ton if he weighed an ounce. I took a few steps toward him and held out my hand for him to sniff. He moved his head back and forth in recognition and whinnied at me while I patted the side of his long face, looking directly into his intelligent eyes. "Hello, Pegasus!" I said, and he whinnied again in response.

"So, Sir Bors is here!" Merlin said over my shoulder, recognizing the great war horse in his turn. "He must be inside!"

"With Lancelot, perhaps?" I ventured.

The old man smiled tiredly. "Wouldn't that be pretty?" He said, and led the way toward the door of the Red Ox.

Inside, the inn was one large dining room with dark wooden walls and floor, and about twenty tables and benches of lighter wood scattered randomly about the space, each table surrounded by paying diners. Saint Swithin's day was a boon to all the local businesses, I would guess. One window facing west was opened to the last of the sunlight, but there was a middle-aged fellow in a plain brown tunic kneeling at the great fireplace on the north wall, preparing to start a fire in advance of the sunset, to ensure the place stayed brightly lit and welcoming. A buxom young blonde in a simple grey gown with a white apron and cap, and carrying a tray of cups brimming with golden ale, greeted us and told us to sit wherever we could find room, and just then my eyes, which had been roving all over the room, caught sight of the nut-brown face and short-cropped head of Sir Bors, seated at a corner table with another knight whose back was to us. My heart jumped for an instant, but on second glance I could see that it was not Lancelot. The other figure was too short, too narrow across the shoulders, too slumped in the seat to be the Great Knight. But I was stunned, and not in a pleasant way, when we approached the table where Bors smiled and waved to us, and his companion turned to look over his shoulder while we approached—and I saw the raven hair, the dark, piercing eyes, and the perpetual sneer of Sir Mordred.

My mind instantly flew back to our last meeting. At that time, Merlin had scolded the king's bastard like a wayward schoolboy, and I had grabbed him by the collar and insulted him—after which he had vowed to slit Lady Rosemounde's throat rather than let me have her, and to skewer me with his sword if we met in the lists. A quick glance assured me that he wasn't wearing his sword at this moment, and I breathed a slight sigh of relief. But still, this did not promise to be friendly chat.

Bors, who knew nothing of that eventful meeting we'd had with Mordred during the Grail quest, welcomed us with a smile as he held up his cup of ale.

"Ah!" He said. "I thought I might find the two of you here. Thought I'd join you in your search. Mine did not bear fruit, I'm afraid."

"No sign of Lancelot at Sir Degore's manor?" Merlin asked, while Mordred stared at me with a mocking curl of his lip.

Bors shook his head somberly. "None. Degore and the lady Constance were perfectly courteous, welcomed me in, and seemed genuinely concerned to find that Lancelot was missing. I do not think that they were feigning." And if Bors did not think so, he was probably correct. One might think that someone as straitlaced and sober as Bors might be fairly easy for some quick, clever trickster to fool. But Bors was the most rational, analytic knight in Arthur's court. It was how he had seen through one deception after another on the Grail quest, and it's how he could be counted on to be right about this situation. Besides, Meliagaunt may have been a lot of things, but he was as transparent as water. If you weren't absolutely certain what he was doing or why, he would tell you.

And so I asked, "What did Meliagaunt say?"

Bors twitched the little, pointed beard on his chin. "He asked me why I would think he'd try to get Lancelot to skip the trial, when his whole purpose was to show how he could stand up to Arthur's greatest knights. To prove that he belonged in the Table, he says. Of course, he seems to be ignoring the fact that there's a moral and ethical component to membership in the Knights of the Table, and that he's fallen short of that standard altogether…"

I choked back a rising guffaw at that claim. Bors the Grail Knight could talk all he wanted about the high moral standards expected of Arthur's group of knights—his was an ideal of chivalry that seemed to match Merlin's as the old man had expressed it at that earlier debate we'd had at the tavern in Caerleon. How had he described it? "Manly virtue in the service of righteousness," that was it. But the irony of that idea, with Sir Mordred present and sitting at the same table—Sir Mordred, the embodiment of every vice I could imagine, who held in scorn every form of courtesy and yet was a member of that band of knights Bors so idealized—was not lost on me.

However, I suppressed my natural inclination to scoff and, averting my eyes from Mordred's scornful expression, merely acquiesced to Bors' assessment. "Well, I have had my doubts about Meliagaunt's involvement from the beginning, so it doesn't surprise me that you found no evidence of Lancelot there." But what of Mordred's involvement? He was a reasonable suspect for any mishap or calamity that occurred in Camelot. If he wasn't guilty of this, he was guilty of something else. And there he sat, taking in our entire conversation.

"And so you've been waiting for us here all day, have you?" Merlin said.

"Well, no, I mean, not here in the inn," Bors blustered a bit, shamed to be thought to have wasted a whole day drinking in a pub. "That is to say, I took the opportunity to explore the town somewhat. Asking about, seeing if anyone had seen Sir Lancelot. I was just telling Sir Mordred here how I visited the cathedral earlier today, and saw the relics of Saint Swithin. Said a short prayer that Lancelot might be found before his saint's day—which is just the day before Saint Thomas's, when the trial is scheduled. I visited the castle too, just to see what it's like. Impressive fortifications, though the great hall I thought was certainly less impressive than Camelot's. I mean, just in terms of its size: can you imagine trying to fit King Arthur's Round Table into that space? Couldn't be done. It's just not big enough for a table seating a hundred and fifty." But then, realizing what he'd said might be interpreted as lacking in courtesy, he quickly added, "But certainly big enough for their purposes here. Ample, I'd say."

Mordred had still not spoken and had on his dark visage an expression of amused superiority, as if he were enjoying listening to the Grail knight's simple ramblings, and wondering what it must be like to actually believe in the efficacy of saints and to be concerned that your speech might offend others. I kept my eyes focused on Bors as Merlin broached an important subject with him. "Sir Bors," he said, "I wonder whether in your gaddings about town you got any news or notion of the whereabouts of our friend Thorvald or his cart?"

Bors had begun to shake his head but if he had intended to say anything, he was preempted by Sir Mordred, who, with a kind of surprised animation, spoke for the first time. "What, the dwarf, you mean?" he said with an air of disbelief. "What do you want to talk to that little beast for?"

While I bit my tongue, Merlin answered, "Because we believe he may have some information about what might have happened to Lancelot."

"Well, I know where the dwarf is," Mordred volunteered. Merlin's eyebrows shot to the top of his forehead with that. I had to replace my jaw from where it had fallen myself. He went on, "I've been making use of his services, him and his cart, since I've been here. There's a fellow in this city who owes me money and has not paid me. I hired the dwarf to arrest him and carry him in the cart to the center of town, where there are stocks for public humiliation. There the debtor was placed and there he'll stay until he pays what he owes."

Sir Bors, who always assumed that people ought to have a rational basis for their behavior, was somewhat confused by this revelation. "But how is he going to have the opportunity to raise the money he owes you if he is confined to these stocks? The whole procedure seems self-defeating."

"Don't overthink it," Mordred dismissed Bors' question. "He has family, doesn't he? Friends? They have money or they can get it. There's a neighborhood of Jews in this town, I've noticed. The family can borrow the hundred nobles from those usurers, if needs be. But he stays in the stocks until then."

"Sounds like cruelty for the sake of cruelty," Bors persisted. "Is this chivalrous behavior, Sir Mordred?"

"And isn't this debtor the brother-in-law of Sir Bedivere and Sir Lucan, your fellow knights?" I finally could keep silent no more, though I loathed the idea of speaking directly to that demon in human form. "And father of the ladies Mary and Elizabeth? How is it in keeping with your knightly oath to torment the families of your brother knights of the Round Table? Where is the generosity? Where is the defense of the right cause?"

Mordred's lips twisted in a sneer as he rose and stood toe to toe with me. "I don't recall any part of that oath that says I must submit my behavior for your approval, *Sir* Gildas," he pronounced the title with exaggerated sarcasm. I glared into his eyes, which were about an inch higher than my own, and my right hand reached down to touch the hilt of Almace, hanging in its scabbard at my side. Still wearing my new, rich mail coat, I felt the equal of any knight in Christendom, and more than a match for this sneering boor, whatever his years of experience. Mordred reached down for his own sword, then remembered he wasn't wearing one at present, and a quick wave of chagrin flashed over his face for an instant before he resumed his characteristic condescending contempt.

He decided to address Merlin, as the ranking figure present. "Well, much as I'd love to stay and exchange pleasantries with you and your little trained monkey, I'm afraid I must tear myself away. Previous commitments, and all that. But if you really are looking for that little Thorvald fellow, you can usually find him here for his midday meal, at sext or so. I'll take my leave for now." And without a backward glance he sauntered out the door.

There was a pause of about two seconds until Sir Bors, breathing a great sigh of relief, said, "Good Lord, there goes an unpleasant chap."

"That's putting it mildly," I answered, heaving a sigh of my own.

"God's molars," Merlin said, sitting down at Bors' table and looking up at me. "Didn't you hear? Sir Mordred has just given us some helpful information. We now know where to find Thorvald!"

"Yes," I said, sitting next to him. "Which makes me automatically suspicious. Why would he do that? There's nothing he does that you can trust. What's in it for him if he helps us find the dwarf? What's his ulterior motive?"

"He wants Lancelot to win that contest," Sir Bors said, and I eyed him with surprise. "Truly. He would like to see the king brought down; that is clear. And if Lancelot saves the queen again, he believes that rumors of their affair will increase until they cannot be ignored—by the king or by anyone else. And that will bring Arthur down. Or so he hopes."

I should have realized that Bors would have thought all of this through, but his insight into the affair between Lancelot and the queen surprised me, though it shouldn't have. He was of all people closest to the Great Knight, and whatever concerned Lancelot concerned him. And in this case, I had to believe he was right.

"Well, that would explain it all right," I said. "So he has made our task easier in one way, but he's added another problem at the same time."

"Sir Lowell of Winchester," Merlin said.

"Exactly—the lady Elizabeth's father, *and* Bedivere's brother-in-law. We can't leave him in these dire straits the bastard has put him in. Isn't it our duty to succor the weak and oppressed?"

"And to aid ladies in distress," Bors added. "The ladies Mary and Elizabeth will be quite distressed to learn of their father's new woes. But a hundred nobles is no small sum. And we need to find Lancelot."

"We'll have to do what we're able in the time we've got," Merlin said practically. Then he gaped at the pub's door and exclaimed "God's eyelids!" And I turned to check over my left shoulder just what had startled him so, and to my own surprise saw Alan of Winchester coming through the door, followed by none other than the lady Elizabeth herself.

CHAPTER ELEVEN

THE LADY, THE USURER, AND THE DWARF

Having heard how Mordred intended to put her father through even more humiliation, Lady Elizabeth had sought to catch us that morning in order to travel with us to Winchester, but believing she had missed us, prevailed on Alan to accompany her to his home town, and they'd left at prime that morning. Of course, I'd overslept, as I mentioned, so she and Alan had actually left more than an hour before us, and had not stopped for lunch. They'd been in Winchester for some two hours by the time we arrived, and had been to the square before the jail, where Sir Lowell sat on a platform, his legs held in place by the hinged wooden stocks that locked around his ankles. Lady Elizabeth, needless to say, was in a nearly frantic state, though Alan told us in confidence that Sir Lowell was in relatively good spirits, considering, and was not terribly uncomfortable. That, plus the fact that the weather continued fine, meant that we could reasonably expect Sir Lowell to spend the night in the stocks without suffering overmuch or without its taxing his health significantly. Which was good, since none of us could possibly come up with a hundred nobles that night. Lady Elizabeth told us that Sir Lowell had sold everything he owned to pay off his debt to Mordred, but had fallen short by a hundred nobles—still a significant amount, probably half the cost of a good war horse like Achilles or Pegasus. Merlin never carried money. Everyone knew I was poor as a serf, and even Sir Bors never had more than a few shillings on his person.

"It looks as if Sir Mordred has pointed us toward the only plausible means of securing a hundred nobles in a reasonable time," Merlin said. "We must borrow it from some moneylender. There is a community of Jews here, is that true?"

A subdued Lady Elizabeth answered, "Several families. Been here since I was a girl." I refrained from remarking that this could mean they'd arrived last week, since the thirteen-year-old was still a girl, as far as I could see. A spunky one for sure, but a girl none the less.

"And in the community there are moneylenders, I imagine?" Merlin asked.

Alan scratched his greasy locks. "There's some as are wool merchants," he volunteered, "an' some are poor and work for the others. But there's at least a couple of usurers among 'em. They ought to be able to lend ya what's needed."

So, over a light supper, the five of us made plans for the following morning. We could not take a chance on missing the dwarf Thorvald when he came in for his midday meal, and so it was decided that Sir Bors, who was most personally concerned with finding Lancelot, would stay around the Red Ox in case Thorvald arrived before we had finished our other business. Alan would stay as well, since he had seen Thorvald leave under cover of night, and could best confront the dwarf if he denied any knowledge of the affair. Meanwhile, Merlin and I would accompany Lady Elizabeth to the Jewish neighborhood to find a money lender and free her father from the stocks. And that is where we left it before retiring for the evening. Bors already had a room, and graciously offered to share it with Alan, and also paid for a small closet for Lady Elizabeth to pass the night. Merlin and I secured a room for ourselves, though it was the last one available, the town being deluged with pilgrims today. Merlin told Lady Elizabeth we would break our fast with her here at prime, an early start being important with so much to do tomorrow. And off the girl went, throwing me a look as she exited that was intended to be either angry or sultry, I couldn't tell which.

***

It probably wasn't necessary for me to wear my new mail armor or my sword the next morning for our visit to the Jewish quarter, and it certainly would have been more comfortable to have walked around Winchester without carrying that extra forty pounds of iron with me. But the distinction of knighthood was so new to me that I wanted everyone who saw me to know that I had that honor. My father had worked months, maybe years on that hauberk, and I wanted as many people to admire it as I could find. And I wanted the respect and authority that such accoutrements could give me. And, truth be told, I also wished to impress the lady Elizabeth. After what Rosemounde had told me, I hoped that I could get her to respect me at least enough to stop being so rude to me.

Bors had already eaten by the time we came down that morning, and he had begged an apple from the innkeeper to take out to the stable to give to Pegasus. I assumed he would stay in the stable in order to feed Pegasus his own breakfast of oats, a practice he was in the habit of in Camelot. It was not just that his destrier was his largest and most necessary investment as a knight. It was also that Bors, like his kinsman Lancelot, felt a real closeness to his horse, and pampered the animal as far as custom and common practice would let him. I made a note to take an apple myself out to Achilles before we left. And to pick up Guinevere on the way.

The serving maid with the white apron and cap from last night was bustling about the pub this morning, crowded as it was with visitors, and told us to have a seat and she'd bring us an egg and some brown bread, which I said was fine, and asked for a third dish for Elizabeth, who joined us a moment or two later. I couldn't help but notice she was wearing a fairly simple kirtle of blue linen with a white sleeveless tunic over it, bound at the waist with a thin leather belt. As a young, unmarried girl, her head was uncovered, but she wore it tied back with a long blue ribbon that matched her kirtle. She looked sober, and without a word, sat down and began with us to make quick work of the morsel of breakfast, and the three pints of small beer that accompanied it. In mid-mouthful, Merlin asked the server where we might find a moneylender in this town.

"Easy enough," she said, and pointed to her right, toward the east.

"You'll find the king's Jews if you head down the High Street that way, toward the cathedral—it's the direction every other pilgrim will be headed today. The first street you come to branching off of High Street to the left is Staple Gardens. Keep going past that and you'll also be passing the jail on the left. And the next street going left after the jail is Jewry Street."

"Aptly named, I assume?" Merlin said.

"Right," the barmaid said. "If you can't find a usurer there, you ain't looking." And off she went, as a customer from another table was calling for more beer.

"Why does she call them the 'king's Jews'?" I asked Merlin, chewing on a crust of the bread. "I've not heard that term before. In fact, I don't think I've ever met many Jews at all."

Merlin nodded. "There aren't a large number in Logres," he conceded. "More in the Rhineland. And a lot more in Spain. And, of course, in the Holy Land. But they are the king's Jews because they are under his special protection. By royal decree they are permitted to follow their own religion, even, as you see, here in the shadow of the cathedral. They may also practice their trade, and one of their chief trades is the lending of money at interest. Since that is against canon law, Christians are forbidden from the practice. But the king sometimes needs to finance things like military ventures very quickly, more quickly than he might be able to collect taxes. So he needs to borrow money, and if the Christians won't lend it to him, then by God's knuckles, the Jews will. So yes, they're the king's Jews, and proud of it."

"Still seems like a questionable way to make a living though, doesn't it? I mean, my father goes to work, he makes something, then he takes that armor he's made and he gives it to some knight in exchange for money. They get something, he gets something in exchange for the effort he's put into making that something. But a moneylender, he gives you some money, you take it, and then after awhile you give it back, and give him some more money to go with it. So what is the money for? The money lender didn't put any work into it, did he?"

Lady Elizabeth, who had seemed not to be listening, piped up languidly, "He had something you didn't have. He gave it to you to use. You used it. You pay him for the depreciation, like if you borrowed somebody's plow and wore down the blade, and gave it back to them with some money for the wear and tear."

Merlin smiled and shrugged. "Makes as much sense as anything. Your Bible does prohibit usury. Many, many times. Aristotle condemned it, too, said it was a sin against nature—since money isn't a living thing, it can't reproduce itself. It's sterile."

I nodded. "If that's the case, then should the Jews be allowed to engage in the practice?"

"The *king's* Jews," Merlin reminded me. "And a better question might be, what else are they going to do? Remember, guilds are Christian organizations. Jews are not going to be allowed to join the shipwrights' or the dyers' or the parchment makers' guilds, or the armorers' guild either, you Cornish bonehead. They're pretty much prohibited from normal occupations in town. So, what's the one occupation not only open to them, but open *only* to them?"

"Well, moneylending, I guess…"

"It was a rhetorical question, boy. Now let's not sit around here debating economics all morning, we've got money to borrow." And with that, we rose and left the inn.

We swung by the stable before following the crowd in the direction of the cathedral, and I held out an apple to Achilles, who took it gratefully, nodding his head in delight with the treat. I patted the side of his nose and as I did, Guinevere got up from the straw she'd been sleeping in and stretched, putting her long front legs out in front of her and raising her tail end high in the air while she elongated her hind legs at the same time. Then she gave her whole body a shake and trotted out of Achilles' stall to join us. I patted the soft fur of her head as she nuzzled me in the side, and all of that was pretty much what I had grown used to from her. But I was not prepared for what she did next: upon seeing the lady Elizabeth, she crouched down in a play posture, leaning on her forelegs like a puppy, and then bounded around happily in a circle around the young girl. Elizabeth laughed—the first time I had ever witnessed that phenomenon—and I had to admit there was a gentle kind of charm in her face when it relaxed and her white teeth flashed in unguarded delight. Guinevere stood up on her hind legs and put her front paws on Lady Elizabeth's shoulders so that the dog's face was level with the girl's, and they stood for a moment looking lovingly into one another's eyes. I had to admit I was a little jealous. I wished the dog would look at *me* like that more often.

As we started up the High Street, Guinevere walked with us with a pronounced spring in her step, and every few steps jumped and gamboled about in a circle around Elizabeth. The girl was happier than I'd ever seen her, until we passed Staple Gardens and came to the jail yard on our left. Sir Lowell of Winchester lay uncomfortably on a platform with his ankles secured in the wooden restraints. A small crowd had gathered around him, made up I supposed of pilgrims on their way to the cathedral, distracted momentarily by the sight of someone who was obviously a gentleman (to judge by his relatively clean and ordered appearance, his proud bearing, and his new-looking blue woolen tunic and brown hose) placed in such a precarious and humiliating posture. A boisterous knot of about twenty-five onlookers had the platform surrounded and were jeering at the prisoner, shouting insults and, in some cases, throwing garbage or other offal at him, ensuring that his blue tunic would not stay clean long.

Lady Elizabeth stood staring, tears pooling in the corners of her eyes. I reached out to her gently, urging her not to look and to keep moving. "You can do nothing right now. The sooner we can borrow this money, the sooner we can secure his freedom," I assured her. "Come, please."

At that moment one of the unruly mob threw an egg that smashed against Sir Lowell's skull, smearing it with sticky stuff and matting his long gray hair. And there was no saint nearby to put that egg back together. Elizabeth gasped, but before she had a chance to react further, another missile—this one a stone—came flying out of the crowd and grazed the side of Sir Lowell's head, so that the right side of his narrow pallid face was bloodied. Belatedly, he found that it might be safest to duck and cover his unprotected head in his arms, curling himself into a ball as best he could with his legs stretched out before him.

Lady Elizabeth hung her head, and I reached out to try to encourage her now to come with us and do what we needed to do. But instead she raised her face, shook off my hand, and set her jaw in the position I had seen it set before, back in Gorre when she had taken her memorable stand against those who belittled Lancelot for riding in the cart. Now she stepped forward and at the top of her voice began to chastise the mob.

"What is the matter with you people? You're going to visit the shrine of a saint and you stop to torment one of your fellow Christians who has committed no crime? Shame on you! Shame on all of you! I call down Saint Swithin's curse on you! You have no charity and you have no honor!" She raised her little fist and shook it at the crowd, whose members began to look at one another fairly sheepishly. But they were immediately taken aback when Guinevere, seeing Elizabeth's tirade, stepped forward herself and, standing in front of Elizabeth, began barking insistently at the crowd. I was surprised, having so seldom heard my borzoi bark, to hear such a torrent coming from her now. Whether she thought that Lady Elizabeth was being threatened, or whether she simply wanted to take her side in whatever conflict she might be in with these people, the hound was not going to stand by quietly when her new favorite girl was distraught.

Fearing that the dog might charge into the mob and cause some damage to them, or they to her, I moved to intercept her and hold her by her collar, telling her in a calming voice, "That's enough, girl. Leave them now and come with us." It was intended for both Guinevere and Elizabeth.

At the same time, Merlin spoke quietly in my ear. "Hold your ground a few more moments, Gildas my boy. I believe they will disperse." And to my surprise, the entire throng, looking whipped and chastened as beaten curs, began to hang their heads and slink away. I looked at Merlin quizzically, unaware of why they might have been cowed into leaving. Could a mob of twenty-five rowdy men be driven away by a young girl's shouts, or a single dog's unwonted yips? But the old man only rolled his eyes. "You Cornish dolt," he whispered. "A knight in full armor, with a long steel arming sword sheathed at his side, is always going to convince a crowd even twice that size to disperse. Be a little more self-aware, can't you?"

"Hmph," I said, with a restrained half smile.

"Come on!" Merlin called. "Let's get this done. We are running out of time." I knew he meant we were running out of time to find Sir Lancelot. This deliverance of Sir Lowell, necessary as it was, was a distraction from our main task, so the sooner it was done, the better, not only for Sir Lowell, who would be rescued from his ordeal, but for us as well, as we would be freed to pursue Sir Lancelot. Today, I recalled with a start, was July 1. Tomorrow was Saint Swithin's day, and the following day was the feast day of Saint Thomas, when the queen's trial must take place, if indeed Arthur let Meliagaunt's challenge advance. It was paramount that we find Sir Lancelot by the end of the day today, if he was to have a chance of getting back to Camelot in time.

Shaking off these thoughts, though, I felt the urge before leaving the area, to call out some encouragement to the hapless Sir Lowell. "We'll be back soon, sir!" I said. "And we'll have you out of there!"

"We'll be back, Father!" Elizabeth cried, the tears now rolling down her tense face. She bowed her head and followed us away from the platform, eastward down the High Street, with Guinevere trotting along at her side.

As we passed out of the jail yard, the next street on the left was Jewry Street, as the barmaid at the Red Ox had told us. We turned the corner and immediately noticed a difference. Here it was not nearly so crowded, since none of the visitors in town were interested in visiting the Jews on their very Christian pilgrimage to Saint Swithin's relics. On this street, only Winchester's Jewish community was busy going about its normal activities. There were only a few people on the street, and I wasn't sure how we were to find a shop specifically involved in the money-lending business. I did notice that the first shop we passed had a slaughtered animal's picture on a sign, while on the door across the street hung a sign that showed a man's head and a pair of scissors. A few doors down was another sign, this one with a tunic painted on the outside. I could easily interpret these signs as denoting the shops of a butcher, a barber, and a tailor.

"Merlin," I asked, a bit confused. "You did tell me that these Jews were not allowed to be members of any artisans' guilds in the city. Yet here are a butcher, a tailor, and I assume a barber. They haven't been apprenticed, then? Yet they are allowed to practice in the city?"

"The community has need of certain services, and these shops deal only with other Jews. Think of your Bible, boy. Think of all the dietary laws there are in the Pentateuch."

"Oh, I always skip those sections," I admitted. "I mean, didn't Christ put us beyond those things?"

"Not as far as these people are concerned," Merlin said. "So they need to have a special butcher who abides by all those laws. There are also particular rules about what to wear, and about how you should wear your hair, so these shops deal with those things, again just for this community."

I shook my head as we walked slowly down that street, peeking cautiously into open doors when we passed them. "It's kind of a strange way to live, isn't it? I mean, don't they feel kind of awkward living their own kind of lives amid so many strangers they're not part of?"

"It's rather a new situation here," Merlin said. "Though Jews have been living side by side with Christians and also with Muslims in Spain for centuries. Your own Saint Augustine called the Jews 'living letters of the Law,' and said that Christians should let Jews live among them as a reminder of the literal sense of the scriptures. Still, a lot of Christians resent their presence, don't they?"

Merlin's reference to Muslims had brought Sir Palomides to mind, and I stopped for a moment to consider Palomides' position in Camelot as it might relate to the situation of these Jews in Winchester. "Sir Palomides must have felt similar to these Jews, at least before he converted to the True Faith, don't you think?"

Merlin, to whom the concept of the "True Faith" was foreign if not anathema, gave me a wry smile. "Palomides had only his brother Safir. And since Safir's death he has no one who truly understands his situation. Even though he is now a Christian, his skin tone and appearance make him stand out as an anomaly in Camelot."

I really had not thought before about how lonely Sir Palomides must be at Arthur's Table. But having been christened, he also had no home to go back to now. I felt for him.

"Palomides does have a special affinity for the Jews he's met in Christendom. He understands their isolation and, I think, envies their community. But remember, he was present at the conquest of Jerusalem. He saw the Jews slaughtered along with the Moors in that city. He has an understanding that few in this age have." I let that sink in as we walked slowly a bit further along the Jewry Street. Unlike the dark-skinned Palomides, the few people out on the street did not look much different from any of the Christian pilgrims now walking along the High Street toward the cathedral, with the exception that the men were all wearing the same sort of hat, a conical yellow cloth hat with a small brim of a stiffer material than the hat itself. I was wondering whether this was a custom of their own, or whether it was some kind of identifying badge required by the city or the church, but just at that moment, we came to an open door with a sign hanging above it that looked like a purse filled with coins. Pointing to the sign, Lady Elizabeth said, "If this isn't a money lender's place, I don't know what else it could be."

In her usual blunt way, Elizabeth had put us on the right track, and we quickly entered the shop. In the small room sat a man of about forty at a long wooden desk. The man had black hair that was cut fairly short on top and behind, though not as radically short as Sir Bors'. In front and in the sideburns, though, the hair was longer and quite curly, as was his dark beard, though that was fairly neatly trimmed. He wore a conspicuous red tunic reaching to his knees, and over the back of the chair on which he sat was a rich but simple blue woolen cloak. On the left side of the desk he had set down one of those same yellow hats I'd seen the other men wearing on the street. On the right side of the desk were piled several stacks of gold or silver coins, arranged neatly in rows, and before the man were placed a lighted candle, a seal, and a sheaf of papers with minuscule notations that I assumed must be ledgers. Lady Elizabeth, who had led us in, was the first to speak.

"We want one hundred nobles!" she blurted out.

"And Tantalus in hell wants a cool drink of water," the man at the desk quipped, deadpan. "If wishes were horses, young lady…"

Merlin chuckled lightly. "Ah, my learned friend, I see you have read the classics. But please forgive our young companion's bluntness. You may have good reason to welcome us. Maybe think of us this way: go back earlier in Virgil, long before Aeneas learns of Tantalus in Hades, to the passage where he first meets Dido, and says 'I am here before you, the one you look for…'"

"Hmph," the proprietor responded, turning his still expressionless eyes on the old necromancer and said with a shrug of his shoulders. "I believe in the passage you refer to, Aeneas and his friend have come unseen in a cloud furnished by the goddess. Yet, you I've seen coming down the street for several minutes now. And what's probably worse," and here he looked up at Merlin with a bit of a twinkle in his dark eyes, "Aeneas actually says to Dido, 'We have not the means to repay your goodness.' Not exactly the kind of thing a moneylender likes to hear, if I may say so." And with that he gave a small, close-mouthed smile and crossed his hands in his lap. "So, where does that leave us?"

Merlin was amused by this witty and well-educated gentleman, and laughed aloud this time. "Then let me begin again, if I may. I am Lord Merlin, adviser to Arthur, King of Logres, Emperor of Wales, Cornwall, Scotland, Gaul, Britany, Ireland, and scourge of Rome itself." That "Lord" surprised me. The old man almost never gave himself the honor King Arthur had conferred on him as his most valued advisor, though others often called him by that title.

"And I am Isaac ben Samuel," the money lender answered. "Master of myself, under God. So, what can I do for you, my lord?"

Merlin continued, "I am here representing one of the king's own vassals, who has fallen on hard times in the king's service, and is currently undergoing certain hardships because of debts he is unable to pay. Accordingly, I am constrained to ask whether you, sir, would be willing to extend me a loan on this nobleman's behalf."

"So you're here for poor Sir Lowell, are you? Demeaned twice now by the king's own nephew over some debt. Shameful! How do you do that to your own people? Hmph. If Lowell had come to us in the first place, nothing like this would have happened to him."

"Well, perhaps we can remedy that oversight for him right now," Merlin responded, "if you are willing to grant us a loan of one hundred nobles, that would discharge Lowell's debt to Mordred, and transfer that to you." Now Merlin smiled as pleasantly as he could manage.

Isaac's black eyebrows shot up into the realm of his curly forelocks, and he answered very slowly and distinctly. "I see some difficulties here," he answered. "Sir Lowell himself is penniless now. It would be impossible for him to repay this loan, no matter how long we gave him to settle the debt. Are you acting at the king's behest? Will King Arthur guarantee the loan himself?"

Merlin did not feel he could prevaricate at this point. "This concern has just become known to us since we arrived here in Winchester. There has been no time to contact the king, though I am certain he would guarantee the loan himself if he were aware of the situation."

"And when you get that guarantee in writing, I will have no qualms about giving you this loan," Isaac said. "But I'm afraid I'd have little confidence in your own ability to guarantee the payment. I hope I don't offend you, but your cloak, for instance, does not inspire confidence in your access to ready cash," and he shrugged again, deprecatingly.

Merlin glanced at his own threadbare garment and had to shrug himself in agreement. "Well, I must admit, you're right. The king provides what I need. What he doesn't provide, I do without. But I assure you, he will make it good."

"As I'm sure his written guarantee will make clear. Once I get it." And Isaac looked up at us with eyes that seemed to hold in them the expectation of our departure.

"But we can't wait so long!" Lady Elizabeth exclaimed. "Father can't lie there exposed to the elements and to the abuse of bystanders for two more days! It'll take at least that long to get back and forth to Camelot!"

"And we have to find Sir Lancelot before we can do anything or go anywhere else," I muttered to Merlin.

But on hearing Elizabeth's plea, Isaac seemed to soften somewhat. "Of course," he said, "if I had something to secure the loan—something of substantial value—I could let you have the hundred nobles now, with your promise to repay the loan—with interest—by a certain date, or forfeit the item put up as collateral."

"Well," I murmured, beginning to understand, "what might we have that would be worth a hundred nobles to you?" Isaac turned to me and his eyes lit up. I felt that perhaps I might regret asking that question.

"You do appear to be the only one of your little group with anything worth bartering," the moneylender smiled, his eyes taking in my accoutrements. "That sword for example. It appears to be of fine German steel, is it not? Forged in the Rhineland perhaps?"

My hand went protectively to the hilt of Almace, and the blood in my face sank timidly into my stomach. Sir Gareth's fine gift? How could I part with it?

"My associate, Sir Gildas, cannot part with his sword. We go from here into dangerous circumstances, where one of us, at any rate, may well find a sword indispensable," Merlin said, looking at me with some sympathy. But what he said, I realized, was absolutely true. Beyond simply regretting the loss of Sir Gareth's sword, even temporarily, I had to acknowledge that searching for Sir Lancelot could require us to fight our way to his rescue. Giving up the sword could be, would be, a serious mistake.

Isaac gave another of his shrugs. "Eh, the sword you can keep," he said. "But that hauberk! Such exquisite work. Beautifully made. And it looks brand new. You provide that mail coat for surety and you can have the hundred nobles right now. That coat is easily worth at least a hundred nobles to anyone. And I can see," he said shrewdly, looking at my face with narrowed eyes, "that it's an item you'd not let go easily, so there's something of a guarantee that you'll be back to redeem it with my hundred nobles, and my interest, as soon as you possibly can." And with that Isaac leaned his head to the side and looked at me quizzically, wondering, I could sense, whether we had a deal.

If the sword had been a stumbling block for me, giving up the hauberk seemed far worse. My father's gift. A gift he'd worked lovingly on for perhaps two years or more. Given away after but a single day? Never to wear it in court? Never to wear it into the lists, or into battle? I realized I had broken out in a cold sweat. Could I not make the same argument for the hauberk as I had for the sword? If we were to meet with kidnappers or murderers tonight in our search for Lancelot, wasn't it just as important that I have my armor as well as my sword with me? But I knew that wasn't true. Without the armor, I would indeed be more vulnerable. But without the sword, I was dead.

"Oh, Gildas!" Lady Elizabeth moaned at my side. It was the first time I had ever heard her address me without the protective cushion of rudeness that was her own mail coat, but I wasn't sure how to interpret her simple cry. Was she sympathizing with the sacrifice I was being asked to make for her sake and her father's? Or was she pleading with me to let go my personal feelings and give over the hauberk to free her father and set her mind at ease?

I looked over at Merlin, but the old necromancer was staring straight ahead, making a point of not looking me in the eye. He knew exactly how much that hauberk meant to me. He'd been there when it arrived. He was not going to tell me to give it up. But it certainly didn't look like he was going to tell me to keep it, either. Because, in fact, Isaac had hit on the only plausible solution to this problem. Elizabeth and her family were essentially penniless. Merlin lived in a cave and the most valuable thing he carried with him was a handful of powder with which he could make Greek fire and scare people into thinking he could harness the power of lightning. Sir Bors might be able to help with some ready cash, but he would never carry that large a sum, and it would make less sense to ask *him* to put up his sword or mail for surety, since he was a better knight than I was and it was more important he be armed and ready to face Lancelot's captors, if that's what we were about to do. And appealing to the king or queen for help would take days, while Sir Lowell needed deliverance now.

When Merlin looked away from me and stared straight ahead, he knew that I knew what the right thing to do was. But he knew I had to be willing to make the sacrifice myself. With a sigh, I unbuckled my sword belt and handed Almace and its scabbard to Merlin, and began to pull the beautiful new hauberk over my head. At my feet, Guinevere whined. I looked down at her and said, "I know, girl. I feel the same way."

***

"God's nose-hairs, Gildas, I thought you were never going to do the right thing!" Merlin crowed at me as we made our way around the corner and back onto the High Street. Meanwhile, the lady Elizabeth, was mooning at me silently with one of those dreamy looks that young girls will get in their eyes, and I don't mind telling you I was inordinately uncomfortable, thinking only, as I did, of Lady Rosemounde in that way, and remembering at the same time what Rosemounde had told me about the queen's plans for me and her youngest lady-in-waiting.

In any case, I was the one carrying the purse with its hundred gold nobles, since I was the one who had put up the collateral and signed the papers that Isaac had drawn up and sealed within minutes of my agreeing to the transaction: a promise to repay him one hundred nobles plus one noble per month interest, but agreeing that if, after three months, I had not redeemed the hauberk, he could lawfully sell the coat for whatever price he was able to obtain for it. I had a sealed copy of the receipt tucked under my habergeon, and had every intention of pestering the queen, Sir Gareth, and anyone else I could until I had collected enough to buy back the coat.

We went to the jailer, gave him the cash to wipe out Sir Lowell's debt, and had the poor man released from the stocks. We helped Lady Elizabeth carry him to his home, which turned out to be a large house, four streets south of the High Street, got him cleaned up somewhat, and set him to rest in his own bed—any servants he may have had at one time had long since left that house of ill luck and poverty. It was Merlin who realized that Lowell may just end up in the same state again without any means of support, his having sold all of his family lands to pay off his previous debts. But Lowell himself had a plan: he was still able-bodied and still a knight. He would attach himself as a vassal to one of the other local knights—Sir Degore perhaps, or his old friend Sir Bernard of Astolat. Merlin thought that an excellent plan, and Elizabeth sighed with relief and a new bit of hope that things would finally return to some kind of normality in her father's house. After that, we left to make our way back to the

Red Ox. It was now well after sext, and we thought that Thorvald may have come to the inn for his dinner—that is, if we could trust anything that Mordred told us.

We left Sir Lowell sleeping peacefully, and I was surprised that Lady Elizabeth seemed intent on coming with us back to the inn. "Are you sure?" I asked her. "Don't you want to stay here with your father?"

She shrugged. "He'll just sleep, probably for hours. Why, don't you *want* me to come with you?" She was back to her old contrary self, I noticed.

"Suit yourself," I replied, as if unconcerned. But I noticed that Guinevere, for one, was unreservedly glad that her new girlfriend was coming with us, and bounced along happily at her side.

Back on the High Street, it appeared that dozens of pilgrims were coming through the gate, and I wondered whether there were enough inns in Winchester to house so many visitors. A good number were pushing into the Red Ox itself, so that we had to wait to allow four monks to squeeze in ahead of us. Once inside, giving my eyes a moment to adjust to the lower light, I spotted Sir Bors and Alan the guardsman sitting at the same table we'd had last night. They were talking animatedly to someone sitting between them, though I could only see the very top of that someone's white-haired pate: Thorvald.

Weaving our way through the throng in the inn, it was actually Guinevere who got there first, and who put her chin on the edge of the table, right next to a beef pie that Thorvald was having for his dinner. "'Ere, now, what's all this then?" The dwarf exclaimed when he saw the dog begging for his meat. "I paid good money for that, an' it don't belong to the likes of you!" But when Lady Elizabeth was the next to appear beside his chair, he frowned heavily and his face turned pale. "Look now, missy, I don't need to be seeing any of you lot. It warn't me as put the law on your father, I just does what they pay me to do."

"Then take up a different trade," Elizabeth shot back. "What you are now is a vile defender of a bullying legal system."

Thorvald, who had found it easy enough to cow powerful knights like Gawain, Gareth, and Lancelot—and who, I was pretty sure, had just been holding his own against Sir Bors as well—now hung his head, chagrinned by the unrestrained judgments of a thirteen-year-old girl.

"We are not here to discuss that," Merlin said, taking charge as we followed Elizabeth to surround the corner table. "I assume Sir Bors and Alan have told you why we want to talk to you."

"Yes, they want to know all about Sir Lancelot, they say. But like I was just tellin' them, I don't know anything about that. I hain't seen Lancelot since he rode to Gorre in my cart to rescue the queen and all that. This is just more anti-dwarf bigotry is what I calls it!"

"You were seen leaving Camelot several nights ago with another figure in your cart," Merlin said, giving no credence to the dwarf's complaints.

"I saw you!" Alan declared. "Tall he was, built like a knight. What do ye say to that?"

"What makes you think that could have been Lancelot?" Thorvald equivocated. "Coulda been anybody from that castle!"

"Like who?" Sir Bors demanded.

"And while you're thinking about that, consider this," Merlin said. "Lancelot has not been seen for about a week now. And no one else has been reported missing from the castle."

Thorvald put on a good show of outraged innocence, even stood up as if to leave, saying, "I hain't done anything, and I don't 'ave to sit here listenin' to these innuendos." But as he stood up to leave, Guinevere stood up as well, putting her paws on his shoulders. Usually she had to look up into people's faces when she did that, but in Thorvald's case, she towered above him and looked down into his startled eyes. She seemed to like this new sensation—her mouth hung open in what looked a lot like a laugh.

"You, too, ya great gangly beast?" Thorvald cried, and pushed the dog away. Then, looking around and feeling hemmed in, he sighed and sat back down. "All right," he said. "But ya must understand that 'e made me promise not to tell. Made me swear on my own mother's grave. But Sir Bors 'ere says 'e might be in danger, and it seems ye're pretty certain just 'ow 'e left the castle anyway, so I'm not exactly givin' anything away 'ere. An' my mother's still alive anyhow."

"You did secret Sir Lancelot out of the castle, then?" Merlin confirmed. "And when was this?"

Thorvald scratched his chin under his long white beard. "Last Thursday it would have been, I guess. So...nine days ago, I'd make it. But it warn't my idea. Nor his, come to that."

"Then whose was it?" Bors pressed.

"I was in the stables in Camelot late that afternoon, sometime after nones, feedin' my Daisy and brushing her down. Well, up rides this knight, and he gets down from his horse and walks over to me. He was in full armor, helmet and all, so he's got his face covered. And he says to me in a deep voice that sounded like he was disguising it, 'I want you to give a message to Lancelot of the Lake.' And I says 'give it to 'im yourself, sounds like you got a voice.' Well, that kinda took him aback, ya see, and he sputtered a bit and then says, "Rest assured, I would, but I must get back on the road immediately, and no one must know I've been here. So, tell Lancelot that I have a message from his Sovereign Lady. Say she demands he come to her in Winchester, and be there tomorrow morning. But come in secret. He is to meet me in the Red Ox Inn tomorrow morning at terce. Tell him.' And then off rides the bastard."

I started at this news, not so much at the words themselves but at what they implied. Merlin, Bors, and I were well aware of the secret of Lancelot's affair with the queen, but for Thorvald to blurt this out before Alan and the Lady Elizabeth was, to say the least, unfortunate. I glanced at Alan, who seemed unfazed by this revelation. Perhaps he had missed the implication altogether. A cloud had come over Lady Elizabeth's face, however, and she screwed up her mouth in a thoughtful grimace. Before anyone could speak, she said abruptly, "I feel a sudden headache coming on. Please excuse me. I think I shall go back to my room," and with that she turned on her heel and left us, her blue hair ribbon bobbing behind her as she made her way through the crowd. I noticed she did not go upstairs, though, but rather went out the door into the street. To get some air, I assumed. Guinevere followed the girl with her eyes and whined. And I turned to Thorvald.

"So, you didn't see his face," I said. "But this knight—was he wearing a coat of arms? Either on his shield or his surcoat? Anything that would make him recognizable?"

Thorvald shook his head. "No heraldic signs whatsoever. His surcoat was pure white, and so was 'is shield. Much like your own."

I blushed at that, but Merlin went on. "So that would suggest he, like Gildas, was a newly made knight, perhaps. Or that he was deliberately disguising his identity."

"Could it have been Meliagaunt?" Bors asked immediately.

"Oh, old Meliagaunt of Gorre, 'im I know real well. I'd'a recognized 'im for certain, shield or no shield, helmet or no helmet, funny voice or no funny voice. This fella was smaller than Meliagaunt. Slighter too, not so broad around the shoulders. Don't think 'e had a beard neither. It warn't 'im for sure."

"It could still have been one of Meliagaunt's stooges. He has several, I understand, that helped him kidnap the queen. Could that have been who it was?" Bors pressed.

"Or what about Sir Degore?" I suggested. "He might have been willing to help his brother-in-law lay a trap for Sir Lancelot?"

Thorvald shrugged. "I can't say. Never seen this Degore bloke. Thin fella is he? Young?"

Merlin, who had been watching Lady Elizabeth's retreat with narrowed eyes, now rejoined the conversation. "Sir Degore has always been an honorable knight. I can't imagine him taking part in any kind of deception against Lancelot. Besides, he is not particularly young. Nearly forty by now, I would imagine. But his build might fit your description. God's nostrils, we're getting ahead of ourselves. Tell us the rest of the story, Thorvald. What did you do with Lancelot?"

"Well, just what the knight tole me to do, whadja think?" Thorvald said. "I found 'im in 'is rooms in the castle. Since our little trip to Gorre, 'e's been pretty friendly with me, ya see, and I'd been used to visiting 'im there more than once. 'E likes to 'ear my stories."

"Of hangings and floggings?" I asked, startled.

"Nah, nah," Thorvald waved the suggestion away. "Of growin' up a little person in a world of big uns. Things I 'ad to overcome to finally get a job nobody else wanted to do. I know your little spitfire there," he nodded in the direction of Elizabeth's departure, "thinks it's a vile occupation. And I suppose it is. But you try getting an apprenticeship when you're my size. Not gonna bloody 'appen, is it?" He glared defiantly at us, one by one, but Merlin impatiently tried to get him back on track.

"Stop babbling and get to the point," Merlin said. "Where is Lancelot *now*?"

Thorvald looked up and blinked at the old necromancer. "It's like I'm tryin' to tell ya, I don't *know*," he blurted out. "I brought 'im 'ere, like the man said, and we met the knight 'ere at the Red Ox. But as soon as we get 'ere, the knight takes Lancelot out to the stables, gives 'im a horse, and says, 'Come with me, the lady is waiting and there isn't much time.' So, off they go. Lancelot tells me to promise not to tell anybody about all this, and then without so much as a 'by your leave' ta me, they've gone, and that's the last I seen of either of 'em. Never gave it another thought, really, till you blokes waylay me today and tell me as 'ow Lancelot hain't been seen since."

There was a moment of silence until Bors stood up and said, "Right. Now we take some decisive action. You, Thorvald, you're coming with me. We're going back to Sir Degore's manor and we're going to confront every man in that place to see if you recognize any of them as the knight you spoke with. And if you do, I will tear that manor down plank by plank until I find Sir Lancelot. The rest of you coming?"

Alan put his palms up as if to say, "I'll go wherever I'm told." I looked at Merlin, who sighed and said, "I don't think it will be fruitful, but it may be worth trying. At least we can eliminate the manor as a possibility."

"Then I guess we're coming, too," I said, and the five of us all began to make our way out, followed by Guinevere, bereft of her new friend.

CHAPTER TWELVE

ELIZABETH

Thorvald insisted on bringing his cart. He could not ride a horse, he said, unless it was a small pony, and he preferred his cart in any case. Merlin decided he would also ride in the cart, claiming it would probably be more comfortable than bouncing around on his palfrey, particularly since he assumed he'd have a long ride back to Camelot once we had found Lancelot. As for this prejudice about it being dishonorable to ride in such a vehicle, he scoffed at such nonsense. "I'll ride in whatever conveyance I like, and if my honor resides in such insubstantial things, I must not have much to begin with."

Alan of Winchester rather liked this attitude, and decided to join the old man in the cart. "Don't have much honor myself," he reasoned. "Ain't no aristocrat. Might as well ride in comfort."

I didn't see that the cart looked all that comfortable but I didn't say anything, and while Thorvald hitched his Daisy up to the cart, I got Achilles out of the stable. *Somebody* ought to have a horse, I reasoned. Not that Bors was about to leave without Pegasus. He was already mounted when I brought Achilles out of the stable, and when Thorvald pulled up in his cart, we started off, taking the west gate out of town toward Sir Degore's manor a few miles back down the road. Guinevere, who had been prancing around Achilles, glad to be back on the road with him, decided suddenly that perhaps she, too, would like a ride, and jumped into the cart with Merlin and Alan.

Straight ahead of us, the sun was beginning to sink low on the horizon as we moved at the easy pace of Thorvald's cart along the road west. Fields of grain were beginning to ripen under July's warm sun, and here and there a small cottage dotted the landscape. We had gone about two miles and were within a mile of Degore's manor when the road passed into a grove of trees and, looking to the right, I saw a cluster of houses around a good-sized manor house at the end of a small path branching right off the road. "What village is that?" I asked, shading my eyes from the sun.

"Astolat," Alan said. And I looked again, remembering the story of that place.

Quite suddenly, Guinevere, who had been riding along lazily, her chin resting on the edge of the cart, shot her head upright, her ears straight back, and stared down the path toward Astolat. Then without warning, she bolted over the side of the cart and began running at full speed along the path.

"Guinevere! Wait! Come back here girl!" I cried, but that was useless. Like her namesake, she always had a mind of her own. I gave Achilles a squeeze with my thighs and off he bolted after the dog. Guinevere stopped about a hundred yards down the path, tearing at something caught in a bush along the path's edge. I pulled up and dismounted Achilles, reaching out to see what she had in her mouth.

"What has that infernal dog found now?" came Merlin's voice from behind me. He had called to Thorvald to stop the cart, and climbed out himself after Guinevere. I looked over my shoulder at him and held up a long, blue strip of cloth.

"Lady Elizabeth's ribbon!"

Merlin's face grew grave and thoughtful, and I noticed with a chill that there was blood on the blue band. I wondered aloud, "What on earth was she doing out here? She must have come this way when she left the Red Ox. But why? What's happened to her?"

Before Merlin had a chance to answer, Guinevere broke away from us and dashed at full speed again down the path toward the manor house at the end of the lane. I looked back toward the cart where Sir Bors, sitting atop his Pegasus, was fuming in exasperation.

"Let the dog go!" he called. "She'll catch up with us later. We must get to Sir Degore's manor quickly."

"You go on ahead," Merlin answered him. "We'll catch up as soon as we can!" And with that, Sir Bors threw his hands up in frustration, nodded his head, and trotted off, followed by Thorvald with Alan in his cart. Merlin turned to me and said, "Lancelot is certainly not there anyway, so there's no point in our going with them."

"He's not?" I responded in surprise. "How do you know that?"

"Because he's here," the mage said matter-of-factly, nodding toward the manor house ahead of us.

"Wha…who…wait a minute, what manor house is this? They said Astolat? So this is…"

"The manor house of Sir Bernard, lord of Guildford: home of the deeply mourned Fair Maid of Astolat and her brothers, the new knights Sir Lavayne and Sir Tirre."

"But what would they be doing holding Lancelot in Astolat? I thought they loved Lancelot here. Or that's what we were led to believe…"

"Elaine, the maid, loved Lancelot. Or at least as much as her adolescent heart could convince itself, and apparently would have done anything for his attention."

"Even to the point of killing herself? As you always say, no one ever actually dies of a broken heart."

Merlin shrugged that off. "We can't yet say precisely how she died. But to continue, Sir Lavayne also clearly loves Lancelot, or at least is devoted to him as his lord and mentor. But Sir Bernard? He was happy that Lancelot sponsored his sons for knighthood, certainly, but how can a father forget that his only daughter's death must be laid at Sir Lancelot's feet?"

"So Bernard is behind this?"

Merlin shook his head. "That does not seem likely. Like King Bagdemagus, his position is too much dependent on Arthur's good will. But like Bagdemagus, he may turn a blind eye on his sons' indiscretions."

"So you're saying that…Sir Tirre is behind all of this?"

Merlin nodded. "God's snowy white beard, think about it, boy! Thorvald said that the knight who gave him the false message from the queen was young, with a blank shield and a plain white surcoat, like a very new knight. Like your own, in fact. Tirre was just inducted into the fellowship of the Table the day you were. From the beginning, if you recall, Tirre was more angry than saddened by his sister's death. Remember his reaction when the boat was found on the river? And it was always Lavayne, not Tirre, who was at Lancelot's side. Tirre may have even been jealous of the attention the Great Knight paid to his brother. But it was the shame of his sister's rejection that angered him the most against Lancelot. Why not imprison him here and so, cause him to miss the queen's trial, shaming Lancelot in his turn?"

I mused on that. "It was Tirre, I recall, who seemed to relish in Lancelot's dishonor at riding in the cart. Perhaps this scheme only occurred to him when the cart episode redounded to Lancelot's credit rather than his shame. But are you certain he's holding Lancelot prisoner, and hasn't killed him?"

"Of course I'm not certain, boy! We just have to hope that's the case. But I do think that Sir Tirre's goal is to shame Lancelot, as his family was shamed, and so he will want Lancelot alive to feel that shame."

"Well, but when did you figure this out? I mean, you didn't say anything at the Red Ox."

"No," Merlin said. "I actually didn't put it together until we found the girl's ribbon here just now. Come, let's move toward the manor. Cautiously, to be sure. You'd better walk Achilles so we approach quietly and don't scare them into doing anything rash in that house. We need to recover the girl, the dog, and Lancelot himself, so we have some work ahead of us tonight."

We walked with purpose but with care along that path, the oaks and aspens on either side of the way throwing long shadows as it moved toward compline. "But why did Elizabeth's ribbon bring it home to you?"

"Well, you must have been suspicious yourself when she left the inn…"

"Why? I assumed she was upset at the suggestion that the queen and Lancelot were lovers."

The old man shook his head again. "Not a bit of it. Thorvald's suggestion wasn't that clear, especially to a somewhat sheltered thirteen-year-old girl."

"She's not *that* sheltered," I argued.

"Don't burn me with the facts, boy! Anyway, if that is what had upset her, she would have gone to her room as she claimed to be doing, rather than heading straight out the door. She knew exactly where she was going. Something that was said at that table made her suspect who the culprit must be."

"Why didn't she just tell us then?"

"You may have noticed yourself," Merlin said, "that she is a rather independent girl. She wanted to see if she was right first. And so she came straight here. Having grown up in Winchester, she knew just where she needed to come. I suspect she may even have known Bernard's family beforehand."

"Or at least knew of them, as an important local family. Even if she did not know Sir Tirre from before, I noticed that they did spend some time together during the queen's Maying celebration, and the time we were on the road to Gorre, and imprisoned there. Whatever made her suspect Tirre, it may have happened during that time."

Merlin, walking slowly with his head bowed, and leaning more than usual upon his staff, murmured, "What was it now? Something about the boot and the lily and the laurel?"

I turned to him in surprise. "'The boot that tramples the white lily impedes the laurel,' I believe was the prophecy you muttered. But that was long before this business of Lancelot began. You think there's a connection? How could you have been foreseeing the answer to a question that you weren't even aware was going to be asked yet?"

Merlin looked up, his eyes now focused on the manor house just a furlong or so ahead of us. "The mystery had already been initiated," he growled. "The mystery of who actually killed Elaine of Astolat. God's elbows, Gildas, our culprit here may be more dangerous than we feared. If Sir Tirre has Lancelot imprisoned, he is definitely 'impeding the laurel': he's preventing Lancelot from achieving the glory that will fall to him when he defeats Meliagaunt in the lists. Bur if he's also the boot that trampled the pure white lily, then it was he who killed his own sister rather than let her live with the shame her rejection by Lancelot would bring her. If he is capable of such an act, then I fear not only for Sir Lancelot's safety but for that of the lady Elizabeth—and your infernal dog as well! Let's get to that house quickly, boy."

The house we approached was not so imposing nor as well-fortified as most manor houses. Sir Bernard was not a particularly wealthy lord, and his house was a waddle and daub construction more typical of an artisan's house than the kind of stone edifice one might have expected of the lord of a manor. Nor were there guard towers or a moat. And there couldn't have been more than two or three knights present, in addition to Sir Bernard and, we assumed Sir Tirre. Sir Lavayne I knew to be still at Camelot. But it was a large house, perhaps one hundred feet wide as we approached and, from what I could see, I guessed sixty feet deep. There were two floors in the house, and as we came to the large wooden front doors with a modern Gothic pointed arch above them, I could guess that it would open into the great hall, where I expected the servants of the house would be preparing to settle in for the night. There were no servants outside to deal with unexpected visitors, and I wondered whether there had been earlier when Lady Elizabeth had arrived. I saw no stable here—I assumed it must be in the rear of the house—so I tied Achilles' bridle to the branch of a small oak that stood not far from the front door, and Merlin took his staff and banged on the door loud enough to wake the dead.

It was about a minute later that the heavy door creaked open and a bent, white-haired crone dressed simply in a black linen gown stood in the doorway eyeing us suspiciously. "Your business?" she asked in a voice that was far from encouraging.

"My lady," Merlin said, putting on his courtier's voice. "My profoundest apologies for having disturbed this house at such a late hour. We are pilgrims in town for the festival tomorrow, and my young friend and I are here in search of a companion of ours whom we have lost, but who seems to have come down this road to this house. Is it possible that she has been here? That perhaps she has sought refuge in this house for the evening? Her name is Lady Elizabeth of Winchester, if that is any help to you."

The woman's eyes narrowed and her jaw seemed to bulge out as she clenched her teeth. She was having none of us. "Begone, ye silver-tongued rascal! We've got no welcome for beggars or highwaymen. Scat, before I call the young master and have him throw you out bodily!" As she began to close the door, Merlin inserted his staff to pry it back open, and as he did so, he stood up to his full formidable height and adopted his booming, intimidating wizard voice.

"Madame, far from being a beggar, I am Lord Merlin of Camelot, adviser and friend to Arthur, King of Logres and your sovereign lord. You will answer to me immediately, without any more of this haughty speech, or I will bring the whole might of Arthur's imperial army down upon this puny manor and you, mistress, will be nothing more than a greasy spot on the floor of a ruined shell of a house. Answer me *now*!"

I won't say she was happy about it, but the old woman definitely changed her approach. She was not going to be the one that turned away the king's messenger. "Come in, then," she said. "But ye'll have to talk to the young master. I don't know anything about no Lady Eleanor or Ellen or whatever it is."

"Then by all means, take us to your young master," Merlin said as we stepped into the great hall. This "young" master, I assumed, must be Sir Tirre. In the great hall were perhaps twenty servants scattered around, preparing for bed. To the left I could see was the small family chapel. To the right was a dining room and, through that room, a buttery and a pantry, which formed a buffer between the diners and the kitchen itself. At the rear of the great hall was an open wooden staircase that led to the family's private solars on the second floor. Beneath those second-floor rooms, I guessed, there would be storage rooms on the ground floor.

Our ancient guide led us slowly up those wooden steps to a corridor with several heavy wooden doors. She brought us to the second door to the right of the stairs, and Merlin, asserting his authority, did not wait for the woman to knock, but thundered on the door with his own staff instead. An angry growl arose from behind the door, and moments later a surly looking Sir Tirre yanked open the door. "What the devil is it now?" he roared as he reached the threshold, but abruptly changed his manner when he was confronted by Merlin and me.

"Good evening, Sir Tirre," Merlin purred, all courtly and polite once more. "Sorry to have disturbed you. We crave a brief word with you, by your leave."

Momentarily stunned, Tirre gazed wide-eyed at Merlin, then at me, then back at Merlin, finally clearing his throat and murmuring, "My lord Merlin, what a surprise to see you here. And Sir Gildas of Cornwall. To what do we owe the honor of your visit?" And with that, he nodded to our elderly guide and she made a slight bow and turned back down the stairs.

"It's a matter involving our traveling companion, the queen's lady-in-waiting, Lady Elizabeth of Winchester. Uh…may we enter?"

I don't know whether Merlin thought we were going to catch him with Elizabeth in his room, tied up or lying unconscious or worse, but of course there was nothing in the room. It was not a large chamber, perhaps no more than fifteen feet wide and twenty feet long, though there was a high ceiling crossed with oaken beams and, facing us as we entered, a huge arched window that extended from floor to ceiling, through which bright sunlight could fill the room (the reason, of course, such private chambers were called "solars").

The room was sparsely furnished, with only a small curtained bed against one wall, and a trunk at its foot. There were no tapestries or other hangings to cover the drab walls. The floor showed signs of having been recently repaired, or at least partially repaired. This building seemed a bit shabby, at least by the standards of lords' manor houses. Still, Sir Tirre waved us into the chamber, where we could at least stand and talk with a bit of privacy.

"So what's this about the lady Elizabeth?" he asked. "She's gotten herself lost, has she?"

"Actually, she seems to have had a bit of help." I produced the blue hair ribbon. "We found this ribbon of hers tangled in one of the bushes along the lane leading here."

"So she was coming in this direction, was she? Curious," Tirre said. "I wonder why she didn't stop at the house?"

"So you're saying she didn't?" I demanded.

Tirre looked at me with a slow fire behind his calculating eyes. "Rest assured, she did not. I haven't seen her since I left Camelot after returning from that ordeal in Gorre. I did get to know her a little bit on that adventure. Morose young thing, I thought. Prone to flights of imagination, as I recall."

Merlin was staring down at the floor of the room. The recent repairs had left it with two different surfaces: A newer, lighter wood—pine perhaps?—covered the floor on the essentially empty half of the room next to the tall window, while an older, darker, more worn oak formed the floor under the bed and chest. The old necromancer took a step or two into that newer half of the room.

"And my dog?" I asked paying little attention to Merlin. "She was chasing Elizabeth down the lane leading to your manor. I don't suppose she's disturbed you here within the last half hour or so, has she?"

"Oh, was that what that was?" Tirre said, seating himself on his chest. "I thought I heard a lot of barking out in the path a while ago. Was that your borzoi hound named after the queen?" He smiled as if he thought the name was quite amusing. But it rang false to me. As I've said before, Guinevere almost never barked. Either he was lying, or, if she *was* barking, something was very wrong. I stepped over to Merlin, the better to look straight across into Tirre's face.

Tirre, still seated on his chest, reached his right arm back toward the poster of his bed as if he were stretching, and Merlin narrowed his eyes. I suspected the movement as well, thinking Tirre might have a weapon concealed somewhere in the bedclothes. Merlin laid a hand on my own right arm, and calmly led me to the other side of the room, closer to Sir Tirre. Then I felt Merlin's hand tense against my biceps, and I knew he was about to take things in a whole different direction.

"In fact, Sir Tirre, our true purpose here is not to inquire after our companion or the dog."

"Oh?" Tirre looked up, blinking his eyes innocently. "So, what then?"

"We have come to discover where you have imprisoned Sir Lancelot!" Merlin shouted suddenly, hoping to startle Sir Tirre, but he seemed unmoved by the accusation.

"Me? Imprison Lancelot of the Lake? You're raving, old man. Lost your wits with age, have you?"

Now Merlin stepped boldly onto the new section of the floor to look Sir Tirre directly in the eye. But just as he did so, a sudden loud and plaintive howl came from the floor below us. Guinevere, having heard Merlin's shout, was letting her presence be known in no uncertain terms, and for a moment Tirre, startled by the noise, was taken aback, and seemed unsure what to do next.

Then a good number of things happened at once. Sir Tirre's hand shot toward his bedpost, which he grabbed and pulled toward him. At that moment the new floor of the room collapsed downward as Merlin, with far more dexterity than I would have thought possible for the old man, leaped to the other side of the room with a single step while I, a bit slow on the uptake, reached for my sword, as I saw that already Tirre had grasped his own sword from behind the chest. From below, Guinevere had indeed now started to bark. With one quick sidelong glance, I could see her trying to leap out of that dungeon, but the straw-covered floor was some ten feet below and even she could not jump that high. Beside her in the straw lay the motionless form of Lady Elizabeth, and I could see a pool of blood beneath the poor girl's head. And against the wall of that space, his mouth gagged and his hands and feet shackled, stood a ragged but incensed looking Sir Lancelot.

I had no time to take in that scene, for Sir Tirre was squaring off to do battle. I don't need to tell you that it was at that moment I deeply regretted having parted with my mail coat earlier in the day. On the other hand, I could rejoice that I had in fact held on to my sword. And Tirre was not wearing armor either, so at least we were evenly matched in that regard. There were few swords in Camelot that could match Almace for quality, but this being the first time I had ever used it in earnest, I could only hope that I had the skill and strength to do justice to the sword.

I faced Tirre with Merlin at my back and the door behind him, the open trap door to our left and the wall on our right. Tirre's bed was behind him and the open space to his right. With the bed and chest taking up space behind him, that left us a small space of about eight feet by ten in which to fight, always with the danger of falling over into the dungeon. And I had the disadvantage of the wall, which would hinder the range of my sword arm. Merlin, seeing my predicament, tried to give me a bit more room by scuttling out the door onto the landing at the top of the stairs.

Tirre continued to stand at the ready, his sword held out in front of him angling across his chest, his feet spread apart with his right foot somewhat ahead of the left to make it easier to come forward with a thrust. Yet he was hesitating, and I realized that, as a brand-new knight with a white shield like mine, this was also his first time using a sword in true mortal combat. That encouraged me, for unlike Tirre I *had* been through single combat at least once before, during the Grail quest. And that gave me a quick boost of self-assurance. I thought that perhaps I could undermine Tirre's own confidence.

"Why do you hesitate? Afraid?" I tried a clumsy taunt.

"Of you? Why, you're nothing but the queen's glorified page boy. You're in my own manor, fool."

Behind me I could sense an uproar as the rest of the household, hearing the turmoil in Sir Tirre's solar, was about to storm the stairs in a mob. I could hear Sir Bernard, lord of the manor, entering below and demanding to know what was happening, and I began to doubt the wisdom of Merlin and me rushing off by ourselves to beard the lion in his own den.

But I'd underestimated Merlin, something I should have known by then never to do. He stood at the top of the staircase, reached into one of the wide sleeves of his threadbare grey robe and, with an elaborate gesture designed to capture the attention of anyone in sight of him, flung a handful of dust down the steps with the bellowed command "Incendia!" and there followed a thunderous clap and a burst of fire that singed anyone close enough to the steps to feel the heat. With a collective gasp, the crowd backed away, no one daring to approach the steps again.

"Stay back, you fools, or incur my wrath," the old man declaimed with newly won authority from the landing. "I am Merlin, right hand of Arthur, King of Logres, and master of all the arts of necromancy! I will rain fire upon you without mercy if you approach these steps again!" I smiled inwardly, knowing Merlin never carried more than enough Greek fire for a single such blast. Fortunately, nobody else knew that.

Turning toward Sir Tirre, Merlin continued his verbal onslaught. "Even now, Sir Bors and Corporal Alan of the Castle Guard of Camelot are approaching this house, and in their company is the dwarf Thorvald, driver of the cart that ferried Sir Lancelot here, ready to identify this man," and here Merlin pointed a bony, accusing finger at Sir Tirre's face, "as the perjured felon who unlawfully kidnapped and imprisoned the king's chief knight."

That may have been wishful thinking—or a colossal bluff—on Merlin's part, but at the sound, Sir Tirre's eyes blinked and lost some of their cold defiance, and when I saw that this was accompanied by a momentary shakiness in his knees, I struck.

I swung my sword up and began to bring it down in an arc toward Tirre's unprotected skull, but he just managed to recover and swing his blade up to parry my edge with the flat of his sword, so that it slid off toward his left shoulder. He then tried to swipe at me with his right hand, but for that move, he had to swing his right back up over his head and then shift his body to the left to bring the sword back in a sweeping arc around from the side.

I knew I should be in constant motion, but the close quarters and the wall to my right made movement difficult, allowing me to move freely forward or back but essentially nowhere else, other than simply ducking and feinting. I waited for him to begin his swipe toward my left side, holding my own sword point forward in my right hand, pulled as far back as I could bring it, my left foot pushed forward. As his blade swept toward me in its horizontal hew, I bent back as far as I could to avoid the sweep and, at the moment the point of his blade began to move past my throat and arc back toward the wall, I thrust forward with my right foot, bringing Almace forward in a straight stabbing motion toward his chest. He had enough control to spin to his left and back, following the sweep of his sword in that direction, and out of the way of my thrust, but my lunge had put me in a position then to sweep the sword diagonally down at his legs, though without much power. He had been hoping to bring his sword back in a backhanded swipe downward at my right shoulder and head from where his sword had ended up after his last unsuccessful hew, but before he could begin, my sword had slashed his right ankle and drawn blood, causing him to stumble slightly toward his right— toward the trapdoor—and the wall to his left hindered the downward sweep of his sword, so that I had a chance to bring my own sword back in an upward hew aimed at his left thigh, which he was in no position to parry. Almace slashed deep into his thigh, and he fell to his left knee, at which point I moved in to grapple with him, shoving him in the hope of pushing him onto his back. But in shoving me away, he slipped toward his right, and tumbled over the edge of the floor.

There was a brief, startled scream and then a dull thud as Sir Tirre hit the floor of that storehouse or dungeon, landing flat on his back. A low groan indicated he was still conscious after that ten-foot fall, but when I looked over the edge to see him lying where he had landed two feet from the still unmoving body of the Lady Elizabeth, I could see that there was no more fight in him.

***

As it turned out, Merlin's ruse concerning Sir Bors and the others bearing down on Sir Bernard's manor house was not such a bluff after all. Having stopped once more at Sir Degore's manor, and after briefly speaking to the knight and any retainers he had in the house, Thorvald had categorically cleared all of them of having been the knight who had persuaded him to trap Sir Lancelot, and with a grudging apology, Sir Bors had given up his crusade to convict Sir Meliagaunt or his supporters of this crime. He decided to hurry back to find us, in the hope we might have discovered some new clue, and on reaching the lane where we had turned off, he saw Achilles tied in front of the manor of Astolat's front door. Wasting no time, he galloped Pegasus up the lane and tied him next to Achilles, then unsheathed his sword and pounded on the front door, demanding entrance. By that time Merlin had cowed the household into standing to the side while he consulted with Sir Bernard, telling the poor man that his son was lying on the floor of his own trap, and urging him to open the storehouse so that we could release the prisoners.

Merlin told the old woman who had let us in the house to open the door to Sir Bors before he broke it down, and this she did just as Bors was putting himself in position to kick the door in if he could. He rushed in with sword drawn, followed by Alan, an arrow notched in his longbow, and Thorvald, swinging the end of the rope from his cart around as if to flog someone with it.

While all of this was going on below in the great hall, I sheathed Almace and knelt down at the rim of the trap. Gripping the edge of the floor, I gingerly let my body hang down into the dungeon. Then I let myself drop the remaining yard or so, landing on my feet. I blinked and stood back against one of the walls, letting my eyes adjust to the dimmer light in the storeroom. Guinevere left the unconscious Elizabeth's side immediately and came bobbing over to me, panting with excitement but also, I realized, with some pain, since she was limping and favoring her left rear paw. "Good girl, it's all right now," I told her, and she licked my hand.

I was most concerned with Lady Elizabeth, but the blood under her head warned me that realistically I could probably do nothing for her right now, and I knew that Lancelot was the first priority at this point. Even before I attended to the Great Knight, however, I knew that I must make sure of Sir Tirre, since it would not do to have him come at me from behind as I tried to free Sir Lancelot.

Tirre lay on his back, moaning softly. As I crept toward him, I found his sword, which had sprung from his hand as he hit the floor and lay several feet away from him. Guinevere followed me as I picked it up and stepped over to his prone body, pointing his sword to his throat.

But he was in no mood—or condition—to put up any resistance. "I yield, I yield," he said hoarsely. "Get me a physician. I think I've broken my back."

I squinted at him for a moment "Move your right leg," I said.

With a bit of effort, he raised his leg a few inches from the floor, then put it down again.

"You'll be all right," I told him. "You couldn't do that if your back was broken. You'll be fine—able to stand on your own two feet when they hang you."

I left him to chew on that for a while, and moved to where the chained and gagged Sir Lancelot looked toward me with eager blue eyes. His brown hair was filthy and hung like a wrung-out mop around his head. I tore the soiled rag from around his mouth and he breathed deeply, then began to spit to eradicate the taste of that gag from his lips and tongue. With a voice raspy from disuse, he said, "I am in your debt forever, Sir Gildas. I've never had to rely on somebody else to rescue *me*. Now I know what it's like to be on the other side. But I thank you less for my sake than for the queen's. My greatest fear was that I would miss the chance to defend her honor. I don't know how long I have been here, but surely I haven't missed the trial, have I?" He was actually shaking—with exhaustion or stress, or fear at having let down the queen, I couldn't say.

"No, no," I said, calming him. "Tomorrow we will get you back to Camelot. The battle is the following day."

"Thank God," Lancelot said, hanging his head in exhausted relief.

At that moment, the door opened from the house, and in burst Merlin, Sir Bernard, Bors and Alan, with Thorvald and two of the lord's retainers. The rest of the household waited outside the door. Bors rushed to Lancelot's side, and Merlin stepped over to Sir Tirre— to press him, I realized, for the key that would open the shackles on Lancelot's arms and legs. And while Bors and Alan focused on Lancelot, and Merlin and Thorvald dealt with Tirre, I was finally able to concentrate on Elizabeth.

She lay sprawled on her belly, her unbraided hair flung about her head like a carelessly tossed garment, her skirts disheveled so that her thin, bare legs were visible, bending below the hems at odd angles. Guinevere had already lain back down at her side and was trying to lick the blood away from a great wound on the side of her head.

I could see that she'd been struck by a hard, sharp object, and though she was breathing, I despaired for her life. But she responded momentarily to the dog's attentions, and her eyes flickered open for a moment. She blinked and looked at me, and I cried out, "Elizabeth! Can you hear me? What have you done?"

She blinked again and gave me a very wan half-smile. "Found the culprit?" she answered in a very weak voice.

"How did you know it was Tirre?" I whispered to her, stroking her hair very gently.

She scowled at me and then closed her eyes as if her head were hurting badly. "What, you saying I wasn't smart enough? By the way he talked, of course. 'Rest assured.' 'Lancelot of the Lake.' Nobody else in Camelot says…" but her voice trailed off at that point and she slipped back out of consciousness.

"She needs a surgeon," I moaned, to no one in particular.

But Merlin loomed suddenly directly behind me, then bent down to examine her wound. Then he opened one of her eyes and let it close again. "So that he can bleed her? That's the last thing she needs. She's bled enough. There is a hermit in the neighborhood, an old ex-knight, Sir Baldwin of Brittany. Bors knows where his cell is. He is learned in the arts of healing—it was he who healed Sir Lancelot of his wounds after the tournament here. Perhaps he can be convinced to come and have a look at this girl."

"I'll ride to get him," said Bors, who had, by now, also come to look over my shoulder. "As soon as we get Lancelot back to the Red Ox where he can get some decent food and a long rest."

As for Thorvald, he was using his rope to tie up Sir Tirre, who had realized he actually could sit up without too much pain and did so now, trussed up and petulant, on the floor of the room, with Corporal Alan of Winchester pointing a notched longbow at his midsection.

But there was a fire burning in my heart that I could not keep controlled. I rounded on Tirre and shouted in his face, "What did you do to her, you villainous bastard?"

He gave Lady Elizabeth's prone body a side glance and then gave a listless sort of shrug. "She…she became a nuisance," he said, spreading his hands awkwardly, it being a difficult thing to do while tied up. "I was coming up the path toward the road and she came hurrying along it, rushing up to me. She doesn't," he paused for a moment. "She doesn't temper anything she says. She rushed up to me and demanded, 'Where have you got Sir Lancelot? I know it's you,' she said. 'Don't deny it!' Well, you understand, I couldn't have her standing in the middle of the road shouting such things at me, it wouldn't do at all. I tried to shush her, to reason with her, to get her to come and discuss it in the manor house, but no, she'd have none of that. She couldn't trust me, she said. I had no chivalry, she said. I had to stop it. I reached out to grab her, and I had unsheathed my sword as well, you know, to frighten her, but she ducked away. All I got was her hair and when I grasped that, she twisted her head wildly, I swung my other hand to try to make her stop and…and I…"

"You struck her across the head with your drawn sword," I said matter-of-factly.

"I did," he said, and looked away with what may have been shame.

"I don't understand this," blabbered an exasperated Sir Bernard. "What has happened to you, Tirre? Where has all this come from?" Sir Lancelot, leaning heavily on Sir Bors' shoulders, had by now gotten to his feet and was standing in what was forming into an accusing half-circle around the bound and helpless Sir Tirre. But it was Merlin who now decided it was time to take over the interrogation.

"Sir Tirre, you laid an elaborate trap to catch Sir Lancelot and to hold him away from the queen's trial. I assume you used this false floor trapdoor of yours to capture Lancelot?"

Tirre merely nodded but Lancelot volunteered more: "I was told that my sovereign lady was in need of my services," he said. There were three of us in the room—Bors, Merlin, and I—who understood that he intended this euphemistically. But he went on, "Imagine my surprise when Thorvald's contact brought me here, to the estate of Astolat, which I know so well. Naturally I knew Sir Tirre, and had no reason I knew of to distrust him. He showed me into the room upstairs. I entered in the dark, and while I was groping about he released the spring of the trap and I fell to the floor below. I was stunned, and by the time I came to, I was shackled to the wall and gagged. I've been there for several days, with only occasional water and a bit of bread or cheese to survive. But I still don't understand why you did this," he said, turning to Tirre. "Do you hate the queen so much that you wanted her burnt?"

"Hate the queen?" Tirre exclaimed, with what seemed unfeigned outrage. And there was genuine pride in his voice when he followed that with, "I was one of the Queen's Knights! Chosen as her elite guard. Do you think I would have allowed anyone to harm her if I could help it? But she is in no real danger. The king will not allow her to be burnt." For myself, I could never quite understand why everyone seemed to be of this opinion. Four years ago, when she had faced the false accusations of Sir Mador, the king had not stepped in to stop the trial. He believed it had to go on, and Guinevere was saved only by the heroic efforts of Merlin and me. Oh, and Lancelot helped a bit as well. But the gist was that for Arthur, the law is the law, and knights, queens, or, I suspected, even kings were not above it.

But Tirre went on: "It was you, not the queen, who were my target. You, the Great Knight, who came into my home and seduced my sister, shamed my family, and then left us in humiliation. And then had the gall to play the innocent all the while. How innocent was it to have worn my sister's sleeve and led her to believe she was your only love? You broke her heart!" This last was shouted, and I could see tears welling in old Sir Bernard's eyes as he nodded in agreement.

"And you mean for us to believe that she died of this broken heart?" Merlin asked, innocently.

"Of course! He as good as killed her, leaving her in that desolation," Tirre insisted. To that, I noticed, Sir Bernard was nodding sadly, tears glistening in his old eyes.

"'As good as' is not the same as 'did,' if I may be so bold as to point out the obvious," Merlin persisted. At that, Sir Bernard groaned, and buried his face in his hands, though Sir Tirre remained unmoved.

"But my lord Bernard," Lancelot addressed the old man directly. "You must admit, I never touched your fair daughter in any untoward manner, or promised her anything more than friendship. You know that she said so herself in that last letter that you wrote for her…"

The grieving father looked up, his head wobbling in confusion. "Letter?" he murmured. "What letter are you talking about? I wrote no letter…"

Now it was Lancelot's turn to be confused. "But…but surely, the letter…the letter that was taken from her dead fingers, the letter she dictated just before she died…"

"The letter," I broke in, looking straight at Sir Tirre, who had shrunk slightly from his previous bold posture. "The letter that *you*, Sir Tirre, claimed was in your father's handwriting!"

"Well…well, what does it matter who it was who wrote the letter? It was she herself who dictated it, so it comes to the same thing!" Sir Tirre, caught in his lie, tried to brazen it out.

"It makes a great deal of difference, boy!" Merlin, swelling to his most imposing height and voice. "It raises the question of why you would *lie* about who wrote the letter. About whether those were the girl's own words, or whether you composed them to make Lancelot look all the more guilty. About what the girl's true state of mind was when she died. And most importantly, about exactly *how* she died. People don't die of broken hearts, boy. How did your sister die?"

"She wanted to die! She said so herself," Sir Tirre, exposed and vulnerable, lashed out in a kind of righteous fury. "The words in the letter were her own feelings. I just put them on paper. She was miserable, and not least because she had shamed her family, her father's house and her brothers!"

Merlin looked intently into Tirre's face for a moment. "Such feelings are common at times of emotional crisis," he mused. "But they do pass. They would have passed in her case. If she hadn't been helped along. I have a feeling she was far less concerned about shaming her family than her brother was. *You* encouraged her grief and her shame. *You* fed her poison to help her in her death wish. You wrote that letter and put it into her hand so that her fingers would stiffen around it as her body went cold. But not as cold as you, her brother and her murderer."

Sir Tirre scoffed at the words, but Sir Bernard began to weep uncontrollably. "How could you, Tirre? To destroy your own fair sister…"

"She was a trollop, you old fool!" Tirre shrieked, turning on his father. Then, raising an accusing finger toward Lancelot, he added, "You know that she offered herself to that recreant knight there! She would have shamed us forever in the eyes of all the world, for some armored churlish bully on horseback!"

"Um…he *is* the son of a king…" I volunteered quietly.

Tirre stared at me momentarily as if I'd missed the point completely, then seemed to clap his mouth shut and sat hunched together, hugging his knees as best he could between his arms, with his hands bound before him.

Of course, I *hadn't* missed the point. It wasn't about birth, it was about public image. This was another argument about chivalry. You are what your reputation says you are. If his sister offered herself outside of marriage to Sir Lancelot, she was a slut. If Lancelot encouraged such behavior, he was a churl. And as far as Tirre was concerned, if he prevented such behavior, if he stepped in and protected the honor of his family, by whatever means necessary—even to the point of murdering his own sister—he was justified, honorable, and chivalrous, providing no one saw through the pious image of courtesy and respectability he had constructed as a whited sepulcher to house the corruption within.

Sir Tirre would say no more. Cowed by a circle of accusing eyes, he merely hung his head sullenly, and Corporal Alan of Winchester stepped forward and performed his official duty: "In the king's name and by the authority of the king's guard, I place you, Sir Tirre of Astolat, under arrest for kidnapping, unlawful imprisonment, obstruction of justice, the murder of your sister, and the attempted murder of this poor maiden lying here. We'll be taking you back to Camelot to face the king's judgment—and his justice."

After that, the drama was over. Sir Bernard's men put up no resistance, and the old man made no argument, merely declared dejectedly that he would make preparations immediately to travel with a small retinue to Camelot within the next two days, in order to witness the outcome of his son's arrest. It was hard to read the conflicting emotions in Sir Bernard's face, twisted as it was with renewed grief over his daughter's death, and distress and horror over his son's heinous deeds.

***

We gently placed the fragile, unresponsive body of Lady Elizabeth, still clinging tenaciously to life, into the cart, where we also carried Sir Tirre, now himself the sort of disreputable criminal such carts were notorious for ferrying to their punishments or executions. He protested, as of course he would, but Merlin quashed him in no uncertain terms, telling him that if he didn't like the idea of being dishonored, he ought not to do dishonorable things. Alan sat in the cart as well, holding his bow half at the ready, just in case Sir Tirre tried to escape, though how far he could get tied hand and foot as he was I could not say. Merlin rode behind me on Achilles, and Sir Bors took the weak and shaky Lancelot before him on his own Pegasus. Guinevere, of course, rode in the cart, refusing to leave Lady Elizabeth's side. And in that fashion, we rode a very grim couple of miles back to the west gate of Winchester. Sir Bors took Lancelot into the Red Ox, and told us he would ride immediately to Brother Baldwin's hermit cell, promising to bring the old healer back within the hour. Merlin opted to go with him, since he knew where we would be taking Lady Elizabeth—to Sir Lowell's house in the city. I loaned Merlin Achilles, so that no time would be lost in ferrying Brother Baldwin back to Winchester. We stopped next at the jailhouse, where we had agreed Alan should hold Sir Tirre overnight, and there, we dropped off the corporal and his prisoner.

Thorvald in his cart, with me following close behind on foot, drove silently through the shadowy streets to the dark house of Sir Lowell. It took a good deal of loud pounding on his door before he cautiously opened it and, recognizing me from earlier in the day, seemed to sense some new catastrophe and threw the door open to demand what was the matter. He wore a loosely fitting robe he had apparently thrown on upon rising from bed, and held a lighted candelabra that flickered when he opened the door. I don't have the words to describe the depth of pain his face radiated when he saw his daughter lying helpless and senseless in the back of that cart. He wept openly as Thorvald and I carried her gingerly from the cart into the house, and laid her down on the one bed in the place, from which he had just risen. Guinevere, who was not to be denied, leapt into the bed to lie at her side. Sir Lowell put the candelabra on a table at the bed's head, and the three of us brought chairs to watch over her as we awaited Brother Baldwin's healing ministrations.

There was nothing to be said, and Sir Lowell was beyond listening to any comfort, so we sat in silence. What surprised me in all this was Thorvald. The dwarf, who had such a hard exterior, toughened by transporting every kind of criminal and by seeing a very rough justice brought down on their heads, so that even the abuse and humiliation of victims guilty of minor infractions could not affect him, was deeply moved by the plight of this girl. "She ain't afraid of nothin' that one!" He explained to me in a whisper. "If sheer toughness can win the day, she'll beat this thing!"

It seemed like days, but could not have been more than an hour and a half before there was pounding again on Sir Lowell's door. "Don't stir," I told the anguished father. "I'll let them in." I opened the door to Merlin, Bors, and a very wrinkled old man with a gray tonsure and a body and face that tended toward roundness. He wore a brown woolen religious habit, and his jowls flopped around a good bit as he talked. But he had keen brown eyes and carried a small satchel that contained, I learned, a number of herbs and potions as well as bandages and other paraphernalia of healing.

As Brother Baldwin set to work searching the bloody wound on Lady Elizabeth's head, Guinevere lay down at the foot of the bed, ceding her place to the hermit but refusing to leave her post as the girl's guardian. Sir Bors backed out of the room. Merlin and I followed him and he told us that he must be getting back to Sir Lancelot. "He has to get a good night's rest and also proper nourishment, so he can make the ride back to Camelot tomorrow and be strong enough to face Sir Meliagaunt's sword on Saint Thomas's Day. But the girl is in my prayers." And with that he was gone.

"Much good that should do her," Merlin muttered.

I let that go, feeling much the same way at the time, and said only, "We must put our faith in Brother Baldwin's skills." Merlin gave a soft groan in the back of his throat, and we moved again into the sickroom.

Looking quite grave, the hermit looked down at the fragile girl, bending over to study her head wound up close. "Can someone give me more light?" he asked. I popped up, and Sir Lowell pointed to a mantel across the room where another candelabra stood. I brought it over and lit the candles from those already burning on the bedside table, and held it as close as I dared to the gash in the girl's skull. Brother Bertrand sighed audibly.

But he set to work immediately, first cleaning the wound as best he could with vinegar, then fixing a poultice that he began to bandage around the wound.

"What is that?" the deeply concerned Thorvald demanded.

"It is a poultice of honey and yarrow," the hermit said absently, focusing his attention on the girl, rather than Thorvald.

"The honey will help ease pain and swelling," Merlin told Thorvald, trying to alleviate the dwarf's own stress. "Yarrow is also called *Achillea millefolium*, Achilles' milfoil—named after the great Greek warrior, you see, because he was supposed to have used it on his Myrmidons' battle wounds. Helps them heal, they say." Thorvald took a deep breath and then let it out. He seemed willing to accept the hermit's treatment. Sir Lowell simply sat with his head in his hands—praying or lamenting, I could not say which.

When Brother Bertrand had finished with the dressing, he stepped away from the girl and faced the four of us, wiping the sweat from his round face with the sleeve of his habit. "The girl is now running a fever in addition to her wound, which is, I will not mislead you, severe." He shook his head slightly to indicate his doubts, and his jowls quivered with the motion. "I believe if she survives the night, we may say she has a chance of recovery. But the next few hours will be crucial."

Sir Lowell moved his chair closer to the bed and held his daughter's hand. I got up to let Merlin sit and to look for another chair or two, for myself and for the hermit. And so began the long, dark watch. No one spoke. Brother Bertrand rose every half hour or so to check the lady Elizabeth's pulse and to test her fever, and each time he returned to his chair shaking his jowls.

It was one of the darkest nights of my life, and not only because of the shadows in that room. This young girl, whom I knew nothing of just a few short weeks ago, had grown in my outlook to become something formidable in my world: a possible wife, if the queen had her way. A possible comfort for the absence of my love, if Rosemounde could be believed. A bold and outspoken advocate in her own right. A presence I, and the court, had only just realized would be sorely missed if lost.

I had dozed off, I can't say for how long, when I awoke with a start. Something had changed. I listened, and could hear nothing from the bed. That nothing was the change: there was no sound of breathing. Suddenly a great and mournful howl split the silence. Guinevere had heard it, too. She sat up next to Elizabeth and moaned loudly and unrestrained to the heavens.

The watch was over. That great soul in that delicate body would breathe no more. Lady Elizabeth of Winchester was dead.

CHAPTER THIRTEEN
TRIAL BY COMBAT

"Whoever has any business before the king's court of justice come forward now and state your case!" bellowed Sir Ywain, acting as Arthur's herald, as the king sat in majesty on a raised dais, wearing his purple robes of state, lined with ermine at the sleeves and neck. His heavy bejeweled crown was on his head today, and he held his orb and scepter, symbols of his royal and imperial power.

A good thirty yards away, on the south end of the field that had been paced off for this trial, on two simpler chairs, sat the accused: Sir Kay, who had chosen to wear his armor and his surcoat, as if, were he called upon at the last moment to defend himself in the lists, he was prepared; and of course, Queen Guinevere herself, who, being accused of adultery and treason, had wisely chosen to wear a simple gown of modest white velvet, with lacing in the front and simple sleeves rather than the exaggerated sort that hung down to her knees on some of her other gowns. She even covered her golden hair with a white barbette and wimple, wrapping her entire head and neck and passing it under her chin. I had never seen her so covered up—usually, as queen, she was perfectly comfortable letting her long hair hang down free and unfettered, often without ornament or braid. But modesty was the requirement of the day, and she had embraced the part.

"Ah, Gildas, I look like a meek little nun, don't I?" she whispered when she saw me. But there was none of the lightness or irony in her voice that I'd come to expect over the years. The return of Lady

Elizabeth's body had cast a dark pall over the mood at Camelot, most severely over the queen's own household, though the anxiety and stress of the past several days had eased with the return of Sir Lancelot.

Our return trip from Winchester had been uneventful. The hardest thing about it had been the logistics. We'd wrapped the remains of Lady Elizabeth in a makeshift shroud and laid her in Thorvald's cart, where we also had to put Sir Tirre, bound hand and foot and tied, as well, to the side of the wagon. The rest of us rode back, but since Sir Lowell was determined to come with us, insisting that he could not leave his poor daughter to make this last trip on her own, I volunteered to loan him my own Achilles for the ride to Camelot. He had been forced to sell his own horse to ease his debts. Lancelot took the gentle palfrey that Elizabeth had ridden to Winchester along with Corporal Alan. As for me, I'd seen and heard so much about this cart that I was curious about riding in it, and I reasoned that by now, Sir Lancelot had dispelled the notion that riding in the cart must necessarily mean dishonor, at least among reasonable people. So I opted to sit in the cart, though not in the bed, where Tirre sat and where Elizabeth's body lay; there was no room there to sit comfortably, especially since Guinevere, still limping a bit and still unwilling to leave the dead girl's side, insisted on lying next to her in the cart. I sat alongside Thorvald in the driver's seat, though that too was a bit cramped, but I think the miserable dwarf was glad of the company, for he had so admired the spirit of the young lady he was bringing home that his mood was severely dampened.

But I was most interested in observing the attitude of Sir Tirre as he sat slumped over in the back. He had not spoken a word since being tied into the cart. Nor, I observed, had he taken his eyes off the body of the girl he had killed. As we rolled out of Winchester's west gate, I saw tears glistening in his eyes, and as we started down the long road to King Arthur's castle, the tears began to roll down Sir Tirre's cheeks. Whether he was weeping with guilt and shame at Lady Elizabeth's murder, or at the murder of his sister Elaine, or at the loss of his own honor and reputation, or simply with regret at being caught, I had no way of knowing.

It was the morning of Saint Swithin's day as we left Winchester, and crowds of pilgrims were coming along the road into town, while we pushed on against the current in the opposite direction. In the noise and bustle of the holiday, I sat beside Thorvald, quiet and melancholy, wondering if there was any way Saint Swithin could manage to miraculously put back together the lives, broken like eggshells, that surrounded that little cart.

***

That was yesterday morning. By late afternoon, we'd arrived in Camelot, and while there was much rejoicing over Lancelot's return, Arthur had seen his weakened state and frowned with worry. Sir Lavayne, ever Lancelot's most vigorous supporter, was mortified beyond all measure by his brother's perfidy, and begged the king to allow him to take up the battle with Meliagaunt in Lancelot's stead, to blot out the dishonor Sir Tirre's vicious acts had brought upon his family. I smiled inwardly, noting how very similar the brothers were, after all, in their obsession with honor and its attendant virtue, chivalry.

Lancelot, of course, would not hear of anyone fighting his battle for him, especially after so much trouble had been taken to find him and return him to Camelot for just this reason. But the king made one concession in Lancelot's favor: rather than having a large jousting field on which the combatants would have to charge one another on horseback to begin the fray, Arthur had constructed this smaller area, framed by his own dais on the north, the box for the defendants, Kay and the queen, and their supporters on the south side, and rows of wooden benches sloped upward on the east and west sides, to allow the greater part of the king's retinue at Camelot to watch the proceedings. In this way, the sore and weakened Lancelot would be spared having to withstand, and to deliver, the buffets of a mounted shock cavalry charge against Meliagaunt. Instead, he could focus on the more skilled combat with the sword and shield necessitated by the smaller field, rather than the brute force of the joust.

And now he stood before the king, with Sir Meliagaunt to his right shouting out his answer to Sir Ywain's demand that he come forward and state his case. He had brought that bloody sheet as evidence, he said, of the queen's faithlessness and that of the king's own foster-brother, Sir Kay, a charge which he would prove against any proxy the two would bring against him. Guinevere sighed, and I murmured in her ear what I knew she wanted to hear, "Your Grace, I know you are as innocent of this charge as your saintly white garments proclaim. I am certain that God cannot permit Sir Meliagaunt to prosper in this trial." At that she smiled with some contentment, though I could see a bit of tension on Kay's face. My lady Rosemounde, whom the queen had begged to accompany her to sit on her right hand, looked at me approvingly and patted the queen's right shoulder when I had done. Merlin, standing behind Sir Kay, lowered his great shaggy brows at me and then rolled his eyes. Having been instrumental in finding the imprisoned Lancelot, he had been asked out of courtesy to watch from the queen's box, and Merlin had accepted the invitation—again, out of courtesy—and seemed intent on being inoffensive, though his expression seemed to imply I was toadying to the queen, whom we both knew may not be guilty of this *particular* charge of infidelity, but was far, far from innocent.

Sir Lancelot stood calmly, holding his helmet under his left arm and resting it against his side and the hilt of his sword, which hung from the belt that girdled his blue surcoat on which was embroidered his crest: three gold fleur-de-lys on an azure background. The same coat of arms was emblazoned on the shield that hung over his right shoulder. The surcoat of blue covered the long mail corslet that hung to his knees, and he wore a mail coif as well that protected his head. The hand balancing the helmet was bare, since he would be using this hand to hold his shield. His right hand, however, was protected by a mail sleeve with a leather palm to help him grip his sword. Having patiently waited for Meliagaunt to finish his rant, Lancelot now stepped forward and in a calm but booming voice made his answer:

"And I hereby fling this upstart Meliagaunt's unchivalrous words back into his face and attest that he lies in his throat. I take my oath before you, my liege, and before all these here assembled, and I swear on all the relics here in Caerleon Cathedral, that my sovereign lady Queen Guinevere is innocent of these charges you bring against her. She did not betray her lord King Arthur with the seneschal Sir Kay, neither at the time you accuse her of, nor at any other time. That both she and Sir Kay are innocent of these allegations I will defend with my life."

"Since there is no reconciliation possible and since each of you maintains the right of your own cause, then arm yourselves, and this question will be tested in combat!" King Arthur pronounced. And with that word, Sir Bors, acting as Lancelot's squire in this affair, stepped from the side and helped Sir Lancelot into his helmet, checking as well to see that all his armor was in place. At the same time, a squire from Gorre stepped to Sir Meliagaunt, fixed his own helmet in place, straightened the red surplice embroidered with the black chimera rampant—which was the coat of arms of the House of Gorre—ensured that his lord had a good grip on his shield that bore the same coat of arms, and then withdrew. The two combatants faced one another and drew their swords. Sir Ywain, from the king's dais, called out, "Now let the trial begin, and may God defend the right!"

The pair of combatants immediately crouched down, their shields before them. In his right hand each held a double-edged knightly or arming sword of some thirty inches or so in length, much like my own Almace: swords made for hacking, not thrusting. Lancelot was taking his time, measuring Meliagauunt's skill and valor, though he probably remembered his opponent's fighting style quite well from their previous battle in Gorre just a month earlier. Meliagaunt, who'd been taken by surprise at that time when he learned quite suddenly that his opponent was Sir Lancelot du Lac, now was far more wary, trying to note or to remember any weaknesses in the Great Knight's abilities. Of course, Lancelot was not at full strength, having been imprisoned and starved for several days in Sir Tirre's dungeon, and the queen was somewhat nervous on that account.

"Oh Gildas, tell me he'll be all right. He's not too worn down by his hardship to withstand that vile Meliagaunt's assaults, is he?"

"My lady," I soothed her. "Remember when this same pair fought to free us only last month, that Lancelot had just gone through the ordeal of the Sword Bridge, and had reduced his own hands to bloody shreds. Yet he had no difficulty at all in bringing this Meliagaunt to heel. Expect no difference in his performance now."

"Well, I for one am praying that Sir Lancelot will slay him in this duel," the queen blurted out.

Rosemounde looked at her with concern. "Surely it would be better if he simply forced him to yield and to withdraw his charges," she offered.

I nodded and added, "My lady Rosemounde is quite right, Your Grace. I know this Meliagaunt—he's looking only for recognition. I think he merely wants to put up enough of a fight to be respected as a knight. His sole motive in all of this was disappointment at having been passed over for the Round Table."

But the queen was adamant. "This recreant knight dared to lay violent hands upon his own queen!" That, of course, was not completely true. He had abducted her, true, but had not touched her person. "Can Arthur keep his due respect as king if he allows petty knights to play fast and loose with his own queen with impunity? There can be no other outcome for this scoundrel!"

"God's knuckles, woman!" Merlin burst out, forgetting all courtesy to the queen. She blanched, but I suppose if anyone could get away with such language to Her Royal Majesty, it was her husband's oldest and chief advisor. "Condemn all disgruntled noblemen in your country to death and you will make a desert of Logres. What real harm has Meliagaunt caused?"

Sir Kay bristled at that. "It may have escaped your notice, old trickster, that I was sorely wounded at this upstart's hands and for awhile feared for my life. Is that harm enough for you?"

Merlin snorted. "It was boorishly done to smite an unarmored man," he conceded. "But you *were* coming at him with a sword…"

"And *he* was kidnapping my sovereign queen!" Kay retorted.

"Stop squabbling," Guinevere commanded. "They have begun to fight. We are still in charge here, unless my Lord Merlin's discourtesies presage an insurrection among the lower classes." Never had I seen her more imperious, and I feared this did not bode well for Sir Meliagaunt.

For indeed, the two knights had finally stopped circling one another and had tried a few tentative swipes with their swords, which each had parried fairly easily with his own shield. Now Meliagaunt, hoping to take the initiative, stepped forward, his shield before his face, and swung his sword downward to give Lancelot a blow to the helmet. But before the stroke landed, the Great Knight had sidestepped so neatly that Meliagaunt's sword swooshed through the air, striking nothing at all, and Lancelot, having ducked to his left, brought his own sword around low, nearly taking Meliagaunt's feet from under him. The knight of Gorre then backed quickly away, and Lancelot, seizing the advantage, strode forward and began buffeting Meliagaunt's shield with blow after blow. There was little Meliagaunt could do but fend off the Great Knight's blows until, having exhausted himself, Lancelot paused momentarily for breath. Now Meliagaunt leaped to life and began his own pummeling of Lancelot's shield, but Lancelot refused to retreat, and traded Meliagaunt blow for blow, until both knights' shields began to show the wear and tear of the battle and appeared dented and scratched, and in the case of Meliagaunt's, showed gaps where whole pieces had been hacked away.

It began to appear that Meliagaunt was tiring. At one point, Lancelot's sword glanced off his shield into Meliagaunt's mail sleeve, cutting through the mesh and exposing the shoulder. Lancelot, easily spying any new weakness, immediately took advantage, and began to aim blow after blow at Meliagaunt's exposed shoulder. He feinted right and then spun about, bringing his sword in from the side before Meliagaunt was able to reposition his shield, and gave the younger knight a shallow wound in the shoulder. In itself it was not much, but it hindered Meliagaunt's ability to use his shield, and Lancelot, relentless as he pursued the profession at which he exceeded anyone else in the known world, pounded Meliagaunt unto his knees with vertical blow after vertical blow, then swung his sword horizontally from the right to knock Meliagaunt's helmet right off of his head.

"I yield! I yield!" The stricken knight cried, throwing down his sword and shield and holding his arms straight up over his head.

Sir Lancelot, his opponent beaten and asking for mercy, stopped, held his sword above his head, and looked toward the king. As far as Arthur was concerned, this battle was over. Meliagaunt's loss and surrender was proof that God had favored Sir Lancelot, and that therefore Meliagaunt's charges were false. But he would not declare the trial concluded without a nod from the queen, who, after all, was the one most affected by Sir Meliagaunt's charge. And the queen made no sign, but rather sat with her arms folded. "Your Highness," Sir Kay said at her left side, showing his yellow teeth in a sycophantic smile. "The king awaits your signal." But the queen sat still as stone. I glanced toward the king, then down to the field of combat, where I happened to catch sight of King Bagdemagus, standing with a strained expression along the side of the lists, his hands folded as if in prayer.

Now Arthur, lowering his brows, saw that the queen was not yet appeased, and called out to the suppliant Meliagaunt in the field. "Sir Meliagaunt! In yielding, do you hereby withdraw your charge of treason and adultery against the queen and Sir Kay, and admit them to be innocent of these crimes?"

Now Meliagaunt hesitated. His face registered hope, doubt, and a certain calculation, and finally he set his jaw with a stubborn determination. I could see it coming and I hung my head. Meliagaunt's stubborn pride was going to get him killed after all.

"I will not retract my charges!" He cried. "You, King Arthur, may make the final judgment in this matter, and will pronounce the legal outcome. But I have said what I have said."

And with that word, Lancelot looked at the queen, and I saw her make a quick motion, holding her thumb down. Rosemounde, catching the sign as well, looked to me, her eyebrows raised in pleading disbelief. "Your Majesty," I said. "You have won. Let him be exiled."

"You do not see the broader ramifications of this, any of you!" the queen hissed. "If he lives then the rumors stay alive. This is how it begins: the crack of the queen's infidelity will bring the Table crashing down. It must be quashed now or Camelot itself is lost."

I looked to Merlin as the last hope. But the old man only shrugged. "And perhaps the abandonment of mercy will bring about cracks on a different side of the Table. Perhaps whatever we do, the cracks will spread from now on. You must do what you will do." And I knew then it was over. Looking down toward King Bagdemagus, I saw him kneel himself, holding out his arms to Arthur, then the queen, then Sir Lancelot. Yet no one noticed him but me.

The only thing that gave Sir Meliagaunt any sort of a prayer was the code of chivalry, particularly as encapsulated in the great Pentecost Oath. Lancelot, like every other knight of Arthur's Table, renewed his pledge each year "to grant mercy to any who plead for mercy." And there was no question in anyone's mind that Meliagaunt had, in fact, been pleading for mercy. On the other hand, Lancelot and the other knights also swore "always to give succor to ladies, damsels, and gentlewomen, on pain of death." Queen Guinevere was asking for succor, was begging for her name to be conclusively cleared. And not only was she a lady, she was Lancelot's own queen. And not only was she his queen, she was his beloved, to whom the code of true love held he should deny nothing. A direct command from the king could have spared Lancelot the stress of decision in this case, but Arthur had clearly yielded the outcome of this case to his queen.

Finally, the Great Knight reached a decision. "I cannot accept your surrender if you will not retract your charge," he said, loud enough to be heard throughout the surrounding grandstand. "And so, if you refuse to recant I make you this offer: if you will fight me again, I pledge to do battle without my helmet or my shield, to allow my left side to be stripped of armor to the extent possible, and to have my left arm tied behind my back so that I cannot use it. And thus armed only with my sword and my hauberk, I will challenge you again, and thereby prove that God Himself is convinced your charges are false."

A collective gasp issued from all the seats in those grandstands, and Arthur himself seemed unsure what to do. Meliagaunt leaped up, snatching this opportunity, as I knew, to become the first knight ever to best Sir Lancelot in the lists, even in such a heavily handicapped contest. "My Lord Arthur!" he shouted. "I accept Sir Lancelot's offer! I retract my surrender, not my charges! I will fight him again if he will hold his word!"

Arthur looked at Lancelot quizzically. "Sir Lancelot," he called. "Will you stand by this offer in earnest?"

"I meant exactly what I said," the Great Knight answered. And he immediately removed his helmet, while Sir Bors came unto the field, followed by the herald Sir Ywain, and the two of them used some leather straps Sir Ywain brought down to tie Lancelot's left arm firmly behind his back. Then Bors carried off Lancelot's helmet and his shield, and Ywain returned to the dais before King Arthur. The king was seated, looking tense. Around the queen's dais, no one had spoken a word this whole time. Rosemounde and I looked at one another fearfully, and when I glanced at Merlin, he had his eyes closed and was shaking his head. The queen stared forward, her eyes riveted on Sir Lancelot, and Sir Kay rubbed his hands over his face and mumbled to himself. On the sidelines, King Bagdemaus had not risen from his knees, but his slumped posture, his head hanging low, told me all I needed to know about his faith in his son's chances.

Sir Ywain, standing before the king's seat, called out once more in the king's name: "Let the combat begin, and may God uphold the right!"

Sir Melieaguant, with a confidence bordering on arrogance, surged forward, his shield before him and his sword arm raised. Lancelot backed off, on the defensive, and when Meliagaunt's sword came down, Lancelot easily parried the blow, then with a backhanded swipe, struck Melieagaunt's shield. Having gotten a feel for the new tactics, Meliagaunt pushed forward with more confidence, for Lancelot's undefended head seemed to lie open to his sword like a ripened melon, and Lancelot seemed to stand flatfooted, waiting for Meliagaunt to aim a blow there. But as Meliagaunt's sword began to swoop down toward the Great Knight's exposed pate, Lancelot shifted to the left, parried the blow with another backhand, then with a spinning move, came at Meliagaunt from the right, smashing the nasal of his helmet into his mouth and breaking three of his teeth. The shocked Meliagaunt stepped back momentarily, which was his complete undoing, for Lancelot now brought his sword around again, slashing down again from the same direction, catching Meliagaunt on his wounded left shoulder and completely shattering his foe's shield arm and rendering it useless. Meliagaunt, now effectively unhelmeted, shieldless, and unable to use his left arm at all, was as handicapped as Lancelot. The wounded knight recognized his plight, and foresaw what must come next, and in a moment of madness or of berserk bravado, rushed at Lancelot with his sword raised, shouting an inarticulate war cry. The Great Knight thrust upward with his sword arm, piercing Meliagaunt's mail corselet and opening a great wound in his belly. The knight of Gorre fell lifeless into the dust. Queen Guinevere heaved a sigh of relief on her raised dais, and from his knees, King Bagdemagus wept without restraint.

CHAPTER FOURTEEN

THE HEALING OF SIR URRY

In the weeks that followed the feast day of Saint Thomas the Apostle, things began gradually to return to normal in Camelot. King Bagdemagus, along with his daughter Lady Constance and her husband, Sir Degore, begged leave and were granted permission to claim Sir Meliagaunt's body and to return it to Gorre to receive a proper burial. The queen would by no means allow her kidnapper and tormentor to receive a Christian burial in the environs of the court or anywhere near Caerleon. And though Sir Degore was himself a knight of the Round Table, and officially remained one so long as there was a Table to be part of, he was seldom seen in Camelot after that day.

Lady Elizabeth, on the other hand, was given a full funeral mass in Saint David's Cathedral in Caerleon, presided over by the Archbishop himself, William of Glastonbury, at the special request of Their Royal and Imperial Majesties King Arthur and Queen Guinevere of Logres. All of Camelot attended the funeral, and wept at the inordinate grief manifested by Sir Lowell and his remaining daughter, Lady Mary, as chief mourners—though Mary, it should be said, seemed to revel in the attention she was receiving from many of the very important people among Camelot's elite, a fact that to some small extent mitigated her sorrow.

I wept myself at the senseless loss of that young and vital girl, who, if things had been different, may at some point have even become my wife. But I must admit to having felt a small twinge of relief, for truth to tell, I was not interested in marrying solely for monetary or social reasons, and did not relish the distraction from trying to look after my lady Rosemounde as best I could when she, too, was married to someone else.

Something good did come out of that heartbreaking funeral, though, since Sir Lowell's plight was finally brought to the attention of the king in a way he found difficult to ignore. He spoke to his nephews—sans Mordred, the man's tormentor—about the situation of this minor vassal who had bankrupted himself in the king's service, and urged each of them in his turn to find something for the knight in their own service, and Sir Gaheris, as it turned out, still had not replaced his squire, Sir Hectimere, after that worthy was made a knight of the Round Table. And so it was that Sir Lowell, having been knighted years before, took the position of Gaheris's personal squire. He was, it was true, somewhat older than was usual for that station, but his experience made him extremely valuable as a personal assistant to Sir Gaheris, and Gaheris gave Lowell control over a small manor of his that had been in the family for several generations and could bring the man some economic stability. Lowell was overjoyed at his new prospects. And who knew? Perhaps one day he might even join his brothers-in-law Bedivere and Lucan as a knight of the Table Round. At any rate, his presence in Camelot was likely to curb some of the boisterous excesses of the lady Mary, who tended to test the queen's patience on occasion as things now stood.

The death of Lady Elizabeth had had a sanguine effect on Thorvald as well. For the dwarf, somewhat surprisingly, had taken the young girl's chiding of his profession to heart, and had renounced his old vocation, refusing henceforth to allow his cart to be used to humiliate felons or bring them to their deaths. Determined now to make his living in another manner altogether, he had conceived of a plan in which he had enlisted the aid and advice of the Winchester moneylender Isaac. Isaac and some of his fellow Jews, who were in the cloth trade, importing wool and other fabrics—including, occasionally, rich tapestries—from weavers in Flanders, had partnered with Thorvald, who now drove his cart regularly, three times a week, between Winchester and Camelot, selling the goods for a profit in Caerleon and at the castle, and running back with orders for tapestries from the king or queen's household, or with raw wool from the pastureland around Camelot to be turned into cloth in Flanders with the Winchester merchants as middle men. Business was already going so well for Thorvald and his partners that he was planning to add a monthly trip all the way to Gorre, to see what kind of business he might drum up in King Bagdemagus's country, knowing how seldom peddlers of any kind entered that land, isolated as it was by that Sword Bridge and Water Bridge and all.

"That young girl let me 'ave it right between the eyes, she did," Thorvald confided in me three weeks after the funeral. "An' I'm damned if it wasn't like the voice of the Virgin Mary 'erself, tellin' me what needed doin' for the good of my own soul." And with that he patted the heavy leather bag hanging from his belt. "It 'asn't done my purse any damage either, I can tell you that!" he added with a grin.

That conversation was actually on the occasion of Thorvald's surprising me with the return of my exquisite mail coat. Sir Lancelot, having heard how I'd been forced to relinquish my precious hauberk as security for the loan to free Sir Lowell in the process of searching for him, had given Thorvald the money to discharge my debt with his partner Isaac and to redeem my armor. The joy of having my father's handiwork around me once more swelled my heart until it overflowed through the tears that glistened in my eyes. Never again, I thought to myself, would I let that hauberk out of my possession, until I gave up knighthood itself. And at that moment, I did not think that would ever be.

The one who initially had the most difficult time accepting Elizabeth's demise was actually Guinevere—that is my borzoi hound, I mean, not the queen. She moped around for days, spending a lot of her time lying on her side and whining. Of course, she was still nursing her injured leg as well. Ultimately, however, she was able to snap out of it and go on, particularly after I took her out hunting with a party of knights a week or so after our return. She was soon in the spirit of the hunt, and was almost keeping up with Aeneas and Dido, the queen's greyhounds, in the chase, so I knew her leg was healing fine. I assumed, like me, that she would always feel that hole in her life, but dogs are better than people at realizing that life goes on, and that we must do so as well.

Of course the other inevitable sequel to Lady Elizabeth's very public funeral was the equally public trial of her murderer, Sir Tirre, disgraced knight of the Round Table. Tirre could have asked, I suppose, for a trial by combat, as was his right as a knight, but knowing that his opponent in such a trial almost certainly, once again, would be Lancelot of the Lake, fresh from demolishing the doughty Sir Meliagaunt with one hand, Tirre grudgingly opted for a trial before the king's court. But the outcome of that was just as much a foregone conclusion as combat with Lancelot would have been. When Merlin and I, and afterwards Bors and Alan and Thorvald, all told our stories before the king's bench, and when Lancelot described his treatment in Tirre's makeshift dungeon, and ultimately when his own father, Sir Bernard of Astolat, testified about how Tirre had forged his handwriting on the letter purported to be dictated by his poor, heartbroken daughter to make her murder sound like the natural result of a broken heart, Tirre had no imaginable defense, and ultimately threw himself on the mercy of the court.

I stood next to Merlin in the great hall at Camelot when the king pronounced his verdict. Unsurprisingly, Sir Tirre was found to be guilty of the murders of his sister, Elaine of Astolat, and of the queen's lady-in-waiting, Elizabeth of Winchester. He was also guilty of the kidnapping of Sir Lancelot as well as obstruction of the king's justice in attempting to prevent Lancelot from appearing in the trial by combat of Queen Guinevere and Sir Kay.

The surprise came in the king's next words. "I have found you guilty," Arthur said, "but we are mindful that you have admitted your guilt and have thrown yourself upon the mercy of the court. In recognition of that plea, and in deference to your family—your father a loyal vassal of the crown, your brother a knight of the Round Table—we are disposed to exercise leniency in this case. We forego the prescribed legal sentence of death by beheading, and sentence you instead to perpetual banishment. You are to leave Camelot within twenty-four hours, or the aforesaid death penalty will be back in effect. You have until the end of August to depart the land of Logres, and until the end of the year to vacate any lands that form a part of our empire. If after New Year's next, you are found within the borders of Ireland, Scotland, Wales, Scandinavia, Gaul, or any part of the Holy Roman Empire, your life is forfeit and the death sentence, again, is in force. This is our final word to you as your sovereign." And with that, though Sir Tirre had begun to sputter something—perhaps it was his gratitude or perhaps just some wheedling complaint—the king had turned on his heel and left the hall. Sir Geraint and Sir Bleoberis, acting as the king's marshals for the day, grabbed Tirre by the arms and showed him the door in a manner that did not encourage him to loiter longer about the castle.

The meeting broke up soon afterwards, and Merlin and I made our way slowly and wordlessly out the door and down the steps into the middle bailey. I was hanging my head and scowling when Merlin broke the silence. "You're troubled, Gildas my boy," he observed.

"Can't put anything over on you, can I, old man?" I shot back, somewhat unfairly taking my annoyance out on him.

"I feel like walking," he said, turning left to tread along the inner wall of the great hall and kitchen. He was leaning more and more heavily on his staff these days, I'd noticed, and I realized that I would have to admit the mage was getting older. Of course, he had seemed about a hundred years old ever since I'd met him. But he had seemed a spry hundred-year-old. Now there seemed to be more of a weight upon him. I watched him walk off for a few paces, then skipped to catch up to him.

"It's this decision of the king's," I grumbled to the old man. "I mean, we've talked a good deal about chivalry and what it means. Shouldn't justice be a part of chivalry? Doesn't true chivalry require that one must do justice? Doesn't it require that the *king* do justice?"

"I take it, young Sir Gildas of Cornwall, that you are implying the king's actions in the case of Sir Tirre were not just."

"Well, of course they weren't," I sputtered. "I mean, look at what Tirre did. He didn't just kidnap Sir Lancelot and, in keeping him, jeopardize the queen's life and Sir Kay's as well. He actually killed our defenseless Lady Elizabeth!"

"He did," Merlin nodded. "Though I think, to be fair, we should recognize he killed her unintentionally, in the heat of the moment."

"But she wouldn't have been there confronting him if he wasn't already guilty of so many other things! And it all started when he killed his own *sister*, for heaven's sake, and tried to blame it on Lancelot. And we don't hang him, or behead him, or burn him at the bloody stake but just let him go his own way?"

"So, justice, in your view, would have been served by the execution of Sir Tirre." It was a statement, not a question.

"Well, look at Meliagaunt," I argued. We had passed the lesser hall by now and were turning right to go past the tower on the northeast wall of the castle. "Sir Meliagaunt didn't kill anybody…"

"Not for lack of trying," Merlin argued. "The wounds he inflicted on Sir Kay could easily have killed him had they been a bit deeper or in a more vital area…"

I shook my head and looked up at Merlin from the corner of my eye. "Weren't you arguing just the opposite the other day with the queen and Kay himself at Meliagaunt's trial?"

The old man smiled. "Don't burn we with the facts, boy," he said, but gently. "I chided Kay for his foolishness in attacking an armed knight while essentially unarmed. But Meliagaunt could have killed Kay as easily as Tirre killed Elizabeth. And Meliagaunt's kidnapping of Guinevere was even more serious than Tirre's of Lancelot. Lancelot was not his royal sovereign."

"Meliagaunt did not murder his sister!" I stressed what to me was the obvious point.

"And yet he was killed without mercy." Again it was a statement, not a question.

"Yes!" I cried, frustrated. The fact was I simply had not gotten over the death of Meliagaunt. I certainly did not number the arrogant young knight among my friends, but I felt some kinship with him. I had held intimate conversations with him. I understood, could even sympathize, with his frustrations and his feelings of being overlooked and underappreciated. I even understood why he had hopped forward to take Lancelot up on his one-armed challenge: if he had won, he would be the man who defeated the Great Knight. He'd never have killed Lancelot even if he had beaten him in the arena. He wouldn't have killed anyone. He just wanted recognition. And yet he had died.

"So, you feel that chivalry was not served in Lancelot's execution of Meliagaunt. Nor was it served in the mercy shown to Tirre? Tell me, then, would chivalry be served if both were executed? Or would it be better served if both were spared? Can you choose?"

I bit my lips. I could see that the old man wanted to make me see the two cases as essentially equal, but still I insisted they were not. "Justice would be Sir Tirre sentenced to death, and Meliagaunt reprieved. And I think you believe that yourself!"

"God's kneecaps, you Cornish dolt, I'm telling you that chivalry demands *mercy*. The king did precisely what his own Pentecost oath requires him to do: he showed mercy to a knight who asked for mercy. How would the execution of Tirre have served the common good in any way? No one was in danger from him anymore. His resentment of Lancelot was grounded in his sister's disappointment, but that endangered no one else and had run its course, and he was no match for Lancelot if it came to that. In exile, he is a danger to no one. But Meliagaunt? He refused to retract his charges. He asked for mercy but would not take back the whole charge that the trial was all about. I argued with the queen that day because I still believed that mercy was the better choice, but she was right about this one thing: if Meliagaunt's charges were allowed to remain in the air…if he was spared to continue to insist on her disloyalty to the king, then Arthur's kingdom could not long stand. He was a much greater danger to the crown, and therefore to chivalry itself, than Sir Tirre is."

By now, we had turned at the southeast corner of the castle and were moving toward the keep, walking in its long shadow. "What you're saying," I mused, "is that in order to preserve the ideal of chivalry, the king himself cannot be completely chivalrous? I mean, if he were, would he not have stepped in to save Meliagaunt?"

"That's one way to look at it, I suppose," Merlin shrugged. "But you might also say that chivalry…well, what is chivalry? It's the ideal behavior that raises human beings above the wretchedness of the slime they were created from…"

"Well, *you* might say that. I don't think it's how I would put it."

"But it essentially is the truth, isn't it? The trouble is, of course, that it's those same human creatures, fighting against their human natures, who have to engage in those chivalrous acts. And sometimes, being human, they just aren't able to."

"Some of us might look at that and say fallen human nature is the problem…" I corrected him.

"You say tomato…" Merlin said. "But what do we say of the queen? It was at her insistence that Meliagaunt was killed, so you regard her as an enemy of chivalry, do you?"

Merlin knew well how difficult it would be for me to criticize the queen, my constant patron and defender. "The queen…well, it is the knights, isn't it? Who swear the Pentecost oath?" A cheap dodge, I admit. Merlin would never let me get away with that.

"Does that mean the ladies are not to be judged by its precepts?" he challenged me. "Isn't the whole system built on the assumption that the knight follows the chivalric code in order to be worthy of the courtly lady that he loves so truly?" He was only partly teasing me. "The assumption being, therefore, that she supports, adheres to, even embodies that very notion of chivalry? Is the queen's treatment of Meliagaunt a lapse, then? Or do we say that chivalry is a code of personal moral and ethical behavior that does not work on the communal level of national politics?"

"But if I remember right, you once called chivalry 'manly virtue in the service of righteousness.' Righteousness has to do with justice, and with what you called the 'common good' a little while ago. That all has to do with the 'communal level.' Doesn't it?"

"Of course it does," Merlin agreed. "And so with Guinevere, as with Arthur, do we need to say that human beings are not perfect?"

"Neither the king nor the queen is perfect. Neither one is a saint. Like the rest of us, I suppose, they strive to bring themselves closer to the ideal."

"And that is where I suppose they differ from most others in their position," Merlin agreed, as we approached the bottom of the steps coming from the great hall, to return to where we'd started. "They at least have the code to aspire to."

"As does Lancelot, I suppose. He had the most difficult task of all, it seems to me. To follow the demands of his lady and queen, or follow his general directive to show mercy."

"Life is not a series of choices between good and evil," Merlin agreed. "Each of our lives is a series of little choices between partial goods, all of which must, by definition, contain partial evils as well. Lancelot, as chief representative of the court, has to make more public choices than anybody else. But they are still those same kinds of choices."

"Well," I concluded, staring back up at the door into the king's great hall. "Better him than me."

***

I know it seems like that ought to be the end of this story. But there was one more thing that happened at Camelot that year that seemed, for me at least, to be the last word on everything that had transpired since Pentecost.

And this occurred on another big feast day: it was the 15th of August, the feast of the Assumption of the Blessed Virgin Mary. King Arthur was in a buoyant mood, bouncing around outside the great hall waiting for the guests coming to the feast, and had made his customary feast-day vow not to sit down to eat until he had seen or heard of some marvel.

That's when Thorvald and his cart came rattling over the drawbridge and into Camelot. But he wasn't carrying some felon or anything like that. What he had lying in the bed of the cart was a wounded knight he had picked up in Winchester, and sitting next to the dwarf in the cart's driver's seat was a young maiden, the wounded knight's sister, who had been traveling with him across all of Europe, apparently, for some seven years.

As the lady told the story, her brother was a noble knight of Hungary whose name was Sir Urry. He had been a knight errant, wandering through the kingdoms of Europe in search of adventure and to make a name for himself, until he entered a tournament in Spain seven years before. He had the fortune in that tournament to meet a certain Sir Alpheus, son of a powerful Spanish earl, in single combat. Sir Urry had bested Sir Alpheus in that battle, but through fate or chance, Urry had killed Sir Alpheus on the field. Urry himself had sustained seven grievous wounds—three on his head, three on his body, and one on his left hand. Still, he repented the outcome of that fight, the death of Alpheus, but his pleas went unheeded by Sir Alpheus's family. The slain knight's mother, the Spanish duchess, also happened to be an accomplished sorceress, as it turned out, and she was not in a forgiving mood.

The duchess cursed Sir Urry, declaring that he would never be whole, his injuries would never completely heal, until the best knight in all the world would search his wounds.

"And so we have been all over," the sister, called Lady Felelolye, told King Arthur, tears beginning to well in her deep blue eyes. She had wavy blonde tresses held in place by a gold wire crespine, and a broad face that seemed open and honest, and wrinkled in concern. She spoke very carefully, pronouncing her words crisply but with a marked eastern European accent. "From the Muslim courts of Spain, to the pagan courts east of our own native Hungary, and then through nearly every court in Christendom, I have carried my brother to no avail. Hundreds of knights have tried their hand at healing him, but they've done nothing but make the wounds break and bleed all over again. We've been told in many quarters that the best knights of all the world are to be found here, in the court of the famous King Arthur, and so we have come by horse litter, by boat, and now by cart across the continent to arrive here, at your doorstep, my lord king. And I declare now, before you and all these present, that if we cannot find my brother's cure here, we will abandon our search and return home, and Sir Urry will resign himself to his fate from this day forward. Therefore I beg you, King Arthur," and with this she fell to her knees, flailing her arms about in a kind of hopeless gesture of distress, "bring your best knights to my brother here where he lies before your court. Let them lay their hands on him here. And if they fail to heal him, let us accept our defeat and leave your land in sorrow and shame."

Now this was, of course, precisely the kind of challenge that Arthur would find irresistible. This was what he lived for, what the

Round Table itself had been conceived for: the public glorification of knightly endeavor. He was not going to pass up a chance like this.

"Then Madame," he said, loud enough to be heard by all who had circled around him and the wagon and the two young foreigners. "I swear by the sword Excalibur that you shall not have made this long journey in vain. I call on every knight present for this feast," and with that he raised his voice to his battlefield command level, ensuring that no one in the middle bailey at the time could have failed to hear. "To make his assay of the wounded Sir Urry. Each knight in his turn shall search your brother's wounds, until that one good and valiant knight shall be found who will mend these hurts. And I assure you, Madame," he added in a more intimate tone, looking with true compassion into Lady Felelolyle's blue eyes, "that knight will be found. You *shall* find your deliverer here in Camelot."

Pages were sent scurrying to every corner of the castle, to track down any knight of the Table Round who might be out of earshot, or was involved in some responsibility or dalliance elsewhere in the castle. Sir Kay the seneschal, coming to Arthur's side, clapped his hands and had four squires bring a comfortable pallet and set it in the middle of the bailey beside Thorvald's cart. Then the squires gently lifted Sir Urry, wincing from the pain, down from the bed of the cart to lie upon the pallet, and there, when the Hungarian knight had been made as comfortable as possible, the king knelt down beside the bed, calling out again in his battlefield voice: "See! I am taking the first pass over the wounds myself, to show you that I expect this of you all! Be ready to follow my lead, each and every one of you."

And so the girl, with a look very much resembling hope beginning to dawn on her face, carefully removed Sir Urry's bandages, exposing the wounds to the fresh air and to the king's touch. Very lightly the king laid hands upon Sir Urry's wounds. And nothing happened.

But then, we hadn't expected anything at that point. "Sir Gawain!" Arthur now called. I heard a bit of a groan from where I stood next to Gareth. He looked over at me, drawing his mouth up into a morose, close-mouthed grin. "Poor Gawain," Gareth whispered in my direction in a hoarse croak. "Sometimes, it's just not the best day to be the Heir Apparent. Always expected to be the first to volunteer, no matter how dangerous or ludicrous the task."

Dutifully, Sir Gawain knelt beside the ailing knight, and went through the same motions as the king had done, but with less apparent expectation—and with the same result. Now the rest of the king's nephews queued up to take their turn. First Sir Ywain knelt down, shaking his shaggy mane in sympathy for Sir Urry's plight, but his sympathy did not make his ministrations any more efficacious than his cousin's. Sir Gaheris followed dutifully, but had no success, and Agravayne, though he seemed eager and fascinated by the whole situation, could not effect any change in Urry's condition.

Sir Mordred, to no one's surprise, was not in attendance, but I was pretty sure that was no loss for Sir Urry, since if Mordred was, in fact, the world's greatest knight, we must be living unwittingly in hell. And so Sir Gareth took his turn at Urry's wounds. I saw him bow his head and knew he must actually be praying, sincere as he was in hoping to help the wounded knight even though, like me, he seemed to think it was a highly unlikely proposition. And, as it turned out, it was.

As a friend of the family, I stepped in behind Gareth and took my turn. Kneeling down at his side, I got my first real look at Sir Urry's face. He had blond hair and blue eyes like his sister, though his hair was shaggy and unkempt, and his beard untrimmed. He had a wound in the middle of his forehead, a longer one on the left side of his scalp, plus a red scar across his cheek, oozing blood. He looked at me with an ironic smile on his face, and with a quizzically raised eyebrow, I greeted him in a low voice. "My lord, I'm truly sorry for your sufferings. I am Sir Gildas of Cornwall, a newly ordained knight. I have no illusions that I am the world's greatest knight by any means. But I will do my best for you, and pray that it may be of some benefit."

The ailing knight gave a bitter sounding snort. "I thank you, my young friend," he said in that very precise accent he shared with his sister. "The truth is, I long ago gave up any hope of finding someone to heal these hurts. Who knows? The old enchantress may have been lying about the cure all along—just one more way to torment me. I go along with these pilgrimages to various chivalric courts to humor my sister, who won't give up her hopes. So please, my friend, let us perform this charade. It will content the Lady Felelolyle."

I gave the honest knight a nod and a wink, and laid my hands to his seven wounds in my best imitation of sincerity, and when I had done, to no one's surprise, nothing happened.

I stepped back to stand with Sir Gareth again, and he looked at me doubtfully as Sir Bors took his turn, followed by Sir Ector, and Sir Palomides. One after another the knights of the Round Table, the undisputed champions of justice and greatest knights in the world, tried their hands at lifting the Spanish duchess's curse. But all to no avail.

However, as I'm sure you realize by now, we had forgotten one thing.

At length, after several dozen knights had come forward and laid hands upon the stalwart Sir Urry—whose face in all this bore an expression of grim resolve and a hope that this, too, would finally pass—one of the pages the king had sent off at the beginning to gather the knights to this spot came back leading the lord Merlin, and with him the Great Knight, Sir Lancelot du Lac. The knight was simply dressed, wearing only a blue tunic and brown hose, as if he'd been interrupted in the midst of dressing. Merlin had a suspicious, self-satisfied look on his visage, and Gareth and I sidled over to him as he joined the throng, while Lancelot, waving off invitations to make his way directly to the wounded knight, took his place in the line that had formed before Sir Urry's bed.

"So what interest do *you* have in this business, you old conniver?" Gareth muttered into the mage's left ear when we'd got close enough.

"I've been thinking that this whole affair had a familiar ring to it," I added in the old man's right. "Reminiscent, say, of the Siege Perilous, where only Galahad could sit? Or perhaps even the sword in the stone?"

Merlin rolled his eyes and scoffed. "What, now I've got to deal with a *Scottish* blockhead in *addition* to a Cornish one? How much foresight do you credit me with, to have arranged this entire rigmarole seven years in advance, to ensure that on this particular feast day, at a time when the court is at a low ebb, these Hungarians, of all people, would show up here at the castle with what is, apparently, an impossible challenge? And why? To give to men and angels some objective proof that here, in the Camelot of the good King Arthur, abide the greatest knights in all the world? And that, by the way, his name is Lancelot?"

Well, I had to admit that, looking at it that way, it really didn't make much sense. But still, the old necromancer had something up his sleeve, of that I had no doubt.

By now, though, Lancelot had finally been prevailed upon to move ahead of the other knights in the queue, for they, like us, recognized that if it was the greatest knight only who could heal Sir Urry, then by whatever measure, Lancelot was the sole candidate.

Where there had been a low, nervous hub-bub prior to his appearance among them, now a hush came over the whole crowd there on the green, and Sir Urry and his sister both looked on Lancelot with a new curiosity. This was different. Hope may have been far from their thoughts, but at least, with this new challenger, an expectation seemed to be raised.

The Great Knight knelt down at Sir Urry's side, and bent his head to whisper something in the invalid's ear that seemed to perk him up a little bit. Then Lancelot reached into the purse that hung from his belt and brought out a small ceramic jar that he emptied into his hands, which he then pressed together in a prayer pose, lifting his eyes to heaven.

"Wait a minute now," Sir Gareth muttered in Merlin's ear. "What's in that jar, old man?"

"As far as Lancelot is concerned," Merlin answered. "It's holy water."

"And what is it really?" I prompted him. The mage drew himself up to his full height and looked down at me, his considerable eyebrows raised innocently to the powers above.

Sir Lancelot began by taking Sir Urry's wounded left hand, and gently rubbed some of Merlin's holy water into it. After a few moments, a pleasant look came into Sir Urry's eyes, and he brought the hand up to his eyes and flexed it, smiling with surprise the whole time. I was too far from him to hear what Sir Urry said, but it looked to me as if his lips had formed the words "It tingles!" as he raised his hand. And Lancelot, rubbing his hands once more with Merlin's "holy water," then laid his hands on Urry's face and scalp, massaging those wounds very, very gently, and again within moments the Hungarian knight broke into a wide smile, nodding with approval, and behind him, I could see Lady Felelolyle bring her hands to her face in disbelief as Sir Urry actually sat up in his bed.

There were gasps and cries of joy from the assembled multitude. Looking around I saw the king, his chest puffing out with pride and an expression of calm certainty on his features that seemed to say, "Of *course* we've found the greatest knight of the world here. It *is* Camelot, after all." And close on Arthur's right side stood the queen, her hands steepled in a prayer pose that echoed the one Lancelot had struck the moment before he had laid hands on Sir Urry. Her eyes were far away, though, as if she witnessed something beyond what was occurring before us, something happening on a metaphysical level.

Now Sir Lancelot, washing his hands in the last of the holy water, searched the three deeper, bodily wounds of Sir Urry, and Urry's discomfort at having those wounds handled was obvious to all who stood around, but within a minute of Lancelot's touching them, a change came over Urry again, and with the most profound joy he shook himself, twisted round on the bed to place his feet on the ground, and rose from his pallet to his full height. He looked around, spread his arms out as if presenting himself to the court, and said in his precise, accented tongue, "These wounds have not felt so little pain for seven long years. I have good reason to believe that they are well on their way to being wholly mended!" And with those words the entire court—knights, ladies, servants, clergy, the king and queen themselves—burst into raucous cheers and a celebration that promised to carry on well into the dinner hour.

"So...holy water?" I said to Merlin.

"Indeed," the old man answered. "With a few special herbs and powders I mixed up myself. I mean, think about it," he said, flashing me a conspiratorial look. "A curse from a Spanish Duchess that prevents the wounds from healing? Please! The only thing that would affect those wounds would have to have been present when the wounds were inflicted, not from a distance by somebody's mother days later. That means the Spanish boy's sword was poisoned when he gave Sir Urry those wounds. Likely the mother knew it, maybe even provided the poison herself. The whole claim about the world's greatest knight was just a hoax to keep the poor knight and his sister scuttling around the continent on a wild goose chase instead of finding a real healer who might find an antidote to the poison. But it had to be something like the poison Marholt had used against Tristram in Ireland, and I knew they had found a cure for that."

"But how did you…" I began.

"I'd heard from Thorvald in Winchester a couple of days ago that these two foreign travelers had arrived, and were likely to make their way here. That's when I contacted Nimue to see whether the Lady of the Lake had any experience of this kind of poison. Apparently she did, and sent me the recipe for an antidote. That's what's in that jar. It just seemed appropriate to give it to Lancelot. Just at the right time."

"Well, Merlin," Sir Gareth chimed in from the old man's other side. "However it came about, you have to admit that this is a great demonstration of chivalry at its best, is it not?"

Merlin gave a doubtful shrug, as if to say he didn't have to admit such a thing at all, but then Gareth added, "Look at all these people! Sir Lancelot is now the paragon of chivalry in the entire world. And why? Because he has done a knightly act proving his value before hundreds of witnesses, in response to a well-known challenge that long preceded his coming, to the effect that only the greatest knight could do this. He has fashioned his worth and his reputation where it stands now unassailable before all the courtly universe. He is now a secular saint, and nothing could be more chivalrous."

Merlin looked in my direction. "I've always held that true chivalry is in the heart. Virtue in the service of the highest good without consideration of personal gain or reputation. Seems to me Lancelot's unsung deeds in the service of the weak or vulnerable—his rescuing of the falsely imprisoned; his courage in crossing the Sword Bridge; his disregard for his own reputation by riding in the cart when it was the only way to achieve the rescue of the queen; even the unsung return of a certain young knight's precious mail coat—these are the marks of his chivalry. But in the eyes of the world, it seems, only the grand public gesture can create the secular saint."

"Even if it's a gesture undergirded by Merlin's own magic," I added.

"Even so," the mage nodded. "It's really not unlike our old friend Saint Swithin, is it Gildas? All the good works he performed in his life among the poor folk of Winchester were not enough. It takes the essentially useless miracle of the restored eggshells to turn him into a saint. I guess Sir Urry is just Lancelot's mended eggshells, isn't he Gildas?"

I just smiled, and surveyed the celebratory crowd. And all this while, Sir Lancelot had withdrawn into a corner, and ever he wept as if he had been a child that had been beaten.

EPILOGUE:
SAINT DUNSTAN'S ABBEY

The shadows of the grove of trees encircled by the cloister walk were falling over the faces of the rapt group of young monks and novices who stood or sat around Brother Gildas, awaiting the call to vespers.

Now in his forty-fifth year as a member of the Benedictine brotherhood of Saint Dunstan's Abbey in Hereford, Brother Gildas had been regaling the younger monks with tales of the already half-mythic King Arthur for at least forty of them. Indeed, both the current prior and the abbot as well had been among Brother Gildas's eager audience in their own younger days, and that fact made it a lot easier for them to turn a blind eye to the youngsters occasionally spending time they should have been devoting to study, prayer, or meditation listening to Brother Gildas spin tales of chivalry and worldly honor, strife, and love. After all, Abbot Aelred reasoned, wasn't chivalry merely Christian charity applied to the secular world? And wasn't the courtly love of one's sovereign lady ultimately just a metaphor for God's love of the Church?

Well, perhaps that last was going a bit too far, the abbot admitted to himself. Still, it was certainly true that Gildas's stories were full of moral messages, so that they were at least as beneficial to his young monks' souls as a number of those tiresome saints' lives, especially the ones that advocated virginity above all as the most important of all Christian virtues, even over faith, hope, or charity.

As for the prior, when the rumor had reached him that Brother

Gildas was telling the youngsters the tale of the Knight of the Cart in the cloisters between none and vespers, his heart had leapt in his breast. Prior Stephen remembered how in his own youth, as a novice, that story of Sir Lancelot's demeaning himself to ride in Thorvald's cart had emboldened his own decision to give up the riches of the world and choose this religious life, just as the crossing of the Sword Bridge had shown him that he could garner the courage he needed to inform his unsympathetic father of his decision. And so he had made his way stealthily to the cloister and concealed himself in a doorway, so as not to be seen by the younger monks and thereby make them uncomfortable or self-conscious during Brother Gildas's tale.

The tale being done, the group of youngsters seemed contented with how it had ended. They enjoyed the apotheosis of Lancelot, the defeat of Meliagaunt and Tirre, and the rescue of the queen and of Lancelot. They also liked Brother Gildas's own role in the apprehending of Sir Tirre, and there were no twists in the story that were especially troubling. Of course, the murders of Lady Elizabeth and poor Elaine of Astolat were unhappy parts of the story, but it wouldn't have been much of a story without them.

But they did have a few questions, as Brother Gildas always expected. The young monk with the large, protruding ears, Brother Balthazar, who tended to ask the obvious, did not disappoint: "So, Sir Tirre," he wanted to know. "Did anyone ever hear of him again?"

"No, lad," Brother Gildas told him. "Not even a rumor. Sir Tirre dropped off the face of the earth, as far as we ever knew. Perhaps he joined a band of mercenaries. Perhaps he was set upon on the road and killed by brigands. Perhaps he married and lived out his days in peace. All I know is, he never again was seen in any of Arthur's realms. And as far as I know, neither his father nor his brother ever heard from him. Sir Bernard, weighed down by the loss of his two children, died within the year, leaving his last child, Sir Lavayne, an orphan. But Lavayne still had Lancelot as his father figure."

"But Sir Tirre was a knight of the Table," Brother Nennius pointed out, his long fingers tapping his thin jaw as if calculating the odds. Nennius always wanted to know the details. It was as if he were writing his own version of the story. "So, who was it who replaced

Tirre in the Order?"

Brother Gildas smiled. "Well, it will probably come as no surprise when I tell you that Sir Urry, by then completely recovered and a doughty knight by all accounts, was chosen by King Arthur to fill the empty slot that next Pentecost, And of course, like Sir Lavayne, he was always loyal to Sir Lancelot, even to the end."

"B..but what ab..bout Sir L..l..lowell?" Brother Notker, called the Stammerer, wanted to know. "I mean, shou..shou..shouldn't he have b...been in l...line for knighthood?"

Gildas waited for Brother Notker to finish voicing his question, though he guessed what he would ask before it was articulated. "Certainly there was a lot of sentiment in his favor. And I'm sure he'd have been next in line, had there been another Pentecost ceremony. But Sir Lowell never did get his chance. And being Gaheris's squire, he stayed loyal to the house of Orkney through everything that happened later."

The red-haired monk, brother Christopher, oldest of Brother Gildas's audience, who'd by now heard nearly all the stories in Gildas's repertoire, followed up on that hint. "You keep talking about 'the end' and 'what happened later.' What is it you're hinting at? The queen and Merlin were both worried about rumors of her and Lancelot. Seems like Merlin was trying to get everyone's mind to refocus only on Lancelot and chivalry. So I guess that wasn't a permanent solution?"

"Nothing's ever a *permanent* solution," Brother Gildas shrugged. "Life goes on. Things happen. But what you're talking about is another whole story, and so it will have to wait until another day."

"I'm not sure I want to hear that one," Brother Balthazar of the prominent ears muttered.

But Brother Gildas knew that at least one more question was coming. Out of the corner of his eye, he looked to his left, where the young monk with his innocent blue eyes and curly blonde tonsure stood with his head down, musing. Brother Abelard always wanted to know about the ladies.

"One more thing, please, before we break up, though, if you don't mind, Brother..." he began.

"Of course, Brother Abelard. You want to know about…"

"The lady Rosemounde," he said. Of course.

"And what is it you want to know about Lady Rosemounde?"

"Well, you didn't really mention her after the trial by combat, when she objected to the queen's judgment. And you also talked about Sir Mordred being away from Camelot—twice. Once when he was in Winchester, and once at the end, when he wasn't present for the incident with Sir Urry."

Brother Gildas could see where this was leading, but waited again, for different reasons, for Brother Abelard to get to his point. "Well," he continued, "where did Mordred's being gone from Camelot leave Rosemounde? I mean, she was under the queen's protection as long as she stayed at court. But did she fall out with the queen? Did she have to resume living with Mordred?"

"She and Queen Guinevere did not always see eye to eye, that is certain," Brother Gildas acknowledged. "But Guinevere would never permit her returning to live with her husband, not as long as the queen held any influence with King Arthur at all. So rest assured, Brother Abelard, Lady Rosemounde remained safe from her brutal husband for some time yet," Gildas reassured the boyish monk. "Now if I'm not mistaken," Brother Gildas added as the low tolling of a bell rolled its deep music over the monks in their cloisters and the orchard that cast such long shadows over them, "we'd all best be off to vespers as quickly as we can. You all know what a stickler that prior is." He said this last a bit louder and more distinctly as his young audience went skittering off with all the speed their professional decorum would allow.

Brother Gildas was much slower to follow. He reached down and picked up his long walking staff from the ground: like his Merlin, he was moving somewhat more slowly in these latter days. He didn't think of himself as a centenarian yet, but by God's knuckles, as Merlin would have said, there were some days when that felt not far away. And so he followed slowly, leaning on his staff, until he reached the closest alcove in the cloister wall. Here he stopped and waited, and after a moment Prior Stephen stepped out to join Gildas on his slow walk to the chapel for the office of vespers. Brother Gildas did not bother to look at the prior but simply walked on, looking straight ahead without expression. Prior Stephen adopted the same expression and posture as he accompanied the abbey's senior monk along the cloister walk.

"So," the prior said after a few steps. "How long did you know I was there?"

"Stealthiness is not among your great virtues, Brother Stephen," Brother Gildas murmured.

After a few more steps, a grin crossed the prior's face, and he let out a low chuckle, turning to Gildas. "You know, Brother," he said with some animation. "When I first heard that story, you said that Sir Tirre had returned in secret to Logres after some time, and had been killed by Sir Lavayne in a duel!"

"Did I?" Brother Gildas allowed the tiniest of upturns to twist the left side of his mouth. "I must have thought that made a better story at the time."

"Well. God's whiskers, man," Prior Stephen exclaimed in good-natured frustration. "Which one is the truth?"

Brother Gildas allowed the smile to creep a little further into his face. "You know, it's been so long I can't really remember," he teased, and Prior Stephen let out an inarticulate "Aargh!" of exasperation.

"But you've been hinting to the youngsters about, you know, the end of things—the last Pentecost. What happens when Guinevere and Lancelot are truly found out. Sir Urry remains loyal to Lancelot, Sir Lowell is true to the Orkneys. The queen reaches a point where she can no longer protect Lady Rosemounde. You have never told that story before, unless I'm mistaken."

Brother Gildas remained unflappable and continued his slow walk. "No," he said at length. "It is a story I have never told to anyone." He took two more steps. "But I think the time is finally coming."

"Well." Prior Stephen said, unable to keep the excitement from his voice. "You must let it be known well in advance. That is a telling I will absolutely be present for. Stealth or no stealth," he added, laughing.

Brother Gildas smiled again, but only out of politeness. His thoughts were on this last of stories he intended to tell. It would be hard for him, ever so hard, but he was convinced now that the time was upon him. Soon and very soon he must revisit the death of Arthur.

251

CAST OF CHARACTERS

Agravain of Orkney: Sir Agravain is a nephew of King Arthur, one of the brothers of Gawain and Gareth. He becomes one of the Queen's Knights in this book.

Alan of Winchester: Alan of Winchester is a corporal in the king's guards, under the command of Robin Kempe. His knowledge of the city of Winchester proves useful in the course of Merlin's investigations.

Alison: Lady Alison, one of the queen's newer ladies-in-waiting, is the petite, dark-haired daughter of an alderman from Bath.

Anne: Lady Anne is the longest-serving of Guinevere's ladies-in-waiting. She has a tendency to take charge when the queen is not around, and the other ladies tend to let her.

Arthur: King of Logres, holding sovereignty as well over Ireland, Scandinavia, Scotland, Wales, and Cornwall, Brittany, Normandy, and all of Gaul. And he is claimant to the emperor's throne in Rome. He is the son of Uther Pendragon and Ygraine, former Countess of Cornwall.

Bagdemagus: King Bagdemagus is a petty king of the land of Gorre, one of Arthur's faithful vassals and a former knight of the Round Table. The elderly king is the somewhat ineffectual father of Sir Meliagaunt.

Baldwin of Brittany: A retired knight who has taken up religion and become a hermit in the neighborhood of Winchester. Sir Baldwin has learned much of the healing arts, and saves Lancelot from his life-threatening wounds at the Winchester tournament.

Baldwin of Orkney: Former squire of Sir Agravain, the surly-tempered Baldwin becomes a knight of the Round Table in this book.

Barbara: Lady Barbara is another new lady-in-waiting to Queen Guinevere. She is a beautiful young teenaged girl, attracted to Sir Pelleas.

Bedivere: Sir Bedivere is one of Arthur's oldest knights, having been with him from the beginning of his reign. He is able to use that long loyalty to obtain positions at court for his two nieces, Lady Mary and Lady Elizabeth, as Queen Guinevere's youngest ladies-in-waiting.

Bernard of Astolat: Sir Bernard is lord of Guildford, befriended by Lancelot before the last great tournament at Winchester. Bernard is the father of Sir Lavayne, Sir Tirre, and Elaine, the Fair Maid of Astolat.

Blamor de Ganys: Sir Blamor is a knight of the Round Table and a close ally of Lancelot and Bors, from their own country. He rides beside Sir Bors in the Winchester tournament.

Bleoberis: Sir Bleoberis is one of the knights of the Round Table closely allied to Lancelot and Bors. He is unhorsed by Sir Lavayne at the Winchester tournament.

Bors: Sir Bors de Ganis is Sir Lancelot's cousin and his closest companion. He is steady, logical, and true. He is also pious, and was one of the three chief Grail knights. At the tournament in Winchester, he wounds the disguised Sir Lancelot.

Brandiles: Sir Brandiles is a relatively obscure knight but one closely devoted to Sir Lancelot. He is chosen as one of the Queen's Knights in this tale.

Clement: Brother Clement is the infirmarian at the Benedictine Abbey of Saint Frideswide near the kingdom of Gorre, and acts as physician for King Bagdemagus and his household.

Colgrevaunce: Close friend of Gildas who was killed on the Grail quest.

Constance: Lady Constance, the daughter of King Bagdemagus (and hence the sister of Sir Meliagaunt), is a former lady-in-waiting to Queen Guinevere, and is now married to Sir Degare.

Cynfor: Father Cynfor was an Augustinian canon and Gildas's tutor back in Cornwall. It was Cynfor's connections at court that helped place Gildas as the queen's page.

Degore: Sir Degore is a knight of the Round Table residing near Winchester. He is married to Lady Constance, a former lady-in-waiting to the queen who is also the daughter of King Bagdemagus.

Ector de Maris: Sir Ector is the brother of Sir Lancelot and the second son of King Ban of Benwick.

Elaine of Astolat: Innocent young daughter of Sir Bernard of Astolat, lord of Guildford, and sister to Sir Lavayne and Sir Tirre. Her tragic unrequited love of Lancelot ended in her death, apparently from a broken heart, and she was subsequently floated down the river toward Camelot on a shrouded barge.

Elizabeth: Lady Elizabeth is one of Queen Guinevere's newest and youngest ladies-in-waiting. She is the thirteen-year-old niece of Sir Bedivere and Sir Lucan, daughter of Sir Lowell of Winchester. Her sister Mary is another of the queen's new ladies. Elizabeth is shy but outspoken and independent when roused. The queen imagines she may make a good wife for Gildas.

Florent of Orkney: Eldest son of Sir Gawain, saved from execution by the testimony of the nymph Nimue, who married him and took him to live in the palace of the Lady of the Lake.

Gaheris of Orkney: Sir Gaheris is son of King Lot of Orkney and Queen Margause—whom he is known to have beheaded when he found her in bed with Sir Lamorak. Gaheris resembles his younger brother Sir Gareth in coloring, but not in temperament.

Galahad: Son of Sir Lancelot and the chief Grail knight, achieved the Grail and died after the quest.

Galahalt the Haut Prince: High prince whose knights are opposed to Arthur's at the Winchester tournament.

Gareth of Orkney: Sir Gareth is a knight of the Round Table and younger brother to Sir Gawain, Sir Gaheris, and Sir Agravain, and half-brother to Sir Mordred. He is son of King Lot of Orkney and Margause, the daughter of Ygraine and Duke Gorlois of Cornwall and so, Arthur's half-sister, which makes him King Arthur's nephew. Gildas was formerly squire to Sir Gareth.

Gawain of Orkney: Sir Gawain is Arthur's eldest nephew and heir apparent. He is son of King Lot of Orkney and Arthur's half-sister Margause, and the older brother of Sir Gareth, Sir Gaheris, Sir Agravain, and Mordred, and father of Lovell, his former squire.

Geraint of Dumnonia: Geraint is a young knight, but a petty king of that region of Logres called Dumnonia. He is inducted as a knight of the Round Table in fealty to his liege lord Arthur in the beginning of the book.

Gildas of Cornwall: Son of a Cornish armor-maker, formerly squire to Sir Gareth and page to Queen Guinevere, Sir Gildas of Cornwall is one of the newest knights of King Arthur's Round Table. Gildas narrates the story and is Merlin's assistant in his investigations. He is nineteen years old at the time of the queen's kidnapping, and remains in love with Lady Rosemounde, lady-in-waiting to the queen, who is married to the villainous Sir Mordred.

Griflet: Sir Griflet is a veteran knight of the Round Table, unhorsed by the disguised Lancelot in the Winchester tournament.

Guinevere: Queen of Logres, and married to King Arthur. Gildas was formerly a page in her household. She is the daughter of Leodegrance, king of Cameliard, an early ally of Arthur's. Her long-standing affair with Sir Lancelot, Arthur's chief knight, is a perilous secret in the court. She is fiercely protective of her lady-in-waiting, Rosemounde of Brittany and of her former page, Gildas of Cornwall.

Hectimere: Sir Gaheris's former squire, who becomes a knight of the Round Table in this book.

Hoel: Duke of Brittany, and Arthur's vassal and close ally from the beginning of his reign. He is the father of Lady Rosemounde.

Holly: Master Holly is Queen Quinevere's aged clerk and doorkeeper.

Isaac ben Samuel: Well-educated and witty moneylender in the Jewish quarter of Winchester, engaged by Merlin and Gildas to loan them one hundred nobles to free Sir Lowell from the stocks.

Isolde: La Belle Isolde was the daughter of the king and queen of Ireland, and was queen of Cornwall, married to King Mark. She was Sir Tristram's secret lover, and died upon seeing his dead body.

Kay: Sir Kay is King Arthur's seneschal, which means he is in charge of the king's household. He was Arthur's foster-brother when they were boys, and Arthur promised Kay's father Sir Ector that there would always be a place for Kay in his court. In this story, he is appointed one of the Queen's Knights. He tends to be something of a braggart and a bully, though the trouble he gets into in this story allows him to demonstrate his nobler nature.

King of Northumberland: One of the kings opposed to King Arthur at the Winchester tournament.

King of North Wales: Another of the kings opposed to King Arthur at the Winchester tournament.

Lady of the Lake: Queen of Faerie, a being of great mystical power. She is responsible for giving the sword Excalibur to King Arthur. She lives in an enchanted palace north of Camelot on a lake named for her. It was in this palace that Lancelot du Lac was raised.

Lamorak de Galis: Sir Lamorak was the son of King Pelinore, who killed King Lot and thus began a feud with the house of Orkney. Sir Gaheris caught Sir Lamorak in bed with his mother Margause and let him escape, but Gawain, Gaheris, Mordred and Agravain killed Sir Lamorak later in ambush.

Lancelot: Sir Lancelot du Lac is the greatest knight of Arthur's Table, and is the secret lover of Queen Guinevere. He is the son of King Ban of Benwick, and his close kinsmen—Sir Bors and Sir Ector— form a powerful bloc of Round Table knights. Elaine of Astolat dies apparently of love for him, but he insists he never encouraged her. Still, the affair causes a rift between him and the queen, which makes Guinevere vulnerable to kidnapping.

Lavayne: Sir Lavayne is the son of Sir Bernard of Astolat, lord of Guildford, and brother of Sir Tirre and of Elaine, the Fair Maid of Astolat. He becomes a knight of the Round Table at the beginning of this story.

Lot: King Lot of Orkney was an enemy of Arthur's who would not accept the fifteen-year old boy as king of Logres. With an alliance of other petty kings, he made war on Arthur to get him off the throne, but was ultimately defeated and killed. He was married to Arthur's half-sister Margause, and was the father of Gawain, Gaheris, Agravain, and Gareth.

Lovell of Orkney: Sir Gawain's second son, and his former squire. He becomes a knight of the Round Table at the beginning of this story.

Lowell of Winchester: Sir Lowell is an impoverished knight whose debts have brought him into legal troubles in Winchester. He was married to the sister of Sir Lucan and Sir Bedivere, and is the father of the ladies-in-waiting, Mary and Elizabeth.

Lucan: Sir Lucan the Butler is, like his brother Sir Bedivere, one of King Arthur's earliest knights. In the Winchester tournament, he is unhorsed by the disguised Sir Lancelot.

Margause: Mother of Gawain and his brothers, Margause was the wife of King Lot of Orkney and was one of Arthur's half-sisters, daughter of his mother Ygraine and Duke Gorlois of Cornwall. Her incestuous affair with her half-brother Arthur led to the conception of her youngest son, Mordred. Not known for her high moral standards, Margause was killed by her own son Sir Gaheris when he caught her in bed with Sir Lamorak.

Mary: Lady Mary of Winchester is one of the queen's ladies-in-waiting. She is thin, blonde, vain, and talkative. The sister of Lady Elizabeth, she is Sir Lucan's and Sir Bedivere's niece and the daughter of Sir Lowell of Winchester.

Meliagaunt: The son and heir of King Bagdemagus, Meliagaunt was been his father's squire for several years and has finally been knighted by his sire. Feeling slighted and insulted by not being selected one of the new knights of the Round Table after the Grail quest, he embarks on an ill-advised attempt to avenge himself on King Arthur while at the same time demonstrating his fitness and his eligibility to be a knight of the Table by kidnapping Queen Guinevere and besting any knight who attempts to rescue her.

Meliot de Logres: One of the knights inducted into the order of the Round Table in the opening of the story. He is a cousin of Nimue, the Damsel of the Lake, and was once saved by Sir Lancelot.

Merlin: Arthur's chief adviser in his early days, Merlin helped Arthur solidify his realm, win the war against King Lot and his allies and the war with Ireland. Rumored to have magical powers and to be able to see the future, Merlin is essentially just a more logical and scientific thinker than most of his contemporaries. He is often called upon to solve the mysteries of Camelot.

Myghal of Launceston: Myghal is Gildas's father back in Cornwall, the armorer and creator of Gildas's magnificent mail hauberk.

Mordred: Sir Mordred is the youngest brother of Sir Gawain and Sir Gareth, the youngest child of Arthur's half-sister Margause. He is married to Gildas's beloved Rosemounde. He is also, secretly, the king's own bastard son.

Nimue: Lady-in-waiting to the Lady of the Lake, Nimue lives in the Lady's mystical palace and never ages. Her beauty enchanted Merlin, who remains in love with her though she has definitively rejected him.

Palomides: Sir Palomides is a Moorish knight who has joined the Round Table and has become a Christian. He was Sir Tristram's great rival for the love of Isolde, and is known as a composer of love poems. He is a close friend of Sir Gareth and, by extension, Gildas. He becomes one of the Queen's Knights in this tale.

Pelleas: Sir Pelleas is known as "the Lover." He is a Scottish knight skillful at the entertaining "sword dance." New to the Round Table, he becomes one of the Queen's Knights in this story.

Pelinore: King Pelinore was an early ally of King Arthur and killed King Lot in battle, thus kicking off the feud between his house and Lot's. His children include Sir Lamorak and Sir Perceval.

Perceval de Galis: Sir Perceval was the youngest child of King Pelinore and was one of the three Grail knights. After achieving the Grail he entered a monastery.

Peter: Peter is Queen Guinevere's former page, who has just become Sir Gawain's new squire.

Robin Kempe: Captain of the King's Guard and of the Royal Archers, Robin spends a good deal of time on guard in the barbican of Camelot, when he isn't training his archers. One of Robin's favorite pastimes is goading Gildas of Cornwall, for whom he has a good deal of affection.

Roger: Roger is the chief cook of Camelot.

Rosemounde of Brittany: Lady Rosemounde, lady-in-waiting to Queen Guinevere, is the object of Gildas's deepest affections. She was married to Sir Mordred in Gildas's absence so that her father could make a valuable political alliance with King Arthur. She remains in that perilous marriage, but is protected by the queen as long as she remains in Camelot.

Taber: Taber is the chief stable hand at Camelot.

Thomas: Young sandy-haired former squire to Sir Ywain, Sir Thomas is made a knight of the Round Table in this book. Because of their similar positions, Thomas has been one of Gildas of Cornwall's closer friends. He is made one of the Queen's Knights in this story.

Thorvald: Thorvald is an old dwarf with a white beard, who drives a cart in which prisoners ride who are being taken to places of punishment. He tells Gawain how to reach the Water Bridge into Gorre, and later transports Lancelot in is pursuit of the queen. Ultimately, he also helps Gildas and Merlin solve the mystery.

Tirre: Sir Tirre is the brother of Sir Lavayne and of Elaine, the Fair Maid of Astolat. Their father is Sir Bernard of Astolat, lord of Guildford, whom Lancelot had befriended before the last great tournament at Winchester. Tirre becomes a knight of the Round Table in this book, and also becomes one of the Queen's Knights.

Tristram: Sir Tristram was nephew to King Mark of Cornwall, and in love with his uncle's queen, La Belle Isolde. Merlin and Gildas investigated his death in order to clear the name of Rosemounde's sister.

Urry: Sir Urry is a Hungarian knight who, having been wounded in a tournament in Spain and unintentionally killed the son of a sorceress-duchess, was cursed so that his injuries would never completely heal, until the best knight in all the world would search his wounds.

Vivien: Lady Vivien is one of Queen Guinevere's ladies-in-waiting. She is French by birth, has green eyes, and enjoys romances, poetry, and gossip.

William Bailey: Proprietor of the Red Fox Inn in Caerleon.

William of Glastonbury: Bishop of the great cathedral of Saint David in Caerleon.

Ywain: Sir Ywain, known as the "Knight of the Lion" because he often goes on adventures with his pet lion, is another nephew of King Arthur, the son of King Uriens and Morgan le Fay, Arthur's half-sister through his mother Ygraine. Sir Ywain is devoted to his cousins Sir Gawain and Sir Gareth.

ABOUT THE AUTHOR

Jay Ruud is a retired professor of medieval literature at the University of Central Arkansas. In addition to *Fatal Feast, The Knight's Riddle, The Bleak and Empty Sea,* and *Lost in the Quagmire*—the first four books in his Merlin mystery series—he is the author of *"Many a Song and Many a Leccherous Lay": Tradition and Individuality in Chaucer's Lyric Poetry* (1992), the *Encyclopedia of Medieval Literature* (2006), *A Critical Companion to Dante* (2008), and *A Critical Companion to Tolkien* (2011). He taught at UCA for fourteen years, prior to which he was dean of the College of Arts and Sciences at Northern State University in South Dakota. He has a Ph.D. in Medieval Literature from the University of Wisconsin-Milwaukee.